C000152958

Jay-Dee heard endless times during his police service he could *tell a good story*. By virtue of the fact he survived 30 years (mainly as a detective) bears testimony to that – especially when he reflects on certain investigations and situations – during a 'lively, eventful career'.

By drawing on so many experiences, he's 'been there, seen it, done it' and now in retirement does appear to be wearing many T-shirts! He hopes when his audience reads his books, they will agree he can *still* tell a good story.

Just turned 60, he now leads a much more gentile, relaxed life compared to before, perhaps at long last not such a mischievous big kid.

In between writing, he walks his two chocolate Labradors, Jasper and Rupert, and crown green bowls. Jay-Dee nearly forgot, (perhaps it's old age,) he enjoys the odd drink; normally 5, 7, or 9.

Jay-Dee's pen name is derived from his two children's middle names. His wife, Lisa, tells him he has been happily married for 36 years (and counting.) – After an odd number of drinks, he is then brave enough to tell everyone; she really is just like one of the family.

Snuff is dedicated to two former officers, both of whom served in the West Yorkshire Police Force. Sadly, over the last few years, both have passed away. I was blessed to have them as friends, and I wrote this book based on shared life experiences and endless work memories that could never ever be repeated.

… Unless of course you wrote a fictional book!

DS Andy Laptew- a larger-than-life engaging character with a fascinating work history, including the fact he was the young detective ignored by supervisors when he correctly identified Peter Sutcliffe to be the Yorkshire Ripper. It stayed with him to his dying day that had they just listened to him and acted straight away- several victims would have survived.

I sat with Andy a week before he died from pancreatic cancer and explained how his numerous accounts of what took place inspired this book. I read to him all the first draft chapters that related to him. They brought a tear to his eye and a big thumbs up – that brought a tear to my eye.

DI 91 Martin Taylor (you will discover the relevance of his collar number) –One of the best detectives I ever worked with. A quiet unassuming man who kept his cards close to his chest and had a razor-sharp mind; forever planning and working out possible lines of enquiry and how to get results.

Unbeknown for years, Martin had Pick's disease before he retired. His detective qualities generated both the introduction of DI Tony Drummond into the storyline and his meticulous approach to work.

Jay-Dee

Signed copy

SNUFF

DI Hawk Series

1st EDITION, SIGNED COPY
for BEN and LAURA..

I didn't sell this to you
but I know you will sell
my house!

Hope you enjoy!.

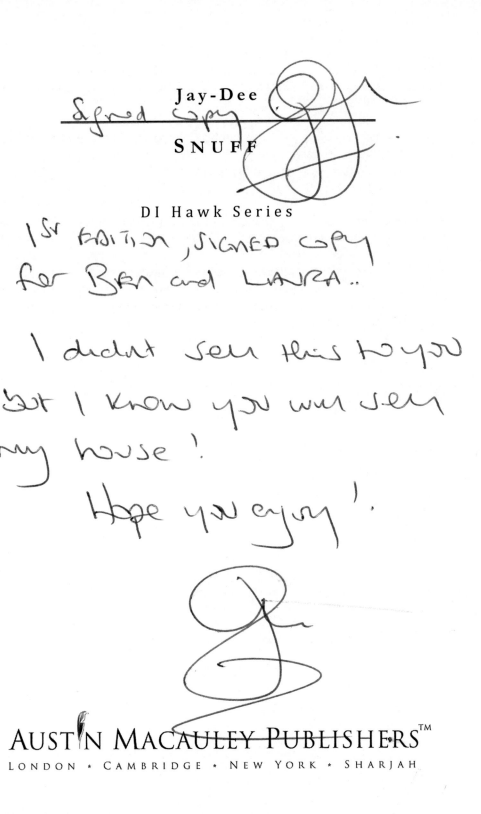

AUSTIN MACAULEY PUBLISHERS™
LONDON ∗ CAMBRIDGE ∗ NEW YORK ∗ SHARJAH

Copyright © Jay-Dee 2022

The right of Jay-Dee to be identified as author of this work has been asserted by the author in accordance with section 77 and 78 of the Copyright, Designs and Patents Act 1988.

All rights reserved. No part of this publication may be reproduced, stored in a retrieval system, or transmitted in any form or by any means, electronic, mechanical, photocopying, recording, or otherwise, without the prior permission of the publishers.

Any person who commits any unauthorised act in relation to this publication may be liable to criminal prosecution and civil claims for damages.

This is a work of fiction. Names, characters, businesses, places, events, locales, and incidents are either the products of the author's imagination or used in a fictitious manner. Any resemblance to actual persons, living or dead, or actual events is purely coincidental.

A CIP catalogue record for this title is available from the British Library.

ISBN 9781398421707 (Paperback)
ISBN 9781398421714 (ePub e-book)

www.austinmacauley.com

First Published 2022
Austin Macauley Publishers Ltd®
1 Canada Square
Canary Wharf
London
E14 5AA

To my daughter, Claudia (Dee), for her undying patience, calm, and control, when sat in my company for nearly a year, when having to transfer thousands of notes thrown at her, both handwritten and typed, on a mobile phone. Proving her value whilst undertaking her master's in advanced project management, putting together this novel from start to finish for submission to the publishers.

For some reason, I haven't seen her since mentioning there's another six books in the Hawk series!

Verb Phrases:
Snuff out,
1. **To extinguish:**
to snuff out a candle.

2. To **suppress; crush:**
to snuff out opposition.

3. To **kill or murder:**
Many lives were snuffed out during the epidemic.

Prologue

Following lots of back-breaking digging in the early nineteenth century, two 'Resurrectionists', Burke and Hare, changed tact – deciding to prey upon live alcoholics instead of buried bodies. With a technique eponymously named as *burking* that achieved traumatic asphyxia; combined with smothering after sitting on their victim's chest, using one hand to cover their nose and mouth, with the other one holding the jaw.

Following capture, conviction, and execution, news of this technique quickly travelled extensively, with peripatetic criminals, including the London Burkers, having another tool at their disposal, adopted and adapted to *snuff out* victims, to make it appear like they had died of natural causes.

Many were taught how to plan and prepare for this effective form of killing, used over a 40-year period by a man, first shown when only a young boy by his dad – to learn all about them before, during, and after principles, and application.

To prevent suspicion and apprehension, to allow continuation of their work; resulting in them becoming a *monster* of a serial killer.

"BEFORE"
LONDON

When we were little, monsters remained quiet and lived under our beds. As we got older, the monsters got louder and moved inside our heads.
Ben H. Winters

Evil begins when you begin to treat people as things.
Terry Pratchett

There is a crack in everything, that's how the light gets in.
Leonard Cohen

1

Workhouse, London, 1880

They couldn't remember why they had left their home in Scotland to travel for weeks before arriving in London, but they would never forget how much their dad's belt hurt when he came back drunk. When he saw that "bitch" had once again passed out after drinking a bottle of gin believing it had been hidden well enough to still be full when he got home.

After initially kicking and punching them both into submission when they tried to protect her, he did what they had seen him do so many times before at home. When he stood over their mother, screaming abuse at her before falling to his knees and placing both hands over her face; before pushing down with force suddenly making her body convulse. With her hands, she began to claw at his face now fighting for her life.

Howard, being older, had seen him do this away from their home many times before, mainly to old men who were down and outs found drunk in secluded yards or streets- until they eventually lay still before his dad beckoned him, after keeping watch. To then help lift and lay them out on the back of a horse-drawn cart before taking them to a big house near their city hospital. Here he waited until his dad returned later carrying notes rubbing his hands together with glee.

'Dead sure way for another easy payday, Son; better than all that digging – plus the poor bastards are in a far better place now.'

Tonight, Howard had to save his mum from this same fate after she turned her head towards them both with eyes bulging, reaching out for help. David who was too young to make a difference and cried out holding his hands to his face begging Dad to stop, but Howard ran towards him, diving headfirst into his face, but facing down so his skull connected fully, causing a loud cracking noise. When his dad's nose gushed blood from both nostrils, he got to his feet unsteadily, to remove his belt.

Howard clearly remembered it was just about bearable from previous beatings if only its leather strap connected with his body, but if the large brass buckle landed on his thin wiry body, it was too much pain to bare; that would send him scurrying away unable to defend his mum any longer.

Tonight though, his mother rallied just in time to save him when stumbling to her feet before smashing one of the many empty gin bottles to hand, over the back of his head, knocking him out cold. Howard in a rage mimicked his well-used technique to kill someone by pushing down as hard as he could onto his blood-red face wanting him to die there and then before his mum dragged him away.

After letting him sip dregs from several bottles, Howard saw David staring at him until he eventually managed a smile with his pain beginning to ease, saying, "Gin helps, little brother. One day you will realise that."

Within minutes, they bundled together all they needed to get away from him for a few days, seeking refuge yet again at the workhouse where her brother had relocated years earlier, but she knew they were welcome to help out with no end of jobs for her and the boys.

Living there, sometimes for a week at a time, gave them a detailed insight of all the chores and tasks that needed to be done to run an effective business. Years later, this paid off for them handsomely when their uncle died young, allowing them to step in, providing a smooth transition to carry on running the establishment. They became well known to most of the charity governors, who readily approved Howard's appointment to become its new work master.

With his own brother Howard going into alcohol-induced decline in his early thirties, David took over the role of manager on his own but rewarded him with a job in their workhouse as a thank you for looking after them so often, with their own mother also given a job becoming head of kitchen.

It was years later after a porter covering their front door took pity on an old vagrant allowing them to occupy one of their day rooms, to offer them a chance to get warm with a blanket and a bowl of food, when they both recognised him as their father after he in turn had noticed them walk past his room, calling out their names.

Both brothers froze upon hearing his voice, with memories flooding back, looking down on an old frail dishevelled tramp reaching out towards them. However, only stares were offered before they turned their backs on him and then walked away in silence before David mentioned to Howard that it looked like he had lost everything, including his belt.

Later that night they both returned after drinking a bottle of gin, knowing what they were going to do when they saw him. David watched Howard once again take the lead to deal with their situation whilst in a crowded room with dozens of other vagrants sleeping soundly all around them.

After placing both hands over their dad's nose and mouth, he held his face in a firm grip, applying extra downward pressure by leaning over his head. It caused him to open his eyes, reaching out towards his son, staring towards him with a look of horror, just before his pupils went into an involuntary rapid flitting movement before his body convulsed momentarily before lying still with his arms dropped down to his sides.

Throughout this 30 second ordeal, his brother whispered into his dad's ear:

"It's best to snuff some candles out for good, you evil bastard. You will never flicker again, so off you go into the dark where you belong."

As they walked back in silence, David reached into his pocket to remove a sharp shard of bone retrieved earlier from their crushing yard. It was where workers smashed bones up with stones, allowing their busy workhouse to generate a revenue by selling its residue and then used to make fertilisers. It was well known they would also remove choice pieces of bone to suck its marrow or chew away at pieces of meat left on them later on after being delivered from city abattoirs and knacker yards.

It was going to be rammed into his dad's skull through his eye socket so when he was found dead it would be assumed another pauper had used it on him. No doubt, during a fight over scraps of meat left on the bone. His brother's technique had presented a far better option, allowing it to appear that he had simply died in his sleep of natural causes, without the need for an investigation, before then being given a pauper's funeral.

Howard had snuffed him out with ease just like he did with candles during his rounds on the dormitory when he covered night shifts in their children's block, where they stayed until 14 years of age before being classed as men to join the others until 60, when they were segregated once again.

This afforded them protection from other inmates kept away from the children, some of whom may well have taken advantage of them, with several sick-minded individuals who were known deviants – wanting access for their perverse pleasures.

Only one person with those proclivities was allowed amongst them. This was known and tolerated because after doing so much for him and his mother over the years, it was his way of paying him back. David turned a blind eye to his brother's heinous actions, now knowing full well having watched this technique on their dad how he stopped them crying out for help when he abused them under the cover of darkness in silence, no doubt when whispering into their ears at the same time, but to comfort them.

David wasn't a religious man but in drink later on he sat alone in his office staring intently at a flickering candle in front of him, now carrying so much more meaning than ever before as he glanced upwards begging forgiveness, before snuffing it out and then slouching forward to sleep fitfully.

Only tonight he had used his hand to 'snuff it out' – meaning hot candle wax connected with the middle of his palm momentarily causing him a little pain. But this was nothing at all compared to the hurt he felt deep inside when reflecting about his miserable life so far, with all that had happened before he even considered what his future held.

Remembering his older brother's words of advice from many years ago, he sipped yet again from another bottle of gin, before falling into a fitful sleep.

2

Small Under Dwelling, Fulham, 1900

Barely a mile away, Simon woke from his fitful sleep laying still and silent after instinctively placing both hands over his mouth, just like his mother had shown him to do so many times, before realising he didn't have to at this moment because he lay on top of their lumpy mattress. For now, at least, he wasn't hiding under the bed with strict instructions, once again, not to make any noise. Often, he would lay there shivering on a cold stone floor when curled up in a ball, with the wooden frame moving slowly at first directly above him but then quicker and quicker, creaking louder and louder all around him.

After a few minutes, he would hear men shout out sounding in pain before they moaned and groaned out loud before suddenly falling silent. At this point, he felt his own heart thumping away when he watched their feet suddenly appear only inches from his face when they swung out of bed before walking away towards their door. Coins were either left on a small table or sometimes thrown back towards the bed where his mother always waited until they had gone before then getting up herself to hold him tightly in her arms. She would weep for ages, with her frail body trembling, stroking and kissing his mop of ginger hair.

As Simon reached out to comfort his mother, she would whisper in his ear that all would be fine, placing his hand over her face then kissing it, then dressing and venturing out to enjoy an early evening sun, before buying bread and meats with coins- either placed or thrown at her. Despite only being eight, Simon didn't fully understand what was going on when he hid and lay silent, but he knew his mother wasn't happy after hearing her so many times praying for them both at night to have a better life and to escape from such a miserable existence.

Simon became confused why every now and then other women who they passed in the street would shout out calling her names. His mother wouldn't explain but he remembered what they said, sometimes threats being made meaning they had to hurry home to throw belongings into bags to move once again. Where they lived now wasn't the best but nobody seemed to know his mother here apart from all those men who still turned up most evenings to see her.

She always called back during the day to check he was OK, often bringing dozens of candles home from a factory where she worked. These were all hidden inside her layers of clothing that he would then drop off at the place where children must have lived in the dark. He still found it hard to say its name 'Orph something' but the man in charge, David, was nice, giving him coins and biscuits (which he shared with his mother having promised he would always look after her) but he didn't like the look of his brother Howard who always drank gin before blowing pipe smoke at him.

All these men calling to see his mother didn't seem like nice men either, especially the one who took his belt off to put it around her neck when he heard her choking before their bed finally went still as his mother coughed loudly. Simon didn't jump out to stop him or shout, having promised to stay out of view and keep silent for her.

They had many rats in their room but he wasn't scared of them after they had scampered around him so many times when under the bed, but later when he was allowed to make a noise, he often stamped down on them hard to kill them all. His mother always telling him that the man with the belt really was the biggest rat of them all but to leave him alone for now. Young Simon had seen this man's feet many times but he had once dared to peek a quick look upwards from under the bed when he left their room heavily in drink, shouting abuse at his mother.

So now, he had also seen his face, one never to be forgotten because with his small dark beady eyes and those whiskers around his face, he didn't only act like a rat, he looked just like one as well. Simon knew what he did to rats, when he didn't have to lay silent under the bed.

3

Workhouse Dormitory, London, 1900

After sipping from his bottle of gin, his hands finally stopped shaking. Sitting back in a comfortable chair, he sent out a plume of aromatic pipe smoke, with one long exhale high into the air before glancing up at all the white flickering candles lit earlier on in the evening. Soon it would be his favourite few hours that made his work so enjoyable, feeling a little tingle in his groin because after all his hard work it would soon be time for him to have a little play.

He glanced across at his metal rod with its conical piece of tin hanging loosely from one end, designed to allow him to place it over flames to put them out silently. This was one of many reasons they called him 'Snuff' because he snuffed out candles.

Another sinister explanation, hardly ever spoken about had generated this name, with no obvious link to Howard, his given Christian name. But many a young boy in the pitch black of night knew why, when suddenly they smelt alcohol in the air from his breath, then pipe tobacco on his fingers; just before his hand clamped firmly over their mouth and nose to silence any cries for help. Before gently lowering himself onto their bottom bunk to comfort them after just taking up residence, normally alone as an orphan, having lost guardians, parents or loved ones.

He would make them feel loved though, in his own way, gently applying more pressure on their faces, until they complied and lay motionless or until more headstrong little buggers who wriggled about resisted longer until finally passing out on him.

However, he always assured them that they were in no mortal danger whispering assurances into their ear before giving it a gentle kiss.

"Don't worry little one, Snuff will not snuff you out for good; it's just to put you out for a short while, just like my little candles."

Others from top bunks would watch on, grateful they hadn't been selected as many nearby placed both hands over their ears to block out his grunts and groans until he climbed out and shuffled back to his room, putting his boots back on and then sipping gin, and smoking his pipe again with a look of contentment on his face.

They had quickly learnt that following a long arduous day's work, you kept quiet or others admonished punishment. Most laboured within the workhouse, but a few lucky ones escaped its imposing regime when hired out for a few coins to work long days in local businesses, who took full advantage of cheap labour, but they tended to offer better food, compared to with what you had slopped out in house, after a wakeup bell gave you ten minutes to get from 'bed to fed'. Here they would join an early morning line, winding its way like a hungry snake, towards a large steaming cauldron of sloppy food thrown into bowls by grim face trustees, often women. One of few times they were allowed into the male block, to ladle out watery soup or congealed porridge.

New young arrivals failing to stifle their cries or sniffles from fear and despair, many still grieving recent losses of a parent were given a smack. Not like one expected from a chastising parent but a thump from a hardened street wise young thug, happy to hand out a punishment, imposing their domination over their new vulnerable arrival. This made them submit to future demands to perform chores as they began to adjust to a new life of servitude, but with many succumbing to such a harsh regime or choosing to end their life of misery.

Some young ones didn't last long but others thrived just like Simon had after winning favour by knowing their workhouse owner, David. Having met prior to his incarceration after being sent to his office as a runner by his mother to deliver batches of candles for over a year, before her demise sneaking them out of the factory, where she worked eight hours a day to keep them off the streets living in a small damp and dingy under dwelling. It was riddled with vermin but she still had to subsidise her rent with weekly visits from many customers, including the rent man she called 'King Rat' who often left his mother sobbing with a new bruise or mark on her neck.

Over several years, Simon had seen or heard so many being abused by Snuff but thankfully he had left him alone since his arrival. Perhaps because his brother had told him so or because he was physically big and strong – soon looking down on their silent abuser, not only when standing next to him but also when laying silently in his upper bunk bed.

They had already decided it was time for this abuse to stop – by all sticking together to sort him out, with it seeming only fitting that Snuff should now have done to him what he had done to so many. It meant that after sneaking upon him in the dark barefoot while laying back in his chair, they held him down with Simon taking the lead before clasping both hands hard, using all his strength over his face whilst leaning forwards and downwards over his head whispering softly into his ear before he died.

"Do worry, because you're going to be snuffed out for good, you dirty bastard."

It was never repeated, but towards the end when he knew he was going to die, it felt as if Howard, when staring up into his eyes, had tried to smile and then kiss the palm of his hand just before Howard placed his hands over his, to give a gentle farewell squeeze.

His death would have passed for an old man who was an alcoholic dying of natural causes falling onto the floor from his office chair, but one of the boys had taken his clay pipe and tobacco. This alerted David to the fact that he had been killed, but when he considered what he had done to so many over the years he did nothing at all. He accepted Howard had met with his just and deserved end, no doubt at the hands of those he had abused.

He had begged him over the years to stop but it was a sickness in his head, perhaps taking so many beatings and blows had led to alcoholism, but he had allowed him to keep his job out of pity for him – paying for his services with only bottles of gin, pipe tobacco and ready access to young children who wouldn't talk or complain.

Over the years some had died at Howard's hands with obvious signs of abuse who they couldn't risk being handed to the authorities for a pauper's funeral for fear of discovery. Luckily an arrangement had been reached with a local cabinet maker – also an undertaker. It meant he could dispose of any such mistakes by putting bodies of small boys in with an adult, to share a coffin to dispose of them without any comebacks.

In return a boy from their workhouse would be sent to sleep every night in the undertaker's basement where he stored coffins made above in his workshop. In this underground damp environment, rats kept gnawing away at wood sometimes even worse faces of deceased, normally eyes first so their job upon hearing any rodent scratching was to protect them by hitting rats with sticks to fight them off.

It was hardly surprising that boys only lasted a day or two before they wouldn't continue - despite the fear and threats of being lashed until Simon was their answer. Several times when delivering candles over the years prior to his mum's demise, he had disturbed vermin within a store cupboard in David's office. When rats ran away from their hiding place as quick as a flash, he cornered his prey stamping them to death, explaining he had done this for many years in their home that had been infested, so he didn't fear them in the least.

Simon was rewarded with a much more comfortable bed and an extra meal every night at the undertaker's when he slept with his coffins. They were normally left empty but nearer funeral dates, bodies would be collected from homes meaning that every now and then a cadaver would also share the same room that he slept in, but again it wasn't a problem because Simon could cope with it.

One night he awoke to what he thought was another rat gnawing on wood, but to his horror, after searching hard but failing to find one, with noise persisting, he finally approached a coffin – holding the body of an old man. He had only just arrived that evening to discover upon lifting its lid that his eyes were open as he stared up at him in a confused state, with his fingernails covered in blood after scratching away at the wood.

Simon looked down at him with pity, all his loved ones believed he was dead and he was so weak and frail now at the end of his life. He did what he had done once before, but tonight it was for all the right reasons after placing both his hands over his face before pressing down to help him make his final journey – watching his eyes flicker just like a candle's flame before the life in him went out, meaning he was now at peace in the darkness.

In the morning Simon recounted in a very 'matter-of-fact' way to the cabinet maker what he had done during the night, describing how he had helped him along by snuffing out the old man who wasn't dead, but was now at peace.

After accepting his big slice of buttered bread for breakfast, Simon hungrily chewed it while walking away back to the workhouse. This meant he missed the look of horror and incredulity towards him by the undertaker, struggling to take in the enormity of events taking place earlier. He certainly took in that between Workhouse and Funeral Parlour, they had created an absolute monster; when still only a young boy, barely yet a teenager.

Fuck knows what he would be like in years to come, when a man.

4

Adult Dormitory Workhouse

Simon Wick's reputation had preceded him before vacating the children's block, now classed as an adult when greeted by David, the House Master, after wishing him a 'happy birthday'. A man showing him kindness since recognising him when they named him Simon, from the day he arrived, remembering his mother who sent him with parcels of stolen candles. He didn't know his own surname but they guessed he must have been about eight, recording his status admission owing to the fact he had become an orphan, along with a brief description – 'Pale Ginger'.

He was sent there following the murder of his mother by their rent collector who put his belt around her neck when he hid beneath the bed, but that old score had been settled recently after working away from the workhouse at an undertaker's. He had choked him to death after chasing him down an alleyway into a secluded backyard returning an experience often suffered by his dear mother of having a belt pulled tight around your neck.

Within months of this happening, rumours circulated that Simon had done it but David protected him from peelers who went through the motions of checking out street talk, but they were satisfied with a cover story given that he hadn't left the premises that day. Plus of course, this rent collector was known to have many enemies – often collecting payments with sexual favours from women, whose husbands upon hearing this must have sought him out to seek retribution and revenge. Odds on, "That's what must have happened?".

David himself had called in and spoken to his adult corridor 'walkers' to keep an eye out for Simon Both were giants of men, big Dave Stainthorpe, a former resident when an alcoholic – but months chained up in a cell had cured that infliction. With his size, it warranted a trustee's job – plus with a club, nobody challenged his position, bringing calm and order within such a hostile environment. Making sure fights and incidents were quickly quelled caused by troublesome residents being dealt with firmly, sometimes exiled from their workhouse, never to be allowed to return if they posed too much of a problem.

Despite strong warnings being given out, David knew that Simon would have some idiot wanting to make a name for himself to stamp down his authority as the 'hard man', so he could then control rationing and perks that new arrivals may bring with them, especially children that had 'come of age'. Normally being put in their place to run errands for them and also doing menial chores because they owned them until the next leader of the pack stepped forward to rule their roost.

As David escorted Simon himself, many wondered what his motive was to protect him so much but few would have worked out that with his already established fighting prowess, physical stature and power, he had potential to be worth a lot of money. Once his old mate called to check him out as a possible new addition to his fighting crew who fought prize-fights around their city and surrounding areas with big money being wagered on the results and healthy purses to the winners.

It was a hostile violent world, but from what he had seen and heard, Simon would be well suited to it, but for now it was all about looking out for his investment for a future return. He would propose a decent percentage of winning purses, all these future plans generated todays escorted walk, and the reason they now spoke in any detail for the first time.

"Simon, I have big plans for your future, I can get you out of here but others may want to cause you harm."

A smile from his young escort instantly vanished before pulling an aggressive face uttering:

"Let them fucking try," before, then assuming a boxer's stance with clenched fists. He began to bob and weave just like a fighter would, throwing out numerous fast fire jabs and hooks.

"Don't you worry sir, Simon will be able to look after himself, you learn that in here."

David produced a small bladed knife used to cut and carve candles that once belonged to his brother when shaping and settling them into holders – handing it to him before winking then instructing:

"I know you're a lot younger and a handy lad, but make your mark early, show them all what will happen if they fuck with you, don't hold back one bit with the first one that has a go. My walkers will look out for you best they can but if you need to cut and carve them like a candle, then do so. Listen carefully Simon, trust me on this – I didn't even extract revenge after you snuffed out my brother."

Simon froze still upon hearing this, often wondering why nothing bad came of it, nobody seemed bothered. He had heard lots of rumours that a 'half gypsy' boxing coach called to see them, looking out for 'handy lads'. Several had returned with bloody noses and swollen eyes, describing how they lost to a young boxer who knew how to fight. Simon had worked out soon that he would get to spar with him, after picking fights with several at a time and beating them on the dormitory wards, he knew he could impress; to win his freedom, but he would never trust anyone, always looking out for himself. To survive it had to be that way, nobody else could step in to help. David sounded genuine; after all it wasn't every day you forgave someone who had murdered your brother.

Simon was well used by now, to stamping down, throttling or snuffing out whatever animal or human that needed dealing with, he knew when to release pressure, but could easily finishing them if he chose. With his new little toy, he could have fun carving away. He really didn't give a fuck about anyone else after what he had already been through and had to do so far from being a little boy hiding under his mother's bed terrified, to now, as an adult, stood holding a knife waiting to enter a dormitory full of grown men, many barking mad and ruthless, regardless of what his actual age was.

As both doors swung open, he came under intense scrutiny when entering, news travels fast in a workhouse. They peered out from the dark, watching his every move, staring him up and down with many realising that what they had heard about him was no doubt true, he looked a force to be reckoned with. Those who felt brave enough to hold his stare longer than others were confronted, but with humour initially. To hopefully save them a beating or a blood shed, with Simon shouting in his best cockney accent:

"What? No birthday cake for the new boy? You fackers!"

Laughter broke out all around him as he was taken to his bed, but left alone with no need to use his knife after handing out a vicious beating with his fists when a retired punch-drunk boxer fancied his chances.

His performance worked, showing off his natural speed and aggression, obviously loving every moment; nobody doubted a sadistic killer in the making.

One day following an escort to David's office by Big Dave the walker, they never saw him again, but some amazing stories were told for many years to come about all his amazing exploits and adventures.

5

Blackfriars Bridge, River Thames Tidal Bank

It had developed into a standoff with Simon Wick refusing to back down – especially now his first two attackers laid out face down. Initially in wet tidal mud, where no doubt they may have suffocated or drowned, had young children from their workhouse not pulled them onto their backs. Before then unclogging mouths and nostrils from putrid mud, inhaled and swallowed along with factory spillage chemicals washed to shore or dumped along the River Thames embankment.

All their stripy shirts – the standard uniform of the workhouse, had easily identified them for what they were believing as kids they would be a soft target. To confiscate their daily finds after 12 hours of hard work scavenging. Anything found of value had been handed already to their 'team leader' Simon, who in turn would later present it all to David. He had sent out all his young 'Mudlarks' to join hundreds of others desperately wading all day long hoping to find coins or anything else of value, normally Flotsam and Jetsam that had been washed ashore from boats and barges using busy shipping lanes.

As with all organised crime in their city, it was territorial as self-made gangsters staked 'manor' claims within their neighbourhood. This was why Jacob Colmore now stood panting heavily knee-deep in mud with an incoming tide rising rapidly around him. In desperation to avoid serious injury or drowning with wet mud acting like a giant suction pad, pulling him further down he told this 'Mad Ginger' exactly who he was, and which gang he worked for, so he had better 'back the fack off' and leave him alone.

Simon had never heard of his gang, but knew from the outset there was no way he was going to give up today's rich pickings just because they had fronted him up earlier on, when explaining he was 'bang out of order' coming to 'their manor', so hand over all they had found today as punishment, but in future they would keep half; with them picking first from the daily booty.

Had this sinking gangster, who had run away from him towards the river, not been covered in mud, Simon may have noticed that large mole on his face to connect with a nickname given to this young street thug, because he had heard of a Jewish gang who constantly fought the Irish all around this area who had Jack 'Spot' Comer as one of its leaders.

Simon realised that besides their tell-tale shirts, his bright ginger hair may have provoked them into conflict – believing he was Irish, who they hated with a passion.

Simon left him alone because he was a spent force before rounding up all the younger children. Sticking together, they returned to their 'manor' – sadly, for most of them it was where they would live the rest of their lives, if they survived its regime.

In view of an embarrassing defeat to the 'Ginger', the gang would have kept quiet about this incident but workers on the adjacent bridge, creating an extra carriage lane, looked down on events as they unfolded below them. Many had seen just how well 'Ginger' had done, a mightily impressive performance, dominating the talk of all the taverns where they drank later on that night.

Amongst this crowd were several 'elders' of their crime syndicate who got to hear of the 'Workhouse Nutter', who despite his age had sorted out their best enforcer who was called in to see Mr Comer senior, intrigued to learn more about 'Ginger'; who had kicked his arse. After this, rumours quickly circulated that he was soon to be trained to become a bare-knuckle fighter by the 'half gypsy' boxing club owner, who was best mates with the workhouse boss.

They would watch his performance with interest, because if he was as good as they said he would work for them in the future. This wouldn't be a discussion, it would be a fact; otherwise, there would be another fire to put out for a dissenter who didn't listen first time. Followed up with a visit to a graveyard showing them a recently dug plot, where they had just dug a little deeper for them potentially to lay at rest beneath the coffin, soon destined to be buried there if they really wanted to upset them again by not listening. Unless they complied and didn't make the situation graver than it already was.

6

Workhouse Master's Office,
London – Simon's Last Day

David explained to his old mate, Seamus, that he had known Simon since being a young lad after the early death of his mother, but he wouldn't be sold to him unless he paid him 'decent coin'. Without doubt this young boy had real value, the best prospect by far, having what it took to become great, not only physically, but mentally. Hard as nails, plus an out and out evil fucker who didn't take any shit from anyone, with many tales reaching his ears about how he had stood his ground with grown men who were no slouches themselves – with them backing off rather than fighting him.

Seamus sat smiling back, letting him talk the talk, but he knew for sure it would be a done deal, he hadn't even brought his boy to test him out, who normally sparred with them to see if they had what it took. David, still attempting to build up the price explained that before he had filled out – you wouldn't look at him twice. A pale and skinny boy with a fiery mop of red hair, but not Irish bred. Many thought his name 'Wick' was given to him because he looked like a candle, with others realising that in the wrong hands he could be just as dangerous, with the old saying that: 'you don't play with fire'.

David didn't recount events surrounding his brother's death, but alluded to rumours about a rent collector found dead in a backstreet with his belt around his neck after being badly beaten. This coincided with Simon returning after his work at the undertakers with bloodied fists, telling his mates that he had just found and sorted out the biggest rat so far.

It was known that his mother had been strangled to death with a belt, with Simon waiting with her in their room for well over a week until the smell of rotting flesh alerted neighbours to her fate. They had formed an opinion that he was waiting in silence for her killer to return to then extract revenge upon him because he had carved a wooden slat from the bed using a knife making it into a long spear. So, they guessed he was going to throw it at him after they found marks in their door consistent with where he had practised throwing it over and over again.

David couldn't hide his look of confusion when Seamus shook hands on their deal with a down payment, even before Simon entered his office. A bonus would also be given every time he fought and won, with the bigger bare-knuckle fights earning the most coin.

They drank whiskey together with Seamus explaining that 'fucker of a Marquis' had driven bare knuckle boxing underground with his stupid rules, it was getting harder to earn a living from it unless he managed to get one of the big-named gypsy boys to turn up for an event at a horse fair.

His extended gypsy family helped him out so he had managed to last in this game as well as running an Amateur Boxing Gym where he would put Simon to the test. With footsteps heard, they turned to watch 'Big Dave' the walker and Simon approach, making an ex-bare knuckle boxing champion, Seamus O'Farrell, smile; his gait and demeanour said it all, but best of all those shark's eyes held the key to the treasure box.

He was a natural born killer.

After beckoning Simon into the office, David explained his life had just changed for the better. Seamus offered his hand to feel the power in his grip, before pouring him his first ever whiskey. He knew enough about this boy already – you didn't knock out two 'Jew Boy' minders on a tidal bank, unless you were a fighter. Those feckers hated the Irish, so Seamus celebrated now owning their future nemesis; he would kick Jack Comers boys to kingdom come, and not before time.

"Simon, you sure can kill as many of them feckers as you want in the ring, sures you can son, to win me lots of money; but not outside it, you're a sures bet – for sure to be sure."

Simon stared down at this strange looking and sounding man, totally confused for two reasons – he knew you normally had to impress him by sparring with his boy, but he had come alone? But most of all, he really couldn't work out why the fuck there had been so many 'sures' in that sentence – fucking gypsies, he'd heard so much about them over the years – all of it bad.

7

Small Clearing, Epping Forest, 1920

Her mother's haunting scream when squatting down to push hard in this dense forest was sadly the last ever noise she would remember her by; with her last ever touch being a vice-like grip on the forearm before she slumped against a large Oak tree, after haemorrhaging to death whilst attempting to give birth to her child.

Refusing to leave their bodies to the elements, Mary armed herself with a heavy broken branch and many stones, before crouching down beside her stillborn brother and dead mother. Mary stared out with her senses heightened, picking up on the slightest of noises from all around them indicating the presence of potential scavengers.

A few hours later, after the heavens opened, she used this pouring rain to wash away blood to see her brother's face before kissing him, wondering what may have been, under different circumstances. Had her mother not fallen pregnant to the squire whom they had worked for before running away, after overhearing him in drink talking about 'eliminating the problem' to protect his position and marriage.

Mary woke with a startle; hearing a noise she knew to be a crossbow being fired as its bolt thudded into the neck of a wild deer collapsing after running past them. It was perused by its attackers who halted abruptly upon seeing them despite her attempt to hide from view using foliage- but not from lifelong hunters, born and growing up in the forest, who had just picked up on all the clues left for them, with freshly cut branches exposing sap giving away her best efforts at creating a camouflage.

Realising the gypsies were now moving towards them, Mary stood holding her sharpened spear in front of her with her ammunition; a large number of stones piled up by her feet. One thing she had learnt over years from many gamekeepers on the Estate was to never trust a gypsy, nor have anything to do with them.

With her long black dishevelled hair stuck across her mud-covered face, she then screamed in fear, making them hold their advance. Seeing her dead mother and new born child at her feet, they quickly started working out events. Both women wore scullery maid outfits bearing a family crest belonging to the man who owned all this land, including the deer they had just killed.

An elder of the clan held out his hand towards her, praising her for looking out for her loved ones, but they would now look out for her – after giving her family a decent burial. He shouted for Bull to start digging as Mary watched a powerfully built man carrying a dead deer, alone, over his broad shoulders. He threw it to the floor to begin to dig like an animal, using only his hands before handing him a shovel with a shake of their heads in disbelief at the simpleton.

They had also quickly worked out that their new family member would now solve the problem of finding a partner for Bull because he was getting more and more of a pain over recent months, wanting to tie the knot and have himself a wife. However, no sane gypsy girl wanted him anywhere near them; at least he would be given one that looked like a gypsy girl who would soon learn their ways.

They couldn't do with him when he was angry or upset, because he could beat the fuck out of anyone; before now he had only ever come second to a big chunk of wood landed to the back of his head.

But God help you though if he got up from that.

8

Romany Wagon – Vardo, Reading, 1926

Now putting in extra effort by pushing away a little harder, the caravan wagon moved even more, picking up momentum with Mary working out in her mind just how much she stood to make, which was the only thing making her smile, unlike the fat fucker who pulled a contorted face and now sweated like a pig on top of her. She stroked what hair he had left before giving a little gasp in his ear. It amused her because her coin wasn't made standing, but when she was quite literally laid on her back. Just like now when willing this fat ugly bastard to finish quickly, just in case the bloke outside gave up waiting for his turn. Mary moaned even louder as she told him he made her caravan rock more than anyone else, as she felt him tense up and finish before half collapsing in a heap across her ample chest; she glanced up at the empty hooks on the wall shelf above her head that thankfully no longer had all the ornaments hanging from them. She had learnt to take them down and place them inside a cupboard box; they had fallen down in the past, but she had educated herself well over the years in many ways, especially how to please them so they always came back for more.

Still only in her twenties and proud of her body, they often told her she was the best, but she also bullshit every one of her clients so took what they said with a pinch of salt; it was all about the coin. She had worked out earlier it could soon be time for a change of scenery, having nearly saved up enough to start afresh. As he crawled off Mary, he called his mate to join them, with his usual jest.

"If the caravans a rocking, then don't come a knocking."

Today, he also paid for his young apprentice who had travelled there with him to have a ride, but on condition he could watch; plus she also got her tits out, so he could play with them. Mary agreed to this because he was paying double, with an added bonus that if he could get hard enough on time that she would fuck him again before leaving. She knew his young buck would only last a few minutes, so she reached across while he pounded away on top with her hand stroking his sagging scrotum. She also stared into his fat face; then moaned and groaned louder than normal as he rose to the occasion, to thankfully end up paying out again. This allowed her to put away a few more extra coins for herself as her 'extras' were now adding up nicely – with her keeper being given a coin a man as he knew how many went inside to fuck her, he watched them come and go as he worked away on the caravan opposite as it neared completion prior to collection by its new owner.

They called him 'Bull' O'Conner because of his strength and dark tan; he worked outside all day, plus a lot of wood stain he used splashed all over his skin, but also, because when not making caravans, he was a bare-knuckle boxer, who would charge in grunting with his head down to finish off his opponents.

His next fight, now eagerly awaited in a few weeks when thousands of gypsies would attend the next horse fair. This would allow Mary the chance to make some serious money when they threw coins at her, after successfully selling all their stolen equines, along with those they had actually bred themselves over the last year.

It was her planned departure date; to hitch a ride with one of the city gents, who would take her to London; which had to be better than what she had in life just now. Because all the women scowled at her – hurling abuse almost daily, calling her Mary Rock, saying all she was good for was making the caravan rock about, not as it was first intended when found in the woods with large stones collected to launch at any scavengers. After being taken in by the travellers, they knew she wasn't one of their own, so was given to the 'Bull' who wasn't going to get a gypsy woman off any of the elders; he wasn't the brightest being prone to fits, but good with his hands as both a carpenter and a fighter. It made, him happy, plus, it had saved a Romany having to suffer the ordeal of him as a husband.

Mary had memories of living in a 'big house' and helping her mum wash and clean for its owners whose own daughter would often play 'teacher' with her, standing in front of a chalkboard, but at least she could now read and write and was even good with numbers. Why her mum ran away with her, she would never know for sure, but had worked out his lordship had given in to temptation before getting her pregnant as she died giving birth in the woods; it had put her own destiny in place which she was reminded of as 'Bull' came into the Vardo, to collect his money, to hand to the elders as he passed her a wet flannel to wash away her days work from between her legs, before he no doubt wanted a go as well, judging by the bulge in his overalls; sadly now knowing too well, yet another reason why he lived up to his bull nickname.

9

Coursing Event, Alder Moor,
Berkshire, 1926

It was a win-win situation for all of them today after muzzling their hounds who had been kept keen after not feeding them for two days. They now strained at their leashes before being released for the hunt with money exchanging hands in every direction, almost as often as the bottles of homemade whiskey frequently passed around their group.

It was good-natured banter as all of today's clans were related through marriage, managing not to fight one another now for over a year leaving them to sort out others who dared to encroach on agreed boundaries. Within these they operated selling wares, plying their trade, stealing whatever they could get their hands on under the cover of travelling after doing the first two legitimate endeavours.

Bets were kept to a minimum today because it was more about a team effort, not a competition, because the number of hares and rabbits they could catch, without them being torn to shreds by the dogs, would pay well. They had realised years ago that there was a lucrative market for undamaged felts with milliners paying decent money for whatever they caught – if they hadn't been savaged or ripped to shreds.

It meant that hundreds of them would soon be trussed up ready for when they arrived out of the city to load them up into carts drawn by horses wearing top of the range expensive tack. Under normal circumstances these would be stolen later on that night from their stables, but not wishing to disrupt future business they were ignored, for now at least.

Mary helped Bull get ready as they set off together with the others before she was left behind at a secret rendezvous point watching over all the horses and preparing food for when they returned with furs later on. When once again she saw well-heeled 'London Boys' arriving early which didn't surprise her one bit.

After flirting with Henry for quite a while now, he was under her spell; he started off wearing his gloves to hide his wedding ring until he opened up explaining it was only a marriage of convenience – with two wealthy business owners cementing future trade and opportunities, with expansion in mind, after families were bonded closer together. They had been children meeting as teenagers, eventually married off.

Mary really didn't give a fuck but played along that she was just a shy girl who had also married young with no say in the matter, but regretted being a 'stay at home' type of girl. But how she would love to visit his city one day; she looked into his eyes, twirling her hair and trying her best to blush.

This had him flushing up before nervously licking his lips, salivating at the thought of her in his arms, let alone when they ended up kissing, after which he begged her to travel to meet him in a hotel, handing her a business card for his place of work a milliner's factory where his office was located.

He assured her that if she called enquiring about work as a cover story, she would be brought to see him after presenting his card, meaning they could then spend the rest of the day together as his imagination ran wild suggesting he would buy her the finest silk lingerie if she wore it for him later on.

Mary eventually feigned a blush but kept his fantasy alive because it was always good to have an exit plan, plus Henry certainly represented rich trappings, making her giggle as she thought of all the hares caught for him as she leaned forward a little more to snare him, allowing a stare down at her ample bosom like hundreds before him who then went on to pay for sex.

They had all known exactly what was going on whereas this naive posh boy didn't have a clue. He would be in way too deep before he even realised he was getting well and truly fucked over by a different kind of animal.

But just like those sweet fluffy hares about to be caught, he would feel her bite; by which time it would be way too late.

10

Horse Fair, Chipping Barnet, North London, 1926

With so much riding on the outcome of this fight, they looked after their man with a comfortable journey to its venue in a Hanson horse drawn cab, with travelling companions under strict instructions to get him there safely, but most importantly keep him off the booze, smokes and women until after his bare-knuckle event.

As Simon was escorted to his tent fully kitted out with chair, treatment table and bandages, Mary who walked past his entourage was instantly drawn to him. He also noticed her smile and her giving him a wink with her mass of black hair piled up high, with her corset drawn tight around her waist to exaggerate her shape with ample cleavage on show.

Mary knew the moment she saw that look of intent on his face that this was the man who would be the first to beat her fella who wasn't at his best just recently, fitting far more often perhaps with the pressure of this fight, plus his opponent's formidable stature and reputation. So much so that she wagered her future nest egg on his defeat backing the 'Wick' hoping he would shine through their bout.

Her undergarments were minimal, allowing her to hoist the dress when her client had handed over enough coin for special treatment with a note 'Mary Rocks' on her caravan door, parked up in a prime location. Not far from the trading ring, allowing hundreds of horny men to call to see her directly after a pay out from the cattle and horse auction. Only now she was up for sale as well, and always in demand with her looks and figure.

That evening Mary stood close to her bookmaker because she knew it wouldn't be long before collecting her winnings as the Bull was constantly battered during the fight to his head in fierce exchanges, as Gypsies sensed their money was lost and yelled for blood to spur him on.

They got their wish as Bull gouged out his opponent's eye with his thumb as blood suddenly splattered into his own face but worked against him as Simon Wick, now enraged beyond control, threw him to the floor. After head butting him unconscious, he let his blood drip down into his open mouth before placing both his big hands over his face and then laying over the top of him, using all his weight to push down as hard as he could.

By the time they pulled him away from over the Bull, he was fitting beyond control after biting off his own tongue that had blocked his throat. With one last convulsion he died, causing a mass brawl to erupt with no money being paid out by default, with those holding the purse now seizing the moment to run off with all the wagers, including Mary's. Suddenly she found herself without man or money apart from today's earnings that wouldn't last long; she needed to act fast.

Later on, after his tent flap was opened, she walked directly up to him after telling the others she had medical skills, before cleaning out his eye socket with spirits as they held Simon down to stop him killing her as well. Then she fastened a patch and bandage to his head, telling him he was in safe hands. She could always make men feel better, and he would be no exception.

Simon Wick stared up at this beautiful woman that had caught his eye earlier, – sadly reminding him he now only had one, but he sensed he had just found someone to look after him as he managed to mutter, before passing out:

'Thank you, gypsy doll.'

11

Boxing Club, Lambeth, 1927

Even with his head guard on inside the ring, he still felt intense pain around his eye socket, but those who owned him stood outside the ring weren't bothered about that one fucking bit. But it caused them real pain, when an average lefthanded boxer chosen to spar with him, could land blows easily on the blind side, to his right. It meant that rival crime gangs would take full advantage of this weakness to bankroll a big win by fully exploiting his injury.

When it was bare knuckle so without any gloves, his other flank would be jabbed at repeatedly, trying to get a thumb into his only eye, then blinding him-leaving him open to an onslaught; that even Simon wouldn't be able to survive.

Slumping down heavily onto his corner stool after only a few rounds, they had seen enough, with their looks and nods confirming what he had already feared, that earning easy money at unlicensed events had ended. They all knew he had been loyal over many years making them a fortune, so they didn't abandon him and gave him a new role within their organisation, now explained.

They operated hundreds of whores across London who either worked in brothels or did escort services for higher end clients at hotels – where they had control of concierges on their payroll who wouldn't throw them out when they touted for business in busy foyers.

They also took big money bookings using one of their many 'modelling agencies'; where explicit brochures showed exactly what was on offer to clients, detailing what they would do for them, covering all sorts of extreme predilections and sexual behaviour. Some girls were even prepared to take a beating, providing they were paid enough money for it.

Simon knew this job offer, to oversee the bitches, would earn him a good wage with many perquisites – included pick of the litter, to pleasure him with any existing or new whores who he could audition before they earned decent money. It was common for new to replace old when no longer in as much demand, but they could walk the streets under close control of their pimps until they were finally past it completely, often found dead or simply disappearing.

This generous offer came with a caveat that Simon had fully expected – having seen how they leered at Mary when initially calling to see him after his fight when tending to his injuries, even then having a little flirt with them.

They wanted her on this 'menu' to be offered to higher end clients, with Simon not doubting for one moment that they would make a meal of her themselves; until something new came along, being served up to occupy their minds.

Simon knew the alternative if he didn't comply with their 'request', with them ruling the roost. They wouldn't hesitate to just kill him off and then take her, so it didn't take long to remove his old, soiled boxing glove for the last time ever before shaking hands on their deal. Just like he had done when they had first called at Seamus's gym with their disgraced son in tow, last seen waist high in tidal mud.

Seamus had taken more persuading, but after a fire at another gym followed by a forced escorted visit to a cemetery to stand over a recently dug plot, with an offer to join the departed real soon, he then agreed they would now own Simon, with him getting a small percentage of winnings; better than getting nothing apart from an early grave.

Simon made his way home dejected, deciding he would break the news to her gently, but having sampled what she had to offer for many months, he knew full well she would be making a lot of money as demand would be high. She was one dirty little gypsy bitch who still had her looks and body – for now at least; plus Maria would be looking out for her, being an experienced madam whose reputation preceded her.

Within months of taking over his new role, his bosses couldn't help but laugh as they heard glowing reports of how well he did his job. Street talk circulated that their one-eyed monster who handed out beatings for fun, was no longer called Simon but 'Cyclops', but only when he was well out of their hearing and out of sight.

12

Wood and Sons – Hat Makers, Blackfriars, London

It wasn't difficult to stage bumping into him, knowing full well he always returned with his 'Leporids' (a word he had taught her when flirting with each other, waiting for the hares and rabbits) on a Sunday evening, to deliver them under the cover of night to his factory.

So next morning the felting process would begin to allow his milliners to make their hats in a highly challenging business as one by one, with diminished demand, this industry dwindled with soaring costs. With health and safety implications kicking in, workshops were equipped with adequate ventilation as per the requirements.

This was following a marked increase of mercury poisoning during a manufacture process. Workers were initially believed to be drinking too much after feeling neurotic and lethargic before displaying physical symptoms of shaking. Covered in legions and now being linked to Mad Hatters Disease, with fewer willing to work with mercury because of its inherent dangers now being well recorded and talked about.

Pulling up outside his factory, the horse recognised Mary first, when picking up on her scent, then her soft voice when she held his bridal before whispering into its ear to calm him down from a long tiring journey after pulling a fully laden cart.

Mary removed her Barnet to show her hair, and Henry Wood couldn't hold back his joy, jumping downexcitedly, before escorting her to his private office inside, where they embraced, then fumbled before she feigned innocence telling him to slow things down. She had only just left her husband so now needed to find work and security before she could possibly commit to a relationship.

Especially with a married man! For goodness' sake, what would people think of her? Her reputation would be in tatters.

This flashed memories across her mind of two or three men at a time having a well-paid orgy with her, fulfilling their every fantasy as she played along, letting them do whatever they wanted, knowing how much they had paid for it in advance.

Still, as per the plan, this was to be played out slowly, as discussed with Simon – whom she had stayed with after moving in with him when not working at their brothel as he earned a crust, running errands for crime gangs. That wasn't enough for them but as he told her many times over, with her help, they could have the whole loaf.

They were streetwise enough to know that a naive loved up rich kid was going to be taken for a fortune, after she had hunted him down and then snared him into her bed, taking him places he had never been before- with a big surprise in store at the end.

Now allowing him to feel her body over the top of her clothes, she let him hear a little gasp then a moan as she glanced down below into the street where a man wearing an eye patch looking up at her with a smile, and then a thumbs up. A man who had just realised that his plan may just work with this gullible slapper's help. She actually believed he was going to honour their deal, running off to disappear; to live their life together if all worked out as expected.

Simon actually knew her dream could become half right, because he would make sure she vanished – never to be seen again, if they pulled the plan off.

13

Felt Treatment Room, Wood and Sons

Rumours abound after only working there for less than six months that there was only one possible reason why young Henry would suddenly take such an interest in checking out hares and rabbits so often, before skinned. That also coincided with the sudden arrival of the 'Gypsy Girl' now shown extreme favours – when allowed to work half shifts and often disappearing on mid-week afternoons. Plus, she never had to cover weekends. They joked that they now handled stolen goods loaded off the carts owned by rich gentry from country estates- whilst she was no doubt handling swollen goods belonging to the owner's son. Suddenly Henry Wood had a full diary taking him away from daily office chores to meetings across the city, but never a definitive place was named.

They all kept tight-lipped, especially after gossip from a foreman who "had a mate" who believed he had seen her in a brothel with wealthy businessmen, was then found face down in a large industrial vat of mercuric nitrate- used to clean and strip the felts before baking them in an oven. A few workers reminded others of the 'Curse of the Gypsies' which had the desired effect to silence them, stemming any chit chat. After caving in the foreman's head with a crowbar and dumping him in the vat, Mary noticed that people were less hostile towards her, as she assured Henry in numerous hotel suites around the city during their raunchy sex-fuelled liaisons, most mid-week afternoons and weekends, that nobody was any the wiser.

Allowing him to believe he was taking the lead, he became sexually addicted to her, and confided he would leave his wife to run away with her, as Mary only just managed to hide her shock and horror – this would completely fuck up their plan, which was why she had been through the pretence of suffering the stench of the mercury most mornings – to play out her part as a humble proud girl earning a wage, but not for much longer.

She had felt many changes since working there, including fatigue and general nausea, but after more bouts of early morning vomiting, she was confident that at long last she had fallen pregnant. It could have been from one of so many clients – even Simon, but this gullible little fucker would believe it was his. He would also have to pay them a fortune to keep it a secret once he was blackmailed. To allow her and Simon to run away from it all together, to live happily in the country, far from all this madness that had plagued them; because like he had told her from the time they first met, there was one thing she could always be certain of – he would love her to death.

14

London Hotel Foyer

Since being told that his tumour was inoperable, with life expectancy less than a year, Harry Hunter had taken a vastly different approach to life and how he dealt with problems. Just like now, when walking out of the hotel foyer, knowing that all the rumours he had heard were true. He wouldn't be around long enough to watch over his daughter or keep this bastard from straying over and over again.

Earlier on his son-in-law had taken every effort to hide his face with a hat worn low and a scarf tied around his neck before venturing out to deal with a cold bracing wind, after no doubt leaving the warmth of her bed. She followed instructions to wait a few minutes before leaving to distance themselves.

Henry Wood could have worn a bag over his head because he would still have identified him having not only studied his familiar shape and gait, plus the fact he was even wearing a bespoke suit recently measured, cut and sewn by his very own hands. Those very same hands that a few hours later shook on the deal to protect his little girl in the future, when he was no longer around.

Harry Hunter was one of the leading master tailors in Savile Row, who now bitterly regretted he had been mainly responsible, through avarice, to use his daughter's marriage to Henry Wood to maximise business affairs between their two respective families.

Sadly, it was obvious now that his son-in-law had thrown himself into a full-blown affair with this 'Gypsy Girl' who was already displaying rich trappings, wearing the finest clothes, furs and gems hanging from her shapely body.

After casting his expert eye across her midriff, he also realised that riches displayed on the outside were nothing compared to the potential value of what she was carrying inside.

This cunning bitch had really taken him for a ride, something he probably wouldn't work out until after she had taken him for every penny possible, but luckily, now with his intervention, it wouldn't come to that.

Even if meaning he ended his own life in a cell waiting to be taken to the gallows, he really didn't care, because he was already a dead man walking, with what he carried inside him. But at least this way he would die knowing he had put right what he had instigated years earlier, that had turned out so wrong for his daughter.

Following the War, many contracts had been made to supply army uniforms, resulting in some close friendships being formed by him, when showing empathy after donating to fundraising events and charities. These represented veterans returning injured or "broken" with trauma of frontline conflict. It meant he now knew just the right man with a gun, who later on that day had just agreed to return a favour to help make his current problem disappear in weeks to come, suiting him down to the ground.

A month later, Harry Hunter held his daughter in his arms with her body shaking with shock, after being told by a police officer attending their home such devastating news. It transpired her husband had been shot dead by robbers when stealing the furs he had gone to collect earlier from a gang of gypsies. No doubt they had double-crossed him, like the officer stated and as everyone knew, you just couldn't trust a thieving gypsy; they really were the scum of the earth.

Harry Hunter fully agreed with a shake of his head, satisfied the cheating bastard would now be put in the ground first.

15

Home of Simon Wick, Lambeth, London

With both his big strong hands clasping tight around her throat, he stared down into her face smiling, before increasing pressure across her windpipe causing her eyes to flutter like so many before who had been snuffed out by him.

Despite her best effort to retrieve her knife from her waist band, used to skin hares and rabbits at work, she felt herself slowly passing out before getting the chance to stick it into this big animal that stood in front of her.

With anger finally subsiding, his grip eased up, allowing her to slump down to the floor gasping, with one hand to her throat, the other with her maternal instincts developing instinctively lay across her prominent bump, just in case the bastard kicked her in the stomach.

Awkwardly staggering to her feet, he told her there was no more value in that little bastard while staring at her stomach, so now was the time to get rid of it, because only a few would pay to fuck her in that state.

Mary played along with what he said, nodding submissively, telling him what he wanted to hear – to buy herself a little time, explaining that all the girls who had fallen pregnant at the brothel used the same back street abortionist, who would sort things out for her quickly. All this had happened after Simon had just heard that Henry Wood had been killed during a robbery. It had made him show his true colours, because like a silly little bitch up to then, she had fallen for all his lies and promises; before now realising he was simply using her, just like she had used so many others in the past to get what she wanted.

Her current physical state wasn't helping though, not only were her hormones all over the place, but she had been impaired and weakened from the effects of mercury, now inhaled for many months. She had seen and learnt all about its side effects from fellow workers who had displayed similar symptoms referred to as 'Mad Hatter's Disease'. It was obvious that others had now noticed her mannerisms with tell-tale indicative traits displayed more often and becoming more pronounced than before – she knew her condition had worsened. They had laughed at her, knowing exactly what she was going through, so much so, they now called her by her new name – 'Mad Mary'.

After Simon stormed out of their house leaving her alone, she packed her bag, then went to his secret stash where he always hid his roll of notes. She stole them, knowing she was now a dead woman if ever he found 'them', because one thing Mary knew for sure, she was keeping her baby, having already chosen its name – after confiding as always with Maria, who had told her many times to run away to start afresh – without him.

Oliver if it was a boy, Olivia if a girl; hoping that whatever she had, they would enjoy a better life, compared to the one she had endured.

16

Mary Rocks Bedsit Dockside, London, 1928

After hyperventilating, just before giving one final push, she clasped Maria's hand – her saviour, the woman who had been there for her since arriving at the brothel months earlier. Mary let out a final gargling scream because her mouth had filled with blood after biting her own tongue by accident. Spitting it out with force, before staring down between her legs anxiously, with memories flooding back of her own mother in dense woods having a still born child.

Back then she had smelt petrichor, the wonderful scent from a lush forest floor as rains fell heavily, turning its rich soil to mud. Very much in stark contrast to a stench all around her now of rotting fish from nearby docks. Sadly, back then a heavy downpour was the only noise she heard when her mother succumbed with a still born child, but today her small room was filled with a wonderful noise of a baby's first cry.

Maria, her 'confidant', passed over her son to be held tightly in her arms, smelling his big mop of bright ginger hair, meaning there was no doubt who his father was, before letting him hear his first ever words.

"Well, Oliver, just like your dad, you have caused me a lot of pain, but in your case, I really don't mind one bit."

Maria lit a cigarette, held in her long holder, looking down on them both – knowing they now faced their biggest challenge – to stay alive; they both needed to keep one step ahead of an evil monster, hell bent on hunting them down.

17

Home of Mary Rocks, Central London, 1934

With a bright shaft of morning light coming through their small under dwelling window, Oliver awoke laying on his side facing her back, admiring her beautiful black hair, thick and tussled, falling down onto her back.

A lone candle his mother lit earlier when nightfall descended had nearly burnt out, flickering away, casting random shadows across damp cracked walls, with its scent hiding foul smells. Not only from stale food inside, but also the stench of excrement outside, coming from a small courtyard where vagrants often slept, often soiling themselves when drunk, when finding a bit of shelter underneath a flight of stone stairs leading to their front door.

Reaching out slowly, he ran his small hand gently over her head, allowing her beautiful hair to fall softly between his fingers, then he leant forward to smell her locks, after carefully checking her eyes were still shut before planting a little kiss on her pale cold cheek. He now whispered into her ear, despite knowing she wouldn't hear him – but that didn't matter one bit when telling her just how much he loved her.

Oliver placed his arm around her small body as she lay motionless next to him, giving her a hug once again, telling her in a soft voice that he knew things would get better for them. "So please don't cry any more when you think I'm fast asleep. You don't have to ask God for forgiveness when leaving me alone for so long, I know you have to go to work most nights."

But he had just stroked her head far too hard, when suddenly a clump of hair fell out, making him sit up on their bed startled, crying out, clinging onto a dark lock.

"Sorry Mum, sorry."

After jumping down from their bed, he quickly turned to face her, but his clumsy movement knocking her to one side made both her eyes open, now staring back at him with an icy cold look devoid of feelings or emotions. He shouted out he could fix it because, look, it hadn't gone out yet, it still had a flame.

Oliver picked up its holder, pouring hot wax from their candle over her head, then, whilst still soft and malleable, he pushed the clump of hair back into position. The wax solidified to hold it in place, allowing the gap to be filled, alongside all his other 'stick on' repair jobs that he had done over previous months.

This latest repair had finally resulted in his small doll's bald head now being almost fully covered again with all the hair his mother had recently lost, since becoming poorly.

Hearing his mother's footsteps descending their outside stairs as she returned home, he quickly threw his doll, left behind by a previous occupant – beneath their bed, before jumping back under sheets pretending to wake up just as she greeted him with a big smile and then a hug, offering him some freshly baked bread for breakfast.

She removed a bright silk scarf covering her almost bald head, now with only a few clumps of hair still left on it before noticing just how tired and frail she looked. Being only four years of age, there were so many things he didn't yet understand, events he had seen in his young lifetime beyond comprehension; sadly, in the very near future his education would begin, to help him understand; but not one that could ever be imagined.

18

Small Enclosed Yard

(Outside Mary Rocks' Home)

It was only a fleeting side glimpse of her face when coming out of a small enclosed courtyard, but the much talked about silk headscarf just seen, made him think it may be Mary. Exactly what Simon had told them to look out for earlier, when he threw a few shillings down onto their tavern table telling them to enjoy a round of drinks on him. With a promise of pound notes for the person who housed her, before playing heavily on a lie, that he wanted to be reconciled with Mary who was and would always be the love of his life after having had a little one with her.

His calumny and deceit continued when describing that sadly she beat his poor child because of her illness after inhaling too much mercury at a factory. This was why she was now known as 'Mad Mary', but he would pay for medical help and even buy her decent wigs – apparently, most of her gorgeous dark hair had fallen out, so she now wore silk headscarves to cover her scalp.

As 'Gunner' Smith accepted his coin, he remembered in years gone by that he had also accepted an offer of payment when his 'pals battalion' were recruited to join regular soldiers after his football team lied about their ages to sign up to fight in World War 1. They became part of an artillery unit for its final years, with battle raging on front lines before his exploits caught up with him beginning with his "thousand-yard stare" with the full effects of shell shock kicking in. At times it reduced him to a dithering wreck, causing his life to spiral out of control, with alcohol his only saviour.

His physicality and vulnerability had been preyed upon by others when he returned to London. Gangs recruited him to dish out punishment when chasing up payments from gamblers lured into high interest loans to repay all their debts to 'underground' casinos and bookmakers. It was how he had got to know Simon, having seen Mary many times over the years on his arm, before she finally broke free from his hold over her.

Simon, now known to many as 'Cyclops', was hated by most, but with his offer of a huge financial reward, it was enough for them to head out to ask questions, to walk streets where you would expect to find working girls whose main income came from drunk punters not fussy about looks. Hers had long gone; plus many wouldn't pay her after realising she was vulnerable, with no pimp looking out for her.

'Gunner' felt sorry for her, not to mention this kid, but he needed money; if he didn't settle debts soon, he would be a recipient of what he used to hand out, but with two previous beatings he knew only too well what was coming his way next. Perhaps it would be a blessing in disguise to let him join so many others who hadn't survived the War.

He was only 30 years of age but now looked old way beyond his years with many flashbacks and spasms sending him to the floor with both hands over his ears crying out like a scared child screaming at anyone near to him.

After watching her walk away, he quietly descended a flight of stairs and he was tall enough to stand on tip toes to look inside a room through a small window. He saw a young child sat on a bed illuminated by a solitary candle – giving off just enough light to convince him that his pay day had been sorted – once he updated Simon.

But Gunner wouldn't mention his son liked to play with dolls, or spoke to them when gently stroking their hair, because that may well get him a beating, instead of a big wedge of banknotes.

19

Home of Mary Rocks

(Next day, early evening)

They both heard footsteps outside coming down their stairs but even before seeing his outline through a window, Mary sensed what was about to happen, making her run for the knife before their door suddenly burst open with him rushing towards her, screaming, after eventually getting to grips with her for the first time in years.

Pinning Mary against a wall by her shoulders, Simon glared down at her while she pleaded to let their son Oliver live – he didn't deserve to die. When he turned his head to stare at the child, she attempted to push her knife into his one good eye; but his fighting reflexes kicked in with her movement, turning away just in time to save his sight, but its blade cut deeply across his cheek, drawing blood – sending him into a violent frenzy.

After placing both hands across her face, he used all his strength to push down hard on both her nose and mouth to snuff the bitch out, leaning forward to place his face next to hers one last time.

Within a minute her eyes flitted, her last conscious act being to stare across at Oliver who stood on their bed frozen to the spot who watched his mother reach out towards him with an outstretched arm, before her hand dropped down to her side, with her knife falling to the ground – just before she died.

After releasing his grip, Mary's body fell to the floor as he screamed out again loudly, because she had been the love of his life, but had defied and stolen from him.

He now found himself drawn to a young child staring back at him wide eyed, Simon immediately knew it had to be his son with that mop of bright ginger hair, plus his very distinctive look replicating his own appearance. It made him gasp and stare in disbelief at what he had created.

Simon reached out towards him with the very same hand that had just killed his mother, smiling when his young son took hold of it after jumping down off the bed and walked towards him.

Holding back his tears, he felt a sense of responsibility never encountered before as he walked him outside, carefully minding his ascent up slippery stairs, telling him it really was his lucky day because his dad was now going to take good care of him. Oliver knew he had just lost the two things in the world he loved the most – his mum and his doll, who he would never see again, but one day he would replace his doll; who would then always remind him of his mum.

20

Hyde Park Brothel, London

Having been a keen swimmer since she was a young girl in rural France, she relished when they opened the Serpentine Lido in Hyde Park. Not just for its warm inviting waters virtually on her doorstep but also from a business perspective. As a busy 'Madam' overseeing a nearby brothel, it now allowed all her beautiful girls to show off their bodies in public, wearing only bathing costumes in mixed swimming groups.

Whilst in deeper waters, they solicited their trade with suggestive whispers followed with quick gropes beneath the surface with clear instructions that if they wanted to see them later, wearing far less for lots of fun, they should speak to an elegantly dressed lady smoking from her long gold cigarette holder, who was now nodding and smiling at them.

Dozens every day would succumb to this plan, literally baiting them in as business boomed, with Maria allowing herself a swim after chaperoning her gaggle of girls back to earn their money. With them being paid a third of what they earned, which was one of the best rates in the city, but their savvy Maltese owners behind many such businesses knew exactly what they were doing. That resulted in better looking women flocking for auditions to seek employment within a highly sought-after boudoir.

Mary Rocks had arrived under vastly different circumstances, soon becoming one of Maria's favourites, mainly because of her upbringing, which bore striking similarities to her own because she was also 'taken in' by others after becoming an orphan, when only young and vulnerable.

For Maria it was a bomb, wiping out her family home during the Great War after she was sent out reluctantly to draw water from a nearby well. This chore saving her life with its blast causing her to fall over into its water, with deep walls protecting her from flying shrapnel and fire.

Her ability to tread water until her loud screams were heard by some local dairy farmers led to her rescue but this also resulted in her capture. Followed by years of abuse initially at their own hands, but then many others after renting her out to numerous sex-hungry farmhands. Her new title of 'Chatte' (Cat) quickly followed by making a reference to her being their "Pussy in the Well".

When she could pass for legal age to officially work from a brothel, she was sold on to service endless British soldiers during the War, one of whom fell in love with her after the 'Madam' at her brothel, who like herself had an English parent, took him in when he was desperate for help following his injury. Maria was designated to nurse him better after he had been shot in his back when deserting his unit.

As the War concluded, he convinced Maria of a better life in London, ending up with him returning home with her, to then be introduced to his older brothers. They now worked for a well-established Maltese family who rewarded her for saving him despite her young age with a 'Madam' position in one of their brothels.

They quickly realised that Maria's multiple linguistic skills could be put to good use as young girls from all across Europe suddenly fled to England with their 'war babies' to seek refuge, to escape physical harm from disgruntled families, not to mention returning loved ones who would not accept nor believe they had been raped, before falling pregnant.

Over many years, Maria helped numerous girls with their children to move on, to escape their vulnerable position after being drawn into a sex industry that sometimes meant having young children held as a threat if any dissension was given. Indeed, she had helped Mary even more recently to keep her one step ahead of Simon who was her brothel manager and enforcer who now pursued her al around London, using his many street contacts – all from society's underbelly, to try to locate them. Luckily Maria found out first any updates when asked to pass a message onto him when not there, allowing her to warn of a visit knowing full well Simon would extract his revenge, possibly on both of them.

But tonight, Maria had failed her after Simon made a payment to Mary's 'Judas' – an alcoholic called 'Gunner'. When handing him a bundle of notes, no doubt confirming he had caught up with her, along with a recent cut to his face near to his eye, perhaps as she tried to blind him attempting an escape. Her own focus was now firmly on Gunner as the bastard wasted no time in celebrating his ill-gotten gain after selecting a young girl before taking her upstairs with a bottle of whiskey.

Before Simon left their brothel his latest girlfriend, barely 16, who looked just like Mary, entered the foyer from a car outside, holding a small ginger-haired child, asking where the toilet was. Upon seeing her face, young Oliver recognised Maria reaching out calling 'Kitty Kat' before he was carried away thankfully with this young chaperone not reacting.

Maria kept out of the way when they left with Simon a short while later, who drove them off into the night. A realisation now kicked in that Maria's own world had just changed, because it wouldn't be too long before this girl either connected to what had actually just happened – commenting that Oliver must know her; or indeed Oliver himself may cry out repeating her very distinctive name. Simon was no fool – he would deduce how his son knew her name, and knew full well how he would deal with her, realising she must be traitor after helping Mary keep out of harm's way.

In an instant Maria made her decision to flee, but not before extracting revenge for Mary. Running upstairs to her room, she put on a swimsuit beneath her dress and then grabbed a secret stash of money from inside a tin hidden under floorboards. This had been skimmed off payments for her girls' services over many years. This nest egg would allow her to move on – to start afresh along with any money Gunner had left on him tonight.

After descending their staircase worse for wear, Maria flirted with him before they left the brothel together after baiting him with another bottle of whiskey plus an offer he couldn't resist; to sample her special skills that he would never forget. Walking together as a couple they entered Hyde Park under the cover of dark, towards its lake.

Approaching its waters edge, Maria slowly stripped down with Gunner looked extremely confused that she wore her costume, prompting him to ask if they were going for a swim together. With a sweet smile she explained only her, before smashing the whiskey bottle over his head knocking him unconscious.

After emptying his pockets of his blood money, she dragged him into deep water as Maria held him on his back, ironically in what was called a lifesaving position, as she swam out with him into the middle of the lake before releasing her hold from beneath his chin. His body sank down into its murky depths below with no sign of life before she swam back to land.

More than anything else, she hoped Simon would spare Oliver because there was no doubt in her mind with his mop of ginger hair and looks that it was his son; sadly now it could no longer concern her. She now had other matters to attend to – with old scores to settle –it meant that the following day Maria boarded a boat to Calais, remembering vividly events from her past.

They would now be in their late forties, possibly early fifties, perhaps even still farming, but they wouldn't be alive for much longer because soon roles would be reversed from when they first found her all those years ago.

It was fair to say it wouldn't end well for them as she accepted a light from a recently widowed chap, well presented, who was returning to his beach home in St Moritz. Flirting outrageously Maria told him she may have packed her costume and would love to swim in the warm Mediterranean Sea. If worse came to worse though – she could always swim naked. Gosh – that would be so much fun – but only if he didn't mind?

Judging by his bulge – he certainly didn't.

21

Small Cattle Farmstead Lens, France – One Week Later

Recently stamped on by a cow, Anton found himself laid up in bed and once again to ease boredom he found himself heavily in drink, with his broken leg. He called out to his brothers to fetch him a drink because both these lazy bastards had not been anywhere near his bedroom for hours, after nipping out together earlier.

But to no avail, until a while later when dark was falling, he heard his front door open before footsteps climbed his stairs. He could tell a woman approached – with her heels making a distinctive noise on wooden flooring with a smell of perfume and cigarette smoke preceding her entrance into his bedroom. He sat up to greet his caller, wondering if they had sent another prostitute to pay him a visit.

It was his birthday in a few days so perhaps they were giving him an early present; it was about time the bastards looked after him when he considered all he had done for them over the last 20 years since heading affairs following their dad's murder- with what started as a fist fight in their local inn, before it was sadly finished with a knife thrust between his ribs into his heart.

He wasn't disappointed in the least now when she smiled at him before walking to the side of his bed, smoking her cigarette from its long expensive-looking holder. It was in fact metal with a gold plate covering. One of several she had used for many years to good effect, including standing out in a crowd of people at a busy London Lido when men were sent her way at the bequest of her girls to discuss 'terms and conditions' before attending her brothel.

Having met and dealt with so many whores over the years in many different ways, Anton smiled back, despite his discomfort and pain he felt himself becoming aroused knowing exactly what she was. A little older than his usual choice but confident that with her wealth of experience he wouldn't be disappointed, after looked her up and down, lasciviously licking his lips in expectation of what was coming his way, asking if his brothers had paid for her to call to see him.

Maria laughed before answering they had indeed both splashed out; but not perhaps as he would imagine. This caused him to stare at her in a confused state before she drew hard once again on her cigarette, blowing a plume of smoke into his face. She removed the holder from her mouth to study it carefully to admire her recent work when sharpening its tip to a sharp point – before stepping forwards and thrusting it deep into his throat, causing him to fall back onto his pillow, clasping both hands across a gaping wound. Blood began to fill his throat as he then began to gargle with it before pouring out from his open mouth as he choked and spluttered – dying slowly allowed her to stand over him to explain that both his siblings were dead at the bottom of the well – having pulled over earlier to help fix her car puncture – before knocking them out with a wheel Jack when they knelt down to inspect her tyre, when realising too late that it appeared undamaged.

At the mention of this well, memories now came flooding back as Anton's eyes bulged with shock, then realisation as to whom she was, with Maria purring like a cat before her 'Meow' when plunging it down once more – deep into his flesh to puncture his neck artery. His face and upper body turned crimson red before he convulsed, then lay still, as Maria spoke out loud to him despite being dead.

"There you go Anton, I got to fuck you and your brothers one last time, only this time good and proper, just as I wanted to do it."

After paying respects to her lost family at a small village graveyard, she composed herself, before commencing a long drive south to St Moritz, pushing yet another cigarette into another cheap holder; but if things went to plan, they wouldn't be gold plated for very much longer.

22

Coal Yard, Finsbury Park, London – Five Years Later

Tightly grasping onto both reins with his large soot-stained hands, Simon looked ahead, trying his best to act as casually as possible, holding his horse steady, not allowing it to pick up speed; despite all that had happened, with his adrenaline still pumping through his body from earlier, he kept on muttering to Oliver sat next to him, but without turning his head.

"Keep them eyes peeled for me, son, today of all fackin' days; watch out for them bastards."

Eventually they pulled across oncoming traffic to enter a large yard with their horse and cart still fully laden with sacks of coal- that appeared to be piled up even higher than before, when they had set off on a busy delivery round, hours earlier.

Their foreman who knew exactly who they were, what they did and for whom they were doing it , had given them this job under duress, after a representative of their gang, a thug with a cosh in his hand, had explained to him when paying a visit:

"Last place you want a fire is in a yard full of coal, wouldn't you agree?"

Resulting in them starting work the very next day on a delivery round; ahead of so many others who really needed the job. This cover allowed them to move around London doing all their nefarious activities – giving them a credible story to plan which home they would target next in the suburbs with so many rich pickings on offer; plus, they could conceal and move proceeds of crime or merchandise needing delivery. This could be firearms or drugs, even bodies every now and then that needed disposing of after either a gangland battle or contract killing.

Today their foreman sensed immediately something had gone terribly wrong to return so soon with so much still stacked up. He quickly saw why after they parked up in the far corner, urgently beckoning him towards them as Simon, for the first time ever, looked worried.

Earlier on, when exiting a crime scene leaving behind an elderly victim after filling her coal bunker – by total chance they had been compromised by a copper walking his beat, whom had chosen the wrong time to call in to one of his many tea spots, just as they were leaving by her back-kitchen door.

Young Oliver with a look of complete horror instinctively reacted by putting both hands to his face to stifle a scream of surprise, because barely a minute earlier he had just put those same hands over that old girl's face inside, when snuffing the life out of her. His dad had also just left behind him, when returning from upstairs admiring one of her diamond rings, taken from a large extensive collection in her jewellery box, so it wouldn't be missed. Even later on, nobody would suspect that a crime had been committed, with so many other valuables ignored, concluding that either a ring had been lost, or more likely a sibling had claimed it already as theirs.

PC Morgan knew straight away he had fallen onto an active burglary in progress – watching them leaving her house to walk towards him, just as Simon used natural light to examine the diamond ring when held up in front of him, allowing to see its true colours, directly relating to its value, just as PC Morgan pulled out a truncheon from his trouser pouch.

But that was his last ever move as Simon, upon seeing him, went into a ferocious attack – landing punch after punch to his face. Falling backwards unconscious, he cracked the back of his head on the edge of a small retaining wall holding a raised flower bed of hardy winter roses. This had always been their recently deceased victim's pride and joy.

If his body was left to be found by his colleagues, it would alert everyone not only to their presence at a crime scene but also involvement in a murder. That would then link them to what had been regarded up to now as many other natural 'sudden deaths' all around their delivery area. This would result no doubt with a visit to the gallows for Simon, making it a do or die situation, quite literally; as they threw his body onto the cart, covering it with full sacks of coal piled up high, before retreating to the safety of their yard.

When their foreman joined them, Simon moved one full sack of coal as the arm of the dead officer wearing his distinctive police tunic flopped out. It nearly made the foreman vomit on the spot, before he then stared with incredulous disbelief as father and son discussed in a matter-of-fact way how to best dispose of the body. A decision to 'weight and sink' him when pitch black in the Thames was made, after making a slight detour on the way home, before tethering their horse for the night in stables just south of the river.

That night they were confident they had got away with it after completing their disposal, with only Oliver realising his police helmet was missing. Both out of fear but with an ulterior motive, he didn't tell his dad, because he knew this would now expose their criminality with potential severe consequences.

He also knew this could finally be his one chance to escape from this one-eyed bastard, who had killed his mother in front of him years earlier. He would never forgive him for that but he would avenge her death, if not by his own hands, then by the hands of others when swinging from the gallows. He had often told him that's where he would end his days if they ever caught him, for once Oliver wanted him to be right.

Since losing his beautiful mum, she had been replaced with a gaggle of women who had also lived in fear, who were often beaten by him, some of whom had also disappeared suddenly. An older one had looked out for him, even spending time playing with him and giving him a cuddle and teaching him things when his mother was working long hours, she helped them pack and move – to stay one step ahead of the monster chasing them all around London.

His dad, when claiming him, had only ever taught him every aspect of criminality – including how to 'snuff out' people to make it look like they had died naturally from old age.

Oliver had memory gaps in his young life – that were now filled in by women who had known his mother in the brothel; sadly, a word he knew and a place he could relate to. He was switched on enough not to mention 'Kitty' who they often spoke about – with his dad on a quest to find her, asking everyone and anyone, after putting a bounty on her head.

He knew his history from overheard chat between girls working the brothel, who concluded Oliver had been brought up by Cyclops, his one-eyed monster of a dad because he had value – practical use to help burgle when climbing through small widows, after carting him around London; playing happy families and lookout.

Oliver, a few days later after killing the copper, had noticed a big man sat wrapped up warm, in a large overcoat inside a greasy spoon cafe sipping from a hot drink, munching away hungrily on slices of toast and staring out from its window. He was looking across at their yard as he watched what anyone else would have regarded as a father with his young son, setting off for an innocent day's work delivering coal all around the boroughs. But for some reason it made him react by jumping up to step outside quickly, still holding his toast in mid-air, totally focused on them. Oliver sensed he must be CID, perhaps hunting down a man and a boy delivering coal, after finding that helmet at the old ladies home where they had called.

*****

A few days earlier, stood outside in the street, DC Andy Laptew felt his heart pounding and his pulse racing, before returning inside to finish his breakfast. Realising he was on the verge of making a major breakthrough – after PC Morgan's helmet had been found beneath a well-tended bed of roses. Owned by its elderly occupant who was one of his regular 'tea ladies' found dead inside; with witness accounts confirming a coal delivery had just been made.

Andy Laptew now concluded he had in fact just watched a murdering psychopath with his son, heading out, using their coal deliveries as a cover. He had deduced from examining the back yard of the elderly victim's house, a large footprint and a much smaller one; this surely related to a man and boy leaving deposits of coal dust and charcoal residue on the stone path, traces that carried vital clues.

With his extensive local knowledge, he only had to watch four main coal yards, because he couldn't approach them directly, intel had connected them all to underworld gangs either controlling or taxing them to allow safe deliveries or suffer accidents on the road, or in the yard, with fires being a common persuader.

Day two of watching workers bag up then head out had paid off, following his dash outside to give him a far better view of them both leaving, especially when the young boy with bright ginger hair turned his head suddenly to stare across back at him. It must have just been by chance, perhaps picking up on his large frame leaving a cafe.

Surely there was no way he could have known who he was, or why he was paying them attention on a cold morning? But his supervisors now needed to be updated straight away, with every team at his station fired up for revenge, Andy knew they would soon be delivering a brutal revenge when getting to grips with their suspect. At least this young lad, no doubt only an innocent party, wouldn't suffer at their hands- perhaps even a Godsend for him to end such an ordeal under the control of this man.

Possibly even giving him a fresh start in life.

23

Walthamstow Police Station, London –
Early Morning

It was something they had never attempted before, but as they all sat together in their CID office at such an ungodly hour, they knew that with so many of them to join in the follow, they had a good chance of success. Especially when they were behind a horse and cart laden with several tonnes of coal. It meant younger and fitter officers would start off on foot with others who weren't exactly built for speed, backing up in many different forms of transport.

Andy Laptew impressed everyone when he turned up for work on a pushbike that coincided with one being reported stolen not far from the station later on in the day. But like he told everyone for years to come it was justifiable in memory of his old mate. They were now told by a tired looking hungover superintendent, who had actually graced their briefing, that they were doing this for many elderly victims, not forgetting a dear fallen colleague.

He told them they would bring this 'one-eyed gangster runner' to justice by trial to teach their underworld a lesson. They now knew who he was and who he worked for, but they also had to consider a duty of care for a young boy believed to be his son – no doubt deeply traumatised over the years by sick, vile events; who now needed to be taken into care, to escape from this depraved existence, quite literally at the hands of his father.

After feigned gratitude for his input, he wished them luck – leaving with handshakes. Now alone with their DI, he then rose to give his briefing which they all knew would be the one that mattered. He told them in no uncertain terms that they would indeed be sending out a very clear message once they got hold of him, before he described exactly how this one-eyed fighting pimp who was a murdering bastard would be dealt with, giving clear instructions that attracted a round of applause with nods of approval.

It brought an entirely different meaning to how they normally went about 'framing' the mad, bad bastards they dealt with, who really needed sorting out.

Something completely new, but they certainly would not fail to deliver.

24

Finsbury Park, London – Three Hours After Briefing

The tension felt became insurmountable, with everyone staring at their lead officer, who now watched them make numerous deliveries in this street. He held his nerve when sitting, attempting to look casual as possible, whilst using a large house window reflection to keep them in view. Following strict instructions given earlier, that they would rather move in too early to take them out rather than too late, to carry a body out.

Dad was mostly in view as expected, with him doing the majority of the work, carrying full bags of coal, weighing at least 100 pounds. This gave what everyone considered to be a true indication that they weren't deviating from the norm whilst doing their round, but he became conscious that the son, had now remained inside longer than normal. This suddenly coincided with Dad taking a detailed look both up and down this street, before also going inside after filling the coal bunker.

Why go inside now to join his son?

Less than a minute later his nerve finally cracked; with far too much at stake as he suddenly stood to light his cigarette, blowing a large plume of smoke into the air, taking off his hat – giving all his backup officers a signal to join him as fast as possible with weapons drawn. Today these ranged from truncheons to metal bars, even house bricks picked up earlier.

Within seconds an Austin High Lot Taxi that had been commandeered earlier by detectives – who now alighted with adrenaline pumping through their bodies, forming a line before they all screamed and charged into the back yard. Many others still arriving behind them, heard a back door smashed down, followed by shouts of pain and cries, when they came up against Simon Wick who now fought, not only for his life like never before, but that of his sons. Despite being vastly outnumbered he held his ground by the door, allowing Oliver to stand well back from the body of an old woman he had just snuffed out inside.

When Simon turned to check Oliver had moved sufficiently out of harm's way, not to self-incriminate himself, a powerful blow to his skull felled him to his knees – landed by Andy Laptew, who had chosen a heavy metal bar over his light wooden truncheon; to stand a chance of extracting revenge.

Simon with incredible strength got back up before lashing out with heavy blows, one of which knocked out Andy Laptew before Simon made one last charge into the backyard letting out a long harrowing guttural shout of anger and frustration using an unbelievable surge of strength, but against a dozen officers who circled him like a captured quarry, before moving in together to finish him off.

Eventually his screams became replaced with only the sound of continuous dull thuds; coinciding with every blow landing to his head and body, rendering this wild animal unconscious. When laid at their feet, supine and motionless a nod was given by their inspector to get their police van in position. Its back doors were opened outwards to expose a solid metal door frame. Picking him up, they all ran at speed directly towards it, now carrying their crazed murderer head first when flanking him like a medieval battering ram, as they heard a loud dull thud after being well and truly 'framed' as he himself was savagely murdered.

They threw Simons body inside their van with his skull badly crushed and with several large fragments of bone exposed through his scalp as viscous blood could be seen running from his mouth, nose and ears as everyone cheered. Someone then made light of what they had done, by quipping it was a job well executed. Laughter followed until their DI raised his hand, before they fell silent; he gave all of them a thumbs up, saying with a smile:

"Who will guard the guards themselves?"

Before warning everyone, they would now stick to a script that he would write out back in their office for them to copy – before submitting it to their coroner, who was a close friend of his. Already primed and fully expecting to hold a hearing any day soon for a dead one-eyed serial killer, leaving behind a traumatised young son, destined to enter into care for help and support.

God knows he would certainly need it after what he had witnessed, endured and been subjected to by his monster of a dad. They could only hope and pray he would eventually make a full recovery from such a traumatic start in life.

25

Punch and Judy Pub, Covent Garden, London

They called it their local pub, meaning its landlord could count himself a fortunate man, not only did they spend a fortune behind his bar; but everyone knew who and what they were so on that account dead-legs and rogues kept away. With another hidden bonus, that held so much value; it became one of only a handful of businesses in London that didn't need to pay protection money, to whichever criminal gang prevailed laying claim to this area being their 'manor'.

This evening they didn't hold back when they demolished their first kitty collected for celebratory drinks after staying tight as a team, making sure everyone typed up reports; every single aspect of this 'unfortunate' death was covered – with an added bonus that paperwork was kept to a minimum with just a covering report for the Coroner's Court with him fully on board from the outset.

With his naval background, Andy Laptew was a match for anyone, so he didn't have to hold back when it came to drinking, but sadly he hadn't yet learnt how to hold back with his tongue, especially when expressing his views and opinions when once again he had his inspector's ear. Who still laughed with that image of him earlier on in the day wobbling along on a bicycle – many sizes too small for his ample frame.

Andy had been cut off mid-flow earlier during a debrief, when daring to suggest they shouldn't believe Oliver had only been an innocent bystander in all of this. He had attempted to explain the relevance of what he had seen him do with a piece of coal, corroborated with a towel he had seen in the kitchen covered in soot, after Simon had wiped his hands clean before they had smashed their way into the kitchen. He was given a rebuke then, only to be silenced, but he now hoped alcohol would soften previous negative reactions to his theory, so once again he put forward that Oliver had to be, without a doubt 'damaged goods', beyond help in fact; realising all along exactly what his role entailed, being much more than an innocent bystander. It fell on death ears before his inspector silenced him, when placing a hand over his mouth, before giving him a stern look.

At this point Andy realised, with their eyes staring intently back at one another, just how much his boss had drunk, with such a glazed look. This was confirmed when he gave his piece of advice, his work mantra always suggested to others to make work a lot less complicated – meaning of course they could spend more time in the pub.

"Keep it shimple, shun, always keep it shimple; we have our sherial killer, so don't overthink it."

Perhaps it was an attempt at a joke when he finished his pearls of wisdom with one final comment, after tapping his finger on his mouth, before walking away to collect more money for yet another drinks kitty.

"Snuff said."

26

Camden Social Services, London

His case officer had spent several months in his company, even finding time to travel with him when he went out daily with CID officers; to point out homes where his dad made him climb through small windows after walking around with a dog lead- a cover story when he pretended to look for an imaginary pet that had strayed.

Other properties were indicated by Oliver who would then freeze before screaming and holding both hands over his head, appearing highly distressed when they parked up outside, before refusing point blank to get out of their car. These were subsequently found to be where its occupant, always an elderly female living alone, had been found dead, initially recorded from natural causes; but now a full murderous catalogue of horror became discovered, as over 20 were detected, quite literally at the hands of Simon Wick.

Background enquiries and research into his life with social services revealed his monstrous profile, showing that he lacked any sense of humanity, compassion or reasoning after a sick upbringing. It had been totally devoid of love and care, but plentiful in evil with acts of horrendous violence, with long term depravation forming the backbone of his life, when growing from young boy to man.

As Oliver hugged his social worker tightly, he buried his head into her body, before letting out a cry of despair once again, learnt from so many young, troubled souls at his orphanage – when they were either caught doing wrong or confronted, with no get out to deny any wrongdoing.

For other kids it had been after a bit of a fight or stealing from foster parents who had sent them back, but for him it was for killing old frail women who weren't happy, often complaining nonstop that loved ones were either lost or no longer part of their lives – knowing that one day they would reunite with lost souls.

Obviously, they had no idea it would be in the next few minutes – by the very hand that had just lit their fire, before the lovely boy washed hands, before approaching them to say farewell. To bid them safe journey, normally drawing a look of real confusion as he helped them 'move on' after his hands were placed carefully across faces, making it possible for them to escape from such a sad lonely life.

His dad would watch with approval before also admiring a few rich pickings carefully chosen. They were only a few amongst so many, certainly not enough to draw any suspicion that a burglary had taken place, let alone a murder.

Once again, this young detective he had first seen when exiting the coal yard days earlier, when he rushed out of a café, leaving his paper and hat behind but still holding his toast stared at him yet again, with utter disbelief. Obviously not being fooled by his performance, but he had more than good reason to be wary – even suspicious of him – far more than anyone else since rescue from his terrible dad.

Before being killed, his dad had taken the fight outside after wiping his own hands clean on a towel, no doubt to give him time to escape, knowing he had to distance himself from doing the snuff by grabbing a piece of coal, to then blacken his hands just washed clean. This was quickly done when his dad shouted to him to stand away from her body; presenting a crime scene, by reversing their roles, so they believed his old man to be the killer.

But this fat detective, when laid out prone in the kitchen, came around on the floor – just in time to clearly watch him blacken both hands. Nothing yet had been said or done about it – really confusing him; it meant for now he may just get away with everything. Who knows, perhaps one day he may even get adopted by a decent set of parents, a possibility suggested by his gullible social worker, in between loves, hugs and biscuits.

When seeing 'toast man' on a bike behind them that day; plus a taxi with far too many people inside, Oliver had worked out exactly who they were- after spending years looking out for them. He had kept quiet because he now wanted it all to end, with his dad out of his life for ever. This had been achieved a lot quicker than he could ever have imagined after watching him being charged head first into a police van's solid door frame, just as he was grabbed by that fat detective before he could run away.

Oliver had easily worked out who 'boss man' was, when out and about with them; it was always really important to know that, having learnt this from his dad. You always did whatever was needed to keep the man in charge happy. This prompted Oliver to dry his crocodile tears before walking up to him, saying in a quiet voice:

'I can show you where my dad dumped that policeman now; it must be terrible for his family not knowing where he is.'

As boss man hugged him and repeatedly thanked him for helping them so much, Oliver threw a quick glance at toast man, really wanting to give him a wink, but he thought better of it pretending instead to cry a little bit more, before pointing out towards the Thames embankment.

Andy Laptew stared up at the sky in disbelief before throwing Oliver yet another dirty look, as he mouthed what he really wanted to say out loud in his strong cockney accent.

'You little Cant.'

27

Lambeth Bridge, London

For years his dad had always given him a running commentary of exploits as they travelled around London, including once a rare bit of humour telling Oliver that memories always 'flooded back' every time he approached Lambeth Bridge. He then recounted building work on bridge expansion, plus hundreds of homes destroyed near its embankments after it flooded in the 1920s. This was following heavy snowfalls in the Cotswolds; the source of their great river that had melted – creating a large swell.

Never slow at seizing another business opportunity, his underworld crime gang employers quickly linked in with building contractors, many of whom travelled in from the North of England with hordes of Irish, soon learning 'the ways' of the city. Basically, this meant that if they didn't find their way to one of many local nominated taverns on pay day to drop a coin in its 'welfare box', it would soon be a farewell to both their kneecaps and a job.

Simon didn't hold back on detail as Oliver was talked through what was done to instil fear into people. Even if they were hard as nails, pissed up, thick as shit navvies who had done manual labour all their lives and didn't scare easily. But after one of them was publicly beaten before having a leg stamped on over a kerb, this loud noise of cracking bone hit home – in more ways than one as coins would then be heard to hit the bottom of their collection boxes.

With his fearsome reputation plus physical presence, his dad was their main 'enforcer and collector', showing no mercy to anyone – all coming back to him as Oliver, now stood on this embankment flanked by detectives. He held his social worker's hand still feeling a stare with an obvious scowl from toasty. Boss man with a look of expectation watched him intently, as Oliver now pointed out at the river to indicate where his dad had tied the copper to hessian sacks of coal – to weight him down, before dumping him into deep water.

Sadly, another memory invaded his mind – rushing forwards from years earlier at this very same spot, when his dad had first shown him what a monster he was. Only this dump had been wrapped secure in sturdy tarpaulin sheets from building sites, with heavy metal rods inside, to make sure their body never surfaced.

Andy Laptew noticed this sudden change in Oliver's behaviour, sensing genuine remorse, not shown before. Tears streamed down his cheeks prompting him to interact with this little bastard for the first time, asking:

"What is it then, kid, what's really upsetting you?"

Oliver flashed him a look of anger before pointing out to the river once again, as he struggled to hold back his emotions.

"You will find my dear mother over there, after I watched the bastard dump her body after snuffing her out in front of me all those years ago. Please Sir, can you get her out of the water as well?"

He couldn't resist getting one over again on this detective by making a point of looking directly at him before saying:

"Thank God you saved me from him."

Andy Laptew felt his hand form a fist but knew it would cost him his job – perhaps even a stint in prison if he punched this little shit. Jail being the last place he ever wanted to be when he weighed up just how many he had sent there, after they had been framed in the normal way, unlike the way they had framed little murdering bastard's dad.

At least they had the last laugh with his dad – he really hoped Oliver read his thoughts when he smiled back at him, rubbing the top of his own head and mouthing 'ouch'.

28

Orphanage, Central London

Before employing a much better cover story to move around undetected in the suburbs of London using their coal delivery service, they had often posed as a concerned father with his young son, out looking for their lost family pet. Oliver would stare up at them pulling a sad worried face, holding a lead in his hand if ever challenged in a house garden or an enclosed yard, prior to them breaking in. Before staff became suspicious of their motive, they had attended Battersea dogs home to select a small dog for free – a prop to help support their story, often throwing it over walls or pushing it through gates and fences into areas they wanted to access before forcing open house windows or pushing him through them, if already open. If nobody reacted inside to a dog running around the house they knew it was empty.

At the dog home they would walk corridors with a member of staff, accompanied by a cacophony of noise with young pups barking, excited when seeing people viewing everything on display, potential owners watching them carefully – observing how they looked and behaved before selecting one; to take away to pretend to be giving it a loving home.

Today at his orphanage, Oliver could fully relate to how those dogs must have felt before he went into 'pick me please' mode, especially when he saw how 'well-heeled' a couple appeared to be – who were now casting their eyes over what was on offer today, as he silently sat with lots of other children in a large room with books, toys, colouring crayons and paper in front of them.

Oliver was far more streetwise and older beyond his years than others who hadn't even picked up they were potentially on the verge of being given a new beginning. This had to be far better than their current living conditions with its boring mundane regime within an orphanage.

When viewing with his dad, Oliver had always been drawn to 'cute puppies' who caught his eye, that stood out from others as he asked his dad, "Please, please can we have that one?" to sound like a 'normal' family hoping to find a pet to take it home and to care for it.

As he now watched them slowly walking towards him, he had already drawn his picture – even coloured it in to add to its full effect, helped by his observational skills he had noticed what lay beneath her silk head scarf, and his expensive bowler hat. So, with such care and attention to detail, it may just get him a desired result today.

Slowly approaching him she grabbed her husband's arm, just about managing to hold back her tears as he timed it well, glancing up at them, showing them his most angelic smile and 'puppy-eyed' look, even giving them a little wave – really hoping it would seal the deal.

A year later, Oliver King, his new name following the completion of his adoption, sat in his new 'family home' to enjoy his free-range egg for breakfast. One he had just selected from a chicken coup – in an enclosed garden behind a large, detached house, where he now lived on the outskirts of London.

It was very similar to many of those gardens he had walked into years earlier carrying a dog lead after traveling out with his dad into leafy suburbs for 'rich pickings'. This flashed across his mind when dunking his toast soldier into his yoke, before glancing across at the kitchen wall, where his artwork drawn in the orphanage on the day of his selection was proudly displayed, now signed.

Oliver King (9 years)

His rapidly completed stick person drawing – two adults, a man and woman holding hands, with a small child between them, who had a big beaming smile on his face, but most importantly he had crayoned them all with a mop of hair that was the same distinctive fiery red colour.

As soon as he had spotted they were also gingers, he knew it would work to get out of the orphanage, before he ended up "snuffing out" one of those annoying little fuckers that kept him awake most nights crying for their 'mummy and daddy'.

Thankfully, he had moved on with his new life, but out of habit he couldn't stop checking the quality of jewellery worn by his new 'mum', or kept safe in boxes inside her dressing table drawers; plus, he always noticed where coins were laid around their palatial home – but now he was learning not to pick them up, but only to look at them, without placing them in his pockets like he used to.

Both his parents were busy doctors who worked long hours and his new grandma lived with them as well; a kind lady who spent lots of time with him – initially doing home study until he started at school. It only took a few months before he could read bigger words, even write with his quilled pen.

Several times his hands would end up covered in ink after his study periods, when the old dear would sit relaxing in front of a roaring kitchen fire, as he would scrub his hands clean and glance across at her. Today, when drying them, he smiled – deciding the time had come. It had to be done. Oliver walked towards her to stand by her side, still smiling, she looked up at him appearing a little confused – before giving her a hug, then a loving squeeze, for the first-time ever, reducing Grandma to tears.

Far better than what he normally did to the elderly – when home alone with them, after methodically washing his hands clean.

29

Final Reports – Oliver King

(1) POLICE/CORONERS

Over a bottle of port in his plush office DI 'Kitty' Kane handed a buff folder to his eldest son's godfather. Who had a silver framed picture of him on his large walnut desk, that had served him well over forty years as district coroner. Their friendship had certainly saved DI Kane a lot of hard work since promotion years earlier, when every now and then he begged a favour.

In-between sips, then draws from Cuban cigars, a present from his old mate sat before him, the coroner initially read quickly what he already knew. That during an arrest, despite repeated requests to stay calm he continued to resist, even attempting to break free.

Despite everyone's best efforts to place him in their van, for safe transportation, the lead officer unfortunately lost his footing. Sadly resulting in the top of Simon Wicks head connecting with the metal frame of their escort vehicle, a police van.

Tragically causing a haemorrhage when fragments of his skull imbedded, causing internal bleeding on his brain. Despite rushing their prisoner to hospital, the doctors pronounced him dead on arrival.

Following the coroner's ruling, he had fully admonished police of any culpable blame and Simon Wicks body had been released from the mortuary, to be buried in an unmarked grave, in a Borough outside of London. A decision made following police disclosures that prior to his arrest he had been caught inside an elderly spinster's home, found dead in her kitchen. They now knew smothering by his hands to be the cause of death. A 'snuffing technique' now connecting him to numerous murders of elderly victims.

Luckily, Oliver his young son had assisted their investigations despite the trauma suffered at such crime scenes. But had disclosed how his dad washed both hands to remove coal dust residue from them. To prevent leaving any transfer clues after delivering fully laden sacks to their homes. Gaining access by offering to start a fire up, but then murdering and robbing them. Forcing Oliver along to look like a normal family thereby providing credible cover, a father and son working together, to hide his nefarious activities.

They had established at dozens of homes pointed out by Oliver, that over a two-year period elderly occupants had historically been found dead inside. Initially believed to have passed away in old age from natural causes. With no signs of a forced entry or apparent injuries. Family members failing to notice any missing valuables stolen or odd items missing. If they did, they just assumed a sibling had gotten to it first before they had.

But thankfully some good had come from all of this, with heartening news when the coroner read progress had been made with Oliver. Responding to counselling despite enduring so much trauma in his early life, a long-awaited adoption had just been completed by a professional couple, both doctors unable to have children of their own. Allowing him to move forwards with his life, surrounded by a loving, caring family environment.

When finishing the bottle 'Kitty' Kane remembered what his newly appointed Detective Laptew had warned him about several times, but didn't have a problem about the boy moving on with a fresh start. After all, he knew far better with his wealth of experience in these matters. Reminding himself – always best not to make work for yourself, to 'Keep it Simple'.

Besides, with such reputable parents and all their trappings of wealth around him he wouldn't want for anything in life, so what could possibly go wrong.

(2) SOCIAL SERVICES

Nancy hurried her final case study today, noticing her clock rapidly approaching five o'clock, before marking the cover with 'FILE' In big red capital letters courtesy of her stamp kit, now allowing her to put away a much thicker than normal folder. One that contained hundreds of detailed reports, mapping a heart-warming journey of the young life of Oliver since rescuing him from his murdering father Simon.

This case reminded Nancy why, for so many reasons, she loved her work. But felt sorry the system had initially failed him to be brought up by such an evil monster. Who himself had slipped through the net with his own poor mother suffering major breakdowns, including spells in a local asylum when a pregnant teenager.

Despite their efforts then, she refused to name the father of her child. But from general comments made they believed him to be a young alcoholic neighbour. A name of Howard had been mentioned by her, after joking he was an old flame who she once held a candle for.

When deemed fit for release with her baby she then broke off from follow-up sessions with her mental health nurse. Only to be found dead a few years later in squalid conditions with Simon cuddling her body. He returned to the Workhouse an orphan before leaving when a teenager, to run with crime gangs across London.

It filled her heart with joy that Oliver had been adopted by no less than two doctors to bring him up. His future family were a beautiful, caring, considerate couple. So much so, they had already requested, that just like well over a million other children, Oliver joined a list, allowing him to be sent away, to live outside of London for a while. To avoid potential dangers from bombing blitz's, with war now looming, just over their city's horizon.

She had never heard of Derwent where they proposed to send him, but a work colleague had walked the Peak District a few years ago and sung its praises. They stayed in several sleepy villages, off secluded beaten tracks. An idyllic, virtually crime free environment, where everyone looked out for one another.

Just as her office clock struck five his file joined many others when put away in a large storage box. Recording thousands of other 'happy endings' in their records office. Nancy now allowed her thoughts to drift in her new man's direction, who had mightily impressed her from the outset with his lovely soft, gentle approach.

Especially towards Oliver, when others were clearly hostile, with terrible attitudes and obvious glares. Especially that fat one constantly muttering under his breath. Nancy even though he may have uttered swear words in young Oliver's direction.

Tonight she may just ask her fella why they called him 'Kitty' but perhaps with her skills she had already concluded it reflected his soft playful attributes.

Nancy took tremendous pride in her ability to suss people out for what they were.

*****

With a ruddy complexion, balding head and obese frame there was nothing feline about Detective Inspector 'Kitty' Kane. Especially with a propensity to bark out instructions to subordinates, until things got done just as he wanted them doing, or suffer serious consequences and feel his ferocious bite.

None of this required during their latest job, with an amazing result-well over twenty murders detected with the file already signed off by their Director of Public Prosecutions.

Confirming Simon Wick to be their serial killer, acting alone, going on a murdering spree in the city and its outer Boroughs.

A succinct one-page social services report appendaged to its rear, fully exonerated Oliver his son. Who, following adoption, took on his new family's name, negating the need for a new identity. Just how Kitty liked it, keeping it simple.

Kitty's nickname- polemic to his physicality and character traits suited him well, but you would only be aware after spending time in his company, during and after work. When many got to witness first hand his propensity to drink alcohol whenever an opportunity allowed or presented itself. But always with his trademark caveat, meaning that within moments of entering a pub he took off his bowler hat, to thrust it towards anyone present when shouting:

'Kitty Kitty' time lads, so drop your coins in the 'hat' before letting out a 'Purrfect' when they began to be dropped inside one by one, before hitting the bar.

Andy Laptew over the last few months had learnt the subtle art of 'deflection' by using someone else as a 'fall guy' to put a little distance between himself and any topic, or opinion, likely to earn rebuke. Especially from Kitty after a few swift drinks, who once again appeared to be benefitting most from his press-ganged collection. Soon passing his hat around yet again, keeping a watchful eye on all present, to make sure everyone complied, and wasn't shy.

After befriending the new boy, a young and keen detective who arrived a few weeks earlier, Andy told him his funny story about 'acquiring' a push bike the morning they caught their infamous snuffer. Having now pulled his puppets strings in that direction, he asked whatever became of Oliver. Kitty in-between gulps of beer disclosed he had just been given an update from 'that case officer lady,' whom he had just happened to bump into last week.

Most present tonight knew he didn't have a problem about putting something into her, which was more than he managed with his beer Kitty's. But a nod and a smile given surreptitiously to one another now was only the measure of how brave they dare be, with no comments made.

"Well, let's just say he's moved on in more ways than one. Following adoption his new parents plan to take full advantage of Operation 'Pied Piper' meaning he soon takes a train journey out of London. That social worker, Nancy I think, did mention a village 'Up North', near Sheffield."

"Apparently beautiful rolling countryside to play in, to keep him safe from bombing raids. To be fair he's had enough going off all around him already in his life."

They agreed it seemed a great choice of place to send him. Weren't Northerners mainly miners with endless supplies of coal to combat the cold up there? So at least with his experience he could now deliver it following that in-house training given to him by his old man.

When laughter died down, they all moved on to tonight's next subject carrying far more importance. Who had got to grips with the new fit typist with enormous tits? For Andy Laptew it became background noise, while working out in his head, which way faced "Up North."

Walking to the pub window he looked upwards to the skyline, before raising his glass in that direction, toasting and wishing them all "Good luck" with the boy monster.

Knowing full well if cold weather didn't finish them off up there, then that little murdering 'facker' certainly would.

30

Treehouse Derwent Village, Derbyshire, 1938

They had been taught many times in their small village school that its name had been derived from the fact they came from a "Valley thick with Oaks". Thankfully, this allowed them to often play in dense woods growing all around them. Today, it explained their choice of venue where they now came together to enjoy the calm and quiet inside a treehouse built high up within a thick cluster of branches. A carefully selected location off any beaten track, ensuring they were out of view high up in a Giant Oak.

It afforded them a much-needed safe haven, after learning sadly at such a cost that they couldn't trust several men who lived and worked all around them in positions of trust; who had preyed upon them for years after finding themselves under their care when at home, at school or even at church.

If they weren't safe when left with their babysitter, a teacher or a vicar, then they had to take to the trees to find sanctuary. To stay close with one another; at least until they had found a way to stop these paedophiles. Unfortunately, they had all learnt that words meaning, not in class but over years of first-hand experiences, not found in any reference book. This was why after completing their building project they now sat huddled close together just like they did in class, in silence, with their paper and pencil laid out in front of them.

Only today's subject was one never taught on any school curriculum – they had to write down how they could kill, then dispose of all these dirty bastards abusing them – sooner rather than later – without getting caught of course.

Sonya Child, who was the youngest of their group – still only seven years of age, concentrated really hard; wanting more than anything her idea to be the best. She had put a pencil in her mouth, a habit she tended to do when deep in thought without realising it – until she tasted lead on her tongue. But this made her smile

88

for the first time in a while; inspiring her to write down exactly what she had planned to make her abusers suffer physically and mentally – plus of course, they would directly relate to why she would be completing the task.

Just before they eventually died, and if it lasted half an hour; just like her ordeals had – then all the better.

"DURING"
DERWENT, DERBYSHIRE

Do not speak of evil, for it creates curiosity
In the heart of the young.
Nakota proverb

Sometimes enemies stand before you, appearing in full sight, easily defeated.
But, often they lie in wait inside your head, hidden completely from view. These
demons remain concealed, resulting in a longer battle, with far more
casualties.
Jay-Dee

He who seeks vengeance must dig two graves –
One for his enemy and one for himself.
Confucius

1

Final Battle, World War One, 1916

Waiting patiently for battle to commence, he remembered what he had been taught over many years – because if you listen and learn from your mistakes, then you stand a chance of winning; but always remember that in the future, if you get the chance to capture a man, then you have to take it – or you can be taken out there and then, in an instant.

Staring at every soldier directly in front of him, he checked that all his own men were in place and in line, before one by one they slowly advanced forward as the battle began; not sure of its outcome or their fate, having suffered many losses with heavy defeats recently; this really could be their last chance for quite a while to salvage a final much needed victory. They came closer and closer together on a crowded battlefield, moving slowly at first from side to side, trying their best to get into a far more favourable position by backing each other up to stay in the game for as long as possible. But one by one they fell silently, steadily being taken out by a worthy opponent, just sitting there in his uniform really calm. With that smug victorious look, smiling back, before his superior number of men, jumped about everywhere, taking over quickly, to easily win another battle.

Despite yet another defeat, he took it well, before dunking his malt biscuit into his glass of milk – then getting told off for dropping crumbs all over their Draught Board. He threw his mum a pleading look, begging her to be allowed to stay up a little while longer – to play another game. Jean Dan became insistent that it was time for bed, because she knew full well, glancing at the kitchen clock, she only had a few hours left to be with his dad – sat there with his uniform worn at home – a stark reminder that he soon had to leave; to begin the biggest battle of his life. World War 1 demands had kicked in with all the extra conscripts needed to back up depleted troops in France.

Even Jean Dan had been affected after agreeing to join the newly formed Women's Volunteer Reserve, with so few men left to oversee responsibilities for keeping the peace – with nurses like herself given extra jobs to "fill in the gaps".

As Corporal Dan glanced down at his young son, Danny, he reminded him that he must keep on practising at Draughts as he handed him the piece that was his 'last man standing', which he then popped inside his small pyjama top pocket after giving it a kiss. He told him to keep it safe, until he needed to use it to get out of trouble, when they next lined up their men to do battle again. Sadly, a few months later Danny knew that this would never happen after watching his mother rip open a telegram, with her cries of anguish telling him dad had fought his final battle.

That night Danny held onto his dark draught handed to him just before his dad had left, clenching it as tightly as possible – for as long as possible, until his hand ached, but the pain didn't matter one bit, because he never wanted to let go of its memory.

2

Buxton Arms, Buxton, Derbyshire, 1930

Negotiating pitch black country roads at speed generated even more loud shouts of anger and pain from the back of their police van, as colleagues suffered the same fate that many drunks had done before them. Normally thrown around for fun when taking the "bumpy ride" back to the station cells, a good ten miles away, or 20 if they did another circuit – just to teach the bastards a lesson.

Tonight though they were driving away from their police station, even leaving a game of cards behind to head towards a small village pub in Buxton. Luckily, another van had just arrived after a six strong serial of public order officers took a 'scenic route' home to South Yorkshire after covering a Derby County v Barnsley match. Its van driver having a brother, who ran a local pub across from the Buxton Arms, meant they were first to respond to deal with a 'big' problem.

Derbyshire-based officers couldn't believe their luck because it was 'Buxton Bob', a six-foot-five simpleton of a teenage farm hand had once again forgotten to take his medication – but had managed to drink a gallon of cider instead, then fallen into another chemical imbalance of rage. Locals knew about this eventuality only too well, including several tonight who were no slouches. Thrown around like rag dolls, after they had attempted to calm him down, with a friendly game of darts ending anything but.

It transpired that Bob couldn't wait any longer to play his favourite game – Noughts and Crosses – so he had wiped out scores on their dart blackboard before drawing his grid, declaring it was his turn to go first – before innocently offering a stick of chalk to an angry drunken crowd who vented their frustration before snapping his chalk in half, sending him into a rage.

Before carrying him out from the tap room into their van, the landlord managed to pull out five darts thrown to repel his advance, embedded in his face, head and body when thrown at him in desperation to stop his relentless assault before screaming and smashing up the pub. Finally, this ordeal ended after being knocked unconscious from a barrage of heavy truncheon blows to his head, by semi drunk bobbies who had managed a trouble-free shift at a football match – to find chaos after a small village darts match.

With a 'thank you pint' all round, for both serials of police they joked about all their homegrown idiots they dealt with. Regardless of which county you covered, each had endless names of 'characters' being mentioned, but not many were as much of a handful as Bob.

One Sheffield bobby who had often been a 'Lone Ranger' when dispatched to pub fights, had decided to stack the odds in his favour after chatting to a local blacksmith who had "weighted the odds" to his full advantage, by drilling out the middle of his wooden truncheon, before filling it with molten lead. This trebled its weight, meaning only one carefully landed blow was needed – normally crushing bones to their body, or, with a head shot knocked them out cold.

Bob had impressed them tonight taking four strikes to his skull before felled, but with this shared modification to their truncheons, Derbyshire officers with their Sergeants consent made necessary changes. They all visited their local iron mongers or horse farriers who were willing to help after which many around their county soon went on to feel the full weight of the law – in ways they could never have expected.

Before resuming patrol, it remained a mystery where dart number six had been thrown, but sadly this was solved later on when Buxton Bob came around in his drunk cell with it still clenched in his anvil of a fist. When startled by a gaoler who gave him the usual early morning rouse, before finishing the night shift.

This meant entering the cell to kick him hard a couple of times when laid out on its floor, to gain a grunt or some sort of reaction – but he got far more than he bargained for as Bob, believing he was coming under attack again in the pub, felt a dart still in his hand.

Jumping up with another harrowing scream, he shoved it twice into his attacker's head, nearly killing the police officer, before realising where he actually stood and what he had just done.

Found to be insane and therefore unfit to stand in a criminal trial for attempted murder, he was given an indefinite detention order to potentially live the rest of his life in a secure mental asylum. Here he was endlessly taunted by other inmates who asked him daily if he fancied joining them for a game of darts, because they had been given one as a present for being so well behaved, hung up on their padded cell wall.

This was after they had all heard how he finished his last game in a police station cell- after hitting a 'Double Top' with his only dart.

3

Tea At Dee's Café, Buxton

William Drummond enjoyed their morning sun sitting outside his Aunty Delia's tearoom, glancing across a large cobbled courtyard to do what he now got paid to do for his foreseeable future – to observe the world go by people-watching, with his new police helmet proudly placed next to him on a wooden table.

A pastime he had enjoyed doing since a boy, when he watched every customer attending at his dad's Smithy over many years where he would help out. Initially with non-manual work by tethering horses keeping them steady, normally whispering in ears or patting their mane as horseshoes were repaired or replaced. After this, children were then rounded up by hard-pressed farmers who were real characters often having to soon return after realising at least one child was missing from their cart.

Farmers certainly didn't hold back when it came to producing future helping hands, with most wives obligated to give them five or six offspring, secretly wishing for daughters with husbands always asking during home deliveries, "Is it a boy, is it a boy?"

He remembered Bob, the only boy with five sisters preceding him, but worth waiting for – a dream labourer standing taller than most men and twice as strong, lacking in intelligence – always managing to get left behind, despite his size; no doubt helped by mischievous sisters to give them some peace. With his siblings desperate to escape his incessant requests to play Noughts and Crosses on what was his only toy, a small chalk board. This meant his hands and face ended up speckled with white dust, after wiping out every game with his big fist, soon running his hands through his hair when deep in thought over his next move.

To use the words 'Bob' and 'deep in thought' in a sentence could only be described as polemic. He lacked any mental agility – being classed as a 'spastic' at school, unable to comprehend anything taught. Often teased when sitting alone in class, with children joking he only knew two letters: 'O' and 'X' because he only understood his favourite game.

Initially nicknamed 'OX' because he also possessed the strength of one – but they eventually eased up on him fearing his punching power. When a young teenager, a new name stuck with everyone calling him Buxton Bob, with many commenting it still contained his favourite letters.

Since joining Derbyshire Police PC William Drummond had read several reports in his village station that Bob was prone to lose it every now and then, especially after one beer too many, but more often than not he would sleep it off in their cells following arrest to eventually calm down, but sadly this had not been the case following his latest arrest.

After accepting his Auntie's little treat, he savoured her freshly baked scone, but he felt his tunic belt getting tighter, reminding him he would have to watch his weight now, because he was doing far less manual work. His decision not to follow in his dad's footsteps after his death was the right one, made for reasons he had never shared with anyone. But it had been clearly exemplified soon after being accepted into his new police job when he was immediately taught a valuable lesson: 'stamp them or lose them'.

Because when stood in his dad's old, now disused, workshop with a hammer held tightly in his hand, he felt it once again in his arm. To such effect that on the final strike onto his stamping kit he nearly missed the target when embossing 91 – his newly issued collar number, as their force had recently expanded.

Worst of all today he had just felt another twinge in his arm, only this time he wasn't doing any manual work, simply holding a China cup full of tea watching surface ripples form before an involuntary shake causing a rattling noise when he returned it to its saucer. This had sent his mind into a whirl about what it could be after calling into a local library several times to read medical journals, offering many differing suggestions.

Some were minor ailments including a pulled muscle spasm, perhaps a trapped nerve, but one sat with him making him break into a cold sweat. He recalled his wife asking him several times over this last year what was he rolling between his forefinger and thumb when his hand was empty. With horror he had read that a 'pill rolling' action (describing a much-used Victorian method for making medication) was an early indicative sign that a person may have Parkinson's disease.

As Aunty Dee walked away after seeking a compliment for her scone, he remembered his uncle had died young from Parkinson's, making him wonder if that was why his dad had committed suicide after watching his older brother suffer so much before his death. Perhaps his own shakes today were now being caused by this same unforgiving condition.

PC Drummond managed to smile when passers-by greeted him because it was such a reassuring sight for them to see a village bobby out on patrol. A young child asked politely, so he got to wear his helmet; but this hurt deep inside, knowing more than ever he had to keep it a secret for as long as possible, to guarantee his police house plus a secure income. Especially after his wife had told him only a few months ago that they would soon have an extra mouth to feed, with it being such a shame his dad would never see any of their children. They planned several; but she had already reminded him with a wagging finger, he wasn't a farmer – two would be the limit.

4

Large Wood Storage Barn, Otta, Norway, 1932

Huddled together tightly in such a confined space, she gently placed her hand over his mouth so he wouldn't shout out, because they only had to keep out of sight a few more minutes without being discovered – to win their first game of hide and seek since the schools had broken up for summer holidays a month earlier.

Every quarter hour, a large wooden clock mounted above an entrance door would single chime, its next noise would indicate they had then lasted 15 minutes without being seen or heard. With her brother's condition, keeping him quiet was certainly a challenge, but recently her dad's new medication for him seemed to be helping; he was noticeably less excitable than before even appearing much more in control.

After positioning lighter wooden planks above them in a criss-crossed fashion, they had made a little den to stay out of sight within a high stacked pile of bigger logs. This elevated vantage point also allowed them a view of six other children below who now scurried around faster than ever, shouting to one another to 'hurry up' to find them.

Sometimes, their anxious calls were drowned out by loud noises emanating from large industrial-sized cutting saws – constantly being fed fully grown, freshly forested, stripped pine trees within their uncle's adjoining workshop.

As Jakob got more and more excited, she pressed harder on his mouth, then smiled before giving him a little kiss on his cheek telling him with a whisper into his ear that they only had another minute to last; they both watched a brass second hand begin its final pre chime circuit, just as the pack hunting them moved ever closer.

Had Sofia not screamed out and then pushed wooden planks away from above her head with less than 20 seconds to go, they would have certainly done it. This was what confused their friends as they also screamed, but with delight, having found them just in time.

Sofia screamed, certainly not one of delight, as she now held back tears, unable to utter a word before then running away – because her brother had just swept his hand under her skirt, to digitally penetrate her with his finger. This had made her react to get away from him as quickly as possible, with her friends chasing after her wondering what on earth had caused this reaction.

Within seconds they all stopped dead in their tracks, before turning when hearing alarms ringing with hooters sounding before silence fell across a normally loud workshop mill to then hear it broken with men who began to shout and scream, with several vomiting. Caused after seeing Jakob running at speed directly towards a large industrial saw; heard by those closest to shout "Sorry, sorry" when climbing its support frame. Only pausing momentarily to stare across at his beloved sister in the distance, he jumped down, straddling its large cutting blade, killing him instantly – by severing him in half from between his legs to his upper body.

Following his funeral, their father Doctor Forde, a leading medical pioneer in mental disorders and behaviours, sat down with Sofia to now tell her about discoveries made recently, when she had been away at her boarding school, before this horrendous incident. It explained why Jakob had been driven to destroy his own genitalia – after many failed tests and treatments to combat his excessive testosterone levels.

It was a separate condition beside other known clinical problems, it attributed towards the major causation factor for his suddenly developed obsession to touch much younger girls, witnessed numerous times during clinical trials by medical staff who had to segregate him because it was escalating steadily, making him unable to control his arousals, but then followed with anger and repulsion – resulting in self-harm between his legs, including all around his genitalia.

Jakob, despite his limited mental capacity, had agreed to be a guinea pig for a new pioneering treatment involving chemical intervention with eugenic sterilisation; to deal with paedophilic behaviours, to treat his worsening condition.

Racked with self-guilt he had violated his own sister must have led him to act in accordance with recent tendencies to target, and now quite literally obliterate the problem, found between his legs.

This inspired Sofia after graduating years later to follow her father's footsteps; to understand and deal with chronic illnesses with linked conditions, but to approach them from a physiological and sociopathic angle. However, her whole direction in life changed in a way she could never have imagined, as erudite well-connected contacts her father knew from within their ministry, urged them to emigrate. This directly coincided with an ever-expanding German socialist party growing and gaining momentum, threatening Europe's peace and calm.

After being offered a place to live with her cousin in Hull who worked there as a freight control manager at the docks overseeing Norwegian exports into the U.K., Sofia was soon awarded her coveted masters place at Sheffield University, but here she self-registered as Sophie Ford.

A new name, a new start, a new beginning – with so much to put behind her; but she now pushed ahead with determination, founded on personal loss after such tragic circumstances from years earlier.

5

J Douglas and Son – Clockmakers, Sheffield, 1935

Upon checking his work diary before setting off, he noticed his son Joseph had previously met their first customer booked in at 9 am, after calling the previous week to place her order for a small brass plaque, engraved and then fitted to her own clock where instructed.

Normally, he would have greeted this client upon returning, to check if his work was to her liking, but his son mentioned over breakfast he would sort it out with her. This was after he had also taken a lot longer than normal to get ready in their bathroom, annoying his younger sister, who then nearly missed her school bus before they set off to work in his car, soon stinking of cheap aftershave.

Moving at lightning speed towards their shop counter to greet her when entering made it all become clear when his dad saw how beautiful she was. His son flirted nervously with a weak attempt at humour, saying this clock could well be a present for him; it was nearly his birthday plus his name also began with a J (which was only what she had wanted engraved on its small brass plate). With a polite smile she played along a little saying not to worry, because 'J' may get a nice present off his dad, after she had worked out a family likeness. He nodded across with a smile at his older 'look-alike' who now laughed, giving a thumbs up confirming her correct deduction.

Persisting to generate small talk, his son guessed she must know all about clocks because she came from Austria, perhaps Switzerland? Before his dad intervened to suggest her accent may well be more Scandinavian – confirmed with a small clap of her hands with a reply of:

"Well done. Norway."

As his son finally took the hint she wasn't interested, he retreated back into their workshop to hear a brief conversation between a lady he thought may have been his first ever girlfriend and his dad, when explaining it was in memory of a loved one, with them both agreeing that thankfully – time really was a great healer.

After leaving, Sophie Ford felt a little sad pondering how circumstances change with time; but this clock would always be a constant reminder of what she aspired to achieve over coming years, because time was on her side now – beginning her journey through academia.

This coincided with James Douglas now glancing across at his son Joseph, his face now covered in a bright-red rash after a reaction with cheap aftershave, before opening his shop window as wide as possible – hoping to lessen an assault on his nostrils. He sadly considered that unless his son vastly improved on both his chat up lines and fragrances, he would be living at home for a long time.

Meaning he would wind his little sister up even more than he wound up all their clocks on display at work, until they eventually sold his business and moved on; because his promise of "one day all this will be yours" hadn't exactly been the truth.

6

Village School, Derwent, 1938

Morning assembly always started their day but had to be flexible, depending upon so many 'up in the air' factors. These including whether the tractor started up, if they were able to herd up cattle in good time, or get up early enough to either walk a few good miles to get there, with others being driven a lot further on slow unmade roads from surrounding villages.

It meant that on a good day, over 30 pupils would attend, aged between 5 and 15, sitting together in a single classroom divided into quartiles. There were a few years difference between each group who began academia, rotated just like their crops. They started off sat by a blackboard before being uprooted towards an entrance door, before they eventually ventured outside – fully grown as young adults into an ever-changing world, awaiting them beyond its threshold.

Today's assembly took a little longer after being told they were all very lucky children indeed; it was with great delight that their headmaster explained they had been fortunate enough to have a recently retired music teacher move into the area. He had fallen in love with Derwent village when calling to see their vicar, an old friend. They had met years ago – initially when both training at a priesthood before he decided to leave to follow his love of music. He had moved all around the country teaching at schools, becoming highly qualified and competent.

Fortunately for them, Mr Pride was more than willing to help out – not only with classroom activities, but further afield and all had been explained in much greater detail in his letter of introduction, now being handed out for their parents to read.

This would allow them a chance to be given private tuition at his home on an evening or at weekends, to learn a variety of instruments, including piano as well as vocal lessons, with even an offer of being picked up and returned home later, if that helped with their arrangements.

Mr Simon Pride beamed with delight, sat on stage facing assembly when they read his CV with its incredible references and praise from former headteachers – all of whom were saddened he had moved on, because he would be missed; truly passionate about his career.

He mouthed almost every word to himself; he knew it off by heart – because since learning to become a printer on a training course in prison, when outed at his previous three schools after abusing his young pupils, he had type set and printed every false testimonial, reference and crest embossed certificate. This was now held by his excitable new head teacher; who had taken it all in hook, line and sinker. He had been accurate when explaining he had travelled all around the country – but that had been mainly in the back of a prison van.

He had chosen his new name to be S Pride because he had been a crossword enthusiast for years and it amused him. An anagram of how he regarded himself when casting a web and waiting for his prey. A 'Spider'. Soon to feed on tasty little morsels, namely young kids living in the scenic village of Derwent.

He was pleased with how his plan was unfolding; so far it had been silky smooth – soon to be put to good use just like his trademark silk hanky, in his breast jacket pocket. His old friend, their village vicar had come up trumps with this village location and he owed him lots of favours, from decades ago during papal training. When he alone took the blame for many of their discretions; to shield him from a full-blown investigation, allowing him to stay, but at his cost, when thrown out, but luckily back then it was an inhouse resolution. But years later he was eventually caught at a music academy, leading to many custodial sentences, but together again they could feed on tasty young flesh. His attention now drawn to a beautiful young girl, already excited with telling a friend she could play the recorder, whilst playing an imaginary instrument; quickly moving her small fingers up and down, smiling towards teacher to get his attention. Well, she certainly had it, confirmed with a little movement in his groin.

She would soon play with his instrument, perhaps at first with his silk hanky shoved into her mouth to stifle her screams; until he no longer needed to use his prop; normally with time they accepted what he did.

Today, the children wore name badges for him to know who they were and with a squint he read hers- before giving Sonya a big smile and a thumbs up. Happy days.

7

Faculty of Social Studies, Sheffield Training College, 1939

Memories flooded back as she sat with other students feeling like a 'Mother Hen' but enjoying every moment as Jean Dan, now in her fifties, began her academic journey to fulfil her lifelong ambition – to become fully trained up as a registered mental health nurse specialising in child psychology.

It was a dual-purpose mission: to help so many unfortunate souls in society who were plagued with mental illness, but also to help her understand and guide her towards finding achievable courses of action to cope, deal and even possibly overcome affliction for young children. Ultimately also for her own son's benefit – who was a tormented soul but Jean felt sure that he was crying out inside for help, sadly though unwilling at this stage to trust anyone.

Perhaps she could be the one.

As their junior professor welcomed her new group, she glanced around her lecture theatre where she had now taught for five years. It had been enjoyable but now it was time to push ahead with all her career aspirations – to take her to the next level, to hopefully be rewarded with a doctorate. She was about to put finishing touches to her dissertation that had stagnated for over 12 months.

After asking for introductions today from her new students Jean Dan didn't need to utter a single word. This was because her heart had jumped a beat after reading her application form, telling her everything she needed to know about this truly remarkable woman with such a fascinating background. On her wish-list, it had ticked every box to help her finally move forwards to achieve success.

Perhaps, she could be the one.

8

Lecturer's Offices – Tutorial, Sheffield Training College

With cross-references supporting her essay submission, using a legal case that she had dealt with personally made it easy for Professor Ford to move their study debate to an off campus meet up.

Where they had discussions, debates and conversations over a bottle of wine as Jean Dan, feeling comfortable with her newfound erudite friend, began to open up about aspects of her former career including an investigation just before retirement – her 'swan song', a local network of paedophiles operating all around Derbyshire.

Numerous hours over many months with their lengthy one to one 'off the record' disclosures gave both women a detailed insight as to what had motivated them to pursue their shared dream through academia. One strove to eradicate completely or minimise unnatural actions of many; whereas Jean Dan wanted to help her son primarily, before moving on to work with young victims who had suffered abuse. This was after discovering several had committed suicide post-conviction of their offenders, ironically when at long last they were eventually safe from them – but had never been given victim counselling or support, that may have saved their lives to help cope with their post trauma demons.

As a 'quid pro quo' agreement, Jean Dan would allow Sofie to call at her home, to share with her classified file case notes and interviews with predatory sex offenders. Perhaps even a possibility that with Jeans contacts – it may secure a one-to-one prison visit with a convicted principal paedophile offender, shown compassion by Jean during a complex investigation. A stark contrast to what the males gave him, mainly knees and punches to his groin and stomach.

This led to him opening up to her, always their plan, using an old 'good cop bad cop' tactic to maximum effect. It had worked when he implicated hundreds of others in a national network. But he never gave up 'Len' who they suspected to be their camera man, taking thousands of photographs. Not only young children – that being bad enough – but also babies, luckily some of them weren't being abused or violated when captured on film.

In return, once Jean Dan had given her son his ultimatum, Sophie would work with him to try her 'step back' initiative, still only in its infancy. But with a willing candidate, with an incentive to become cured, to be able not only to join but then hold his position within a police force, she would test her model out on him. This detailed case study could be just the kick start needed to climb up the academia ladder to eventually make senior professor.

It was a controversial approach pushing at many boundaries, but after hearing recently from her parents about atrocities and horrors being committed at home, it put things in perspective. This was after her country was invaded by Germans to implement Hitler's plan to impregnate Scandinavian women by SS Soldiers to fulfil his dream – to create a purebred Aryan race now officially documented as 'Operation Lebensborn'. Compared to her proposed actions, they were nothing when you looked at what was currently going on in the world.

Many would be shocked with her concept, but it paled into insignificance with Hitler striving to breed out impurities to create only pale-skinned children with 'pure' blood.

Sophie glanced at a clock after hearing another quarter hour chime; this being her constant reminder to work hard in pursuit of success, after losing one poor tormented soul, meaning the world to her.

Who knows, with time she may manage to save Jean Dan's son – before it was too late.

9

Prison Cell, Strangeways, Manchester

Sat waiting for her in his cell, Steve Dale ran his tongue once again over his gum that used to hold his two front teeth. It was still soft, tasting of blood only having them kicked out a few weeks earlier when at long last, following many failed attempts they finally managed to find his prized stash of photographs.

He accepted other cons every now and then would get close enough to land a few blows, even though he had a 'voluntary segregation' status awaiting an appeal to go ahead against a ten-year sentence. But he knew if prison staff kept on allowing them to get near him, it wouldn't be long before they killed him.

With his latest threat to make an assault complaint taken seriously, they had now eventually done their job, albeit reluctantly – to keep him isolated. This was until it had transpired during his court case that one of his 'victims' was a prison officer's niece from Sheffield. A phone call from him had resulted in a 'message' arriving in the shape of a guard's boot – delivered with a beating in his cell when kicking his teeth out.

But this time, no formal complaint had been made, knowing only too well his 'keepers' would kill him. No doubt making it appear that he had hung himself at night in between their one-hour cell checks.

Today, he took a calculated risk – because he knew his visitor had been sent in by the 'old bitch', who had played nice cop before putting him away when begging him to give up 'Len' who had taken thousands of photographs of children. All of them in various stages of undress, with some being abused. Several of these had been found in his works locker at school; this damning evidence convicting him with his trial judge taking exception to a head teacher interacting with children as he had done or fantasised about loving them. Deemed depraved and sick for now, until society finally understood 'they' had a totally different approach to 'love' without parameters or boundaries.

Since the request for a visiting order landed, his thoughts became dominated by her; not too difficult to achieve when you were alone in your cell 23 hours a day. With no window, and sadly now with nothing to look at to help stimulate his thoughts. But he had made his mind up about what needed to be done; logic dictated that eventually his secret stash would be brought to police attention, who this time may pick up on a few clues – that would convict his stepson known by only the cover name of Len – thankfully the old bitch from CID had never identified him, but sometimes though, you never see what's directly under your nose.

Len set up in business many years earlier as a professional photographer, who initially did landscape before studio portraits of families, he diversified with his own predilection, drawing him towards children. So, he specialised in christenings, birthday parties and school photos before hitting upon a genius idea to advertise in kindergartens to promote his business services. Offering professional images of young children really opened the door to a sweet shop as parents paid for studies of their babies. This allowed Len to fully exploit his access to and time spent with toddlers. It meant young pre-school children were delivered like little gift wrapped presents to his studio. With his girlfriend oblivious to his abhorrent motives, she helped out by babysitting siblings, allowing him to focus in a way he really wanted to on subjects, sat gargling away naked in front of him.

It only took a minute for him to capture on film what many others would cherish for years – keeping safe prized possession gifted to them through the lens of a camera. Thankfully, CID never connected this cover name to him or indeed his place of work, a small business premises in Matlock. It even became a tea spot for several local bobbies with a few, then becoming customers for family portraits.

Ironically it meant Len often stood directly in front of those who wanted to capture him; whilst capturing them on film, at a time when he became the most sought-after protagonist of indecent images that circulated across the north of England. Where his work was quickly fed and distributed across many paedophile networks craving his 'artistic' offerings.

Today Steve Dale had to risk giving Len a message, requesting to pay him a visit in prison – to warn him he needed to make urgent changes to his studio décor because one of his coveted recently seized images had inadvertently captured a damming reflection –when Len took it, of a young girl sat posing by a toy-sized dressing table. She wore sexy makeup, but nothing else; but he had overlooked that in the mirror you could see Len's studio behind her, with its distinctive print visible on its shop wallpaper.

In prison they intercepted, monitored and skim-read all his mail, but visitors with no convictions or known connections to any underground groups were paid far less attention. Plus, with Lens name not being linked to his own, meant he could use this 'professor' bird as a carrier pigeon, to deliver his request.

If he had put it in writing when following normal protocol to instigate a visit, that person's details would be passed to a police prison liaison officer who would check them out; whereas a random visitor applying for a visiting order may be checked out, but only in weeks to come – by which time necessary precautions with a bit of DIY redecoration at his studio would allow him to stay well ahead of an ever-chasing relentless pack.

Len really was accomplished at doing that, being as crafty as a fox.

10

Visitors Hall, Strangeways, Manchester – Noon

Under normal circumstances, prisoners on 'special watch' would be afforded a segregated visit to comply with rules in accordance with their status; to protect not only them (as many hardened officers had to be reminded), but also their family and friends – who were more often than not reluctant visitors into such a harsh regime.

Where parents and loved ones also had hatred and anger vented towards them with a commonly held belief they had either 'created or covered' for a monster who preyed on young children, with many inmates praying they got accolade and recognition for being first to get to them – to end their miserable existence.

This would be their 'badge of honour' so they would then be given an elevated status, with respect being afforded. This was normally never attained with most of those striving for this praise regarded as lower-end criminals on their scale. With lifers, normally Gangland members, especially those who were Manchester-based being what they aspired to measure up to.

Today's prisoner, 1331, sat nervously with his back against a wall in the far corner of a visiting hall with many other inmates turning heads to stare at him. Several ran fingers over their throats to help him fully understand they would eventually catch up with him. Because he was such a dirty little bastard, that would pay with his life for what he had done.

Even the stunning looks of a lady that entered their hall to sit opposite him, didn't escape snarls and underhand comments. Sophie Ford had been primed before her visit about what abuse she may well receive, but she didn't react, maintaining eye contact at all times; with a small nervous-looking man apart from when he stared down at a desk in front of him.

The current Strangeways governor, both young and keen, had ambitious aspirations of being elevated from this Gaol to work within the Ministry of Justice to oversee future penal reform. This was why he found motivation and time to meet a leading professor; currently doing her thesis on psychology – all covered in her letter of introduction when submitting her request to visit her proposed case study, who now sat before her looking terrified.

It was only a half hour chat, begun by explaining who had sent her, making him laugh; did she really think he hadn't worked that one out by himself? Knowing full well she was from Sheffield University. He asked if 'Old Bag' who was doing her degree there (Jean Dan told him about her future plan following retirement when trying to befriend him) could die anytime soon? He couldn't resist holding back with his hatred and venom towards her, when discovering at his trial what she had done during their search – producing hundreds of extra exhibits, found both in his locker and at his home, most of them planted by the bastards.

Yes, he possessed photographs that some people may not understand – representing natural beauty, not only to him but also many other like-minded individuals, who he shared them with. It helped them all admire 'innocence of young sexuality' waiting to be enjoyed by those wanting to appreciate it first, with age just being a number. With such archaic, myopic, legislation that dictated genuine feelings when passion sometimes just couldn't be suppressed, but sadly reviled by most of society, who turned hostile towards them -only regarding them as demonic criminals.

Professor Ford, her chosen titular today; carefully selected to appeal to his ego, feeding his craving for attention, as she had already correctly diagnosed after speaking at length to Jean Dan he had 'histrionic personality disorder' – seeking attention from others, believing he was worthy of an audience, but only with her full focus. Despite an elevated academic standing he wanted and craved to be regarded as just an important individual, more than deserving of her indulgence.

This craving now tactically fuelled further by Sophie who lowered her own head slightly, telling him how honoured she would be to work under him to help her fully understand his dilemma – let alone his struggle in life; now being regarded as an outcast. When millions read her report, obviously fully focused on him with his plight, after his ordeals – they would clearly understand his perspective.

It concluded with a clammy palmed handshake, but she also felt something else, having just passed her something small. He obviously didn't want anyone else to see this after agreeing she would be allowed to interview him within prison to assist with her work. It allowed him to put forward an explanation about an 'illness' he had been labelled with, but there were a few conditions and caveats; she had fully expected these having already put things in place with their ambitions governor who didn't want to lose kudos, with this chance to progress his own career from its already elevated position.

So yes, he would be reinstated with certain privileges including a 'cell with a view' with a guarantee he would be protected from attacks in future, with a private room for meetings from now on, away from prying eyes with 'finger across throat' threats.

Yes, providing he engaged weekly to her satisfaction over a six-month period, he would then be transferred to a prison closer to his home – making visits a lot easier for his family, with this leading to a final unexpected request.

But yes – she would call to see his stepson from a previous marriage who lived just outside Matlock in the Peak District, to tell him he was agreeing to see her for help, like he'd always begged him to do. He then explained to Sophie he now really wanted to put things right between them after so many years, hence his hope that he would consider face to face interaction if he would apply in writing for a visiting order. All she had to do was visit the address just given.

But Sophie saw distinctive changes during this final request, when compared to his others – despite this one seeming relatively minor. Because his demeanour, body language and voice carried a far different meaning, it displayed a higher degree of urgency and importance than you would expect, indicated by preparing his hidden message passed on a carefully concealed folded piece of paper, with a home address for her to call at before returning to Sheffield.

Sophie Ford bid him farewell, reflecting about what she had just heard and seen, which meant she didn't even hear further abuse directed towards her when leaving – but did notice Mr 'ever so keen' governor waiting outside, urgently awaiting an answer – had he agreed to her ground-breaking intervention programme? (He had already decided on its title for when performance examples were written to help support future job applications.)

Sophie Ford smiled, suggesting it may be best to have a chat in his office as she now had a few urgent questions for him. Later on, this paid huge dividends after he confirmed his two front teeth were missing after a recent altercation during a cell search – but no complaint made. He had overreacted, falling when contraband was found and yes how very astute because they had seized photographs from his cell. Her egocentric governor passed them over immediately, after hearing Sophie would deliver them when calling to see the original investigation officers, with whom she had regular contact.

Indeed, they were the ones who had asked her to visit him, hoping that 'Prisoner 1331' would eventually soften to her interaction; to name a few names of those who still had their liberty.

When passed the envelope with a few photographs inside, Sophie didn't feel bad about just feeding this gullible governor a little bullshit. After all, it wasn't as if he had held back himself, dishing it out with such a crap story given about 'missing teeth'.

Sophie Ford sat in her car before unfolding a small piece of paper handed to her earlier – now feeling confident this man he wanted her to visit must be a key player in their network. Could this be a desperate attempt to forewarn him after seizing his photograph, had this triggered concern?

Jean Dan had been unable to identify Len, who was a conduit for all their material, who had kept so many supplied with perverse fantasy images – first seen through the lens of his camera?

She studied the main photograph taken from him of a young girl sat facing a camera, seated innocently alongside a small dressing table, but wearing only a thickly applied dark lipstick with a large pearl necklace looped several times around her neck, hanging down towards her midriff.

But most importantly of all, she had spotted a major clue – supporting her deduction; that Len had taken this picture of his young model – in his photographic studio.

Sophie Ford glanced at herself in the internal car mirror, when just about to apply makeup and light lipstick (having deliberately dressed down before entering prison).

She froze with such a vivid image of that poor child in the photograph, innocently sat playing – oblivious to perverse actions all around her. Sophie stayed make up free, now feeling sick in her stomach – just before checking her roadmap to determine her best route to Matlock.

Confident that on reflection, with what had been found – she could really help; by soon getting to see the animal responsible for taking not only this sordid image, but no doubt many thousands of others.

11

"Take a Peak" Studio, Matlock –
Two Hours Later

Wearing a headscarf with sun glasses, she walked across a scenic cobbled square, admiring an artistic sign displaying such a cleverly chosen name for a photographic studio located in the Peak District. It had some wonderful landscape photos on display – capturing natural beauty from its surrounding countryside that drew in many thousands of tourists, every year.

This would be Sophie Ford's cover story if she had to speak with anyone inside, but using only her native tongue – Norwegian, feigning a very poor command of English to keep it short – before leaving with her map held in front of her, just like a totally lost confused tourist, walking away with a smile, perhaps a little wave.

After visiting his home address with no answer to repeated knocking, Sophie was lucky enough to return to her car just in time to see a lady she knew lived there. Looking through its lounge window earlier, a portrait photograph had confirmed that hanging on a lounge wall. Despite arriving home and parking up her drive, there was no need to speak after also seeing a 'Take a Peak' business card on a window ledge – this included the shop address in Matlock. Most importantly, when walking towards her front door with key in hand, she noticed she wore a large pearl necklace, but her heart sank even more after her car's back doors flew open as two young children, a boy and girl both under five, excitedly ran inside giggling.

With great sadness she recognised the little girl – seen naked in the photograph.

A short while later when posing as a lost tourist, stood outside its display window admiring many framed photos of amazing views, Sophie Ford raised her sunglasses – to clearly see some unique wallpaper inside with a distinctive camera and tripod print. This was identical to what she had noticed in a toy dressing table mirror reflection, on a photo seized – during an earlier cell search. It now meant she had sufficient evidence to present Jean Dan with a full picture supporting her belief Len could be fully identified. Just when a man came into view standing by a display counter inside, who gave a beaming smile followed with a warm handshake to another customer, who held a gift-wrapped picture under their arm.

Hopefully, if things developed well, it may not be too long before others got their hands on Len, who could then be sent to prison, gift-wrapped for others – to help him lose a few teeth, just like his step dad.

With all the evidence now available, they wouldn't even need to frame him.

12

Operation "Capture", Derbyshire HQ, 1939

As a debt of gratitude for her assistance – with an amazing contribution to identify an elusive Len, their appreciation was shown when allowing Professor Ford to attend debriefs with Jean Dan, after they fulfilled their objective. Capturing a major player who had operated amongst them for over a decade; posing, quite literally, as a legitimate business concern. But he was now sat in a prison cell, concerned for his life, knowing full well what was going to happen to him if not protected, starting from now until his lengthy sentence was completed.

Using an age-old tactic, detectives walked his girlfriend past his cell door a few times, allowing her to scream abuse; they even slowed down to point and nod towards his chalked name above the door. This made him fold far quicker than expected – meaning she was soon released, having been an innocent victim. They knew that from the outset; they called it their 'ways and means act' and she didn't hesitate to give a statement against him, after showing her one of his creations. They called it 'lipstick and pearls' – the photograph of her own daughter; born just before being selected by a monster of a predator, taking full advantage of her life predicament after she had fled away from a violent husband to seek a safe haven.

A raid on his studio resulted in hundreds of photographs – not to mention dozens of 'customers' with a specific wish list, detailing what they wanted on film with mailing addresses. This allowed for controlled deliveries to prove receipt after warrants were executed within minutes to show they had opened their 'order' with many hiding them to prove culpability leading to a conviction.

As part of her 'post-arrest deal', Sophie Ford attended his cell after charge to meet her resident 'guinea pig', who would now fully cooperate with her psycho analytical studies, including monthly visits in prison until her doctorate was completed. It now allowed her to probe and investigate, attempting to understand a mindset driving such perverse behaviour.

After lighting his cigarette, she allowed him to stop sniffling before explaining in no uncertain terms that from now on, she could be his lifeline. He would benefit from her 'pearls of wisdom' – with this phrase having its desired effect. He obviously fully understood its meaning after bursting into tears, before throwing himself at her feet.

Sophie Ford winked at Jean Dan, standing by his door – who would be an understudy for her thesis; they gave one another a thumbs up, before staring down at this pathetic creature, laid out on his cell floor below them.

They mentioned in a later conversation, over a celebratory drink, that you normally did find a snake on its belly.

13

Central Train Station, Sheffield, 1940

His throat felt bone dry again, but what concerned him more was how he could feel his heart thumping away. With his ever-present trademark – the white silk hanky, now held tightly in his clammy palm, he dabbed away frantically as more beads of sweat formed on his furrowed brow. It ended up this way after many years of frowning at pupils hitting wrong notes attempting to teach them piano. Today, he knew more than ever before he had to hold it together. Suddenly a steam train came thundering towards them before coming to a halt in the crowded station, causing plumes of sulphurous white smoke to engulf everyone. He wondered if this white nebula effect just created resembled heaven – but he knew the likelihood of him finding that out would be remote.

When this hazy mist lifted all around them, he quickly spotted two other paedophiles on the very same platform, who didn't make eye contact with him – as agreed during a catch up, only the previous night. Filled with lubricious chat when excitedly babbling away with mounting uncontrollable excitement about what was soon going to be gifted to them on a plate – to feed their incessant appetite.

Following a shrill blast from a station masters whistle, they now intently watched doors being thrown open, slamming hard creating a cacophony of sound against metal train panel sides – out of beat, but a wonderful noise in the circumstances. Extra guards brought in to control swelling crowds, also blew away frantically on their lifelong service whistles, attempting to take control of this hectic situation. It soon became apparent that adults on packed platforms were the main protagonists – now unable to control their emotions unlike line after line of subdued children slowly emerging into view, clinging to appointed escorts. They held each other's hands to form a human chain, becoming overcome with the scale of activity all around them.

Eventually, the trustee's, who wore a badge to prove it – namechecked them against a government-issued register having 'Operation Pied Piper' embossed upon its cover, under an impressive gold crest, displaying a royal coat of arms. With lanyards that held badges hanging from their necks, one by one they were ticked off – confirming safe arrival – before given a smaller name badge, pinned to outer clothing.

A stern-faced police officer in full uniform meticulously countersigned each entry for those children who would soon be living in Derbyshire. A nervous excited music teacher moved forwards slowly to collect his ward after he had produced his own identification, with his confirmation letter. Already vetted, then approved to become a guardian – before finally a child had been ushered gently towards him. He took in scant details on his badge, with his name having no real relevance, unlike his age, that made him lick his lips again.

Most children had now been reduced to tears, but his little present remained stoic-faced, holding out his hand to formally introduce himself to his new temporary guardian; knowing he had agreed to take him to live in a safe haven – far away from his new parent's home in London where possibly a bombing blitz may take place under coming months, possibly years.

Mr Pride offered to carry his young man's bag, but he held it up easily to make a point of showing he could manage. This didn't surprise him one bit, after feeling such a firm grip during their handshake; plus, he hadn't been shy when making direct eye contact with him during introductions.

Walking towards his car, he glanced down at his ginger-mopped little present; letting his imagination run wild, thinking about what else he would soon be feeling besides his firm grip over coming months – perhaps even years if this war dragged on. Had he still been a religious man, he would pray it continued as long as possible, but only for selfish indulgent reasons.

Today's events at Sheffield station had brought a whole new meaning to that old saying about 'riding the gravy train'. They now approached their driver, a good friend and fellow paedophile, who honked the car horn – obviously over excited and a little too giddy, now seeing their beautiful new play thing get a little nearer.

It could only be described as a dream come true for them, and many others just like them, taking full advantage of what they could volunteer to look after. A perverse heaven, a place they would never see – because with their predilections they may well be going in the opposite direction – but for now he did know they were going to Derwent with 'little mister independent.' Confirmed by putting the case in the boot himself, before shaking their driver's hand.

Perhaps a slightly longer shake this time, on account of him pausing momentarily – when noticing he wore a dog collar and a large gold crucifix.

14

Home of Jean Dan, Derwent Village, Derbyshire

Both were a constant reminder of an antithesis present during her life, when staring at them in her bedroom mirror reflection. Jean now looked down at two pieces of metal that hung from her necklace, laying side by side – representing two polemic worlds; sadly witnessed first-hand, one recently causing her so much turmoil, pain and suffering.

A simple crucifix – an open obvious display of good, next to a small key representing pure evil, causing her watery eyed gaze – to avert towards a large oak chest – now padlocked shut. Its content accumulated over her 25-year police career, serving as a reminder that good could triumph over evil when she put monsters away – men who inflicted pain and suffering on so many, with most victims sadly young children.

Her chain of thought broken when she heard excitable giggles and then loud laughter coming from downstairs. Her day now began with several local children dropped off by parents, before heading off to work with many having to travel into towns and cities around them. Limited jobs only available in local villages – as farmers and small businesses with so many offspring, normally being self-sufficient.

Her own son was on hand to help out for now, before he pursued his ambition to follow his mother into the local police force. A letter had just landed stating he was due a home visit in coming weeks by a senior officer, before a decision could be made in relation to his appointment. Jean knew it was only a formality, having spoken recently to a chief inspector, a personal friend, who years earlier had been her Sgt when she first joined Derbyshire's rank and file.

As her son chased after children, they spilled out into her garden as she watched him scoop them up one by one to put them in his "dinosaur cave" –

which this week was a clothes rack, propped up in a far corner next to a wooden shed, with a large towel draped across its frame. Today, "Rex" of the Tyrannosaurus dynasty, hunted down his prey, one by one – until all were caught. Subconsciously, as she stared down, her hand once again held both pieces of metal on her necklace, as she battled in her mind with a distinct possibility, all was not as it appeared to be, with evil lurking close at hand, disguised in so many different ways.

Sometimes, perhaps even as a dinosaur – playing an innocent game with young kids, who were brought to a trusted childminder, every weekday – for safekeeping.

Jean Dan may well be watching another constant battle once again in life – taking place with good and evil in juxtaposition, with her holding the key as to whether her son did continue in pursuit of his career, or she confronted him with the many reasons she had locked her 'memory box' in her bedroom. Now convinced he had been looking into it for quite a while, before made inaccessible to him.

Had its gruesome contents, he'd no doubt seen and read over many years, corrupted his mind, perverting his soul to make him what he now was?

God forgive her – if she had been the cause – but perhaps her local priest could give her guidance in her moment of need. Jean had found great comfort in religion during life, helping her cope and deal not only with demons from yesteryear, but also those now appearing in her present.

Now hearing a car pull up outside, she opened her front door to greet their much-talked-about new arrival, with all her other children giving in to curiosity – ignoring well-established game rules, with a loud mass breakout from 'dinosaur cave'. Laughing and giggling excitedly they ran up behind her to greet the new boy who suddenly reacted by standing like a boxer – looking like he may throw punches, before he realised they weren't a threat and only rushing to see him. Jean Dan ushered him inside, telling all her giddy children to calm down before she playfully rubbed his mop of bright ginger hair before announcing:

'OK, everyone, calm down please; this is our guest who will be living in our village for a while. I've explained to you already all the reasons why he had to move to the countryside; where it's a lot safer to live – so please put on your name badges we made yesterday, so he also knows who you all are.'

They all concentrated hard to get their sticky paper labels on straight – bearing their handwritten names displaying a bright assortment of crayon colours, decided by whichever one they had grabbed from the tin, now proudly worn and checked – before reading an official-looking plastic badge pinned to his coat, telling them this new boy's name and his age in capital letters.

'OLIVER KING (10 YEARS OLD)'

Whom, out of habit, since arriving only a few minutes earlier, had already taken in the gold crucifix with its central half-karat diamond – not to mention her ruby and emerald platinum ring, worn next to the 18-karat wedding band, before he wondered if the old girl lived here all alone – in this big house.

15

'Dinosaur Cave', Jean Dan's Garden

Hearing a 'dinosaur' roar outside – both children having been caught earlier wanted to escape his cave – to be free, to carry on playing this game with all their friends. They sighed – staring at one another in silence beneath several towels, which covered a clothes prop before a young boy eventually asked a younger girl:

"Are you keeping a secret? Because if you tell me, I really, really promise I won't tell anyone. Honest, honest, cross my heart and hope to die, stick a pin in my eye."

She quickly peeped outside, to make sure he wasn't anywhere near – just in case he heard them, before whispering back with two hands, one either side of her mouth:

"Yes, but I promised to keep it to myself because if I tell anyone – it will lose its magic, so I can't use it to escape, but I don't know if it's a magic colour yet."

"You check yours and I will check mine," he whispered back in a voice full of mischief and excitement.

She wanted him to go first, but after a flurry of exchanges – including an offer of his chocolate bar in his lunchbox, that sealed the deal. The temptation just too much for a lover of chocolate. Standing up to pull her tights and knickers away from her body before reaching down to retrieve a 'magic coin' – this would now be her first sight of it, after he had placed it there earlier on – but only when safe to do so with absolutely nobody else around them who may see it – which would then destroy its powers. After looking down she couldn't hide her disappointment – just like the look on her fellow prisoner's face, when they both saw it was a white 'coin' – which was in fact a wooden disc from a box of draughts they always played with first thing when they were dropped off, before having a fun game of 'chase and capture'.

They both knew only too well – after months of being told by him that only black magic worked, meaning it had to be a dark coin that could be used after three of them had been caught. This then allowed them one by one to go with him, for him to check for 'hidden magic' as he called it. Only one of them would be lucky enough to have this 'magic coin', but they never knew who. They often wondered who was lucky enough to have magic with them today.

Tyrannosaurus Rex knew full well – but also knew that particular little child would be last to be captured today. Every week he would continue to hide them, when one on one in his piano room he would gently place it between their legs after patting it a few times to make sure it wouldn't fall out, when they ran around after starting the game.

Every time he played draughts with his mum on an evening, he would always smile, knowing full well where each piece had been placed earlier on – adding such a thrill to both games.

16

Parish Church, Derwent – One Month Later

After watching him rip open his letter – bearing its force crest and then hearing him scream out with joy, she knew it was now imperative to make a decision, that could potentially make such a difference for so many. It would be one of her most difficult, but was always the case when it impacted on loved ones.

Daniel Dan's hands shook with excitement when closing his eyes to picture himself in uniform; not only for himself but for his dear friend, his like-minded special confidant who had helped him make this difficult journey, arriving where he wanted to be. He was now in a position to fulfil all his cravings and desires, accepting who and what he was.

His scar on his wrist bore testimony to his struggle when once unable to cope and deal with his proclivity for young partners – an attempt to end his life. In more ways than one he had been saved to allow his existence; his raison d'être to survive to stay alive, to continue.

His mentor both kind and understanding, after all his own life experiences borne out of abuse – teaching him how to adapt to his situation and then move forward in a far better way, without inflicting pain or suffering, to become far more loving and gentler.

Unlike so many others whom he had now met, his own interest and compulsion to experiment with children had come from the most unlikely of sources. His first arousal visual when reading reports and seeing images seized to be presented as evidence to courts – by his very own mother. Initially for safe keeping, but then out of habit, she began to keep police files at home, even following her retirement without sending them to be archived, realising they may come in useful with future studies.

Also kept tucked away were two other souvenirs, her handcuffs and epaulettes. Daniel had spent many happy hours accessing this memory box until one day he found it padlocked shut – initially causing concern for him but nothing was said; plus, with her kindergarten being set up from home, this convinced him it was just a precaution, preventing children straying to find unthinkable items when running around and playing in their large home.

It would be a bottle of red wine celebration when he saw his friend later on tonight as arranged, but with plenty more to discuss, because he would now be able to access many "honey pots" as they called them, such as children's homes. Even young offender secure units and borstals – it really presented an endless list of opportunities now gifted to them.

As Jean Dan stared across to study his face, she wished it was possible to read his mind, so much appeared to be racing through his head before he made excuses about leaving to pick up some shopping. Later on, she ventured out herself to put trust in her religion, knowing fully well her confidant would be free after his early evening service, just before he did his rounds to see parishioners laid up at home, but who had requested a visit from him.

Prior to calling, Jean Dan picked wild flowers to lay them at her dear husband's grave, despite it being over 20 years since losing him in action during the war. She took comfort from spending time at his grave having already reserved a plot next to him, when her turn to leave this world, to depart this mortal life, to join him in spirit.

Later that night, after sharing with their priest her fears and concerns about her son, he offered a pillar of support, agreeing fully she should now confront him – but offer him counselling and help with her young university professor. He knew all about her from previous updates and shared secrets, relating to how they had met during her degree and a joint operation- with Sophie herself having worked for years doing studies for a mental health doctorate with paedophiles.

After explaining he was setting off on his rounds Jean left but the priest returned to his living quarters upstairs where he poured red wine, having breathed sufficiently from when his excitable guest had brought it around earlier to celebrate unbelievable news. Smiling, he said:

"I knew all those years at drama school would pay off. I acted as though all her revelations about you were the first I'd heard, but just so you know she's going to confront you real soon to suggest you get some help."

Daniel Dan smiled back raising his glass; he had heard everything about his mum's friend, this professor, a more frequent caller over previous months – so he would play along to appease her – he had managed to fool her most of his life; so, a little longer wouldn't harm, but bless her, she really did love him despite everything she knew about him.

After all, he was the little diamond in her crucifix.

17

Crown Court, Derby – R V CLEGG

Prior to taking her place in its small public gallery they allowed her access to their adjoining prosecuting barrister's interview room off a large court foyer, displaying a notice board listing the case to be held next as RV CLEGG for sentencing, after entering a guilty plea to every charge they had put before him.

After sliding a piece of paper towards his former partner that only listed one item, she signed the disclaimer with a trembling hand followed by a flood of tears. Professor Ford, had correctly anticipated this reaction, so now handed her a paper tissue already tucked up her sleeve. A final parting gift to dab her eyes before leaving the room. Before she paused at its door to gather her composure, to eventually speak – but with venom. Not only as a woman, but a loving caring mother, who had been used; but far worse, her daughter had been abused.

"Promise me you use it to good effect, I beg you – please make that bastard suffer as much as you can; let him feel pain for what he did."

After giving her a hug with a promise she certainly would, Sophie decided there was no time like present before opening an exhibit bag – to wear what had just become hers, before taking her seat carefully chosen in court. It guaranteed the bastard would see her when stood in the dock. She used a compact mirror to check her appearance, just before a court clerk told everyone to stand. Then their learned judge walked in to take his seat, a signal for everyone else to follow suit. Silence fell in anticipation.

Moments later, with court officers flanking him, Clegg remained impassive when sentenced to 12 years imprisonment, but when he glanced across to see Professor Ford wearing distinctive dark lipstick – he looked shocked. But when she brought a large pearl necklace now worn, up to her mouth to kiss it, he then collapsed in tears.

Delighted with his reaction, she spent over six months using her technique of 'contain-blame-shame', when making him face up to consequences of his actions, before restorative intervention brought in next to promote self-reflection then change. With excellent progress made this went on to support her thesis, with Jean Dan being cross referenced, giving her credit as an understudy for a paper entitled:

'PEARLS OF WISDOM – A REFLECTIVE APPROACH' (Contain-Blame-Shame)

Following glowing accolades both women were recognised for academic work regarded as outstanding; with their own University honouring them by holding a ceremony, attended by leading scholars.

A photograph taken captured a poignant moment when they posed together with a large pearl necklace draped across their shoulders – with a thumbs up and a smile for the camera.

When alone, following numerous questions and chats with eminent psychiatrists, Jean Dan thought about her son, prompting her to ask a question, now regarding Professor Sophie Ford as a good friend and confidant.

"Are you ready for your next challenge Sophie, but a lot closer to home?"

Jean then opened up completely about her dilemma, having snowballed since their initial chat, because it would now need a lot more than a few props to sort out a real challenge- when dealing with a serving police officer, far more difficult to contain when out and about on patrol.

18

Country Path, Buxton, Summer 1941

They walked together full of joy along a path, away from him with two rolled-up towels, wearing only just a small pair of swimming trunks. The passing motorist slowed down in his car to find himself staring at their amazing alabaster like young bodies – with pert little bottoms. They laughed and joked oblivious to the fact they were now being stalked by a paedophile, who felt a warm tingle in his groin who he parked his car to follow them at a discreet distance.

Despite disappearing from view, he knew from local knowledge, where they would be heading – you really didn't have to be a detective to work that one out, which of course he wasn't.

Having only just recently joined Derbyshire Constabulary he was still wore a uniform, but now had a car to cover a greater area as a patrol office. A greatly beneficial factor, contributing to his other hidden life; indeed, he would certainly have missed today's opportunity if he had been simply plodding around on foot in one of the town centres. Under those circumstances far too many people would be around – with virtually no chance of having presented two little treats like these boys; now going for a swim in an isolated location, well known to locals, himself included.

He glanced at a warning sign on his approach to this reservoir's wa ter's edge reminding everyone of inherent dangers of swimming on a hot day in ice cold water, but this really would be the least of their worries today, bless them.

Watching both boys standing knee deep in the reservoir, skimming flat stones, they counted out loud how many they had bounced before sinking – when he called out to them. This startled them at first, but they then waved because it was the really nice young policeman who they had seen many times near a playground in their village.

Who really liked to watch them play – even rubbing sun cream into shoulders and legs to make sure they didn't burn when it got too hot, telling them all they had to be really careful; because sunburn was dangerous.

One of many things in life that could hurt you – when sometimes you just didn't see the danger until it was way too late.

19

Coroner's Court, Buxton – Four Weeks Later

They heard evidence from farm hands, who had responded to the sound of his whistle, frantically blown by the officer – attempting to drag two boys out of the water. They went on to explain how he persisted for well over ten minutes doing mouth to mouth resuscitation. But sadly, despite his efforts – it was too late to save them; they were well beyond help as a pathologist who carried out their post mortems reiterated how dangerous it was to swim in cold water on a hot day.

He suggested perhaps that one had gone into spasm and then cramps; before sinking, before his friend dived down, attempting to bring him back to the surface. He then perhaps went into shock, after taking in water, resulting in both boys drowning together.

This account appeared to be corroborated by PC Dan who described finding them far out in the reservoir – way beyond standing depth- when one suddenly began to splash about before disappearing underwater. The other shouted for help before arching his body, then submerging himself out of view by diving down into its dark water.

Regardless of being a strong swimmer – holding many badges with a certificate in life-saving from being a scout volunteer, and despite his valiant efforts, Constable Dan just wasn't able to revive them.

In recognition of his unselfish heroic actions, he was put forward for recognition by the Royal Humane Society after already being commended by his own chief constable.

After giving his evidence they asked if he wished to add anything, prompting a heartfelt apology to both families, present in court, that he was unable to do more for them – he had had given his everything – he had tried his best.

He didn't mention to everyone present in the court that he had actually first seen them barely waist deep in the reservoir. He had warned them of the dangerous algae present in the water – so he called them over to join him on its bank. Here, he checked to make sure that the younger boy hadn't got any down his trunks; sadly, he had found some – so began to wash it off him until his older confused friend – knowing this seemed wrong dragged him away.

This then caused both of them to swim off in panic, choosing to tread water instead of returning to him on the shoreline, until eventually they tired, then swallowed water; when screaming at him to leave them alone. They went under one by one before he waded in, to remain nearby to ensure they had stopped moving – knowing full well that they were dead; but most importantly his secret died with them.

After seeing tractors parked up and farm workers having dinner in the distance, he quickly reacted by blowing his whistle, to create a cover story – suddenly throwing his own arms about. Before dragging them to the bank and going through lifesaving motions administering mouth-to-mouth resuscitation on two dead children. Timed perfectly with the farmers, now standing over him, before offering reassurances to comfort him – they clearly saw he had tried his best to rescue them – they could see both boys had drowned.

That evening he hung both certificates at his mother's home, who under 'normal' circumstances would have been so proud of her son, but Jean Dan knew he was far from normal – instead they were a constant reminder that perhaps all wasn't as it appeared. Jean had every confidence that her son would soon feel the benefit of counselling by her university professor; who was going to be working hard with him using her new stand back methods – to help him see the error of his ways.

Sophie Ford had to agree with Jean Dan, that events didn't seem comprehensible and far too much of a coincidence, when her son who displayed paedophilic behaviour just happened to be with two young boys – wearing only swimming trunks – who had ended up dead when realising there may be witnesses, hence he created the cover story.

Jean held the necklace crucifix in her hand, before gently rubbing a finger over its small diamond – dreading to imagine what her son had actually done, exacerbated by the fact he did it when wearing the uniform she had respected and loved all her working life.

Tears streamed down her cheeks, asking herself if she had been the cause of his infliction. Sub-consciously she now held the padlock key to her memory box, alongside the crucifix on her necklace.

But now, it hung down a lot heavier than ever before.

20

Home Of Jean Dan, Derwent

Before joining, Jean had suspicions to such an extent, she nearly whispered in her police predecessor's ear to block his appointment. But her maternal instincts of belief kicked in to protect him, after sitting him down to give him a final ultimatum. If her instincts were true, then at the very least he had to resign. But first he had to seek medical help and counselling from her friend, who she knew could help him.

It became resolved when giving his solemn word never to lay another hand on a child, but he would get counselling, agreeing to travel monthly to Sheffield. To visit this professor who would use ground-breaking work to help control this attraction and urge towards children.

This 'step-back' recovery plan meant he would now get sexual gratification from initially only watching a child, but never any touching or penetration. A voyeur role.

Hoping in time this would stop his own paedophilic involvement even more with regular masturbation. To satisfy unhealthy urges when looking at photographs of children initially. Once unhealthy cravings were dealt with it then allowed to aim for his engagement in normal adult interactions.

Controversial ground breaking work, many wouldn't agree with, but so far tested patients were complying. They had been convincing when assessed by others to deem how much of a danger they now presented to children.

A few weeks later, Jean never knew that the polite new boy, she had recently got to know since his arrival from London, had been touched over his clothing. With her son watching his abuse when at his piano teacher's home, but it formed part of his treatment. Complying with Sophie Fords request he now adhered to this – or a negative update from her to his mother would result in his career ending.

Oliver had impressed Jean in so many ways, not least tonight after calling to check with her during a recent bout of flu that she felt OK. Before offering to make her a cup of tea with a few biscuits. This made her smile, knowing of course he would get to enjoy this same treat. But bless him, he even washed his hands thoroughly after a bit of chocolate had melted on them when dunking another biscuit in his hot drink.

Approaching her slowly with a smile on his face, she sat peacefully in her chair with a warm content smile. But a short while later her eyes fluttered, just like they always did, before death.

Oliver whispered softly in her ear that she knew her son was a dirty fucker, who had watched him being touched up by the music teacher; when he sat in front of a piano, but it wouldn't be long before they killed them all, thanks to her needing a grave- to be dug real soon.

After washing up his own cup and plate he left no clues that anyone had called to join her. Oliver felt another tingling sensation in his groin when looking down at Jean Dan – slumped at peace in her armchair. He felt a real sense of achievement, managing to snuff her out with only one hand for the first time ever – but certainly not his last.

It brought a tear to his eye, certain his old man would have been so proud of him. He removed her necklace before nipping upstairs to open her memory box. It had fascinated him for ages to discover what she kept inside. It exceeded expectations – it came with a bonus after finding a set of handcuffs. These would soon be put to good use to shackle dirty bastards – to be dealt with differently; compared to how police would normally sort them out after capture.

Oliver resisted the temptation to pocket her necklace, admiring the gold crucifix with an encrusted diamond, but knew it would alert far too much suspicion if not found on her body. Before leaving he slowly ran his fingers through her hair and smelt it, with his eyes closed. It made him cry out loud like it always did afterwards; by allowing them to join loved ones, with this making him think about his poor mother. Never given that opportunity, taken when only young but ever present in his thoughts.

21

Acorn Club Meeting, Large Oak Treehouse – Tuesday

Sadly, a candle had been left lit on his piano at home overnight, with its dripping wax damaging several key wires that now needed replacing before it could be played. But they were all told "the show must go on," meaning their weekend recital would now be at the Church Hall. It wasn't a problem, in fact it was music to their ears because their Vicar, his good friend, would finish his evening service in time to allow them to put a few finishing touches to their production. Plus, he would stay behind to help out, so like he had joked it really was a blessing in disguise – they all really hoped that would be the case.

Tonight, they all agreed this presented too good an opportunity to miss as they excitedly chatted away in their tree house, they were looking forward to putting in place those final and finishing touches.

Following Jean Dan's unexpected sudden death – Oliver had introduced part two of his plan, because her grave had already been dug early to take advantage of a break in torrential rain, also forecast for most of the coming week, with flood warnings issued across their county.

By damaging several piano wires a few days earlier, it meant that with the Christmas concert nearly upon them, they had fallen into his trap by holding practice where only one other piano could be accessed, at their church hall – directly next to its graveyard. It meant that once they had killed them, they only had to drag both bodies a short distance to then dispose of them beneath Jean Dan's grave, after digging down a little deeper. A disposal method for bodies put to good use by criminal gangs in London – spoken about by his dad when his former boxer trainer teetered over one, to be told he would be buried if he didn't comply with their demands – Oliver didn't share this memory with them.

Everything was covered in detail when they sat together like Acorns in their large Oak tree; with Tony being gently directed by Oliver to state the obvious – that 'recital night' presented them their best opportunity, especially with both abusers present together, so near to a graveyard.

Like Oliver stated, it really was a blessing in disguise before telling them what he had planned, and how they could do it – providing them all with an air tight alibi. Huddled together they listened intently to what he said, then applauded him for how quickly he had come up with such a genius idea, distancing them all from any possible involvement.

Sonya reminded them though not to forget her part of the plan – just before pulling out lots of closed Acorns from her coat pockets making them smile, had both her hands not been full she would have clapped along with all the others.

22

Village Shop, Derwent – Saturday Morning

He only did only a few hours work for a couple of shillings, but this morning his time spent behind its counter would prove to be invaluable. For once he studied the '50' crossword puzzle in the local Derby Herald newspaper – spread across its back page with its 50 clues, described by most as 'challenging'. Only a select few people knowing the meanings of words such as "cruciverbalist" were likely to complete more than half of it – before filling it in, when answers were printed in Wednesday's edition.

Its near completion had become just one critical component forming part of an intricate plan. Just like many other things that had to be done to create a credible cover – helping put distance and time between them and deeds they planned to execute later that night. With execute a good choice of word; giving a decent clue as to what exactly they intended to happen.

Several shop regulars laughed when they saw Tony Drummond staring down with a vacant look at a large crossword, mostly remaining blank. A few would playfully tease that they would start him off with a few answers as it began to fill in slowly – meaning others later on were shocked but also intrigued that he had done so much, so they then studied one's he hadn't got with a few more extra clues completed.

After finishing his shift, he left with a few coins, a bar of chocolate, a packet of crisps and two newspapers. One had its crossword well over half finished. It meant if all went to plan, it would give the police a vital clue. Exactly what they wanted to happen if they were going to get away with a double murder, under everyone's noses, in a quiet snoozy village. With two down, holding a cryptic double meaning – but they were all confident they would manage to fill it in soon – no problem.

23

Workshop, Derwent Village, 1939

It was just like an Aladdin's cave – with every imaginable tool in various states of disrepair, along with thousands of nuts, bolts and screws; his 'bits and pieces' he knew one day would come in handy. For that reason, he never disposed of anything because you just never knew when you would need it. He always told this to his wife, who often begged him to tidy their back garden, now holding the overspill that even his large workshop had no chance of accommodating.

Bob Coyne – known as 'Odd Job Bob' – had a heart of gold, but like a lot of his tools he wasn't the sharpest, having never troubled schoolteachers much, but mainly because he had never bothered to attend. Unless he was dragged there screaming by his mother every now and then, just to have a few hours peace and quiet at home with his dad, who didn't mind him 'bunking off' to help him put back together anything dropped off earlier for repair by the villagers.

This nickname incorporated the fact he also had an 'Odd' look and manner - with a nervous tic and a stutter. His twin boys hadn't inherited his tic with only a mild speech defect with one of them – Tim – now having tests done, appearing lately to be more and more withdrawn; bed wetting and having mood swings – plus a stutter recently becoming noticeably more pronounced.

Bob didn't know much apart from every aspect of mechanical engineering along with extraordinary skills at making and fixing pretty much anything broken or not performing like it should. He hadn't grasped why his two sons, Tim and Tom, were called the 'Tanner Boys' with their 'Coyne' surname, because of course, two 'tanners' made a shilling- often called a 'Bob'. They had given up on trying to explain this to him, but they loved him to bits – especially when they saw his delight when allowed to be an honorary member of their 'Acorn Club' but only to help them build an impressive tree house deep in the local woods.

They knew he wouldn't remember its location since last there to finish it off over a year ago, taking it way beyond his normal memory span.

Bob didn't know why his son was 'going backwards' as his wife described him when angry , when pegging out even more washed sheets after soiling them once again overnight. Nobody knew the reason apart from Tim who was being sodomised – by the very same priest that had just called earlier to ask Bob to dig a grave for Jean Dan. They planned to hold her funeral over coming days – to be laid to rest next to her husband's, when this unrelenting rain finally eased up.

They shared this fact with the other members of The Acorn Club; who were the only ones knowing what else was going to be put in there beneath Jean Dan's coffin. This would be happening after the Tanner Boys put together an assortment of Bits and Bobs, meaning soon the time would come when they could make good use of them – to quite literally execute their plan. It had recently been carefully planned after a few meetings in their well-built tree house, more so since their new member, recently arrived from London had contributed so much, and was more than keen to give them a helping hand.

24

Recital Night, Church Hall – Saturday

Both Vicar and music teacher were surprised to see that despite atrocious weather, they had all turned up in good time after organising themselves well, with a couple of car shares. They stood outside by an entrance foyer waving at parents from beneath an umbrella, as they held a heavy front door open for them. As children ran down a church path towards them – carrying their musical instrument cases before parents drove away, knowing they now had two hours of peace and calm at home, before the storm returned after collecting them.

It would be far from peaceful and calm inside their village hall, indeed, both abusers would have been really surprised about what had been brought to tonight's recital. This included several heavy metal bars, two sets of handcuffs, numerous Acorns, lots of plastic sheets and a dripping wet shovel, hidden outside under a graveyard bush, along with several pairs of sturdy wellington boots and five sets of heavy-duty waterproofs.

Both men stared at each other in total disbelief when small but heavy lead bars were taken out of drawstring recorder covers – with handcuffs from a violin case, just before Oliver and Tony stepped forward in silence to strike both men over their heads with the lead bars. This knocked them down to the floor where they were quickly put in handcuffs – with both hands held firmly in place behind their backs.

After waiting for them to come around, Sonya, as promised, took the lead after they had agreed to implement her tree house idea. She took great pleasure in ramming small, closed Acorns, into their mouths. Pushing them down one by one as far as they would go – with her abuser's eyes staring up at her in fear at what was happening to them. Sonya knelt beside both to read her speech they had all helped her with – as remarkably, in the circumstances, she managed to speak slowly and calmly.

"You shoved a silk hanky in my mouth before abusing me, just in case I cried or screamed out loud. Tonight, our Acorn Club is returning this favour – so when we beat you to death in a short while, you will die silently, at the hands of those you have already killed inside – but together we are strong."

Both men bled from the mouth, as they bit down on Acorns with silenced cries for help, attempting to make pleas for forgiveness; shouts of pain stifled and inaudible , as they wriggled about completely naked on plastic sheets laid down over a church hall paraquat wooden floor. Looking wide-eyed towards one another, both realising they were just about to meet their maker. As children hell bent on killing them formed a circle, staring down with anger – but also relief, knowing at long last, revenge in the sweetest possible way would be extracted; finally gaining retribution, for the years of violation suffered.

One by one they struck down hard with heavy metal bars, starting as discussed with lower body, before gradually working upwards, allowing both to remain conscious longer, enduring prolonged excruciating pain. Numerous bones broken to make them suffer as much as possible before a final round of dull thuds. When they struck the bastards in a free for all with ferocious force – but now on their heads, causing skull bones to collapse and splinter inwards, until eventually they became exposed, long after they had died.

This was followed by silence – then a group hug as adrenaline pumped through veins. Bodies shook after realising those on the plastic sheets eventually lay still.

Oliver appeared the most in control and calmest at this point who carefully went over the disposal plan. With three of them taking it in turn to dig down several feet deeper in Jean Dan's grave – both bodies carried in blood-soaked plastic sheeting outside, and dropped into the deepened grave, then covered with freshly dug muddy soil – until out of view. Finally, they beat down the looser earth, smoothing it level – to make its base appear just like before. With tools, weapons and clothing bundled into canvas sacks, then hidden in undergrowth; until they could dispose of everything and burn clothing deep in the woods – when next visiting their treehouse.

They still had a short period of time left before collection, so turned the Vicarage lights on next door – where Oliver, almost identical height to the Vicar, now wore his clerical clothing. Thankfully, it still rained heavily when standing in shadows, holding his umbrella to appear just like the parents had seen before; when all the others left, running towards waiting cars. Oliver, not in view himself would say, if needed, that he had waited inside – until walking home later on with his guardian, their music teacher.

All the children told parents, both in the cars and at home – it had been by far their best recital, having managed to stick together – generating a really good beat.

But they didn't elaborate any further on that note.

25

Music Teacher's Home – Early Sunday Morning

Having lived there for many months had helped, especially when paying more attention than normal over recent weeks to his daily habits and routines- with some strange peculiarities (but he wasn't best place to comment about that). He was ready to implement his plans. The most important final phase. To create a smoke screen to help them avoid detection let alone attract any hint of suspicion, after raising an alert that his guardian had gone missing – with him not saying a word to anyone – having suddenly vanished.

They knew the police would suspect them- the last people of all to see them alive, those who needed to be firstly eliminated before any suggestion of foul play. With time however, they expected a conclusion to be made that something untoward, even sinister, had happened.

Several parents should hopefully be very convincing when giving accounts – that their Vicar was last seen waving goodbye from his church steps; in effect leaving Oliver, the only remaining child and final witness to last known movements.

This presented a challenge – but after months of practice, he was confident that the note penned by himself would pass as genuine – to satisfy police the music teacher had written it that morning, explaining he had 'popped out to get milk from vicar,' confident he would now be up.

To support this Oliver had made a milky tea with three sugars, before pouring most of it away – along with the remaining milk – to leave an empty bottle with a kettle filled with water, placed on the stove, to appear like his brew that morning had to wait – until his friend rescued him with a cup of milk.

Most ingeniously though – they used a half-completed crossword puzzle, given to him by Tony Drummond along with an untouched paper. Oliver ruffled and folded it many times, making it appear read and well handled – especially with half its large crossword completed. After Oliver meticulously printed correct answers, once again imitating his music teacher's style of capital letters – with a pen left on his kitchen table. This made it appear he had made a first attempt to complete it, something he did regular as clockwork, every Sunday morning.

Everyone knew how competitive him and the Vicar were – to show who had completed most of its clues when they compared answers following evening service. Many in the congregation had witnessed this weekly when parishioners would also mention how close they had got to finishing it – with several being reminded, with a smile, where they were; having never got anywhere near that far before.

With his sheets rumpled and his bed still unmade, it looked like he had retired with his milky sweet tea, waking to do his puzzle before realising he had to pop out to get milk.

Similar corroborative work had been staged last night at the Vicar's house – to make it appear that his bed had also been slept in, and he had already put psalm numbers up for their well-attended Sunday prayers on an Order of Service board; with bibles placed on pew seats for his congregation – its large front door unlocked, also to show he was ready for his flock.

In his kitchen a full pint of milk was placed on a worktop with his side vicarage door unlocked – to conclude their music teacher had called to beg a favour. After that, everyone else would be left to fill in the gaps to speculate what happened next; because neither man would ever be seen again.

The Vicars disappearance was first reported by his organist to Oliver an hour later, after calling at church, when looking for Mr Pride, who had failed to return home with a bottle of milk.

A day later, Oliver moved in with Tony Drummond at first to be looked after, turning out to be fortunate; they both got to hear first-hand updates about what was happening when officers called to see Tony's dad for a chat and a catch up.

Enquires led to a startling discovery – with all not how it seemed as "Mr S Pride's" true identity became discovered, with him being a recently released convicted paedophile, who had used forged papers to gain his position at their village school.

Decades earlier it transpired he had been directly involved with their local priest in a scandal at a southern Church, where many choirboys alleged abuse. Sadly, ignored when brushed under its 'papal carpet'.

These startling revelations became public knowledge – in such a close nit community, opening up many conspiracy theories with every one taking culpability away from their Acorn Club, as to what may have happened to them. Both had many reasons to run away, perhaps with gangs of vigilantes potentially from all over the country made up of victim's families – keen to hunt them down, or had they had run off together fearing exposure?

The Acorn Club knew they had pulled it off following Jean Dan's funeral – when watching her coffin lowered into the ground – laid over the top of two men, the likes of whom she had buried many times during her police career. Another priest hastily brought in to conduct her well attended service, with a lady professor, who had recently become her friend speaking kind words about her; a very sombre gathering, with Daniel Dan collapsing by her graveside. Everyone believed he must have been overcome with emotion – perhaps suffering a breakdown – but five children stood together dressed in black – who had just stared directly at him mouthing "You're Next" – knew differently. It certainly wasn't emotions; it was a combination of gut-wrenching shock and overwhelming fear.

Because this last remaining bastard was now fully aware they had sorted out his other two partners in crime, and he would now know for sure what they had coming his way.

He was on borrowed time, plus he would know that his new police uniform, wouldn't save him either.

Daniel Dan – a dead policeman walking.

26

Coyne Family Home – After Jean Dan's Funeral

It had become a last-minute rush for the Coyne family, who really weren't accustomed to dressing up, meaning Cheryl Coyne took a lead role making sure her husband looked presentable before tasked to make sure he made a decent knot on both son's black ties. At least they could all attend Jean Dan's service to pay their respects looking smart for once – without standing out from everyone else. Bob would have to run inside church to get changed back into his trademark overalls with work boots to fill in her grave afterwards.

Tim and Tom had wanted to help him with this job – just like they always did whenever possible; but not today, with Tim fiddling with his tie all the time – leaning back into his dad who stood close behind him reaching over his shoulders, concentrating on trying to make his knot as neat as possible. At this point Tim closed his eyes – imagining he was being given a lovely big cuddle – much needed, because he felt so upset about what was going on in his life.

Dirty horrible personal things that made bullying about his recent stutter at school seem like nothing – when compared to what was happening to him when their Priest got him alone. Later on, when home after the funeral he quickly changed into his play clothes – before going outside, alone for once – without his brother, to head for the workshop before they all returned from church.

For once he really needed to be alone.

One of his many scout badges related to how well he could tie knots. Taking hold of thick rope, originally used to tether horses, he made it into a 'sliding noose' – before its other end was looped high over a large exposed roof beam. It now meant that for once in his life he could soon be of use to them all – to stop him from 'going backwards' – something he had heard his mum say many times about him recently.

His Acorn Club had discussed several times how they required another grave – just what they needed now to make sure Jean's son could also be put deep in the ground. To stop him from doing anything to another child ever again, well, this way they would get their wish.

Without hesitation he jumped down from a large set of stepladders he had once helped repair – with his knot sliding tight around his neck. His final memory – a happy one – his dad putting both arms around him earlier , as if giving him a big loving cuddle.

After entering his workshop an hour later – Bob fell to his knees upon seeing his son's body hanging down before him – knowing full well this was something that couldn't be fixed. He cried out in anguish making his wife and Tom come running to join him, both immediately sensing something terribly wrong had happened.

27

Jean Dan's Home – Two Days After Funeral

Tom pleaded and begged them all – to help kill him straight away, after rushing into their workshop with his mother to find his brother, but they told him it would give them all away unless it was planned properly. Oliver and Tony told him they would discuss their options because it would seem far too obvious – if once again another person, let alone a local police officer, suddenly went missing just as another burial took place for his brother. Also, Daniel Dan had to be aware now that they were after him, meaning he had kept out of their way – until no doubt – he went on his offensive in an act of self-preservation.

Tony though, decided to act alone after watching his house looking empty tonight, with no lights going on when darkness drew in, giving him cover to climb inside through a small open window at the back. This led into the kitchen with Tony entering with a rolled-up newspaper – left open for him to see its large crossword page on a wooden table, where they had sat together to play many board games – including draughts, with pieces later hidden to let them escape.

It's 'Two Down' clue – encircled in red, with its corresponding grid squares affording enough space to complete it with 'YOU'RE NEXT.'

Sending yet another clear message – they were on a mission to avenge what he had done to them, meaning he would be killed by them sooner rather than later.

He had no magic piece to let him escape.

His plan backfired because after his mum's funeral they never saw sight of Daniel Dan again. It became public knowledge he had resigned from Derbyshire Police, with a letter submitted. This coincided with a quick house sale to support his written intention he was going to travel the world 'putting his past behind him.'

Unlike crosswords they had used so far – at least his disappearance meant that their puzzle was solved. They had worked out he would never come near them again.

28

Home of Jean Dan –
Two Weeks After Her Funeral

After locking her memory box for possibly the last time she placed a comforting hand on his shoulder when he glanced up with tears in his eyes, before handing her its key removed from his mother's necklace prior to her burial. He now held the crucifix in his hand, that now hung from a chain worn around his neck before bringing it up to his lips, kissing it with so many memories flashing across his mind.

Her crucifix had a small diamond in its centre. She had told him since a young boy it represented him – explaining he was central to her life and faith, so it would always protect them, surrounding them with love.

Within a week a sale had been agreed for her house, when snapped up at a reduced price to become a holiday home for a professional couple from London, having relatives nearby who had made them aware it was available to buy cheap.

Now sitting at his kitchen table, he glanced across at a well-used clothes horse leant against a wall, making him bring his hands to his eyes, trying his best to block out what this represented in his life. It helped to justify completely the course of action about to be taken, it was 100 percent right – he fully accepted he now needed her professional help as well as counselling and treatments, needing to disappear from this area immediately.

His mother had been an excellent judge of character, an extremely perceptive woman; it was one of many reasons she had chosen to confront him when sat at this very table – when ripping open his acceptance letter. Now, within a short period of time, his journey had come full circle when staring down at a pen and blank sheet of paper she had placed in front of him to write a letter.

No doubt a 'do or die' moment for him – certain if he didn't do as was asked of him, then he was going to die. He glanced across at a box of draughts knowing that no number of dark pieces were going to help him escape from the clutches of those he had abused over many years. With time, they had all grown strong together since an arrival; that new boy who seemed well ahead with his development in so many ways – having already extracted revenge on two of them with only himself remaining.

Professor Ford was going to honour what sadly turned out to be her dear friend's last wish, to apply her ground-breaking techniques with her son, after fearing, quite correctly he'd abused his position of trust. An award for the reservoir incident had been the catalyst – with his mum applying her former police skills when correctly deducing he must have followed them to the water's edge – well out of view from the road.

Earlier on, Sophie had noticed him looking at a Clothes Horse and the box that held draught pieces, now supporting many subconscious memories that Jean had also alluded to – explaining how she had watched him playing games with children to cover and deflect behaviour. It was a common tactic often deployed by paedophiles, plus his glance towards the kitchen wall where his award had hung – confirming his mother was correct about his devious actions involved in this incident.

Those framed certificates, along with a few pieces from a game box, were now in her briefcase; representing only a few of her props going to be used during her ground-breaking approach soon to be activated. With her willing guinea pig, she would take treatment to a new level; an agreed 12-month programme. He would encounter extremes like never before; it would either cure, break or kill him.

Dithering, with his pen hovering over a blank page, she commenced with her role of maintaining effective control over her subject. Sitting opposite, giving a clear command to listen carefully to what she said before writing down what he was about to hear. Sophie dictated to him his letter of resignation, slowly incorporating into it key signal signs with stress related wording and para phrases – to clearly show he had suffered a mental breakdown, hence the decision to move on, away from the public eye and scrutiny.

More accurate a statement than he could have ever imagined, with what she knew was coming his way, especially if her psychotherapy didn't work to alter his mind set. After that it would then mean moving on to another part of his body with a set of injections below his waist – following on with her dad's pioneering work – chemical castration.

Daniel Dan had played at being a monster when others ran away to get out of view, but he was just about to meet his match. Only this one wouldn't be roaring like a dinosaur; instead, she would be speaking calmly when wearing a clinician's white jacket, plus he would be in clear view all the time having nowhere to run or hide.

She walked him to her car with all the contents of Jean Dans memory trunk now in several full boxes in the boot, however, one of her prized police keepsakes – her handcuffs, were missing. These had once been proudly held up and shown to her when allowed to read some of her old case notes; who knows in time they may turn up, for now, they were certainly the least of her concerns. This fact hit home when glancing across at her passenger – now holding onto her crucifix yet again for comfort. But that would be taken off him later on, along with everything he wore – before entering a padded cell naked in the basement of her home. Once locked inside she may spare him the hosepipe punishment on his first night – unless of course he showed any signs of dissent – meaning he would then be punished.

She had promised Jean, who had insisted her son got the full treatment to cure him – it really didn't matter how wet he got – that would be the least of his worries.

***

Several years later, hands that had once extracted revenge were now squeezed together even tighter, both in anticipation and fear, when they eventually exhumed Jean Dan's coffin. They stood huddled side by side on a hillside, staring down on Derwent church graveyard. Grips eased, and they exhaled with relief and joy when gravediggers hadn't reacted differently after lifting it out. Before placing it on a horse-drawn cart with all the others, in various states of decay.

Following evacuation notices, events had moved quickly, meaning villagers in and around Derwent had to vacate homes and relocate businesses. Allowing for a mass flooding operation to take place to form a large reservoir, deemed necessary they were told to support industrial areas far away in the Midlands. Essential production had to be maintained for munitions and armoured supplies to feed ever-growing demands created during World War 2.

Only a small price to pay, compared to the cost of defeat, and its dire consequences if this became an unthinkable eventuality.

Five conspirators had now become three with one of them, later on, clutching to a hand painted sign. Carrying such meaning after his younger brother had sacrificed himself, believing it would benefit them all.

Tom had spent weeks moving everything from his Dad's workshop, with any hopes his Mum had this forced move would allow a scaling down shattered. When every single item managed to find its way into their new home, and adjacent workshop.

With a painted piece of wood, added to its hoard, displayed on a wall. But sadly in memory of the person that hadn't made the journey with them out of Derwent.

The Acorn Club never planned to talk again about their dark shared history. A well and truly hidden past, not only buried beneath soil, but also under thousands of gallons of water. There really couldn't be a better hiding place for two bodies...

29

Children's Psychiatric Ward, Sheffield – Friday Afternoon

After tugging down hard on her hair once again – a few more small clumps separated from her head, before staring down at them with a vacant look, when slowly rubbing them between her fingers before writing another manic entry in her 'Anger Diary'. She pressed down hard with a felt pen as yet more flashbacks and memories of abuse were hastily captured on its pages as inky smudges made parts of this tragic story illegible, when trying to wipe tears away that had fallen onto her rapidly filling journal. With numerous doodles and drawings all across its pages representing cadaverous faces with wild staring eyes and clock faces – with numerous hands indicating either early mornings or late evenings.

It had been a rare case of childhood abuse accounting for less than two percent of recorded cases of paedophilia – with a female assailant. Lisa Sykes captured yet another moment representing her systematic abuse by her nanny, who had lived with her wealthy family in their country house, outside of Barnsley. Unbeknown to them they had facilitated her mission to gain access to children by employing her when joining a reputable agency after working for years as a home help – with social services who rated her highly.

Following several bouts of self-harm with "cry for help", cuts to arms and legs these were recognised for what they were after she collapsed at a family gathering when her uncle's new girlfriend, a psychiatric nurse, took her to bed for a sleep – correctly interpreted their meaning. This identified the cause of them after Lisa came around in bed – screaming when she woke; believing this lady sat next to her on her bed in a darkened room, was her nanny. Once more, about to go through her well-rehearsed motions of pretending to be an attentive guardian when preying upon her.

162

It transpired following her arrest that most of these violations took place when she had brushed, then plaited her long hair – both on a morning and before evening meals; when family members sat together often for the first time that day. Both parents always leaving home early to commute to cities with her much older siblings back home from private school.

Lisa's hair became psychosomatic to her years of abuse, hence was now pulled out daily and then placed in her diary next to drawings of her nanny. Depicted with wide eyes that stared back at her from a dressing table mirror – when sat brushing her hair for an hour at a time during which her hands moved all over her body after a bath with only a towel wrapped around her body, as she shivered from fear then cried.

It was a challenging case for Sophie Ford but she believed they were now at long last making progress after studying recent diary entries with clinicians. They now showed more self-control over her writing, plus less anger with her pen movements, fewer faces, with even less hair pulled out. Still early days – but they were all optimistic; Lisa was coping better, but they accepted she would always be deeply affected by her ordeals.

With apologies for cutting this monthly meeting short to attend to another case study, Sophie would do her continuation progress report over the weekend, therefore she took all relevant diaries home with her.

This was in fact where her latest case study would be sat in his locked room in her basement – but would be allowed out for a few hours to walk around spacious grounds at her home, but only with Professor Ford's supervised company. Later on, they sat together for an evening meal to reflect on his treatments from psycho analytical sessions during the previous weeks – before moving into 'consequence of actions' mode – when she read entries to him from Lisa's diary.

After finishing crying, a trait becoming more common recently, she then showed him strands of hair, then a few of Lisa's drawings to really emphasise this young victim's pain and hurt because she was still suffering three years post abuse.

Watching this effect on him – she agreed it would be safer to spend another night in the padded cell. Once inside, when naked, feeling vulnerable – he curled up in a ball screaming, before crying like a child with both hands over his head after noticing small clumps of this 'tragic child's' hair that she had strategically laid out on his cage floor.

As Professor Ford watched him through a spy hole in its door, she felt really excited about the noticeable progress made with her patient before casting her eyes more intently over his body. This made her realise just how much better he was looking on the outside, after losing so much weight and doing such rigorous training.

It actually made her more excited in other ways as Daniel Dan whimpered away for well over an hour as she chanted 'Contain, Blame, Shame.'

It was a shame that his mother – who had instigated this treatment, wasn't here to witness its progress.

30

Crucible Rink Baths, Sheffield City Centre

After paying for his own spectator viewing, plus one under 12 swim for an hour, he had to shout to be heard above incredible noise levels generated by dozens of screaming hyperactive children. They ran staff ragged after delving into each other's swim bags, to then use elasticated goggles as catapults. Hard boiled sweets (sherbet lemons) were loaded – then fired, around a crowded foyer with staff threatening life bans if they didn't stop, who narrowly avoided direct hits themselves before showered in a white dust, when bright yellow sugar coatings on sweets exploded upon impact all around them.

His extra ticket helped with the illusion created today that there was in fact a child with him, especially when he called out into incessant chaos holding the swim ticket – before he walked behind groups of children. He pretended to beckon one towards him until he turned a corner to climb stairs towards a seated spectators gallery looking down onto the busy pool.

He selected a seat opposite its shallow end, where hundreds of young children managed to break every one of a dozen pool rules clearly displayed on posters everywhere, followed by a cacophony of whistles blown by staff; who had to watch their every move because, as lifeguards, they knew they couldn't stand another serious injury or near drowning incident – that would certainly cost them their jobs.

This was his first venture outside for well over six months following an intense treatment regime, but he was confident that even former workmates could be sat watching their kids all around him without ever recognising him. His appearance had changed so much, now being at least four stone lighter with long hair, plus a full-length thick beard. He would take great delight in eventually shaving it off but for now, it served its purpose- hiding his face well.

Placing a child's pink coat, a Disney World towel and a small princess bag next to him, he continued with the masquerade he watched over a young girl. Copying other genuine parents every now and then, with lots of waves and claps when standing – given to children craving recognition for swimming a width underwater – or not doing a belly flop after diving into its shallow end (breaking another pool rule,) generating another whistle blast.

After complying with instructions to sit there for a full hour, he then went through a staged pretence of tapping his watch and shouting into the distance – making out his child had to get out of the water straight away – to meet him outside in five minutes, or there would be trouble.

Once outside she joined him on foot from her parked car approaching with bated breath, awaiting eagerly for his update. He couldn't wait to share it, she had already noticed obvious physical transformations, but also major changes on the inside when holding both arms out before hugging her with joy exclaiming.

"I've just watched hundreds of young boys and girls for an hour in swimming trunks and costumes – without being aroused in any way – with no sick fantasies played out in my mind! Professor, you are a genius."

Sophie Ford glowed with pride, holding back tears before hugging him back, even planting a kiss on his forehead to avoid contact with his itchy whiskers. They now hid his blushes and a genuine look of confusion – when sat in her car – feeling aroused by an adult female for the first time ever in his life; but he wouldn't share that with her just yet.

It was early days, but he knew this major change may just mean he didn't have to be injected in his testicles to have eugenic sterilisation. Because he had agreed to this if all else failed. He noticed she now let out a little nervous giggle far more often and brushed her hair back, giving him lots of smiles – just like now – before she drove them back to her palatial home. With its basement padded cell, where he hadn't spent any 'contain' time for quite a while.

Daniel felt genuinely excited about what the future held. Finding himself turning towards her yet again he admired her side profile. Sophie chatted away incessantly – until they arrived back at what they now regarded as his home, and no longer a prison.

166

31

City Centre Squat, Sheffield

Barbara Dawson lit another candle with her lighter, always kept in a small leather pouch hung from her neck, now such an important part of her life. Without that she didn't have her key component, a flame – to heat up her precious drugs, making her life just about bearable; with many scars on both her wrists, a constant reminder when it wasn't.

Today she didn't have any coins to feed into her meter but that was the least of her concerns – because she didn't have any heroin either; to feed her raging habit- to put into her veins or even traces left on any foil to inhale through her running nose.

She examined her face in a cracked mirror using only a flickering light from her last candle, casting darting random shadows across her profile. Enough though to see recent injuries inflicted by her pimp, who had caught her out pocketing punters extra money – after paying her above an agreed normal going rate to dress as they wanted before doing as they demanded – that was far from normal.

She believed it was being clever – but was stupid not to realise her pimp met up with her customers later on that same night to sell them drugs at a shebeen. Here, he found out about her indiscretion, resulting in her nearly ending up in hospital after beating her like a dog on her usual corner, in front of many other street hookers – teaching her a lesson, and as a warning to others there was a severe consequence for any form of deceit, her injuries now evident in her reflection.

It made Barbara wonder who was damaged the most, her or the cracked mirror.

Later that morning after giving two of them oral sex as they lay on rancid mattress next door, they then allowed her a burn on their foil to 'chase the dragon'. It still held small traces of heroin from their drug abuse the night before, plus a swig from one of the many bottles of whiskey stolen from a local supermarket the day before. After word quickly spread that a burly security man, who guarded its exit had thrown a sicky for a few days after winning on the horses. This meant they could 'grab and run' – with no one to stop their escape, until he eventually returned after pissing up all his winnings.

She planned to take full advantage of this news and after drugs and alcohol had quelled her cramps and withdrawal shakes, she like so many other 'down and outs' was drawn to the store – like a moth to a flame. Barbara wore her poachers' jacket with six pockets on its inside, making her stand out like a beacon on such a muggy warm morning, causing a highly stressed store manager fully aware of how much had been pilfered the day before, to watch her like a hawk, before swooping down to catch her red handed.

With the weight of her coat after filling it with so many stolen bottles, she wasn't able to run away, before dragged unceremoniously by her long straggly blonde hair along his supermarket floor – then thrown into an office. Initially she held it together acting like a street cat fighting for survival, offering him a 'fuck and suck' if he then set her free.

Sajid Khan looked down at her with pity and disdain because she couldn't be any older than his own daughter, perhaps 15 years of age. He ignored her sordid offers before ringing his local police, who after being plagued with calls to attend there the day before took nearly half-an-hour to arrive. During this time Barbara Dawson lost her feral edge – soon breaking down and turning into a kitten, crying out for her mother before sucking her thumb like a young child.

Staring for ages at Sajid's array of silver framed family pictures on his desk, she could see him beaming with joy with all his children hugging him as they also smiled for the camera. Barbara began to compose herself before telling her life story to a complete stranger – but one who she had judged to be a good man, unlike all those bastards that had preyed on her since a young girl, coming from such a privileged background.

After self-modelling her looks, hair and dress sense from being only a young girl on her favourite toy, she soon picked up her nickname that also became her street name, but for vastly differing reasons as everyone called her either 'Barbie Doll' or 'Dolly'. Sadly, the first one to play with her before many hundreds of punters was her dad, resulting with suicide attempts or smaller cuts- her cry for help injuries before finally being sectioned by her mum. A last ditched desperate attempt to save her from self-destruction after paying for private counselling sessions, revealing the cause of her downward decline was her dad, quickly arrested, but killed himself in prison before standing trial.

Several hours after being detained at the store, a police sergeant rang her mother, who had reported her as a missing from home, indeed, she was regarded as a "High Risk Misper" in view of her well-documented vulnerability and only 15 years of age, with drug and alcohol dependencies.

Sheila Dawson waited until she stopped crying, but these were tears of joy that her little princess was safe, before making yet another phone call to her daughter's private physician. She had never let her down yet, with her endless intervention and professional help over many years, who agreed to take Barbara into private care to begin work trying to break her out of this destructive cycle before it was too late.

Sophie Ford assessed all she had been told over this phone call, then collected Barbara Dawson's case notes from her office at home, carefully considering not only her approach and direction for all her upcoming treatments, but extended her thought process towards a man stood in her kitchen. He was preparing yet again another low-fat high fibre dinner to ensure he continued to shed even more weight, as he smiled at her in his white apron.

This gave her a eureka moment when she formulated a plan to allow him to hear first-hand, face to face, all about devastating life changing effects brought about by paedophilic actions. Eying him up she guessed he was now no more than a 38 chest; it meant she would pick up a medium-sized clinicians' white jacket before he also attended with her to begin "Barbies" treatments.

Next time she interacted with her on a private juvenile psychiatric ward, her new assistant would be introduced, who would then make detailed notes after listening to every single sad word.

Describing monsters, who preyed on young children with their abhorrent actions, just like the one who would be sitting opposite and holding his pen, making copious notes, who had done exactly the same for so many years.

She looked forward to seeing how he reacted – not only then, but over coming days when he read everything back to her – morning, afternoon and night.

32

Train Station, Sheffield

Perhaps Oliver King shouldn't be so harsh on himself for making such a schoolboy error, because when all said and done – despite so much happening in his life already – he still hadn't become a teenager. Now he acted his age, snuggling into his mother's side – with the train home gently rocking them together. She lovingly ran her fingers through his hair – he could really relate to that – to let him know he would be better off home in London after all that had taken place.

Both his parents could have accepted a terrible tragedy when his new little friend hung himself in his dad's workshop, they now knew his problems, but to also discover that his foster carer was a convicted paedophile – was just too much. Hence todays reason why she had rushed up to meet him at Sheffield station; along with a lovely family he had stayed with for a few weeks. Their son Tony still looking deeply shocked after discovering his own dad had also hung himself. It would appear he also had problems – Parkinson's Disease, something she had encountered first hand in many hospitals in London, causing many years of suffering – with it being such an unforgiving illness.

Oliver had given Tony a hug before boarding his train, waving goodbye to him, seeing such grief across his face – he wanted to, but decided not to explain why he had killed his dad. After following him into his old Smithy workshop to stage that he had also hung himself – placing a noose made from old tethering rope around his neck to strangle him manually. A task made easy with his weak emaciated body, before he looped then tied one end around a roof beam using stepladders, to carry and suspend him when already dead – then pushing them over to lay on the floor. To appear as though he climbed them before kicking them away to end his life.

It was deliberately made to look very "Tanner like" so people would believe it had been a catalyst; another troubled soul who decided it was time to end their miserable life – after suffering so much recently with his illness.

Luckily Mr Drummond's hands shook so much with his Parkinson's condition, it made him spill milk earlier that day over a crossword newspaper. The one filled in by all the shop customers. Along with notes Oliver had made covering his plan on how to kill their abusers. Oliver had brought them with him for fear of discovery from its hiding place at his music teacher's home – just in case they searched there for clues. He had made a schoolboy error by leaving them in his new bedroom on his desk, before planning to burn them later that morning. They now displayed an obvious clue they had been seen – with tell-tale splashes of milk across them, following an act of kindness, a glass of milk with a biscuit, brought to him by Tony's dad who had not said a word and left the room. But he must have seen them. His eyes still worked.

It became too much of a risk to ignore that he may say something about what he had found when his police mates called – like they always did, possibly if thinking he alone had murdered them – motivated by his abusive foster carer; but either way it was self-preservation primarily, but for others as well, including Tony, his son.

They would never know about Jean Dan or William Drummond, nor for that matter about so many others he had killed over the years. His mum now poured him a drink of water – spilling a bit with the train's involuntary movements – making him smile. He glanced over at two elderly ladies playing cards across their aisle. One of whom wore a beautiful diamond cluster ring mounted on an aluminium band – making him smile even more before gently rocked with the carriage's movement into a deep sleep.

It had been a hectic and eventful few month, but it would soon be forgotten in time. In any case, he was confident they would be replaced with so many other memories – created by his own actions.

"AFTER"
SHEFFIELD

To hunt successfully you must know your ground, your pack, and your quarry.
K.J Parker

Once more into the fray,
Into the last good fight I'll ever know.
Live and die on this day.
Live and die on this day.
The Grey

Sometimes the hunter, becomes the hunted.
Actaeon

1

Shoulder Of Mutton Public House, Sheffield City Centre, 1972

It had been easy to work out where they all drank after a shift. Not only on account of several regulars who joked before they landed, it should have been named the 'Coppers Arms'. But because their jovial host, after posing a year earlier for local press photographs, had proudly displayed that framed newspaper story in full view behind his counter, when surrounded by a crowd of 'suits' all raising a glass.

Its clever headline read:

Former Detective Now Behind Bars. But Happy To Serve For Many Years!!

Its text described how he had invested money into three failing City pubs. Each given a change of name, relating to his Welsh heritage; Red Dragon and Lamb and Flag competing the trio with the one he stood in now, the Shoulder of Mutton.

Detective Sergeant 'Hawk' couldn't help but wonder how much he must have sequestered over his service pre-retirement without getting caught, not only enough to acquire Freeholds, but also to fully refurbish, then rebrand.

Clever man. Shame in a way he wouldn't be part of his new squad in a few weeks when he joined Sheffield City CID as its Detective Inspector, following his move from Greater Manchester, but it came with a caveat, that within his first two years he passed a local examination board. When you were given a number of scenarios to deal with by role actors testing your ability. With staged scripts, presenting a problem that needed resolving before a panel of judges assessing your competence to do the job, in his case that of Inspector rank.

He lacked any Uniform experience when promoted directly from DS to DI, but had enough time to sort that out, one way or another. He always found ways to achieve success, to find out what he needed to know. Exactly the reason he now stood in this pub looking and acting how he did.

To blend in with today's surroundings he wore one of his many, much used 'prop' outfits, including large thick-framed, tinted, National Health glasses. Given another airing to cover his bright blue eyes. By far his most noticeable feature, potentially giving away his identity. He had called in twice already over recent weeks, to order drinks, before chatting away with similar dressed, heavy drinking regulars, certainly not following fashion.

Nor big on looking after themselves, hence he had removed his dental bridges from both upper and lower gums so he didn't look out of place with his missing teeth. His new drinking companions tooth loss down to a complete lack of dental care, his for operational reasons that still made him shudder, with distant memories taking him back to sacrifice's made years ago. A secret never to be revealed, but one that without a doubt had helped make him what he had become today. With a focus and determination to always succeed, sometimes at any cost.

They had offered to fit titanium implants of the highest quality by a leading medical dental surgeon. But he expected no less when 'they' dropped a hint "perhaps don't rush to have the work done." Quipping that his loss could also be his gain, when he sunk his teeth into future juicy cases.

Today Hawk decided to speak here with a Northern Irish accent, harsh and abrupt. One well known to him from when a child flitting around the Emerald Isle.

With drinks flowing, he soon became one of the gang. Accepted by his new found friends, especially when buying them all a round of drinks. When sharing that a big accumulator had paid well. Earlier on he'd memorised the names of three winners triumphing at York the day before, at long odds. All having Irish trainers whom he would make out he always followed.

One who enjoyed a regular gamble had bothered to ask about his nags of choice. So his cover story, a subject now known off by heart became tested. But could be told with confidence, giving it credibility, and most importantly protection for his imaginary character. A lesson taught to operatives to blend in when infiltrating groups, so crucially you didn't stand out so prevented drawing unwanted attention to yourself, or worse still suspicion.

Luckily he'd learnt from those who had been undercover, during a few previous operations. Sadly his last one exposing bad apples, corrupt officers, working for criminals by selling information, even if it meant compromising fellow workmates. Hence his sudden promotion and transfer.

Hawk wondered if three pubs would have a Welsh theme name had his Mum chosen Sheffield instead of Manchester twenty years ago, after fleeing Ireland. Had he joined this Force and not Manchester, to suss out their jovial host who may have ended up behind different bars. Hawk regarded himself quicker than most with a sixth sense, one of his many positive traits.

But fully aware of many negative ones though, personified when throwing back yet another whiskey, before eying up a busty barmaid. He had to smile reminding himself how he now looked, making it mission impossible to get to grips with her.

But not when he didn't hide himself behind heavy stubble, teeth missing, glasses, flat cap and a well-worn duffel coat, purposely cross-buttoned. In a month's time when shaven, suited and booted with piercing blue eyes on display and making contact, it would be game on. By then she'd know exactly who and what he did for a living, making Hawk confident he'd get to taste and sample the goods.

For now he settled for a packet of Salt and Vinegar, generating another work memory about the case that had got him promoted but transferred. He hadn't regretted his actions, then seizing an opportunity to move onwards and upwards.

Another step up that promotion ladder, taking him towards Superintendent. A rank carrying rich rewards in so many ways. When he got there, it would cause both fear and trepidation for others, with whom he had old scores to settle.

A loud boisterous crowd broke his chain of thought, but generated a welcome sight in a large gilt-framed mirror, hung above a line of optics. Skilfully angled downwards, no doubt by an X officer. No doubt using it to watch his back, when venturing out to collect and stack empty glasses on his bar. Exactly the reason Hawk sat where he did, to pay attention to those behind him who had just entered, without making it obvious he did so.

His quarry making it easy for him when they all came to the bar before letching at this young barmaid, well chosen by an old mate. Not in the least phased by attention, when giving back more banter than given. Even feigning shock and horror when asked if she'd like a "stiff one" before pushing a vodka optic twice to dispense a double measure. To explain with a 'Cheers' she didn't normally do shorts, but when she did one was never enough.

Directly aimed at "Titch" who had just splashed his cash, only to be insulted by her. Hawk couldn't help but notice he was indeed vertically challenged, but took it in good spirits, so to speak.

A ruddy faced rotund man, with a voice matching his stature bellowed out.

"Like most things love, that's gone straight over his head!"

Despite what must have been such a frequent punchline everyone laughed too much, for too long. Helping Hawk work out this had to be a soon to be leaving Inspector, still completely oblivious to his fate.

Hawk had been told when meeting his new to be Divisional Officer, that DI Boyle was subject of an internal audit enquiry over fraudulent expense claims. To then mention his old DS had retired just in time, before held to account. With suspicions confirmed by opening up a chain of pubs. Sadly though for DI Boyle he would not reach the finishing line, his race well and truly run, because past indiscretions had not only caught up but overtaken him.

DI Boyle would be spending time behind prison bars, hence the reason why Hawk couldn't have pre-meets. Obviously this would let the cat out of the bag. But it fit in well with his plans to watch them in their natural habitat. It allowed him to work out who and what they were, before putting up brick walls, hiding behind them until comfortable with a newly arrived boss.

Especially after doing background checks, to find out why not only promoted, but then transferred out of Force. It would make them both suspicious and nervous, two traits causing detectives to hold back too much, not daring to do their usual 'tricks of the trade' to get results.

These ranged from criminal detections to gaining critical information, helping solve much bigger cases such as Murders or Conspiracies. When secrets and evidence was hidden out of view in deep, dark, murky waters, associated with the crime world. Meaning you couldn't delve down there where it mattered most, if paddling about playing it ultra-safe, wearing arm bands near the surface.

Hawk had decided he needed to hit new ground running, by knowing beforehand who could be used to influence others by peer pressure. To gain well established trust within close knit circles. Identifying team players a critical task, so he knew who to stroke as opposed to dissenters, who would be well and truly slapped.

If nothing else, one consistent story would be relayed from his former colleagues in Manchester when checking him out: "Don't fuck with him, he's switched on and street wise but a mad 'eejit' of an Irishman. If you cross him, he will then nail you to it."

Hawk would offer them a chance to be on his team, to run with his pack carrying the baton, or it would be inserted where the sun doesn't shine. They had a choice. He had a way with words when needed.

After watching and listening for over an hour Hawk, staying in character, weaved and shuffled slowly outside when hearing one member, now identified as a Sergeant shout out towards him:

"Fucking hell, Roy Orbison looks blind drunk again."

Hawk had already concluded he would be a non-team player, appearing far too loyal to a corrupt Inspector. Often seen deep in conversation in conspiratorial fashion with a retired sergeant who had got away with it, plus he flashed the cash far too much, and his suit and shoes stunk of money.

He may tell him, just before quickly getting rid of him that Roy Orbison wasn't in fact blind, but chose to wear trademark dark glasses as a prop, a bit like himself.

Hawk knew for a fact in the words of the song he would be the one who would end up crying. When walking out of what would soon be Hawks new office, for the last time. But at least an early dismissal would save him the discomfort of having a baton shoved up him.

No doubt he would relay to everyone else what a bastard Hawk was, but by then they'd remember what his old Manchester team had told them. To help everyone agree, once their former sergeant had left to start an office job at training school, it really was for the best.

Before asking yet again if Hawk would like another black coffee. Knowing he drank it that way to allow a nip of whiskey to be added, whenever he 'fecking' wanted.

It was all about gaining effective control of any situation – a work ethic and approach that had become Hawk's life mantra, after dealing and coping with so much over the years. Often remembered when running his tongue over both his dental plates.

2

Hare Tattoo Studio, Sheffield City Centre, 1973

Having suffered numerous addictions over so many years, Hawk considered himself lucky. Because having paid for something to be used on him with a needle, thank God it only dispensed inks and not drugs.

After an hour he finally succumbed to an unbearable pain, before crunching down with his teeth on a leather bit. Handed to him earlier by the tattooist sat opposite. Now unable to mask their 'I told you so' smile, having assured him it would be eventually needed, to help with discomfort.

His dental bridge nearly came out, when biting hard but thankfully he moved it back into place using his tongue. One of many tricks learnt over the years.

Hawk summarised they were possibly a failed medical student, having given such a long-winded soliloquy. Describing all about receptors travelling up his spine, to activate sensory inputs in his brain.

At least biting down hard showed he'd listened for once, but as per usual had ignored most of what instructions were given. A more than common trait at work, when supervisors gave orders, before doing things in his own inimitable style, believing he knew best.

Today he'd failed miserably earlier by not adhering to pre-tattoo protocols, following a solid hour's drinking in a nearby pub, just before attending.

Most bar owners knew him, in fact at one establishment a landlord had already held a pint glass below a draft Guinness pump in anticipation. Before surprising him when asking for a double vodka with a dash of lime. But when drunk down after a few pills were popped into his mouth made for a more than familiar sight.

A small pulsating needle now felt more like a hammer, when making contact with his sternum. But he sat still, staring back with a look of defiance. Even giving a wink then a nod of his head when asked if still okay to continue with his tattoo.

Alcohol and pills had increased his blood flow, now requiring extra dabbing, with his tattooist working out this customer had been drinking. A white spirit, possibly vodka, having already smelt lime on their breath earlier when exhaling a few times. A normal reaction to combat increased pain and discomfort.

Without stopping allowed them to finish his amazing tattoo in one sitting, over a four-hour period. A photo of a bird shown earlier, on a ripped-out page from an ornithology magazine now displayed across his chest. An image created using primarily dark shading and tones, with softer hues bringing it to life. Highlighting its lethal talons, both open, fully extended downwards towards his naval area, over several upper and mid ribs.

A beautiful, but deadly Hawk.

Once finished both artist and customer admired it, with Hawk smiling back at himself before a full-length mirror. Skilfully using its reflection to keep a trained eye on events behind. It paid off, watching two blouse buttons quickly undone.

Now turning, to face this beautiful lady before him, Hawk complimented her. On both his tattoo, and what he could now clearly see just above her ample cleavage, with a pair of Hare-like ears popping up into view.

"Well, you are full of surprises, looks like we both have designs relating to our names. Most people know me as Hawk."

She smiled, with an involuntary lick of her lips before flushing, all good pre-cursors to indicate sexual arousal.

"Well Mr Hawk, my nickname is 'Bunny' given to me when a young girl because my surname is Hare. More recently given to me for more grown-up reasons."

"Well Miss Bunny, I'm sure you know that Hawks love to hover over them."

Now her turn to have a flow of blood, with an obvious reddening on both sides of her neck, as her pupils opened, with Hawk's blood flowing in the opposite direction.

Attempting to sound coy she asked:

"Is that when those cute fluffy bunnies end up getting well and truly fucked over?"

Smiling back at her, after just confirming she was well and truly game on, he then handed her his wet, indented leather bit. It drew a look of confusion from his next prey, before his turn to give instructions.

"Bite down hard on that, Bunny, just in case it's needed in a short while. To stop your loud screams from hurting my ears, that may cause me even more pain. You know all about those receptors."

She couldn't help but laugh, replying with a "Cocky bastard, aren't you," thankfully confirmed when reaching out to grope hard between his legs. Before playing along, putting the bit in her mouth, then keeping wide-eye contact with her lover during his full, undivided attentions.

Hawk had called at Hare studio when her services had come highly recommended by several test purchasers. Who worked on their local drugs team, plus an old friend, an undercover officer he knew well. All inking up over recent months to get into character. Altering appearance's, helping to distance themselves from who and what they were in reality.

Such a clever shop name, using her actual surname, Hare, and its hidden meaning, relating to gender, with a play-on words being one of only a few female tattoo artists in such a male dominated industry.

After feeding on her for well over an hour they hit local pubs for drinks, before they parted, with Hawk promising they would be meeting up again soon.

Especially now, knowing how well she had just demonstrated her grown-up nickname of Bunny. Performing just like one, so he would certainly be calling to see her again.

It brought a whole new meaning to having a 'touch-up' with your tattoo artist.

3

St Marie's Church Hostel, Sheffield City Centre, 1974

With a lockdown policy in place at 10pm they knew it had to be a more productive approach to begging, with time against them. Years of living on the streets, before taken in by their Church, giving them a warm dormitory with a comfortable bed and two blankets, secured conformity with most of its regime and house rules.

But hardened drinkers needed a secreted bottle of spirits to help them through long nights. When cramps and shakes kicked in making most of them desperate for a sip to ease pains, with a craving for alcohol outweighing subsequent consequences.

Three discretions resulted in a one-month exclusion, with self-inflicted addictions in most cases leading to a self-generated return to the elements, resulting in them having to live back outside.

Tonight they had all agreed to pool their efforts by covering a bigger area. Knowing from years of trial and error the far more favourable locations. To gently ask for "just a few coins" when staring with pleading eyes, to help them afford a bite to eat, having not eaten all day. Complete bullshit, with only a liquid meal on their menu, at least forty percent proof. If they were hungry for non-alcoholic offerings, they got a bowl of soup slopped out from a row of church volunteers for supper. Bless them and Praise the Lord.

Fast-food outlets paid off well on a night with people commonly in drink, along with betting shops and amusement arcades. Especially when lucky punters may just hand over some of their winnings.

Tonight's 'caring sharing moment' on a packed dormitory turned into a full-blown fight, with the only thing handed out a barrage of kicks and punches. These were all aimed at 'Weasel' upon realising the selfish bastard had just gulped down half a bottle of Vodka. Before passing it around an alcohol dependent group, all desperate for a slug. Who all screamed out in horror, before he then cried out in pain.

During this violent melee one of them gave Weasel the bottle back, but after it had been smashed, then thrust several times at his face, one severing an artery in his scrawny neck. It meant that at least he did share his blood with others, covering five of his attackers.

Attending officers dragged everyone outside towards Police Vans before driven to their station, to throw each one into a cell. They joked with a bemused Sgt, who couldn't believe he had to book prisoners in tonight, they had all been caught 'Red handed' at the crime scene.

He replied with only a tirade of colourful language and scowls. Not one to upset too much, a supervisor who packed a punch. Sometimes not only for prisoners but staff when they agitated him too much. So they saved their little joke for later on about tonight's victim Weasel being a piece of vermin.

Miraculously the 'Pond Life' rule applied yet again, when a good for nothing drain on society pulled through. With emergency surgery saving him, from being another murder statistic. Good news for Inspector Hawk Shay though, helping keep numbers down with an added bonus that he got another detection for violent crime.

This however came at a cost today for Hawk, with his entire workforce now tied up dealing with five withdrawing prisoners, who now rattled more than bars on their cell doors, shaken endlessly by them to get attention, crying out for medical help. Wake up calls at their Hostel included numerous plastic cups full of pills and potions, needed to help combat every conceivable alcohol and mental health related condition.

Between them they were an almanac of illnesses, meaning to everyone's despair down the cells, that until a Force Surgeon waved his magic wand to make what they needed appear, they couldn't get near to interview them.

Several old school detectives dropped hints to Hawk with conspiratorial whispers perhaps they didn't need to be present. Detailed entries could be made in pocket note books to cover admissions, before an afternoon court appearance for a remand to Prison. Allowing a celebratory piss-up that evening, that for some would last late into the night.

Apart from those trying to save what they had left of failing marriages, when leaving early to a jeer of drunken abuse from the vast majority. Long past any point of salvation with wedding rings worn on chains, or kept as momenta in office drawers.

Since their new Inspectors arrival social activities had really taken off, with far more serious drinking sessions. It meant they often woke up slumped across office desks if they hadn't pulled. Sometimes they couldn't remember whether they had or not, but with various stains found hidden away, apart from obvious visible lipstick smears, it gave them a good clue.

They joked over strong black coffee, often laced with a hair of the dog whiskey, that as ABCD's (A Big City Detective) perhaps they really should be able to work it out.

The jury had only been out a short while with a unanimous verdict returned about Hawk. Not only one hell of a boss but also a great bloke to be around. Leading from the front, with what he had up front with his looks, never failing to score. Women flocked around him leaving his colleagues in no doubt he got results all round. Not only with 'birds' he preyed on, but villains he hunted down, also ending up in his clutches, and at his mercy.

He mucked in more than most to help out just like today. Volunteering when heading out into town on an errand, to collect the endless 'scripts' for prisoners, after Mr Atkinson, Force Surgeon, prescribed what they needed. To help make them fit for interview, without vomiting and shaking too much before admissions were made. (some cell staff joked that was just the detectives)

One way or another it would be written up that way, regardless of anything to the contrary said, to convict them all for a wounding. Had their victim not been a street rat it may well have been a charge of attempt murder.

Hawk sat alone in his office, with everyone else busy down the cells, before he put the extra 3 foils of Valium collected a short while earlier from a pharmacist into his drawer. After crushing two just removed under his crystal glass tumbler. Before mixing them in with his Malt whiskey that he swallowed down in one gulp.

He had worked out correctly 5 lots had initially been prescribed, but that number easily changed into an 8 with a single stroke of his pen. With an unsuspecting chemist kept occupied in conversation after Hawk showed him his Warrant card to identify himself. Normally a uniformed gaoler would attend, but a cover story told how they were all snowed under with 8 alcoholic suspects. With a few gory details thrown in to complete his deception.

His pills one of his many addictions, with another one soon to be fed. When inviting their surveillance team to join them for drinks. Knowing full well Maria with a body to die for, had stood out several times over the last few weeks, giving him more than a passing glance.

Tonight she may well get his full undivided attention, because if all went according to plan later on, she would certainly get to see his new tattoo hovering above her. Including what would be standing out directly in front of her.

4

King's GP Surgery – Opening Ceremony, Sheffield, 1974

It turned out to be a well-attended event with their guest of honour, a labour MP, seizing an opportunity to gain maximum political coverage and momentum before local elections. Making full use of an offer months earlier to link in with both doctors by paving their way to help iron out any creases, making it a smooth transition for them. All his contacts in local planning offices made a change of use from a row of semi derelict shops into a brand-new medical centre with four treatment rooms and a good-sized car park a formality.

His reward was a staged well-coordinated local press attendance, plus lots of news coverage before managing numerous interviews with publicity photographs to capture this grand opening with no doubt their soon to be re-elected MP snipping a red ribbon across its entrance doors to loud cheers when flanked by its two proud doctor owners and son.

Everyone was delighted especially now because this would ease burdens on other over stretched medical centres and GP practices all around Sheffield. It would help secure quicker appointments with new initiatives introduced, easing patient accessibility processes for prescription only medicines. A fulltime trained practice manager overseeing this project, as he explained to a swarm of reporters how a 'home delivery service' would operate.

This idea was praised then fully backed by both their medical council and local health authority, so much so its pioneer, Oliver King, had already linked in with other practice managers, who agreed to roll out this ground breaking idea with a 'shared information' working protocol. This facilitated a networking system to allow nominated medical staff to work on a Rota basis, providing a more practical effective service, not only geographically but timely with weekend deliveries also being made to increase clinical capacity.

Both parents sang their son's praises who had decided not to pursue his medical career after initial training in London but had travelled north to join them both with his mother returning to her home town to eventually end her career by serving her local community. She had grown up here as a young lady before moving south after meeting her future husband a cockney, but doing training at Hallam Medical College.

Oliver King stayed behind to lock up after everyone had left, sitting proudly at his desk, glancing down at several box files with already over 500 patients enlisted within their large catchment area classed as 'mobile'.

But what drew his full undivided attention was their 'dormant domicile' patients – all applying for his ground-breaking scheme after completing an application form to be assessed, then hopefully approved, for home deliveries.

Most importantly, he knew that besides this hundred or so, already applying at their surgery this figure would soon be magnified many times over when other practice managers replicated his process, meaning endless opportunities to put his cunning plan into action – because old habits die hard with sexy memories flooding back of his 'good old days'.

This made his blood flow to his groin making him fully erect. Oliver rubbed his hand over opened envelopes mailed from so many elderlies who had written in asking to be seen at home. He now closed his eyes, softly smelling the paper inside envelopes, imagining in his warped twisted mind what they looked like before meeting them.

He would certainly comply with all their requests calling to see them to prescribe his own unique approach – by giving them a helping hand whenever possible.

His body shook with excitement, picturing a small toy doll soon to have more clumps of hair stuck all over her head.

5

King's GP Surgery, Sheffield, 1975

It had been an amazing first year for their new practice as Oliver watched both his adoptive parents clink champagne flutes, having for once taken a night off to enjoy this moment. So much had been achieved in such little time since they had moved up to Sheffield, bringing the girl back to her Yorkshire roots.

Having waited years since her own mother had passed away, obviously now in her thoughts when glancing skywards no doubt thinking how lovely it would have been for her to celebrate with them. Oliver had already worked out in his head it had been forty years since his own mother had been murdered. How he wished she had looked down to see just how much he had done in her memory A continuing tribute to honour what she had done against the odds to bring him into this world in the face of so much adversity.

Allowing him to get into people's faces.

Despite his adoptive parents hopes he didn't follow them into a medical career when ending his training to become a doctor. Deciding to explore the world, but at least he had returned to their fold to make a fresh start. Traveling with them after taking the plunge with this Surgery.

Oliver had to leave the hospitals he had trained in following allegations against him of malpractice were reported after several incidents. When surviving family members questioned his approach, not to mention his presence when found numerous times alone in relatives' private bedrooms.

A close call foiling several planned snuff's, when blending in well with a white coat in medical surroundings with malice and iniquity. To continue with his reign of killing forced to subside for years. Now though, once again, he had the opportunity, and couldn't resist the thrill and lure. Not only the actual physical act itself but the build up with its interactions, filling him with deep emotions and feelings like he had never experienced in any other way.

How couldn't he return to this area, to be in an amazing advantageous position with so much access to so many. A dream job for a psychological killer, with a craving for elderly frail women. Living alone and who readily invited him into their homes without him having to carry a sack of coal or light a fire like he used to do. With so many sweet memories now flashing across his warped mind. With more recent ones tangible and borne out by his impressive collection of much craved souvenir hair snipping's continuing to grow before given pride of place.

He knew his mum would be looking down, wearing that silk headscarf and smiling – fully understanding and forgiving all his contributions in her memory.

6

Rose and Crown Pub, Cross Pool Sheffield

All his work colleagues often joked when they went for a few beers after their depot siren sounded to signal clocking off, they should still wear ear mufflers. Because in drink, Jon Greenwood became even louder than normal. Without a doubt he was the heart and soul of their group, a popular man despite him possibly suffering a heavy fall with a bang to his head when a child, resulting in him being a Blades fan (Sheffield United) whilst all his workmates supported their other city team, that also took its name from a local cricket club, Sheffield Wednesday.

They appreciated though he had won a lot of gritting contracts around their area with his brother running a busy bar within the nearby Royal Hallam Golf Course, who tipped off its owners; he had a contact to prevent cold weather falls on their large private car park. This was following a local solicitor, claiming thousands off them after a heavy tumble on ice, with their public liability insurance not paying out when found negligent by not taking reasonable measures to help prevent an accident in cold frosty weather.

Likewise, tonight's 'host with the most' had put a good word in with his Brewery managers, securing a deal for over 30 pub car parks to be made safe, especially those being more family orientated, where Dad took wife and kids out for a bar meal when he wasn't playing in a Darts league game or having pre drinks before a very important football match.

Tonight, they raised pints toasting him once again after getting yet another decent contract following a bloke from a local GP's who had called in to see him to shake hands, after agreeing to make use of their services. Plus, he knew several other clinic managers just like him, who wanted to make customer parking bays ice free, with lots of patients fit enough to attend in person, but they were elderly, weak or infirm – with some being all three.

As Oliver King drove off, he was delighted, after weeks earlier booking Jon in at their Surgery for tennis elbow with an inflamed tendon caused by excessive overuse after years playing sport, but also doing manual work when shovelling grit at their yard.

But this had led to a fortunate discovery relating to grit being supplied, but it would however have polemic consequences for some patients.

Many would benefit from safer car parking facilities, freshly gritted when venturing out to attend the surgery, but sadly a few would not be as lucky. They would die in their own homes over winter months.

Because it was a well-known fact, sub-zero temperatures led to a marked increase in old people's deaths for a number of reasons, but that figure had just increased by two.

Firstly, this grit spreading company who got advanced weather forecast's five days ahead, shared projected cold spells with its customers, so they knew in advance when gritters were attending with a two-degree temperature a trigger mechanism.

Secondly, this would also allow him to plan in advance to trigger a home visit, but with a difference, because he wouldn't be leaving medication to help them, he would be calling to put an end to their miserable sad pathetic lives. Everyone would then attribute this to "natural causes" when once again another cold spell had wiped them out on a sub-freezing night.

When you were actively killing as many as he was, you had to be cunning and clever to cover your back, not alerting anyone to what you were doing by drawing suspicion upon yourself- with this latest information helping him more than ever with his plan, his raison d'être.

Especially when there was so much more work for him to do, with so many out there to give them a hand to help them out, before being carried out in body bags from their homes to an undertaker.

He simply moved things along – a little quicker for them.

7

Home of Beryl West, Loxley, Sheffield

So many memories came rushing back to him, finding himself once again sat in front of a roaring fire, sipping tea with his host; an elderly lady, who spoke with tears in her eyes about her family, most of whom were displayed on grainy photographs within silver picture frames, clustered together on a small table next to her comfortable well-worn high chair.

Pausing to ask her caller if he would like another slice of cake – because it really was the least she could do, thanking him for calling so promptly to sort out paperwork from his surgery, making sure medication was delivered to her home or she could choose to nominate a relative or friend to help out. Living alone in such an isolated location, presented problems for her with a difficult journey not to mention her limited movement with those arthritic knees.

Oliver King sat pretending to listen whilst admiring her gorgeous white hair – but he knew that today he wouldn't be snipping any as a little souvenir. Suddenly his thoughts focused on something just mentioned earlier when she held a small picture frame. It had thrown him out completely but now he sought clarification about what he thought she had just alluded to.

He had already established that Beryl was 91 years old, being the youngest sibling having three elder sisters but surely, they weren't still alive?

"Beryl, did you just mention they couldn't be nominated at the moment, but they are normally always there for you when needed for so many other favours. Surely, they're not still alive?"

She couldn't hide her smile, clasping her hands together and said, "Oh, yes, indeed, in fact, I'm sure they will last forever; well, perhaps, at least until they get one of those telegrams from the Queen. They are all in their mid to late 90s but sadly don't drive anymore, it's a real shame because they only live a few miles away in Derbyshire but, like me, there are now really bad on their feet."

Oliver King could hardly contain his own euphoria before making a little note of their names and addresses – explaining to Beryl it was always lovely to know a bit about patient's families just in case of any emergencies.

He didn't explain that he knew for a fact that the Queen wouldn't be sending any of them a telegram. Serial Killers knew no boundaries, let alone one only a few miles away. A few trips from South Yorkshire into neighbouring Derbyshire wouldn't be a problem. Plus, it was always safer from a 'self-preservation' point of view – to put a little distance between you and your many victims.

Back in the day, his 'safety net' had been his old man, always there as a fall guy for him but obviously he was now operating alone so had to stay 'one step ahead' of a chasing pack. Police these days were much savvier and more switched on, hence his reason for not always preying upon surgery clients. Hence, why he always gently probed just like he had done to discover 'new opportunities' within their extended family trees.

He felt accomplished and fantastic, so much so he took Beryl up on her kind offer, knowing full well she had just saved herself, without knowing it, this being really good news for both of them – for vastly different reasons.

Her cake making skills were exceptional – she would now be around long enough to bake many more for him to sample. No doubt when he called to comfort her over this coming year to check she was coping OK.

After suffering such a sad loss, or three.

8

Bamford Allotments, Derbyshire –
Sunday Eve, Summer 1976

With a hosepipe ban in force, he now felt it was necessary to call a meeting with his fellow allotment owners, after learning that one of their loose lipped partners had said too much during one of his wife's coffee mornings. It turned out they had devised a rota to water their own vegetable plots but only when he was at work, for fear of him taking some action against them if caught turning on the tap to break the law.

Sometimes the life of a policeman in a close-knit community could be difficult, having many disadvantages when you inevitably got to hear everything, this time words spoken over a slice of ginger cake.

Often, he would be trusted but not now when it came to prize marrows with such fierce competition at village fete's he was being exiled, cast out like a leper when all he wanted himself was a decent crop from his King Edwards and Sweet Peas; these being his wife's and daughters' favourites – to keep them happy.

Tony Drummond made small talk initially about a recent plague of ladybirds swarming their area, looking for food. With such a mild spring, now followed by their hottest summer on record it had wiped out their normally plentiful aphid food supplies, including local crops. Tony Drummond got straight to the point. He assured them he really didn't give a 'flying fuck' about any water rationing so don't hold back, and make sure they watered his plot, to ensure he also got a decent crop return.

With laughs, then handshakes all around he became one of their trusted confidants with normal service reinstated before he called into work at his CID office, where several of his staff had made an executive decision to spend a good chunk of their coffee fund on several boxes of ice pops. It helped to cool them down after office fans stolen during the week from every other room in their station were found and then retrieved one by one. CID were number one suspects for any in-house theft or underhand, sneaky behaviour.

As expected, his new young and keen CID aide continued with a life long tradition of 'brown nosing' his inspector. Within five minutes of arriving, he brought him 'by far the best flavour' ice pop made using only natural juices. He accepted this before reading a large pile of incident print outs from all over his division over the last 48 hours.

Doing this chore now made for a far less 'Manic Monday' if he just spent an hour getting an overview of what had gone on since beginning his weekend off. Firstly, he read about a serious assault after a fight between two neighbours when one was caught watering roses until his hosepipe was severed with some hedge cutters. This led to a full-blown fight, resulting in secateurs clipping off a finger 'pointed in a terribly threatening manner' as written down to a reply after arrest and caution.

Working his way through a mass of other reports, under any normal circumstances – a turn out by mountain rescue following a request by local 'water fairies' (fire brigade) to eventually air lift four stranded metal detectors, trapped in mud, would not have held his attention or even caused him any concern. Let alone the enthusiasts' comments that they had heard all sorts could be buried under the exposed mudflats.

That was until Tony D stared down in abject horror at this innocuous report – before realising they had been rescued from his old former village of Derwent. Evacuated decades earlier when flooded to make a reservoir. But with this baking hot summer – parts of it were now being gradually exposed – with its water sinking to its lowest ever recorded levels.

He froze as an ice pop melted in his hand. Gazing in utter disbelief at what he read on fax machine pages – that were now tinted bright orange from lots of "natural juice" that had just run down his forearm, without him even realising.

But he did realise that other well-connected people could be in serious shit – just like himself – if they found what lay buried beneath an exposed graveyard; where years ago they had exhumed 68 bodies known to be buried there and had taken them to another graveyard – before all surviving occupants were forced to vacate their childhood village and its surrounding areas.

But five children had known only too well that two others were also buried – but not in the conventional manner. Both men were handcuffed; with arms behind backs and beaten, screaming into mouthfuls of acorns. Now their shackles would cry out to metal detectors to come and find them. When they picked up on high pitched noises in their headphones, indicating something substantial may be found. Like any enthusiast they wouldn't resist a return visit, believing an ancient burial site and a high-value treasure trove may soon be up for grabs.

DI Drummond now needed to contact his fellow conspirators from years ago, who still lived in their area, with one who only visited briefly from down south never to be seen again. Luckily for him he had moved on a long time ago with nothing to fear.

For once Tony Drummond became unique, by virtue of becoming a Detective Inspector who hoped and prayed there would be no more detections in that particular area. Prompting him to instruct a uniform night shift to deploy an officer to stand guard at the graveyard to deter any other trophy-hunters hoping for a major discovery.

Because he knew full well, they may just find much more than they could have ever imagined.

9

Central Police Station, Derby –
One Hour Later

It had to be a very simple instruction for her client this evening, because he wasn't the brightest. Exemplified when once again caught burgling his mother's house. When thrown out and disowned years ago after he killed her beloved young cat then threw onto a coal fire. Following that initial arrest they noticed, when dragging him fighting into custody, just how badly he had been mauled. It must have put up a fight, inflicting numerous deep scratches around his waist and lower groin area.

Rumours abound about what he may have been doing before killing it, giving rise to his nickname 'Kit Kat'. But Kelley Keegan tried to convince everyone he got this name because he loved to eat those chocolate bars all the time when a child and they were his initials. Too many knew this other story to believe him, with those fully knowing just how strange he was in manner having no doubt about what that poor kitten suffered. No doubt after which he panicked before killing and disposing of the evidence.

Despite Sonya now kicking his leg over and over again, when sitting next to him for this latest offence, he just didn't shut up, so talked himself into another 'Charge and Detain' for morning court. His rotund gaolers told him it was curry night, so if he had any money in his property, he could chip in. Because they had heard he didn't mind putting a bit into the Kitty.

A joke completely wasted on him, with a confused blank look. With Sonya stifling a giggle, not even bothering to say a word or complain on behalf of her client.

As solicitors went, they didn't mind Sonya Child's, on account of her being a regular visitor down the cells and a local girl. Decent and fair, not power-mad like Ricky Green and others, turning out from Cities to represent hardened criminals. Who paid out big money to have done whatever they needed to beat the system and get off any charges levelled at them.

Once escorted from their cells she didn't have to stifle a laugh at the Kitty joke any more. With the gaoler half apologising but was delighted his piss-take at her clients' expense had amused her. Having always fancied Sonya, loving women with a fuller voluptuous figure.

But her laugh soon stopped when seeing the look on DI Drummond's face. Who had found her after ringing an emergency call out number, to establish which station she had attended for an interview. Taking her arm, he ushered Sonya away with great purpose into a side room. Where she heard Tony say something she had hoped and prayed for decades would never be repeated. When he looked directly into her eyes and shaking his head whispered:

"Our Tree House Gang needs to come together again urgently. We may only have days before they find them. This drought may expose us in the worst possible way."

An image of two dead men shackled in handcuffs, with badly crushed skulls dumped into a grave flashed across her mind. With all five of them cheering at what they had just done to their abusers.

She of all people knew exactly how strong evidence left at this crime scene would be against them, if those bodies were found. No matter how many times they were all kicked on their legs under the table. And even if they managed to stay quiet during interviews, they were just like her client's mother's kitten from all those years ago.

Well and truly fucked, before getting badly burnt, with no escape possible.

10

High Rise Flat, Mount Estate, Sheffield, 1976

Luckily for him today, this body had been hanging from the back of a bedroom door for nearly two weeks until discovered. Making it easy to deduce, and fair to say he wasn't a very popular resident. A loner, rejected by most of society for over twenty years. His life had spiralled downwards resulting in him living like a hermit. This meant minimal interaction, apart from with staff serving him on a regular basis at his local chippy, or nearby pet shop, whenever buying food for himself, or his stray feral cats.

It wasn't often Force Surgeon Atkinson considered himself fortunate on a Sunday morning to be turning out to a 'Stinker'. With a combined nasal assault inside the flat coming from his obese, rancid maggot infested body, rotting fish and chip papers and an overpowering smell of cat piss soaked into a sticky carpet. Today though a blessing in disguise, when once again he gently let out yet another chicken vindaloo fart. After yet another belly rumble, but his last release had not ended well, causing him genuine concern, and a grimace.

Thankfully his predicament, just like an awful lot of murders in this City over recent months had gone undetected. But 'Mr Cat Man' wouldn't be adding to this sad crime tally, because it hadn't been hard to work out from several clues his death was self-inflicted. It meant that burglars who rang in anonymously to report his body, had forced entry after a failed attempt at self-autoerotic asphyxiation.

It had gone horribly wrong after passing out and hanging himself, before slumping forwards and dropping a small piece of orange held in his mouth, luckily ignored by all his feral cats. No doubt one of the few times, and certainly the last, he had ever put fresh fruit into his mouth, judging by his size.

Supporting photos were taken to back up his deduction, including previous holes where his weight had pulled coat-hooks out of the bedroom door. Mr Atkinson held back releasing more pungent vapours, when a Detective Sgt, with a massive nose approached. Who may well have suffered more than most with that size of proboscis He seemed far too smiley, appearing to be in too cheery a mood. Soon accounted for when he couldn't resist describing in great detail his conquest last night. Picked up in a nightclub who found herself on the back seat of his CID car, after giving her more than a lift home. Annoyingly "Pinocchio" felt the need to wink at this point, just in case he didn't understand an obvious sordid meaning.

Now a single man himself for far too many years, his night-time titillation and only conquest involved doing a red-hot curry sat home alone. Made even worse at this time of year, when having to raise a rather excellent glass of red wine towards the living room mirror to toast himself, with yet another lonely 'Happy Birthday'.

The bottle of red wine being the only 'full bodied treat' he enjoyed these days, and the only imminent female company his mother this afternoon. When once again he made his weekly pilgrimage to visit her.

If nothing else she would offer him a big slice of freshly made cake, after already playing her usual 'guess it's flavour' game He held back from saying chocolate, with this featuring on a list of shopping done for her a week earlier, along with half a dozen eggs and self-raising flour. Another clue drawn from the fact his Mum didn't eat this type of chocolate with its sharp-tasting flavour, owing to its high cocoa content, unless baked in a cake.

When leaving he used a graffiti-covered stairwell, and felt another rumble in his stomach. Prior to some local 'pond life' coming fast up the stairs, because once again the communal lift was faulty. They certainly weren't worthy of restraint as he descended, farting loudly. His footsteps were loud, a combination of hard leather soled shoes and a concrete stairwell, with an echo generating enough sound to hide any give away noises. But not it's hideous stench just when the 'brain donors' who pushed rudely past him, walked directly into its pungent smell. Before they turned angrily and shouted back at him from above.

"You dirty, smelly, old fucker."

With a broad smile and a wave he really hoped he got to meet them all again. Sooner rather than later, when laid out for him in his professional capacity. Like so many other pond lives who died protecting their 'manor' from rival feral gangs, who also dealt drugs. Apart from when they were busy breaking into lonely old men's homes, who were easy targets for them.

Perhaps he now needed to consider taking early retirement, to spend a bit more time eating cake with his dear old Mother.

11

Doreen Atkinson's Bungalow – Day Before (Saturday Afternoon)

After listening to her son for many years she had finally got into a habit of putting on her latch, before opening the front door at her large, detached bungalow in its own grounds off a country lane. But not today, when hearing the caller at her door, as regular as clockwork. By far the nicest young man she had met over many years. After Andy her son of course, and she would get his ingredients out for his cake after her visitor had left.

Had it not been for the caller she would have begun mixing them all together in the kitchen where they now stood. This turned out to be such a shame for Doreen.

Because if her caller had seen them all on the worktops, he would have asked a few questions. To then discover her son, a Force Surgeon with the police would be calling tomorrow. Meaning that after he delivered Doreen's medication, he wouldn't have washed his hands then 'Snuffed' her out when sat comfortably in her high chair.

So ultimately his alibi cover actions were all wasted. These including the removal of her tablets from now until Sunday Morning from her pill dispenser. With a carefully placed glass of water at her side, to make it appear she had died of natural causes the following day, to suggest she had in fact taken this medication.

He also left a vital clue to show foul play had taken place when making his usual nosey around a victim's house. Because he found a bar of dark chocolate, and he just couldn't resist breaking off a few pieces before driving away. Popping them into his mouth, to savour the strong taste from its high cocoa content.

He knew Doreen wouldn't have minded him pinching a few squares, despite only recently getting to know her. She really had been such a lovely old lady, but sad and lonely. Missing her late husband – but that had just been fixed for her.

Sitting alone later on in his bedroom he opened up his sunglasses case ever so carefully. To lift up what now lay on its cushioned base to help protect lenses. He stared down excitedly at a gorgeous lock of silver hair just snipped off Doreen's head with his small scissors. One of many accessories available to him on his multi-tool pen knife. But only his scissors had been used over recent years, and on a regular basis.

Oliver King now smiled when running his finger over a small clump of hair ever so gently. This never failed to bring a little tear to his eyes, before glancing across at a cupboard draw. Before holding his finger now shaking from adrenaline pumping through his body to his mouth in a *shhh* fashion, whispering conspiratorially, "Got another little present for you."

He felt himself getting fully erect and he felt a little embarrassed about that, but who wouldn't be when this happens with your mum in the same room.

At least he didn't have to hide under her bed anymore; he had crawled out from that hiding place years ago. But many had, and indeed would in the future, wish he had stayed there, never to be seen again.

12

ACC'S Office – Monday Morning, Sheffield Police HQ

Despite most inspectors always having a manic start to a working week known as 'Dalmatian Day' with 101 things to do, he was summonsed urgently to see his assistant chief constable at HQ. Stressing to drop anything he had planned, this took priority, it was urgent. This had resulted already in several near fatal accidents as his concentration en route lapsed as one by one he recounted horror stories heard over many years of officers being "found out" before being called in first thing Monday morning, either to end up arrested or suspended.

This particular ACC from its command team, was known to be the 'hatchet man', who told them often as they then slumped into a chair, after initially being made to stand to attention, to hear exactly what was being alleged against them and by whom.

In between horns, blasted after last-minute swerves with heavy breaking, DI Fergal Shay began thinking of his 'worst case scenario' as he convinced himself his major breaches of protocol and discipline codes had been committed years earlier, with his co-conspirators, bless them, no longer alive – following endless years of alcohol abuse with stress related illnesses.

Since his promotion to inspector, it was fair to say he had been creative – 'pushing at boundaries' – whenever possible, especially with detection figures or prison write offs. Fucking hell, every single supervisor in CID did this to varying degrees – especially when reaching higher echelons of police rank, most of whom had often been promoted for how well they had done when doing this exact same thing.

Many marital affairs had cost him dear now, drawing his mind finally to a recent encounter with a female promotion board 'role actor' when making out it was by total chance, he had bumped into her on a night out. But after using his contacts and after following her – for a few weeks on pay days – he knew where she went for drinks in busy city bars just like the one she had visited before he spilled a drink over her, all staged to make conversation.

It was a careful slow build up as he waited over a month before finally declaring that besides her 'day job' in requisitions, she was trained to take part in practical tests, learning her part, acting out a scenario for promotion candidates. This tested how they dealt with a practical supervisory problem, with others marking how well they performed.

Besides her own role she had read other 'actors' lines when testing their recall (as Hawk really hoped she had) resulting in pillow talk with lots of whispers – guaranteeing him success then substantive promotion to Inspector rank. Promises of a future life together, all an act – with him performing a loving committed role – foreign to his character – but well enough to fool her.

After drinking Vodka, then popping pills before being found by her girlfriend who was a house mate, fully aware she had been well and truly 'used and abused' – Hawk now feared the worse. But why come forward and expose him only now years later? He had been told on his phone call that this meeting was work related and 'they' were waiting for him. Was it going to be a direct challenge with her present – before his possible demotion after cheating or worse still when living with her – would she recount what she had picked up about his habits and underhand practices with a prostitute informant? If so – he was fucked. Those consequences didn't bare worth thinking about, he may well end up hand cuffed after slumping into the chair.

Hawk took a deep breath – before fixing his tie, then entered his ACC's room to let out an audible sigh of relief because she wasn't sat there sniffling into a tissue. Just before he went back into panic mode once again as "axeman" introduced him to their force surgeon, whom he had met several times before – generating fear when explained this meeting had been triggered after discovering something that related to his relative.

This couldn't help but make Hawk think to himself:

"Mother of god, please don't tell me she is your daughter."

He soon discovered she wasn't, because it related to his dear mother and another ten or so elderly women who had all lived alone in Sheffield. What his ACC told him next caused his mouth to drop open before he did make use of that much used chair, as Hawk himself slumped down into it with a look of total despair.

But, thankfully, without the normal career ending thought when asking one's self "have I just thrown away my career." Hawks question asked was a completely unique one – and with a strong Irish accent.

"For fecks sake – have I got a maniac of a serial killer snuffing out loads of old women all around Sheffield – for fun?"

Which, all things considered, from a very selfish perspective had to be a far better prospect, compared to a suspension before a possible prison sentence.

At least now – he remained in the job and could get out there to do what he did best – and catch the sick bastard.

13

Bowling Club, Monday Evening, Buxton, Derbyshire

Mavis felt well and truly pissed off when 'Skinny' Betty had got the job before her, especially when finding out later on after interviews, that their new coroner in Sheffield was primarily a leg and bum man- who preferred women who were 'svelte'. No doubt then, her fuller 'voluptuous frame', as she called it, was an explanation as to why, despite having greater experience, with far better typing skills, she wasn't chosen. Over such a skeletal, flat- chested, constantly on a diet bitch, who only ever applied because she had told her about it.

After an initial 'cooling off' period of their friendship, despite knowing one another since joining girl guides, it was eventually rekindled when their bowling season started again. They swallowed pride to renew a winning partnership, going on to win an inter-district pairs competition yet again, with Mavis allowed to take home a shared cup for six months first, because Betty did feel guilty about getting a far better paid clerks job – after flirting with her new employer when interviewed.

After nearly missing an evening league match, Betty turned up with some major breaking news that night because she had been told by her new boss that 'shit really had hit the fan' before having to run around all day pulling files.

A deranged psychopath of a serial killer was operating around Sheffield doing something called 'snuffing' on elderly women living alone, with their mad man responsible possibly having some sort of 'medical connection'.

Before taking to her bed that night after thinking about recent events all around Buxton and its surrounding areas, this convinced Mavis she should call to see her DI, whom she did clerical support work for besides doing their coroner officers administration filing.

She had recalled that over this last year or so, a lot of women including three sisters, remembered by everyone as Girl Guide Leaders, had passed away suddenly; they had also lived alone in isolated homes, so she would pull their sudden death reports to let him browse over them.

Perhaps it was just a coincidence but she would let Tony Drummond decide on that, he was meticulous, but lately had seemed rather distracted, even distant since about a month earlier when some metal detector enthusiasts had been airlifted from an exhumed Derwent graveyard. This had led to a uniformed presence guarding this site bringing a new meaning to "graveyard watch" because under a full moon, an officer clearly bored had walked around looking at uncovered plots to discover an exposed shattered human cranium.

This resulted in a forensic pathologist attending with archaeologists, who then carefully dug down to discover two handcuffed skeletons buried side by side as rumours spiralling out of control. They were badly weathered, but looked like old style police issue handcuffs. It kickstarted a frenzied paper hunt to identify who they may have been, let alone who it was that had murdered them.

Derwent village, evacuated in early 1940s had been flooded following a government order being approved to create another much-needed reservoir to supply an ever-growing demand from a rapidly expanding industrial midlands. Home office ministers feared a knock-on effect on "munitions production" in later years if World War 2 continued indefinitely.

In fact, if memory served her right, she was sure there had been talk that a very young Tony Drummond and his family had lived there before being made to relocate. She had a vague memory of once calling at his home to see a framed photo of his family stood outside an Iron Mongers with Tony, perhaps, only five or six smiling at the camera while tethering a horse.

Mavis had visited because they had just won a mixed pairs Police Bowling Cup who she had regarded as a friend over many years. Sadly, he had now given up bowls, she guessed with long unsociable hours not to mention non-stop relentless ever-increasing demands, these were no doubt the reasons behind it.

Mavis feared something was terribly wrong with Tony after watching him more closely at work, when he started to act out of character, as if he carried the weight of the world on his shoulders.

14

CID Office, Pre-Tuesday Morning Briefing, Sheffield

Before taking their main briefing, he called in his 'movers and shakers' who he referred to as his 'C Team', whom he knew could be trusted and were always willing to go above and beyond whatever was needed. With Cunning and Connivance when necessary to Collar, Catch, and Convict Criminals. With the last C- having 'unts' after it, but only ever said in closed circles.

DI Shay still spoke with a soft Irish accent despite leaving Ireland when a teenager, who only broke into any hint of 'Yorkshire Twang' for maximum effect when going head-to-head with slouches; normally if he considered them to be work shy but when he was pissed off, angry or often really pissed, then his full Irish Brogue broke out.

He had been named 'Hawk' at training school by a slightly more intelligent than normal instructor, whose mother was Irish, so he knew Shay's Gaelic name origin was in fact derived from this prolific hunter. Plus, with his piercing big blue eyes, dark hair, good size and with an appealing soft accent (when it suited) it meant he always had incredible success with women.

Everyone agreed he preyed on 'plenty of birds' so it was more than an appropriate sobriquet fitting in with his behaviour back then, but even more so many years later with an unrelenting appetite.

But with three failed marriages behind him, along with a recent small paunch after finding his extra weight when hitting 40, his personal life and health was a disaster. Heavy smoking and too much of a liking for malt whiskey contributed to this. With his bottom drawer bottles always kept in gift boxes so they didn't give away their presence, preventing them from rolling about causing distinctive clinking noises if they connected with his much-treasured engraved tumbler.

Everyone knew his success at work; he had never faltered with an impeccable record – with many detections for both acquisitive crimes plus major incidents affording him nothing but respect and recognition from his peers. An investigation, he was about to oversee, without a doubt his most high profile and challenging. With immense pressure coming down on him from superiors above knowing its magnitude, plus enormous public interest guaranteed to be generated. Emotive hostilities would be vented towards them if this story broke too soon.

It was imperative, as his bosses had just told him, to keep its lid on, to keep it tight, gaining first and foremost an upper hand with covert investigations if needed, before they did anything to alert or spook this dangerous offender. He was a cold calculating serial killer, who had employed asphyxiation many times before to murder numerous elderly women using what was known as a 'snuffing' technique, where he cupped hands over his victim's mouth and nose. So far this was always in their own homes without raising any alarm, until he had chosen his wrong victim, because her son had picked up on vital clues unlike all the other victim's families, who with their relative's age and ill health, believed it was 'natural causes'. Just like attending officers had.

After finding his mother dead, Mr Atkinson had noticed many things incongruous to her normal habits and behaviour, alerting him to foul play. Her body was too cold with no early onset of rigor mortis present, which he knew full well indicated she had been dead at least 16 hours. It meant her killer had staged her Sunday morning's ingestion of medication, soon to be confirmed in a week or so pending toxicology results.

Was this to distance themselves from her murder scene to give the killer time to prepare a false alibi?

They had washed their hands before laying them across her face. A bar of soap by her kitchen sink was placed behind taps next to wall tiles on the right but Doreen Atkinson, only four-feet-ten, could not have reached that far back, plus was left-handed, so always placed it opposite on her left-hand side.

If still alive beyond Saturday afternoon at the very least, she would have started to prepare making his birthday cake, and would never have eaten any ingredients, especially one so high in cocoa content.

Mr Armstrong, forensic scientist, had presented deductions with conclusions based on personal knowledge. Her killer must have been known to his mother with no signs of forced entry, he was right-handed with a liking for dark chocolate, possibly with medical connections.

A short list of other recent sudden deaths fitting this MO's strict search criteria had already thrown up a cluster of another ten elderly women within their homes, all of whom initially recorded as sudden deaths from natural causes.

After making phone calls to potentially other victim's family members, Hawk could hardly contain his excitement having already uncovered a suspect who could be their serial killer- but as always, a hunch was fine but proving 'beyond reasonable doubt' was a critical gap that had to be bridged, to stand up under court scrutiny.

With all his 'C' team around him he knew that was more than possible to achieve, when leaning forwards in his chair to speak in a quiet manner, smiling across at his DS, whose big nose was equally matched by his big bragging mouth, before asking him a question, already knowing its answer.

"Are you still trying to fuck that fit young reporter at the Sheffield Herald?"

This was followed with stifled laugher all around the room because they all knew he was, as 'Hawk' continued:

"Well, that giggle confirms it, which is good news indeed, so make sure you do get to grips with her in a few days' time. Besides giving her your dick, also gift her with a bit of red-hot information 'off the record'. Let her know there's a serial killer who we are all hunting down; let's call him something catchy. How about the Sheffield Snuffer?"

(Nods of approval, it was a catchy name)

"Because, by then, we will be out there ready to watch and follow every single move made by this crazy fucker here."

With that, DI Shay unfolded newspapers to show press releases from a few years earlier covering a grand opening for a new doctor's surgery in Sheffield. Its owners – two GPs – were photographed stood by a large reception desk, sat behind which was their son, holding a telephone to his ear as if taking calls to book patients in for future appointments at their new practice.

An interview with these doctors, who had relocated from London, covered how they were proud to offer home delivery service for prescriptions if patients were infirm or unable to collect medication. Hawk now jabbed his finger at their son taking a call in the photo as he declared with a much more noticeable Irish accent.

"This crazy ginger-haired fecker here is Oliver King, their son, who's 'handing out' more than pills when paying all of them old dears a visit, because there's no doubt in my mind that he's our 'snuffer'."

Hawk had been told to keep it all hush hush, to put a lid on it all until they were ready to make a move, but with his trusty team helping him, he was soon going to announce to the world by leaking it to a local reporter they had a serial killer on their doorstep. This was before he then applied more heat to blow that fucking lid right off, to make sure he nailed the bastard.

It was fair to say DI Shay really didn't listen very often to those above him, much preferring to do things his own inimitable way. This had paid off for him many times before, so why for fucks sake do things any differently now?

A hunter, who had prayed on so many others, was about to be hunted down. But like all good skilful hunters, he would make sure he didn't know that fact until it was way too late to avoid being captured.

15

Park Hill GP Surgery, Sheffield, 1:50am

Both of them knew exactly what they were doing after selecting a surgery, that was at least six minutes' drive from its nearest police station, having just done a recce and cruising past to see all their patrol cars parked up in a rear yard. Uniform plods normally worked 10–6 nights with a 1am meal dragged out until 2am – with all those detailed to meal, then invading early, carrying bags full of food from various takeaways. Ripping open kebab and pizza boxes and ignoring healthy eating lunch boxes – packed earlier by loved ones.

These knowledgeable burglars even had with them a police radio tucked away in their car with a large roll of brown tape, along with their faithful jemmy. It had served well recently after targeting doctor's surgeries all around Sheffield. All of them had Class A drug cabinets with full books of blank prescriptions, not to mention a practice stamp making them high value. To authenticate whatever druggies wanted to write on them – to be dispensed from chemists after purporting that a GP had signed it for them.

Parking a short distance away, checking there was no activity in surrounding areas they now hooded up and then attacked its rear window after covering it with adhesive tape. This held its glass in place with only a muffled cracking noise after forcing off its hinge and clasp lock, separating it with their jemmy from a wooden frame.

They both knew from experience that a 'silent alarm' had just been activated, it would take 10 minutes before going audible but even with a direct line activation to a control room, their earliest unit following dispatch wouldn't arrive within eight minutes. Especially when hungry drivers took a few minutes to shove mouthfuls of food whilst still hot down them – before running outside to patrol cars to drive at speed without 'blues and twos' to approach in silence, hoping to contain, then catch intruders caught when still within the premises.

Once inside – the two burglars knew exactly what to do, getting what they wanted quickly, doing what they needed to do just before a sudden flurry of police radio activity helped them when officers updated a control room, giving ETA's, allowing the two burglars to return outside with a few good minutes to spare.

It gave them time to get back to their car, putting any damning evidence out of view in its boot, before DC Cox of Sheffield City CID – whose turn it was to work three evening shifts this weekend – removed his ski mask, before speaking with clarity and purpose into his police radio.

"DC Cox and DC Harding in attendance at a burglary at Park Hill Surgery Silent Alarm, I can confirm it's a forced entry on its rear window, identical MO to others with taped up glass. All units attending, please maintain silent approach with responding units to hold an outer cordon position at front and sides of building, we will stay at the rear. Control, please, dispatch our dog handler ASAP; intruders may well still be inside."

As control thanked them for this update, they were amazed that not only were CID out and about on a night – but they actually had a radio with them – because normally, by now, they would be in a dimly lit club and hoping to pull before closing time.

DC Harding parked their CID car by a window they had just forced open. He told his partner just how professional he had sounded on his radio, perhaps he should consider a stint back in uniform? This wasn't even funny, but they did smile at how well they had added to an ongoing smokescreen, that active burglars were busy in their city after stealing 'drugs and scripts'.

They later feigned such disappointment that nobody was inside- even a keen dog handler and his four-legged beast looked upset; he hadn't got to bite anyone – but for some reason kept on paying both detectives far too much attention. They both agreed later it was a good job that dogs can't talk – because he had definitely sussed them out.

A busier than normal pissed off scenes of crime officer failed to lift any prints but commented it must be the same team responsible with identical MO's, including same sized jemmy being used.

Both detectives agreed; but knew full well it wasn't the same team – because two other staged breaks had been done by their colleagues on other teams, like them, following their DI's instructions. When Hawk told you what to do, then you did it without question, or you would be getting measured up for your shiny new uniform. After that you would then get to talk on a radio all the time when out on mobile patrol.

They wrote this burglary up in their CID night report book, giving a green light to activate 'Operation Smart Student' – a play on the fact that 'Class A' drugs were being stolen. These would be found in months to come – much to the surprise of one or more miscreant when their homes were searched under warrant, who fully deserved a prison sentence. Hawk had already spotted a few that may come in handy when he was feeling under the weather or unable to sleep.

Their Divisional Crime Prevention Officer was dispatched promptly to visit several city GP surgeries to inspect premises. He would give out instructions, hoping to drastically reduce any victim impact by educating practice staff how to keep documents safe using a 'clear desk' policy, with digitally coded padlocks on filing cabinets.

As luck would have it, his first call was at Doctor King's practice, where under any normal circumstances it wouldn't have taken long to assess what needed to be done – with all its new modern fixtures and fittings. But following detailed instructions from his DI, Hawk, he ended up spending a lot longer there than necessary, because he also knew exactly what he was looking for, before eventually finding them.

A box file detailing all their 'home visit' patients – who had taken advantage of their new prescription delivery service initiative. When alone, as staff became busy with endless patients attending, he explained he was fine to be left by himself to write up his report notes.

These included a few addresses copied from a home visit index list, that on first glance, did seem to correspond to sudden death locations – at homes around Sheffield.

A lot of thought and planning had been put into this covert operation; including an officer being sent in prior to his visit for a sick note, once Hawk had first ascertained after checking previously submitted doctor's notes – to cover absence – that he did attend there as a patient. Before returning to see a GP when pretending his best to look and sound like he did actually have a case of man flu – when he managed to read a wall chart, showing staff shift patterns to confirm 'OK' wouldn't be working today.

This meant an extremely helpful crime prevention officer could now use his vacant desk, as a good example of how easy it was to access so many documents containing personal information – with most drawers left unlocked where files and folders were stored, not to mention sensitive details visible on papers left on tabletops.

Most important during this staged visit he made a vital discovery of several pill dispensers clearly marked from Mon to Sun, with each day having am, pm and eve compartments – identical to what they found at the initial crime scene at their forensic scientist's mother's home.

Hawk, it would seem had been right from the very outset, it appeared that Oliver King was indeed a leading suspect, who may well be their serial killer.

Later on, after updating him one to one in his office, Hawk thanked him for doing excellent work – before being left alone to gather his thoughts. At this stage they only had circumstantial links with no solid evidence, on account of many others also having access to so much information and pill dispensers.

King had been clever when generating this shared information scheme, it created a blanket excuse to deflect from himself – to rebut any allegations that he was their serial killer. He could calmly sit there and smile back across an interview table, having control of his own defence with compelling counter arguments and a switched-on barrister who would easily keep him well away from a prison cell.

Hawk knew a prolific hunter like this – with inbred survival skills – had to be taken out of his comfort zone by being panicked; so, he would act like a startled rabbit in bright headlights, allowing him to swoop down to catch the bastard, when least expected.

After that – he could play and toy with his latest prey – who eventually would be skinned alive. With teams out and about working hard, researching his background, they were slowly gathering evidence – to eventually put a wild free running animal somewhere they would never want to be.

In a locked cage, with no hope of release.

16

King's GP Surgery, Car Park, Sheffield City Centre

Following a reconnaissance – they soon realised just how busy this car park got; both during the day and early evening. The practice itself had numerous patients attending for scheduled appointments, but because it didn't charge for customers it became a much-sought opportunity to park for free. Because directly opposite a shopping mall charged its customers an hourly rate. In typical Yorkshire style they circled and waited, pretending they were calling to see a doctor, to avoid spending a few coins.

This resulted in several bays on its far side, furthest from any shopping-mall entrance doors, being clearly marked with large whitewash writing on its concrete floor as 'Staff Only' A lady, presenting herself as a downtrodden housewife laden with several bags of shopping, now slowly shuffled along towards this area. Chewing her gum with vigour, looking up every now and then to avoid slowly manoeuvred cars shuffling to position themselves, to claim first prize, a free spot.

Her two bags full of contents had all been carefully selected, not today, but many months earlier. When showing amazing initiative, to come up with this idea, using one of her supporting props, a cheap carrier bag from a local store. It dangled from her arm, and after word had spread across surveillance teams, many others, employed what became a much-used tactic. A genius solution to allow them to effectively follow a 'targets' car on a dark night. When normally it blended in with many others with illuminated tailgates only seen from behind, when joining endless long queues in busy rush hour traffic.

Especially when those they followed drove such a common car like Oliver King's, a bog-standard Ford Escort. With its ever present, ubiquitous tail-gate cluster of rear lights and indicator seen everywhere on an evening. When finishing work to head off home like so many others.

Unlike others though he was a serial killer.

Now they could make it possible for his car to stand out from anyone else's, by making it unique. Helping to follow him for hours on a night when watching his every move, his every visit. They knew only too well, at any time, another life potentially may be in danger. Pressure mounting with time passing, meaning he may strike yet again if they lost him, even if only for a short period of time.

As DC Marie Whittaker walked past the 'Staff Only' allocated area she continued with her chewing action despite her mouth now being empty. Because moments ago, she let go of one carrier-bag handle, so all its non-breakable contents, packets of dry food and tins fell out. Before picking them up, but only using one hand initially, until her chewing gum, momentarily held in her other was stuck onto the offside taillight of his parked vehicle.

This meant that later on after setting off when illuminated, it would stand out a good mile away, with its distinctive black dot drawing them towards it, making their job a lot easier.

Now leaving the car park she continued with her exaggerated mastication action but only pretended gum still occupied her mouth. Before updating her team, a short while later, over a car-to-car intercom system it would now be possible to "stick" with this bastard. Before popping another piece of gum into her mouth, only this one was for keeps.

She let her mind drift imagining what she may well be doing with her mouth soon, after going out of her way to update Hawk on their daily debrief. Those amazing blue eyes paying her more attention lately. It would have been obvious to anyone, let alone a highly trained surveillance officer. One who desperately wanted Sgt rank and a coveted place in CID.

Bar-room talk with girly mates all in the job after consuming plenty of drinks often had them giggling, when repeating a much-heard rumour. With many confirming its accuracy, regarding promotion, working in such a male dominated profession.

"You have to go down, to go up."

She hoped by now he'd got the hint, let alone fully understood how she got her 'Yo-Yo' nickname, after pleasuring so many with her mouth. Another rare time when she removed gum, but only for a few minutes with most of them.

17

Coroner's Office, Sheffield, Mon to Wed, 12 Hours a Day

Every delivered box-file had been rammed full with potential elderly female victims as inputters began to realise the extent and scale of future murder investigations. All initially recorded as non-suspicious with only a 'sudden death' report submitted. An ever-growing tower of forms piled high, before allocation to investigators, it soon built up, becoming a monster of an Incident Room to hunt down a Monster who had generated so much misery. Upsetting soon to be retired Police Constable Steve 'Shifty' Allen who had mistakenly thought becoming the coroner's office assistant would be a great way to keep his head down. To continue just as he had started out nearly twenty-four years ago by doing only the bare minimum. This had soon earned him his Shifty nickname ,because if anyone ever mentioned doing some sort of work then he soon shifted.

Sighing out loud he now sat deflated for days, working long hours with an Incident Room recorder reading every 'Form 49'. Containing only scant details that a patrol officer, or if available to attend a coroner's officer had filled out. Completing basic standard limited questions relating to surrounding circumstance. Ninety Nine percent of the time this would not give any cause for suspicion of foul play, meaning barely a one-hour initial attendance with reports duly filed in his office. After checking with a relative about how to put together a bar-graph he now applied himself to do more work over his next few shifts than ever achieved before. To finally complete his task on an 'Action Form', made him realise a monumental shit storm had started to come their way.

Tapping gently on DI Shay's shut office door he really had hoped he wasn't in, but sadly he heard him shout out with a much stronger than normal Irish accent 'Get yer self in here Shifty boy'.

He had been forewarned that if you heard an obvious strong brogue then be far more wary than normal, when Hawk eyed you up and down if stood before him.

When Hawk studied this work-dodging excuse of an officer stood before him who now looked worried, his own stomach churned. Because his more than obvious non-verbal signals told him it wasn't going to be happy reading when he studied this chart, now clutched rolled up in sweaty hands. It didn't bode well.

18

Incident Room, Thursday, Sheffield Police HQ

It was like a reunion do for most of these seasoned detectives, who sat together in an incident room beneath a plume of smoke as cigarettes, cigars and pipes were lit. Those who could only afford to buy tobacco at the moment to make their own were fully aware that soon they would be rolling in it, with overtime payments and out-of-pocket expenses, plus mileage. They had heard on the CID grapevine this was going to be one hell of a major investigation, perhaps, by far, the biggest they had ever worked on.

Rumours had spread that a serial killer from Sheffield had prayed already for many years on numerous victims. They suddenly fell silent as a man whom most of them respected, but feared if ever crossing him, came through a door; soon followed by a team of high-ranking officers, no doubt wanting to hear in his opening speech not only facts known already, but what they wanted answering more than anything else.

"How are you going to nail this bastard to the cross as quickly as possible, before we get crucified ourselves by both press and public." Guaranteed to happen when word got out just how many he'd murdered, without it even being noticed.

DI Fergal 'Hawk' Shay immediately asked for windows to be opened before he began to unroll papers. Individually laid across a large desk, centrally placed for everyone to see in this crowded room, helped now with plumes of smoke eventually clearing. They watched intently, focusing on a detailed bar graph, appearing before them. This showed column after column next to each other, with a figure on top of each in PC Shifty Allen's distinctive hand.

'Months and Years' appeared along its horizontal axis, with lines of vertical columns corresponding to a descriptive that read 'Sudden Death Report' (Form

49) Down its vertical middle they observed a bright red thick line separating thirty-six monthly columns representing three years. Another line, a mean figure, indicated a 'rolling average' for all Sudden Death reports. DI Shay addressed everyone.

"Welcome to 'Operation Germ' I had these windows opened so you could clearly see all the information on this chart before you. Sadly, what's now presented before you has gone unnoticed for these last three years, indicated by comparing both sides of the central red dividing line."

"Before this middle date, Sheffield City with its surrounding area, contained within a six-mile radius, had a rolling average of thirty-two 'Deceased'. Female occupants living alone, in their own home, who were over sixty years of age."

Hawk paused suddenly for dramatic effect as a realisation kicked in all around him. Because hardened men, detectives for many years now looked with total disbelief at graph columns beyond this divide line.

"Yes, I can tell by all your looks that a sudden realisation is now hitting home. Because over these last three years you can all see an obvious fact staring you in the face. Our rolling average sadly jumps up to thirty-six. This represents a gain of four, meaning its up over ten percent."

"Following the recent 'Snuff' murder of a lone elderly female, it kick started this Major Incident, allowing us to set search parameters. It means by our best scenario we may have a Serial Killer 'Snuffing Out' one victim a month, so potentially thirty-six murders. But worst-case scenario, if he's responsible for doing all four extra victims a month it means well over a hundred. I'm reliably informed if that's the case it makes him far more prolific than any other Serial Killer."

Many without realising it raised hands to mouths with absolute bewilderment and shock. DI Shay pointed out their actions saying "Exactly, what you're subconsciously doing now, represents how he's doing it."

Just when nobody believed it could get any more intense DI Tony Drummond from Derbyshire Central CID entered the room flanked by his Superintendent. With a quick introduction he proceeded to unroll his own bar graph over DI Shays. Made to correspond exactly, with identical format thanks to two coroner's assistants. From neighbouring Forces, but bowling partners and close friends for decades. Who had bothered to update one another about a series of events going on 'next door'; generating an audible gasp all around the room with an identical pattern clearly visible again over this same time period.

Displaying another marked increase, this time over twenty percent, taking monthly averages from ten to twelve.

Most importantly occurring within a few miles of a boundary line separating Derbyshire from South Yorkshire Police Forces.

DI Shay now had to stop himself raising a hand to his own mouth in disbelief when taking in this development, meaning their combined actual upper figure could be nearer one hundred and fifty.

DC Hepworth also raised his hand to his mouth, but to draw on his skinny rollup with a little smile. Realising he would soon be able to afford filtered cigarettes.

With a joint Force connected enquiry his future mileage claim had just doubled, not to mention all his expenses and overtime. Who knows, sooner rather than later he may end up getting that dream holiday caravan. Not to mention that long overdue blowjob from his wife as a thank you. Happy days, a win-win situation, plus of course they may even catch this sick evil fucker.

19

Fashionable Apartment, Sheffield City Centre

Remembering his wish list, she continued to play along with his fantasy games so stopped off at a local mini market to buy a few items, because she sensed there was a major story coming her way, as well as a horny detective Sgt after paying her lots of attention followed by his corny chat up line that being a reporter meant she was just 'his type'.

Normally that wouldn't have led to any further conversation, let alone several dates, before deciding to 'take one for the team' as her editor encouraged – in pursuit of major headlines. Kay Bailey worked at the Sheffield Star, with her first few years being uneventful after her dad's golfing connections got her a job, with his wealth getting her a bijou professional executive suite. Described as such in a plush laminated sales brochure, now hers, despite only being in her early 20s. Kay Bailey now smiled, overhearing a shop owner speak to his son when she patiently waiting at his clustered counter, with a hastily assembled basket of items.

"I know it's long hours, but I need you to cover next week, while I'm away on my pilgrimage. Mecca Innit."

Following a defiant look he reiterated his demand, saying with a theatrical swirl of his hand.

"Don't forget son, one day all this will be yours."

Sajid Khan now turned his attention to a polite customer for once. Who unlike most of his giro-regulars normally tried to rob him or shout out rudely demanding to be served, leaving his son to slowly walk away towards a storeroom and sulk, with the weight of the world on his young shoulders. No doubt willing only a few more years wait before he finally got what he'd been promised, since a young boy, helping out non-stop at their corner shop.

As Sajid punched prices in one by one for her selected items, it may have just been Kay's imagination. But he seemed to smile, perhaps understanding why exactly she had called in with a last-minute shopping list. After bagging up a can of whipped cream, a selection of chocolate bars, a jar of honey, a banana, four AA batteries and several large candles.

Watching her walk out quickly he couldn't resist wishing her a 'lovely night' before she turned to stare at him, but flushed up. Confirming his thoughts, realising he no doubt tried his best to imagine where all the candles were going. And whether or not they would be lit.

Sajid himself counted his blessings that all his daughters married young. Not having to do this dating thing with their husbands having already been selected.

Once home Kay tidied and heated up a casserole made that day by her mother. Before setting her table, knowing full well everything else had been bought to play his sex games. Before lighting the candles and putting them in her crystal holders. She knew for certain this would be the only place they would be shoved tonight. But he'd emphasised just how important it was she got them.

It seemed obvious he now wanted to share some major "breaking news". So for that reason, he got to make a kinky fruit and chocolate cocktail out of her, before smothering and covering her in honey.

No doubt exactly what the dirty old 'Paki' at her local store had pictured in his mind earlier on. When stood before him trying to look all innocent. But at least tonight after Detective Sgt 'Pinocchio' had left she could then crack open her four pack of batteries. Not on his list, but certainly on hers, and needed for her own pleasure. To operate her vibrating Deluxe Edition, four speed, rotating headed Dildo (Black).

With his micro-dick, felt several times when rubbing up against her, along with a few hand tweaks- to try coax him into sharing the story, Kay knew for sure some back-up would be needed. To finish off what he'd started when gone. With her old reliable mate to hand, who she'd rather have a cosy night in with, any night of the week.

So to speak.

20

Bethel Street Police Station, Sheffield

They waited together in a cold front foyer after one of them had been asked to call in 'just to clarify a few things' – as part of their ongoing investigation. It had already hit papers sending a wave of fear around Sheffield after it had been leaked to an attractive female reporter, whose name and picture accompanied its headline, that a serial killer was at large killing many women. As DS Copeland beckoned them inside, he didn't recognise his solicitor, so possibly he normally worked from behind a desk or didn't cover criminal work. As instructed, he played his overworked detective role well by yawning, and looking at his watch constantly.

Oliver King had been at his parents' home when he got the call, so his mother had asked one of her long-time friends to attend tonight with him who had overseen a few legal matters before opening their GP Surgery, specialising in conveyancing.

Mr Carter normally dealt with civil and commercial matters but had liked his mum since when they were young, and grew up together in a small village in Sheffield. Before going off in different directions, but delighted, albeit with her husband, she returned to open their Clinic. Especially when its catchment area covered his parents' home when his dad became ill – when they afforded him endless visits and palliative care; with Cancer wiping him out in six months. They made his final journey painless with his Mum now becoming a "creaking gate". Despite a growing list of pills to help her along with endless ailments, they had told him only recently she still had years left.

This latest news had filled him with both frustration and despair every time he got home. Sadly, a modest terraced property shared with his second wife – who like his first, now made his life a total misery; now letting herself go physically, following bouts of depression and comfort-eating – with alcohol readily to hand, causing her weight to balloon to well over twenty stone.

His mother held the key, quite literally to his release, from his ongoing torment and ordeal in life; her longevity adding to his suffering and frustration – because she stood on stoically, refusing to lend him money, or even sell her home along with its connected land, potentially worth a fortune. Confidant planning permission could be obtained to develop a dozen properties.

This belief borne out recently by a woman he wanted to run away with – now seen several times privately after they initially met at work, attending land disputes for clients; mainly fractious neighbours with planning issues, with her representing their local council highways office. After a few cosy meals they began a full-blown romantic and loving affair – ironically, she told him this had never been planned, but they couldn't build a future together, unless he left his wife.

Tempted to tell her that's what he banked on, when inheriting money, but held back. Since meeting her his mind had gone into overdrive – remembering the old joke 'where there's a Will there's a way' – now willing her to die soon, to make his dreams become a reality.

This evening the detective gave a lack lustre display, when going through the motions, asking standard questions on a hand written list of Actions – In-between a few yawns, explaining he worked from an Incident Room. There wasn't anything to worry about, they simply asked people a few questions to be 'Traced, Interviewed, Eliminated (TIE)'. Within a few minutes Oliver King duly obliged by answering them all, before the detective thanked them with a handshake – to leave them back in the foyer. When suddenly his 'client' asked to have a word in private, to clarify if that would now be the end of it. After assuring him no doubt it would, and with a grateful shake he felt the power in his hand. The same one that earlier had nervously gripped so hard on a chair arm, to such an extent that his knuckles had turned white – clearly showing he must have felt under considerable pressure during this routine questioning.

Oliver King had no reason to feel that way, when simply asked if he'd visited certain villages, on specific dates. This coincided with 'suspicious incidents' they now investigated – following press headline reports – it certainly had to be linked to unexplained deaths of elderly women.

His car colour, make and model common – but similar to one seen several times by witnesses, days before or after 'events' related to an enquiry. Mr Carter had made a connection to these three women, not yet realised by this so-called detective. But his client didn't mention why he had good reason to be in these area's – because he knew all three women. Mr Carter knew this for sure, because all had known his Mum and following his own Dads funeral he'd met them briefly when they quaffed sherry – all complaining about their own aches and pains, but praised the newly arrived 'angel' who had flown up from London – with his strange accent; who delivered all their medication – but always had time for a chat and a cup of tea.

So – this nervous powerful man, who for some reason wanted a solicitor with him, had not mentioned to himself, or perhaps most importantly to this officer – that he worked for his parents, with a genuine valid reason to account for his movements when making deliveries for patients who couldn't attend their surgery in person, all registered surgery customers.

Bidding him goodnight, Mr Carter hung back to wait for his lift, with his own car in a garage for its MOT. Hopefully his wife may even turn up sober, when a chill ran down his spine after watching such relief on Oliver King's face earlier, exhaling loudly once assured – that should be it.

Carter knew from this leaked story, that victims were old infirm women, who had been 'Snuffed Out' by restricting their breathing, until passing out and dying – but initially it appeared from natural causes.

Driving his wife's car home later on – she snored loudly from the passenger seat, and he thought about his girlfriend. She – slept like an angel, sometimes nudging her to check she was OK. This directed his thoughts elsewhere, to a much darker place. When his heart began pounding much faster than normal, realising a hand shaken earlier had no doubt been the one responsible for 'Snuffing Out' so many elderly poor women living alone – taking lots of medication.

Just like his own mother.

21

Home of Oliver King, Sheffield

After remaining calm for so long, and as cool as a cucumber, he now knew that following a local newspaper headline he had panicked for no reason – a little earlier. Especially when sat with that docile detective simply going through motions to eliminate him along with no doubt many others, who would have to be spoken with.

One thing learnt over many years of being a look out – not to mention a serial killer – was to be a people watcher. This had stood him in good stead, especially visiting the elderly, but his earliest recollection had paid huge dividends. It had always remained with him when he saw 'toast man', that big fat detective moving quickly carrying a piece of toast outside. He was showing far too much purpose, plus he would never forget that look of horror in his eyes a few days later after working out, for sure, he was responsible for snuffing out that old dear and not his dad.

Without a doubt – toast man – saw him kneel down to pick up a piece of charcoal, then used to blacken his hands to distance himself from killing her with an alabaster face without a mark on it – but why on Earth was nothing said or introduced as evidence? All these years later it still really confused him how he became treated as a normal child before granted adoption status – with the rest of his existence mapped out as his destiny, allowing him to fulfil his passion in life, to bring about other people's demise.

Only just recently though – he had seen a man come to their surgery, who was far too chatty before his sick note for flu was collected. He had paid not only him far too much attention, but also their shift pattern chart he kept glancing at displayed on the wall. Upon checking out his client notes he discovered he was in fact a local policeman. On its own that didn't present a problem, but to then discover they had been paid a visit on his day off with items obviously moved around his desk during a crime prevention initiative; this was far too much of a coincidence.

It was time to act, meaning he had to cover his tracks with a few items needing to be moved, with a few people needing to be seen. To remind them they were all in a very delicate position after he had read about a recent discovery of bodies in a grave exposed following severe drought in Derwent, where he had been sent to as a boy- ironically to keep him safe.

If his other 'Acorns' didn't play ball, one in particular, and do what he asked of them, then just like a village from his past- they would all end up high and dry.

22

Small Park, Outskirts of Sheffield

They jumped into life when their Static Ob's van crew broadcast 'Out Out Out' to instigate the start of their surveillance. Initially they deployed on foot, and picked him up leaving the house. Perhaps after many years of studying a person's body language, Non-Verbal Communications and gait they had now developed a sixth sense. Because they all sensed he now walked with purpose, moving a little faster. Corroborated by the small Jack Russel now dragged along rather than walked at normal speed. First witnessed when not allowed to spray over the neighbouring bush. No doubt an ongoing territorial battle, with their dog always seen to piss over a tree in his garden.

He appeared to be a 'Man on a Mission'.

A fleeting glimpse of his back beneath a neon light did allow for a small rucksack to be noticed draped over his shoulder. This definitely had an object inside it with what appeared to be an outline of a small box pushing against its outer canvass lining.

With numerous props and covers to hand further members of their team were sent out into this dull overcast night. When the Target headed into a local park where later on, they saw his dog fastened to a bench. Before he suddenly appeared from a well walked path between trees to then return home, this time allowing his dog to spray away and mark its territory.

DC Hutchinson, in full jogging gear, ran slower than normal and feigned fatigue when doing a few laps of a cinder track. This circled a grassed area opposite where his dog had yapped when left alone. No doubt unhappy with tonight's walk.

After keeping eye-contact on a copse of trees with its thick undergrowth, she had maintained a count in her head before he reappeared. Head down along a path and brushing his coat clean after pushing past lower branches. She had just got to 'Mississippi One Hundred and Eighty' in her rhythmic count.

They only had a poor light tonight with no moon to help, but were fairly sure he no longer had a rucksack. But impossible to work out his choice of path prior to him emerging, with two heading in opposite directions. So this meant a large 'dump zone' with his three-minute window of opportunity. Perhaps a minute's walk and then a concealment, before returning to where he entered.

Perhaps their Task Force Officers could map it out when daylight, then comb and dig away until they found it. Because once again intuition told them during a debrief later it had to be something of great value and importance. Oliver King without a doubt had been desperate to keep it safe but secret.

Later on, Oliver King sat naked in front of his bedroom mirror, ignoring his whining dog. He stared back at himself, holding back tears. For decades he hadn't gone without having her to hand on a night. He didn't like spending time alone, already missing her. Unable to cuddle and hold her next to him in bed. To sniff and stroke her new hair and whisper in her ear that everything would be okay. She knew he'd always look after her, doing whatever was needed.

This prompted him to glance across at what he'd just picked up earlier from a littered forest floor. Near to where he had just buried her. Now holding it in his hand with eyes closed, its distinctive smell evoking a distant memory. Now flooding back as he heard excitable voices in their treehouse when agreeing Sonya's idea was the best, meaning she got to go first, to ram the first one down into their throats as far as possible, so they knew how it felt.

Tomorrow he would turn up at their 'gang leaders' place of work, to hand him this little reminder. They had all vowed to stick together, to help one another at all times. With him now a senior officer he expected no less from him.

He didn't want connecting to any other 'incidents' potentially bringing him down- especially if they found out about his past life in London. With so many dark secrets from his murky background, before they adopted him.

DI Drummond wouldn't recognise him at first, but when handed this Acorn he would be left in no doubt about just how much damage he could cause them all. If he didn't fully cooperate and protect him. Having read in the papers that Derwent graveyard had been exposed during the drought, attracting lots of metal detector enthusiasts resulting in bodies buried with their arms in handcuffs.

He had fobbed them off back then with a story about how he got the other set of handcuffs, but they may work out the true version of events if they were identified as Jean Dans. This again may connect him to her death.

He had made lots of holes in his Mums box and wrapped a little bit of silk around her head to hold her newly acquired hair in place before burying her. Plus a small rucksack should keep her dry and warm. Only until things got sorted. He knew she would be missing him just as much as he missed her, with them having such a strong bond.

23

Di Drummond's Office, Police HQ, Derby

He assured everyone that he felt 'OK' as he made his way back to his office, but he began to feel sick again in his stomach when he realised whose name those two initials stood for; after just meeting without any doubt, the evillest man he had ever met in his life, who had preyed upon not only loved ones in his own community, but also elderly women across England.

His London background now uncovered recently by incident room detectives, making excellent headway with even more evidence collected; momentum now gathering with his arrest inevitable. Now staring down at this acorn, he realised both his and other people's worlds could be on the verge of collapse – at Oliver Kings hands, which were those of a serial killer. Now known to have been one, even by the time he had landed in Derwent as a young boy, all those years ago. Those same hands from decades earlier, that had already snuffed out so many, including as he had only just discovered – their dear old babysitter – and former police officer Jean Dan. Done to kick start a revenge plan to murder their abusers facilitated by him, to create a space, to bury them beneath her grave – also explaining how he had acquired the extra pair of handcuffs.

This could now be proven beyond any reasonable doubt, having just had interim forensic reports from a pathologist that one pair of handcuffs recovered from one set of skeletal remains – confirmed embossed digits were in fact her collar number.

Oliver King had fooled them into believing he had acquired them after attending with his guardian the piano teacher, at the request of Daniel Dan, his good friend, to play a recital during a function at a social suite within Derby HQ station at an officers' ball. Claiming he wandered off alone to find an open police locker, from which he removed a set of handcuffs. But now he knew Oliver King had removed them from her bedroom where she had kept them in a storage box with all her other memorabilia – after he had no doubt used her key worn around her neck. Tony Drummond pulled himself quickly together after this initial shock. With his covert operational background unknown to most – he possessed requisite skills, after all he had planned under pressure, when other people's lives hung in the balance. By complete contrast Hawk overtly showed who and what he was, and how he felt – but he had a polemic approach, keeping everything hidden. He was now already deep in thought and formulating a plan in his mind – because it may just be possible with careful planning, and with a little help from his old 'acorn' friends and one other to incarcerate King in hell, for the rest of his life. He now realised they could use and manipulate events from their past to good advantage.

Despite using his dad's handcuffs with their shared collar number and the age-old tradition to 'stamp them or lose them' – luckily, for now, scientists couldn't read the digits – but even if they did it could be covered by presenting Oliver King as a 'lone agent' having stolen them – from where, at the time – he had regular access to his home. Plus, they could all put him there alone with both victims – after the final recital – and he did actually live with one of them. An obvious deduction could be made – he had extracted revenge on one of his abusers. One major challenge ahead would involve a cunning plan – after he convinced his fellow DI Hawk, who was more switched on then anyone he had worked with – to accept his offer – to help convict Oliver King. But if he could pull it off then at the same time, it would guarantee he never spoke a word at court, against his fellow Acorns.

He became quietly confident Hawk may only work it out, after the event – but he would cross that bridge when he came to it – because he was just about to make one hell of a journey – carrying a lot of responsibility, not to mention dire consequences if he fucked up.

24

Handmaiden Public House, Sheffield, Thursday Evening

Only after hastily arranging this meet in his local pub, near to his work, did Carter realise how apt its name had become in the circumstances. He now waited for Oliver King to arrive, after convincing him over a lengthy phone call there really could be mutual trust between them. After explaining in great detail how he knew him to be their 'Sheffield Snuffer'. Naming the three victims mentioned in his interview who were all old ladies, who were actually patients at King's Surgery. One of whom had described him in person as a saviour for delivering medication to them.

He had put all his cards on the table, telling King his mum stood in the way of an escape plan for his future happiness, with the new found love of his life. Who had just given him an ultimatum, meaning action now needed taking when he was away on holiday abroad. It provided the ultimate alibi, especially when King could make it look just like so many others before, a natural death from old age. He told him that after all she suffered from ill health and took copious amounts of medication. She ticked all the right boxes, and with King's help he really wanted to put her in one.

In the interests of 'self-preservation', he convinced Oliver King that should he suddenly meet his own demise, then the executor of his will had instructions to send a letter. Just recently deposited with him, to the lead investigating officer a DI Shay, to fully expose his criminality. Carter knew another safety net was in place with this evening's meet in a busy public place, to ensure a deranged psychopath didn't lay a hand on him, unlike all his other victims.

Having arrived early to secure a table had been a good idea, because this pub was loud and lively. With more and more stood at its busy bar jostling to be served. Many others occupied stools around the table where he now sat facing an entrance door. Until eventually an irate looking Oliver King arrived, pushing his way towards him with a facial expression like thunder, causing Carter concern. Before slumping down next to him, nearly knocking an old man off his stool when studying his newspaper, doing a crossword puzzle.

As King offered an apology to him it fell on death ears, quite literally, when fiddling with his hearing aid, now making a high-pitched whistling noise then falling silent. No doubt caused by dead batteries, but he ignored him, cursing under his breath about today's youth showing no respect.

"Fucking traffic, I've had to circle three times before getting parked, please don't tell me you chose this pub for its name?"

Carter relaxed, now realising he wasn't vexed about meeting him. It appeared he had accepted what had to be done for him, without putting up a fight. Who knows, perhaps he derived joy out of doing it, so didn't see it as too much of a problem. But perhaps a cash incentive, offering him ten percent of her homes sale value once the deed was done had possibly helped to cushion any reluctance.

Either way, within minutes King had taken from him a spare house key to gain entry, but that shouldn't be a problem. Having already paved his way, explaining to his mother his friend from her GP's would be dropping off a Pill Box. To help regulate medication with him away, to make sure she didn't overdose.

Her gave King her address verbally, he didn't want anything written down for obvious reasons. Avoiding at all costs any self-incrimination evidence showing him to be complicit in any way following her death. After shaking hands, he allowed Oliver King to leave first, fully knowing his services were needed before his return home in one week's time. He flew out on Monday with his wife, hoping he could keep his own hands off her, because spending time with her on holiday would be unbearable.

When King left, he sipped his pint of beer allowing himself a smile, raising his glass to self-toast himself. What he had just arranged to take place over coming days would change his life forever.

But this had already been guaranteed in a way he would never have imagined as DS Alex Jowett still sat across from him on his stool, staying in character sipping down his dark rum. Before slowly moving towards a busy bar with his rolled-up newspaper now tucked under his arm. With its weekly large Crossword, that paid fifty pounds in a prize draw if correctly completed, when submitted.

He had filled most of it in tonight, but he wouldn't be winning a penny, with every single answer wrong after what he had written. But he had just recorded in its numerous boxes almost every key word spoken and heard when sat opposite. This alone, when exhibited should convict them both for a conspiracy to murder at least. But he guessed Hawk would still run this operation a bit longer, to swoop down on his prey, Oliver King, at or near a crime scene.

He correctly worked out he wouldn't be home much over coming weeks before returning to his car, to remove his props. A faulty hearing aid always making a short whistling noise when pushing its button, a false beard, and an old man's hat and coat.

Earlier on, using his vast surveillance skills DS Jowett concluded King, who they had just followed circling around endlessly to find a space, would call into this busy popular pub. It had allowed him time to be dropped off in his much-used disguise. Noticing attentive stares directly towards him when entering the pub from a nervous 'suit and tie' intently watching its front door had paid dividends. After getting his drink he sat as close as possible to him, sensing correctly he was waiting for someone to join him.

Perhaps he was an Insurance Broker or a Solicitor? But who knows, with a foot surveillance about to commence on him, when leaving, they may soon know exactly who this 'unknown' was.

DS Jowett allowed him a ten second start before leaving himself by a different door, just in time to admire a beautifully shaped peachy arse, courtesy of DC Whittaker now walking away following him, after taking up a good position outside, to hopefully take him to his place of work or car. Either one would eventually reveal his identity.

Looking at Maria did actually make him feel like an old man, as he sighed again letting his imagination run wild. Knowing exactly what good positions he would like to take up with her. One of which would be directly behind her, but definitely not as taught in any surveillance training manual.

25

Carter and Jones Solicitors, Sheffield Office

After carefully applying makeup and paying particular attention to her right eye to make it look realistic, she arrived half-an-hour early on purpose, to sit in their busy reception area hoping it would display photographs of their firm's partners and staff. Sadly it didn't, meaning she would have to wait until being called through to see her solicitor, who had managed to squeeze her in after hearing she was now being subjected to physical violence after a land dispute with a neighbour, but didn't want to involve police.

Had he been a criminal lawyer, they may well have identified him last night as most of their team were long serving officers, who knew most by sight, but nobody had recognised him. DI Shay with his usual sixth sense, so often paying off asked they check out Oliver King's brief, who attended for his police TIE interview days earlier. It was a good idea because being suited and booted he dressed like one, plus after taking him away on foot she had seen his face several times before losing sight of him, not too far from where she sat now at these very same offices.

Using fictitious details Maria Whittaker feigned her 'victim' look of despair as she studied every face from behind a recently dampened handkerchief. A few courteous solicitors escorted clients towards an overworked middle-aged receptionist, who hastily used the office diary to note their next appointment promising a follow up call as a reminder.

Money mattered, with a generous legal aid claim for both a call plus a real bonus of a returning client who generated a healthy hourly rate before entering into costly protracted divorce proceedings. Sadly, for them these wouldn't apply to her when she managed to suppress her joy when Mr Carter emerged from an office to meet what transpired to be his wife, turning up unannounced to get him to sign their travellers' cheques. His passport had been used to order them as explained to their front of house receptionist. They needed this break with his poorly elderly mother being a real pain, causing him stress.

As Mr Carter's next client was called through, his receptionist was going to apologise; they were running a little late, but DC Whittaker had already left after gathering all she had needed.

For many reasons she looked forward to updating Hawk that it was a definite confirmation. Mr Carter had handed a key to King, he was a solicitor so his hunch once again was right. Maria hoped hers was that he fancied her like mad because she was more than willing to become one of his prey after redoing her makeup, then unbuttoning yet another button on her blouse, before going into his office. He was stood waiting for her update with a big smile and a gentle squeeze on her arm as she sat down.

After being taught how to best use mirrors and reflective surfaces to maximise what was seen on surveillance, she was delighted to see him stare down at her bum when stood behind her, then her ample cleavage when at her side- when she used an office window, acting like a mirror with bright morning sun shining on it. Perhaps her sixth sense wasn't too bad either; plus, if she performed well in other ways, she may just get that long awaited promotion soon within her grasp. In due course it would be mentioned she really didn't mind being under him, one way or another. But for now, she leant forward to pick up her handbag from in front of her to draw his admiring looks even more.

Hawk himself admired her subtle moves picturing her doing what everyone spoke about, to earn her 'Yo-Yo' nickname. A game they both now played out and he didn't mind one bit, always a more than willing participant. Plus, with her policing ability she deserved a promotion, but he wouldn't mention that for a while.

Until he got tired of pulling her string.

26

Di Drummond's Office,
Derby Central Police Station

It wasn't obvious, but to a trained eye, having just watched him leave his office, it had been spotted. So he now stood exactly where Hawk had after pausing when something had caught his eye, making him stop momentarily before continuing at his normal pace, walking away before closing his door behind him.

As DI Drummond stood in exactly the same position, he saw this month's detection figures visible on a clipboard near his filing cabinet, several marked up in bright red, showing where he had fallen short of divisional targets, but he couldn't imagine for one moment why a fellow DI would study these, they surely held no interest.

Suddenly his heart was in his mouth after he averted his gaze towards that cabinet. He stood just tall enough to see partially inside a terra cotta pot now empty that had held a plant he hadn't watered for a month, finally losing its will to live before wilting, then being thrown out by his cleaner.

A conservative guess put DI Shay at least five inches taller than himself, perhaps six-foot-three – that accounted for his next move as he held his position but stood on his tip toes. This opened up a view further down into his earthenware pot to show it wasn't in fact empty. Because it now brought into view an Acorn, delivered to him earlier by Oliver King, making it clearly visible laying there on its side. It had been tossed there after his return from meeting him, just before his crime prevention officer joined him in his office with those latest figures now hung on their clipboard.

But why would this Acorn mean anything to DI Shay? Who had also glanced several times towards his wall mounted pictures telling a little of his life story, he lived in the country, had several children and had an allotment, so nothing of importance.

Only Tony and a few others knew their gang's Acorn Club name from decades earlier, plus with an arborist report still awaited only then, potentially, would they identify what had been pushed down their victim's throats from residue found around skeletons. This in itself wouldn't connect anyone directly to their historic murder.

So why had Hawk reacted? Perhaps he was letting his imagination run wild, imagining worst case scenarios at a time of uncertainty, worrying about what Oliver King may do or say when captured. It was putting him under a great deal of pressure, causing more noticeable involuntary tweaks in his arm. He had first noticed them years earlier, resulting in him giving up crown green bowling.

Oliver King would firmly believe he could serve him better, to help him any way possible in his capacity as a senior detective, with access to evidence and witnesses. It meant he would want him 'on board'.

This would drastically change when their damning statements were made against him, but without a doubt they needed to come together again as a matter of urgency but would give a treehouse a miss as a meeting place, perhaps settling for a restaurant to meet Sonya and Tom.

As Hawk drove back to Sheffield, a small but necessary detour was taken when his almost photographic memory kicked in to recall surveillance logs he had recently read. These had far more information and greater detail than an initial verbal update about their follow to a local park; when Oliver King was seen to enter then disappear before returning into view three minutes later.

He also knew from the surveillance earlier on today that Oliver King was seen parking near a parade of shops, where his team then got blocked by a delivery van, meaning they lost sight of him for 20 minutes until his return. Hawk had discovered that using a snicket located between local shops led you to a subway, eventually giving access to DI Drummond's police station within minutes.

Had Oliver King called to see his old mate who he knew from all those years ago when sent to live in Derwent as a young boy?

It was only a small village, so surely that was more than likely but urgent enquires in London should furnish more information after one of his 'C' team had read an interview King's mother had with Sheffield journalists, who published her life history featured in a 'Women in Business' story. This had touched upon initial heartbreak that they couldn't have children before adopting Oliver, who was briefly relocated to Derwent as part of 'Operation Pied Piper'.

Hawk himself had researched this war initiative finding out most children were sent to live away from home for four years until World War 2 ended. So why had King come home so soon?

This was another of his urgent actions, but he didn't want to alert his fellow inspector; he just felt something was wrong, it hadn't yet dawned on him but he would figure it out in the end. Perhaps his plan to spend time with him tomorrow on a trip to see an old, retired detective may pay off.

But for now, he was standing in a park after counting up to 60 to allow a one-minute travelling time before a return trip from where King was seen emerging on a path. This gave him a minute to hide whatever had been in that rucksack carried from his home. Hawk looked exactly at a spot where he was going to direct his team to start digging after staring up at a large oak tree surrounded by overgrowth near its huge base.

Where hundreds of Acorns had fallen to ground, forming an almost blanket cover beneath where he sensed they would find whatever Oliver King was so desperate to hide that night. Hawk now certain he had picked up, and then delivered, that Acorn to DI Drummond. It wasn't dried up or brittle even in that warm office with any age to it, appearing fresh, plus he had a blood hound's nose; he could smell its distinctive odour just like now with all those around his feet.

His senses normally got him results; they were now telling him he would have to watch his new willing partner carefully because unlike Acorns, this really wasn't an open and shut case This was why his 'C' team would be trusted to follow Tony D to his home tonight after work. He wanted to see how close to where Derwent had been he lived and who he met. His allotment photo in his office had a 'Bamford's Best' sign displayed, showing it was near to where flooded Derwent had been located.

Hawk made himself smile, thinking about that allotment and this case in general before saying out loud to himself:

"Well, Hawky boy, the feckin plot thickens!"

27

'Beachy View' Care Home, Brighton Sea Front, 1976

On this rare occasion he hadn't hidden her dentures, but in any case, it didn't stop her peeling yet another orange, before loudly sucking on the fruity segments. Luckily her name provided another great opportunity to allow a more than apt nickname. An old habit from bygone years, when in another life every new recruit had one given. Some remained with officers their entire service, regardless of whether they liked it or not.

Retired librarian, Lucy Sampson, always gave a disapproving stare when he called her 'Juicy Lucy' Perfectly timed now, when she made the orange disappear before them. She often passed numerous comments, but a combination of fruit, and strong Brummie accent made it impossible to grasp its full meaning. But enough to show she really wasn't happy with him. Join the club girl.

Because that fact applied to pretty much all of them, dumped here and forgotten by families who only paid the occasional visit, no doubt remembering the classic saying 'Where there's a will, there's a way'. A sentiment echoed by his sister, after just making her long pilgrimage down from South Yorkshire, with her brown bag of grapes. At least she'd munched on less this time, so he may even attempt to do a part-exchange with Juicy for his fruit of choice. Or, like normal, just wait until she crashed out when her pills kicked in. He knew where she hid her stash.

Later on, after returning his gaze from their birdfeeder outside, towards his side table, he realised straight away some bastard had just eaten his last custard cream off his plate. He stared around a large room, badly in need of decoration. Where, with another twenty prisoners, who they called residents, he'd been dumped yet again. For a few hours, to sit staring out of its large bay window, in the hope they eventually fell asleep, to make it easier for them during their working day.

Only two were nimble enough to get to his side and back. With most of them slumped half-dead, or comatose and dribbling, after this afternoon's tea trolley, with no more than two biscuits allowed, had also served up their medication.

It reminded him of when young in service, a still innocent PC gaoler serving up drinks to prisoners in busy cell areas, with a very similar approach. You get what you're given, no requests, no deviation. But don't worry, you will get a taste for tea with two sugars. Because no doubt (you little shit) just like all your thieving predecessors you will be staying with us many times over coming years.

Smiling at this memory, he wondered how much longer he would be served his sweet tea with two biscuits, because he was now heading downhill rapidly. But he still had a sense of humour, playing along with two admirers, Jayne Wynne and Jen Dudley. Clocking up over one hundred and sixty years between them, making him their 'toy boy', a mere pup by comparison, at only seventy-two.

Both women eagerly watched, waiting for his response. With their less nimble friend Mavis Drage, peeping wide-eyed over her Agatha Christie book Murder on the Orient Express. Trying to look on covertly, but her giggling gave herself away. Andy smiled to himself, cracking yet another joke in his head, because she certainly wasn't a trained observer. Before throwing them all a suspicious look, feigning anger and then surprise. Jayne was clearly seen to dispose of 'evidence' with a quick hand to mouth movement. Followed by a chew and a swallow, her eyes sparkling with delight.

"Facking Hell! Daylight robbery! Call me an X Detective, but I do have two prime suspects. It's that old classic 'Distraction Job'. But ladies I've got news for you, it's still classed as 'joint enterprise' so you're both as guilty as Fack."

His exaggerated cockney accent made those still awake smile, but made his 'cream girls' (a play on 'dream girls' from yesteryears) giggle away, because they now had what they wanted most, his full undivided attention.

Jen, who had asked earlier if a chaffinch had returned to feed outside (yet again) clapped her hands. Praising him for yet another brilliant detection, with Jayne, her partner in crime, beaming with delight.

Andy Laptew, now on a roll, kept his banter going, with a little wink towards Jayne, followed with a suggestive.

"Oh well, my old girl, it's nice to see you still swallow when you have to."

Even Cyril, who hadn't responded much to anyone or anything for days, suddenly sat up laughing at that one. Just as Andy got yet another rebuke, when told to watch his language and manners, by a stern-faced house matron. Who turned on her noisy heels to answer their front doorbell. Andy waited until well out of earshot and sight before raising two fingers with a defiant 'Fack you Nurse Ratched'.

Even those who hadn't seen 'One Flew Over the Cuckoo's Nest' still found his actions and comment funny. Giggles were silenced though when returning, flanked by two smartly dressed men, suited and booted. Immediately catching the cream girl's eyes with a series of elbow nudges then a flurry of whispers to one another, wondering who they were, and what they wanted. Even Mavis came out into the open when putting down her book to take in the view, far better than the beach.

Retired Detective Sgt Andrew Laptew now smiled at them both, knowing immediately by sight who they were. Indeed, after a recent visit from his sister calling down from South Yorkshire with a newspaper, he had a more than good idea why they had called to see him. Its Sheffield Snuffer headline had given him one hell of a clue.

With focused concentration his mind now surfed through a life-time of past events recalling his early CID years. To remember a name given to a young miscreant who made it good following adoption. After escaping from his dads clutches when running a network of street urchins across central London.

'Oliver Twist' they had called him, a play on his first name, his surname back then had been Wick. Andy always thought a candle connection more than appropriate for that little bastard. Because he never doubted once, despite his young age he had 'Snuffed Out' numerous old women. But nobody would listen to the 'new boy' in their elite CID office. Soundly ignored and told to move on and get stuck into a mountain of jobs piling up on his desk.

Amanda Jayne their matron, appeared even more stern faced than normal when asking him to join both men and herself in her office. Slowly making his way Andy wondered just how many more that little bastard had gone on to kill.

Andy really wanted to escape from all this madness around him. Sadly though they still hadn't imprisoned an Indian Chief who stood seven foot tall in his boots and liked to chew gum, to carry a large heavy water-therapy unit over his shoulder. To throw it through their large bay window, with its beachy view beckoning.

He found himself humming a distinctive tune in his head from the film's final scene when 'Chief' escaped from the Mental Asylum. To run back home to join all his family on their Reservation, never to be seen again. Jayne and Jen both told Andy to 'Hurry Back' when reaching out to him, as they would miss him loads when gone.

He knew what they meant, but also knew he would soon be departing in other ways.

But got another shriek of delight when he told them both, that when he did return his thorough investigation would certainly be continued. This meant he may well end up taking down all their particulars. Even this made Cyril smile and jump up in his seat, who then gave him a thumbs up, asking if he could join him.

"Facking Hell," Andy thought to himself, a bit of hope for 'Nice One' yet. He may even end up playing for Tottenham again if his recovery continued.

28

Senior Investigator's Office, Sheffield HQ

Driving back to their incident room one of them was filled with joy, DI Drummond with abject worry, knowing that soon his world may collapse with all he held dear coming down, crumbling on top of him just as earth had fallen down onto their 'victims', all those years ago- when buried in those graves until discovered with such damning evidence behind their backs. This connected Oliver King, who was, after Andy Laptew's account, definitely their serial killer who had gone on to kill so many. Not for personal gain, but as was suggested by a criminal profiler brought in to assist their investigation, motivated for sexual gratification, stemming perhaps from adverse childhood experiences.

As DI Drummond pondered over their five-hour return journey, he formulated his 'get out of jail' plan for himself and his other 'Acorns', who did what they did to avenge wrongs against them when isolated, violated and desperate for them to stop. He knew exactly the person who would do what was needed to save them all, but first and foremost she would do it for revenge against an evil bastard that had snuffed out her confidant and dear friend Jean Dan. Who had helped launch her career as a leading psychiatrist, who was now the most published authority in her field of mental disorders. He clearly remembered her visiting Jeans home over and over again all those years ago and he had seen how she had wept at Jean's graveside, plus her kind words about her dear friend at her well-attended wake afterwards. Luckily nobody else would now make this connection decades later, allowing her to be classed as an impartial 'independent expert witness' without any conflict or interest in King's case following his arrest.

Tony Drummond, after joining CID years later, connected Jean Dan's and Sophie Ford's conspiracy when working together to self-help one another, especially after a link was made between a studio owner and thousands of depraved pictures of young children, following a visit with a man in a high security prison whom she was allowed to see having been caught years earlier by Jean Dan. So a pupil had taught her lecturer first-hand about her investigations, which linked in with her academic studies and research.

After returning they sat with a SIO for nearly an hour, concluding when both men shook his hand knowing they could now prove their case after an amazing statement taken from a long-retired Andy Laptew. He had shared in full what he had seen, what he knew, but sadly what he was told to forget as his supervisor took full credit, applying an age-old approach of KISS (Keep It Simple Stupid) A practice since policing began to allow so many to escape attention or conviction for all their wrongdoings. When you had a result already and you've won, why overplay it; why on earth make loads of work for yourself when you've already nailed someone, who, this time, had made it even easier for them after dying from his injuries, with only a covering report needed for a coroner. Just four sheets of typing, put in a folder to be forgotten about until one of their team collected it from a criminal record's office, whilst doing research into Oliver King with Social Services Coming up trumps for once with a record about Oliver's blood parents. An old clerk at records, himself a detective back in the day had sung Andy Laptew's praises; they both shared a love of Opera; having kept in touch with him over many retirement years, who updated them about to where they could now find him in his beach view home. Apparently true to form he was causing mayhem after his recent bout of illness, which hadn't suppressed his wicked sense of humour and antics.

Old DS Laptew had wept after reading, then signing his statement after being told just how many more had met the same fate as they had seen first-hand all those decades ago, with 'hand' hitting home with its obvious meaning, but now he had given them a golden opportunity to put away a murdering bastard in prison for the rest of his miserable life.

It had stayed with Andy Laptew all his life how he had noticed at the elderly victim's house, his dad's hands were both covered in coal dust when they first arrived, but young Oliver's were clean- fully supporting that he had just prepared himself for killing her by washing them thoroughly before placing hands over her face. With Oliver going on to tell them whilst clinging to his social workers hand, this was what he had seen his dad do many times, explaining to him how this was essential- so as not to leave traces on their faces when they were 'snuffed out'.

Andy Laptew's damning evidence all these years later, including how he picked up cold pieces of charcoal, then used to rub all over both his clean hands, to hide his guilt, would finally be used against him. Using 'Similar Fact' evidence along with 'Res Gestae', it was an airtight case when they introduced so many irrefutable but circumstantial comparisons, to outline such a highly unique modus operandi, with proven accompanying actus reus which a decent prosecution barrister would formulate into a compelling legal argument. No doubt using one of their long laborious soliloquy's which would normally conclude that it was quite simply 'an insult to common sense' not to find this defendant guilty as charged.

With personalised identifiable handcuffs belonging to Jean Dan found on one skeleton, who herself was found with no injuries before her sudden death; would allow an obvious inference to be drawn, with Oliver being a frequent visitor to her home, that he had snuffed her out first to steal her handcuffs, to use on his guardian music teacher, a convicted paedophile. Along with his partner in crime their Vicar, whom must have been abusing him before he extracted revenge on them both. Needing a grave, hence the reason he killed her, all part of his devious plan to facilitate two murders with this being its kick start mechanism to complete his mission to dispose of their bodies. Oliver's social worker had him assessed after being taken into care before adoption, writing he was a 'fit member of society', despite initial findings he may have some 'mental instability' in later years with post trauma psychological stress, after all he had witnessed at such an early age.

This report really was gold dust for Tony Drummond. It allowed him at the end of their meet to casually throw into conversation, almost as an afterthought, that they may be criticised if after arrest, at the very least a further study wasn't completed- just to circumvent a common defence tactic to plead insanity. This was approved by their SIO, who did what so many had done before him, as he later wrote his policy book to show that he had thought of this, which he would use as a good example to support his promotion application due to be submitted in a few weeks.

DI Drummond knew their force was now on a tight budget with so much money having already been spent on overtime with rumours of detectives ordering luxury caravans already, but luckily he knew a key professional who was a leading expert, who he made out with a nod and a wink he would wine and dine once again to secure her services for peanuts. Even volunteering to use his forces own budget, which as he had hoped resulted in him being given that Action following King's arrest but to be completed before Kings initial plea hearing. This normally took place a month or so after being remanded into custody. It would negate his defence barrister introducing a defence of insanity in an attempt to make him unfit to stand trial.

Tony Drummond didn't mention that with Sophie Fords help, she would find King unfit to stand trial. Because he knew full well if this 'air tight case' got to court his defence team would expose everything. Meaning a realistic danger of bringing him down when close to retirement. So he would puncture holes in the prosecution case to prevent any revelations bound to come out during a protracted Crown Court fiasco.

Nobody would ever listen to, or believe any ridiculous cries of protestation from a certified mad-man of a serial killer. When desperately trying to deflect blame onto highly respectable members of society. No less than a solicitor, a police inspector and a business owner. All fuelled by his warped deranged mind, seeking revenge- no doubt after reading accounts in their statements. These would cover how he bragged about stealing sets of handcuffs during his stay, before picked up by his adoptive mother and returned to London. Having lived with them only a few months, seeming such a strange boy from the moment he landed. Always finding any excuse to visit Jean Dan, but sadly now they knew only too well why.

This plan could work, and would happen with Sophie Ford on board, working her magic, especially when he explained to her who had killed Jean Dan – meaning Oliver King sectioned to a Mental Asylum. To find himself in a straitjacket , in a padded cell. To stop him 'Snuffing Out' lunatics whom he would soon be living with for the rest of his miserable, tormented life.

No less than the evil manipulative bastard deserved. Tony Drummond knew this full well, because it took one to know one.

If Hawk knew how he worked and how he thought, Tony was more than sure he would be mightily impressed. Such a shame they had only met at the end of his career, and under such circumstances. He had no doubt Hawk would have been a brilliant undercover officer- with his help and guidance of course.

29

CID Office, Sheffield

To escape every now and then to get away from a busy Incident Room, going back to their normal day to day working office proved a godsend. It allowed them to sit in a safe haven with long established work colleagues to talk openly about others who had been brought in to help. They didn't know them personally so couldn't trust them. During discussions to put forward thoughts and ideas about how best to catch their killer using any tactic they could get away with.

All were surprised that Hawk planned to catch King at a 'crime scene' but firmly believed he had an 'Ace in the Pack'. A definite target King would push ahead to kill , sooner rather than later, on behalf of Carter his solicitor, who now had a hold over him.

Sometimes you never disclosed to others thoughts on your mind, unless you were confident they wouldn't crack or spill their guts. Especially if things went wrong, or suspicion fell upon them of inappropriate acts. Potentially they could compromise an investigation, or worse still have them suspended. But they were doubting this risky move, fraught with danger.

With Hawk they knew he would back them to the hilt, doing whatever needed to protect them. It reciprocated their trust in him, giving them confidence to comply with his requests to achieve success when they hunted down their prey.

They didn't doubt his skills or initiatives, having never seen him shy from any sort of confrontation, always keen to push at boundaries until opponents were beaten. Every now and then, normally in drink a recollection about what he had seen 'back in the provinces' with references to an uncle would be made, but this never developed into a full story.

As Hawk walked into their office they were well practiced to not even flinch or react, because it would have given away their conversation about him. A brave move, with potential consequences, that could result in getting measured up for a shiny new uniform. DS Jagger skilfully changed conversation mid-flow, to recount a salacious account of what he did to his new girlfriend's older sister. After coming home drunk with her sibling passed out upstairs, when trying to keep up with him earlier drinking tequila slammers.

Describing how he then slammed her, introducing the contents of a fruit bowl making their leader pause to hear the 'juicy bits' before shaking his head. Smiling at hearing this same old rendition, no doubt bullshit, but funny.

Hawk slammed his own office door shut behind him, before slumping into a chair to stare down once again at a letter just collected from their mail room. Penned by his eldest daughter, sixteen years of age. Despite his endless pleas she still refused any contact- not wanting any reconciliation following a bitter divorce with her mum many years ago. With two other daughters from other failed marriages shunning him as well. Ironically meaning he'd achieved a full house of failed relationships, meaning he now lived alone as a consequence.

He cradled a glass of whiskey in his hand holding it with a much firmer grip than normal, with his stomach churning from upset. Exacerbated no doubt by a lack of sleep and far too many pills. Momentarily losing self-control he threw his crystal-cut glass, against a far office wall. Instantly regretted because it carried sentimental value, a leaving present from colleagues in Manchester. Whom he had worked with before promotion, holding him dear, they had a Hawk engraved on his gift .

It had just made its final flight.

His current team fell silent upon hearing its loud smash, knowing they should get the fuck out of there quickly, until he calmed down.

Unfortunately, DI Drummond now entered their CID office with Mavis, who had a spring in her step, and a smile on her face. They were warned that perhaps now may not be the best time to see him. He wasn't in the best of moods, but she beamed even more when waving aloft a piece of paper. Saying they needed to hang on a second to watch a transformation, after breaking some news. Before randomly throwing in a 'Be Prepared' that confused the hell out of them. So out of natural curiosity they ended up sitting back down.

Only a short while later they heard a loud cry of delight come from his office, after Mavis shared her memories of the 'Owl' girls, with younger sister still alive and well, being a patient at Oliver King's practice. But Mavis had just visited her to discover Oliver King, a frequent caller, had been given all her older sisters home details as 'points of contact' With all three recently found dead in their homes, all in their mid to late nighties- it simply had to be too much of a coincidence.

Hawk now became more tempted than ever to bring him in straight away, but it would all be circumstantial evidence. He had just used this very same fact to win a hard-fought battle with his supervisors. Who eventually, only marginally, agreed to extend his surveillance another 24 hours. Going with Hawks animal instincts, when telling them it would pay off. To achieve their ultimate goal, by catching this murdering bastard red-handed.

He used a coffee cup for his next drink of whiskey to toast Mavis, and had she been twenty years younger he would have got around to thanking her properly.

Unless of course he got completely shit faced- then who knew, especially with his chaotic lifestyle gathering downward momentum.

30

Bowling Club, Ladies' Practice, Buxton

They were 'ladies' as they often teased one another when expletives couldn't be held back during a highly competitive game, especially against rival teams in their local derby matches which, ironically, because of the league they played in, were mainly from Derbyshire. This afternoon though nobody coined their 'ladies' phrase to remind a fellow player of expletives as several muttered 'Fuck' out loud as they watched 'Boring Bob' walk through their gate. With a big smile and a cheery wave, oblivious to the fact that everyone did whatever was needed to avoid spending too long in his company before he went into one of his 'sleepy soliloquys' about subjects that had no interest or meaning to them. Repairing radios or making kit models of aeroplanes really didn't hit any spot for them, which was one of many reasons his late wife had joined their club years earlier just to get out of the house from under his feet to escape him for a few hours. Sadly, passing away last winter during a cold spell, she had given him his name as 'Boring Bob' with it being even sadder that he felt an affinity still to her ladies team, for whom she bowled, hence his arrival once again after visiting her grave not too far away.

Luckily, they had a valid excuse to send him off on an errand, to despatch him quickly. Explaining their Club Raffle first prize, a bottle of Sweet Sherry, had been won by Mary Carter who lived in Dore just over the boundary in South Yorkshire. Such a lovely drive, no more than half an hour away, if he would be an absolute darling?

Bob remembered her, she too had become a keen spectator following her recent illnesses, who like him would often turn up to watch matches when his wife had been playing. In fact, he recalled a conversation with her before she suddenly disappeared one day, when mentioning her old vintage radio's problem with crackly intermittent reception. So perhaps he could check that out for her when dropping off her prize. As a final sweetener, to get him to fuck off they told him that when he got back at 6 pm, he could join them for tea and homemade cakes. This made his little face light up, collecting her winning bottle before setting off in his car to deliver it.

They all promised one another to be finished and away at half five to head to the village pub, after he had swallowed their lie, because he certainly wouldn't be swallowing any cakes. Later on that night after several drinks they still couldn't stop laughing about sending a 'Bore to Dore' who they all liked to ignore.

But over coming days, after hearing a few whispers, followed by a strong rumour about what had happened in Dore later that day, they couldn't wait to catch up with Bob to find out all about it first-hand. So much so they now watched out in eager anticipation towards their entrance gate. Awaiting his arrival to serve him up tea and cakes they had now made. It had been on every local radio station as well as in Newspapers with talk he may well be interviewed on TV all about it.

Forgetting all about how a lady would comment, they just couldn't fucking believe it.

31

Home of Mary Carter, Sheffield

Despite it being a bit of a rush, it had gone well when primed to expect him with his pill dispenser; to help with daily allocations of medication. But she still went on to vent her anger towards her son, who really was a 'useless lump'. At least though he had bothered to visit her albeit briefly. But it had only been for the first time in several weeks.

Just before departing on yet another one of his bloody holiday's meaning his poor old mum had to fend for herself. Like she now told her visitor she would be having the last laugh, planning on going nowhere soon, certainly not into an old people's home.

He stood listening at her kitchen sink, fully realising why he had been sent in to sort out his problem, after insisting that whilst there he didn't mind giving her a hand (this always made him smile) before going on to pretend he would wash a few pots. A pile conveniently stacked up ignored, but it allowed him to wash his hands, sticking to a well-practiced routine. Making sure they were clean before he would then savour his slow walk towards her with a smile on his face, with a look of confusion on hers- before 'snuffing her out'.

Oliver watched a steady flow of tap water stop, then start again with a splutter to become barely a drip. Mary saw a puzzled look on his face, prompting an explanation it often happened with a drop in water pressure after flushing her upstairs toilet. For some reason this made him look horrified even more, after hearing heavy footsteps coming downstairs.

"Don't worry it's only 'Boring Bob' from the Bowling Club. I'm guessing the girls fobbed him off by sending him across on an errand to bring me some cheap sherry I won in a raffle."

As Bob entered her kitchen with his sickly smile his life was about to change for ever, beginning with his nickname. Soon he became a most sought-after companion for catch-up and drinks; just to hear again what he witnessed over the next few minutes. His account changed many times but he would never tire of describing it.

This included firstly a man wearing a crash helmet, diving head first at great speed through a kitchen window, just as a sledgehammer then began smashing away on Mary's door- before suddenly it crashed open with four big men bursting into her kitchen and screaming loudly. Who all jumped on a man when walking away from her sink towards him, with dripping wet hands.

Even Bob was gently taken to his knees, then held as this ginger-haired man, who must have called when he was upstairs using her bathroom after drinking far too much tea, was repeatedly thumped, then kicked to his head and body. Before being handcuffed and dragged outside in a most unceremonious fashion. After this they all began to shout excitedly, holding up a pill box found next to him on Mary's kitchen floor. He then heard them all shout out they had just caught their 'Sheffield Snuffer'.

Stood outside Hawk had adrenaline pumping through his veins like never before, causing his whole body to shake following his most daring operation. It had only just been given approval from his brow beaten bemused senior management team. Who yesterday had stared in total disbelief at their senior detective, willing to put his whole career on the line as he implored them to fully back his judgment.

DI Shay congratulated all his surveillance team, who one by one suddenly appeared from bushes, undergrowth and trees in the rear garden, that had afforded them a view into Mary's kitchen after following, then watching their target being allowed inside by an old lady.

This was after holding up a pill box to show her why he had called, becoming their cue for a 'Rapid Entry Team' to get into position. They had established it was a heavy-duty wooden door, solid oak, so they backed it both ways; implementing a new technique by launching a colleague head first through a window wearing a helmet, along with protective clothing including gloves and lots of padding.

PC Iain Blenkin, known as 'Rudolph', because he was so small in stature; he surely must have stood on tip toes like a ballerina to make their height limit to join, an obvious choice to be thrown into her kitchen. After landing he was shocked to see an old man in her kitchen because they had missed Bob arriving just before they had parked up after following their target to this house; its number coinciding with what had been written down in a pub on a crossword puzzle.

DI Shay now gave full attention to his quarry with arms handcuffed behind his back, who was laid out in the garden until beckoning for him to be brought up to his feet. Hawk made a deliberate point of slowly walking towards him before then stooping down to go face to face with his captured serial killer. He stared into his cold shark like eyes before placing one hand towards his own face and then gently covering both his nose and mouth before saying with a strong Irish accent:

"Caught you both red-handed, as well as clean-handed, you murdering fecker."

Oliver King defiantly stared back, smiling before throwing down his challenge.

"Prove it, you Irish cunt; you're no match for me. Last time I was stopped leaving an old woman's kitchen when she was dead inside and I still walked away Scott free."

His smile disappeared as Hawk winked at him before replying:

"Mr 'toast man', your old mate, that big detective, who you didn't fool for one minute, sends his kind regards. He remembers that day well. Andy told me only recently how he saw you blacken your hands all those years ago. He can't wait to tell those jurors with great delight all that he witnessed, and all he knows about you. Let's just say your past really is going to come back to bite you on your arse, because regardless of any excuses and whatever defence you come up with it won't wash a second time, Oliver, my old son."

When saying 'my old son', he did so in his best attempt at a Cockney accent. Hawk also made a deliberate point of staring down, then touching Oliver King's hands.

They were both still wet having just been washed.

32

Holding Cell, Sheffield Police Station

It was bedlam all around him, as he sat in a large holding cage with a few drunks and shoplifters, who latched onto their "new arrival" starting by having a polite conversation. But soon cut to the chase after asking if he had any cigarettes on him, but then paid him no attention when told he was a non-smoker.

Apart from one little idiot in a football kit including boots, who had picked up on his accent, explaining he had a rich aunty that lived 'down south', who had disowned his family. Today though that really was the least of his worries after head butting, perhaps even breaking a referee's nose during a match. Worse still, four opposing team spectators were off duty coppers, who had locked him up. He went on by assuring everyone present, but with nobody really listening, it was a good job there was four of them- otherwise he would have got the better of those 'pigs'.

As Oliver King was being booked in, he remained calm, glancing at a blackboard to see their cells were nearly full with everyone's name displayed with a summary of why they had been arrested. It was deafening as prisoners kicked cell doors, calling out for a light or hurled abuse at gaolers, who walking past their hatches ignoring any request and uttering 'Busy' without even bothering to turn heads towards them.

As a young PC (who he later discovered had an elderly grandmother suspected of being recently killed by him) glared at him, he took great delight in writing on their prisoner board in the largest block capital letters possible within his allocated space, OLIVER KING-SHEFFIELD SNUFFER.

Oliver King averted his look to the floor as a cell Sgt told him to empty his pockets onto their counter, telling him he was being kept for questioning before letting him know that if all went well, he would never be released again after what he had done. When all his belongings were thrown in a bag, it drew his attention to a bright green plastic key fob. This was a present off a patient, who he knew was a defence solicitor, who by all accounts was good at his job. Oliver King asked for him to be told he was here because he wanted representation. This seemed to anger the cell staff even more, convincing King he must be decent at what he did .Perhaps this explained his 'Tricky Ricky' Green, nickname.

Suddenly, he was taken hold of firmly before being half-dragged, half-marched down a noisy corridor and pushed with force into his cell with its door slammed shut as hard as possible behind him. A polite request for a drink fell on death ears with not even a 'busy' given as a reply.

Sitting there alone on a small wooden cell bench he realised that no doubt he would soon be joined by one of those idiots he had seen earlier in their holding cage after being given their last vacant cell. It wasn't long before he worked out in advance who was going to be sharing with him, after hearing a clatter of football studs in the distance getting louder and louder. He watched his cell door open as an annoying little fucker, who needed "four to get the better of him" at his football match, who had been dragged along by only one of them. Who then threw him against his cell wall. Just for good measure he was also given a hard slap across his face, making him cower in a corner and whimper like a child.

Eventually gaining his composure after a bout of shouting abuse (but only when his escort officer was the other side of their cell door after again slamming it shut), he sat on their bench rubbing his cheek before saying:

"Fucking hell, mate, I saw what they wrote on that board when booking you in. Are you that Sheffield Snuffer everyone's talking about? I bet they gave you a right fucking kicking when you were arrested. I got a good beating before getting here, not to mention that slap just then, and all that for only hurting someone with a bit of a head butt."

Oliver King really wasn't in any mood for this little wanker, deciding to put an end to any conversation with a long stare at him before saying:

"Let's just keep quiet or I may have to show you how I snuffed them all out, so not another word; is that understood?"

His cell companion slid away from him as far as possible, nodding his head before staying quiet for a good hour before he was asked through their hatch by a gaoler if he wanted a solicitor. This was declined and he was taken away for interview, but this time no shouting or abuse at the same officer who had slapped him earlier.

As this red cheeked prisoner entered the interview room, two stern-faced detectives sat staring at him, before he turned to the gaoler, who then shook his hand laughing after apologising for slapping him so hard as he jokingly pointed at Hawk, who couldn't stop laughing, to explain himself:

"He told me I had to do it but fucking hell, it was a good idea, even your cell mate looked shocked when it landed."

DC Thompson of the drug squad, an old mate of Hawks, rubbed his cheek, having already worked out who was behind it, but with a recall to duty on his day off, plus double time, to dress up as a footballer for a few hours to sit with a killer in a cell was well worth it- before giving them his update.

"You've got the right man banged up there for certain; he's already threatened to snuff me out in the cell. By the way I've never seen it as busy; did you lock a load up so we had to be banged up together?"

Hawk smiled and said, "No, I've got eight early turn plods to fill all the cells for two hours overtime with strict instructions; they keep on kicking doors and hurling lots of abuse through hatches."

DC Thompson accepted his cigarette as he realised just what a clever, crafty fucker Hawk was, who true to form pulled out his hip flask taking a swig. It was to celebrate with his Sgt they had got the bastard, as their other 'prisoner' reached out for a sip.

"Sorry, Tommo, none for you; we can't have you going back and smelling of booze now can we, but perhaps, this kind gaoler PC 'Busy' Tasker may just make you one of his coffee's without pissing in it or even 'rimming it' with his dick, like he normally does for all his lovely prisoners."

Pc Tasker gave an incredulous look before smiling, then walked towards the kitchen to make that coffee, but how the fuck did he know about that?

33

Cell Area, King Interview One, Sheffield HQ

After sticking a 'reserved' sign on a small interview room door within their cell area his DS looked confused. Knowing full well that besides Oliver King, who wasn't small, his solicitor Rick Green would definitely be in attendance, and everyone knew his stature, one hell of a giant of a man. A bigger than life character and an 'in your face' personality, not to mention enormous build, whose reputation preceded him. To such an extent even Hawk vented anger when discovering 'Tricky Ricky' would be representing King. Let alone this imminent prospect of sitting with him in a room, just about to happen.

They had previously only stared or glared numerous times at one another across courtrooms, bars and even streets, when with their respective entourages. Never before had they spoken directly, let alone been in such close proximity. Albeit Green attended their cells on a daily basis it was extremely rare for Hawk to enter this arena, to conduct an interview. But today these two gladiators would do battle.

Having identified King from the outset, let alone putting his career on the line in order to catch him red-handed, Hawk felt it only fitting he now finished off what he had started. To make sure they nailed an evil serial killer for good, and of course he got another chance to wind the fucker up and stare directly into his shark eyes.

He wanted to get 'up close and personal' so this answered his Detective Sergeant's confused look earlier. When watching him lean forward's to literally go 'face to face' with the bastard. He gave King this title for now, but in time it would transfer to Green who would get his full attention. Everyone knew he had got far too big for his boots, after he bragged to everyone he wore size fourteen.

Hawk quipped he would end up regretting that when he'd finished with him, because he would be sticking his own feet up his arse, so bigger the better. He had already set things in motion months earlier with a plan to lure him into a false sense of security. For now though he sat tight on this initiative until seeing how things progressed. If Green could be removed from his post, or he had a hold over him things at work would be a whole lot easier.

After both King and Green had completed their 'pre-interview chat', many considered it had been his first attempt at one-upmanship . When spending an hour together, before buzzing to let them know they were ready. So Hawk and his Sgt repaid the favour and then kept them waiting longer, until eventually entering, carrying several evidence bags- but giving no clue about what they contained, with PC Tasker on hand to open their interview room door.

Before closing it behind them Hawk asked him to make Mr Green and Mr King a drink (accepted by both) with Hawk giving him a wink. Everyone agreed afterwards this levelled up their scores, knowing full well how he would make it, as per normal.

Rick Green made a point of standing to his full height, looking down at Hawk who glanced up at him with a smile. Unable to do much about an obvious few inches' difference, but would bring him down a peg or two in many other ways. This would begin immediately, planning to destroy his client sitting directly opposite across a wooden table. Leaning forwards to get even closer to King, Hawk completely ignored Green from the outset. Even after proffering his hand for an introductory shake. Green smiled but stared angrily, having just been deliberately blanked, knowing he had one hell of a battle ahead with a man he'd heard so much about.

After giving King a police caution with a noticeable Irish accent, King acting under strict instructions, indicated clearly that he would indeed remain silent, because he didn't plan to say anything. Before making an exaggerated movement with both his hands placed over his mouth, seizing this moment to wink at both officers. Hawk smiled at his first venture to get a reaction from him, within barely a minute of entering the interview room when he sarcastically commented:

"Ahh look at you trying to be clever there from the outset Mr King. I bet you would much rather be doing that sort of thing to some dear old defenceless lady in her own home, rather than to yourself. But hey I'm guessing you'll be the only one doing a lot of things to yourself, starting from now and for the rest of your miserable life."

Hawk returned the wink when staring down directly into King's groin, before kissing the back of his own hand. It worked well, making King react, now going into a tirade of abuse towards him. Hawk noticed Green using an age-old tactic, by banging his leg into his clients, reminding him to shut up and say nothing. Hawk suddenly turned to Green, saying to him.

"Wow, you'll both end up with bruises on yer legs at this rate Tricky, if you carry on reminding him to shut up banging him so hard under the table."

After this the gloves were off and chaos ensued with endless abuse thrown by everyone. But every now and then this did get interrupted with a couple of relevant questions about a few 'Snuff' murders around Sheffield. During verbal melees Hawk clearly picked up Green had baited him with several comments, suggesting he was losing it, after throwing his best cut-glass crystal whiskey tumbler against his office wall. Also asking if he could afford to replace it on his pittance of a wage, with this making Hawk glare at him in anger.

Returning upstairs to their CID office with exhibit bags still unopened, they now decided to change tactics for their next interview. Having only managed to ask a few relevant questions over half an hour. But at least they had all got a lot of pent-up anger off their chests.

It had to get better, it couldn't get much worse, that was for sure. DS Jagger had also picked up on several reference's about smashing that whiskey tumbler. He couldn't help wonder how Green knew. It made him consider if he had someone on his payroll inside their office?

He would have been well and truly gobsmacked had Hawk told him then and there how Green knew so much. But he would share that detail with him, about who had been spilling the beans over a few drinks later on. When finishing their interviews, but he knew this would only be achieved if they did actually manage to ask enough questions.

Before it descended into an all-out brawl, and he really didn't give a flying fuck if it went that way. Both his gloves were off and he wouldn't wait for the bell to throw the first punch.

34

Cell Area, King Interview Two

Without them even realising it, things had already got off to a better start because they weren't offered a drink of tea, which confused PC Tasker, who had already had a drink of water to oblige the expected demands placed on him today.

This time King appeared subdued, even Rick Green remained seated when they entered the room, allowing them all to stay calm to cover so much of their wealth of evidence against him. Pulling out file, folders and handwritten notes, all connecting him to so many murders as they began to convince King that it was a lost cause. But they saved their best for last reading from a detailed statement telling him it had been taken from retired DS Andy Laptew, making King speak for the first time.

"Mr Toast, don't tell me he's still alive."

They assured him he was because he had taken great joy in giving such a detailed damning statement against him only days earlier, outlining how he had murdered an old lady in London just before World War 2 when his old man died during his arrest.

King held up his hand, it was his turn to lean across their desk before speaking in a strong Cockney accent, saying:

"Died! You're having a facking laugh; he was executed in front of me, then they all lied to a coroner to cover it up; he was the killer, not me. Your 'fat lad' ex-copper has had an axe to grind against me since then, so his statement is worth jack shit."

Hawk had been uncertain as to when he was going to play his ace to nail this bastard for good, but after just watching his outburst of emotion for his old man, who he hated, he knew now was right. With a significant pause for effect, he pulled out a box with holes clearly made on its lid before shaking it up and down, so you could clearly hear it had something inside banging around as Hawk put on a scary voice before staring directly at King saying:

"Looks like yer mammy has made another comeback after you buried her by that Oak tree. Would you like to give her a hug or stroke her head, Mr Oliver Wick? I bet being left alone was a real hair-raising experience for her."

This brought every member of staff running into their room after King's loud harrowing scream. He couldn't control his anger as he dived forwards to grab hold of his precious doll as Hawk got out of the room with every gaoler needed to drag their prisoner back into his cell as even Mr Green looked bemused and off guard.

So much so, Hawk really had to resist his overwhelming temptation to land a sly punch on the bastard. Nobody paid them any attention, even Green himself stared down a cell corridor at his client, who now acted like a man possessed. This time they returned to their office agreeing it had gone a bit better, but they needed one more interview before they could charge him later on tonight.

They couldn't wait to see his reaction when showing him what they now knew to be Jean Dans old handcuffs. Plus, his glasses case, with its utility tool that still had traces of hair on its scissors from recently "Snuffed" women. One of whom didn't get to bake her son a birthday cake. Hawk's birthdays had all come at once, before instructing everyone on his Incident Room to make sure they were free later on for one hell of a piss-up. DS Jagger then convinced him not to begin their next interview wearing handcuffs with an Acorn in his mouth.

Hawk assured him he had said it in jest, he would never stoop so low before throwing him a wink, explaining he had to nip out for half an hour to do a bit of shopping.

35

Cell Area, King-Post Interview Three

After many years of defence work, he thought he had seen it all but after they had thrown everything at his 'prize client', who was going to have one of the biggest most prestigious trials ever held, he looked across at Oliver King hiding his repulsion felt towards him, but he knew full well he didn't get paid to like them.

They had now covered well over a dozen cold hearted murders with Jean Dan's holding an important key to his defence. It linked in directly with his 'Derwent Experience' after being sent there as a young boy, but most importantly it would allow a damning case against his fellow 'Acorns' to be used to destroy police credibility.

DI Tony Drummond's statement, just read, made it obvious he must have colluded with his fellow DI to cover up his own actions from years ago when they killed their abusers- only to now pin it all on his client, using him as a scapegoat for their own actions.

He had always been taught by his mentor that if you can stop their first 'domino of evidence' from falling, then any others directly in front remained standing. It meant your client at the end of this line, no matter how long it was didn't take a fall. It would take a lot of work, a lot of research, but with one hell of a pay day.

Thankfully he had King on board, not to say a word at this early stage, about him joining an 'Acorn Club' tree gang. Otherwise it allowed them plenty of time to re-group to sort out their stories, chopping down any defence tactics at trial. Far better to make amazing revelations at Crown Court, to call shell-shocked, last minute unsuspecting witnesses. Including Sonya Child's who he'd come across many times at Magistrates Court. Who would crumble before a jury to win an amazing victory. To elevate both his standing and position within legal circles, bringing in a flood of contracts from barristers seeking his services for pre-court work generating rich rewards.

He knew King to be a serial killer and that a loved-up Solicitor, soon to return from holiday, would no doubt roll over to give evidence against his client. But they would clearly show, from notes made in their overhead 'crossword evidence', Carter had been the main protagonist. Preying upon his vulnerable client when meeting him in a busy pub where things were misheard. King only egged him along and refused to comply hence only called to help his mother with a pill dispenser, just like he had done with so many others.

With numerous practices and employees having access to hundreds of clients personal detailed information it could be anyone accessing a shared database. Held between five GP surgeries all of whom covered Sheffield City, along with its surrounding boroughs. Including its small villages, with lone occupants on medication. Presenting an opportunity to enter homes to commit heinous offences. But only if those could be proven against his client and Hawk's fancy coloured bar graphs fell well short of that evidential burden placed on the prosecution. This wasn't some sort of school project, it would become a full-blown Headline topping Prime Time TV sensational trial. With lots of twists and turns on a winding road, heading directly at that smug fucker Hawk. He planned to shoot him down, and pluck him feather by feather in front of a startled jury.

Arrangements had already been made for him to sit face to face with another animal known as Mole, who would be paid well to do what he did best. Dig up lots of dirt but during the day and night. Plus his little 'Ace in the Police pack' who may deliver lots more when watching Hawk's reaction after taunting him about smashing his engraved whiskey tumbler. It confirmed what she shared within a day of his outburst to be accurate and true. With her continued help he may shatter Hawks dream of convicting King. Even if they somehow got a result, with everything now known about his client's sad upbringing could be dynamite, to blow their case apart after what 'Oliver Wick' had been through as a child. It really did read just like a Victorian tragedy before saved and eventually adopted.

If needed to be read out chapter and verse to twelve good men and women on their jury, he would have to make sure they had been given a box of tissues. But that old dear of a Clerk Betty, covering Northern Circuit Crown Courts wouldn't be allowed near this trial. Green discovered recently she used to be a paramour for a few old school detectives, one of whom paved the way for Tony Drummond to become a good friend and valued future contact.

All these hardened detectives operated in a dangerous world, needing a safe haven for endless drinking when prone to tell a tale or two. Often these whispers got a little louder after whiskey chasers and one of his clients' dad did the pouring. His son had recently landed a fabricated charge and sentence, but now as the landlord of their retreat he more than willingly kept him fully updated. Including all he knew about Betty, with 'old tales' about who had called around to benefit from her company in many ways. Including jury gossip and updates during trials to help them plan how to present evidence before they were sent out to reach a decision.

One of many pieces of evidence he now pulled together not only to bring their case tumbling down, but to sort out Hawk for good. He had to be his biggest nemesis, to have him moved on or sacked his ultimate goal to make his future time in Sheffield much easier. He planned to take the wind from under his wings to ground this Irish bastard, before stamping all over his nest.

With his size fourteen shoes this would be so easy to do. Hawk had at long last met his match.

36

Wonderland Store, Sheffield City Centre

He entered the busy city centre toy shop with many screaming children pointing at everything on display, asking if they could 'please have that one'. Only to then be dragged away with parents wishing they had never entered this store in the first place. With partners trying their best to hide what they had bought, without them seeing, soon to be, Christmas presents.

Hawk didn't have that problem because his children were well beyond 'buy me a toy' age. Who probably wouldn't ever be allowed any gifts he bought them again. With his three X wives bitterly moving on and never wanting anything more to do with him. After realising what a lying, cheating bastard he was, not wanting his offspring to ever know their dad. To allow them all to rebuild broken lives with new partners. He knew they thankfully now appreciated what they had, instead of himself, a hedonistic bastard. Who they married young, when taken in by his charm before his demons kicked in, and he treated them like shit.

With a letter from his eldest daughter folded in his pocket acting as a poignant reminder of venom being vented towards him. All things considered he knew many didn't regard him as a bird soaring high, but a snake sliding about on its belly. But he did leave the store with a carrier bag full of toys after buying three dolls, selected because they had long hair, his main reason for choosing them. Their recipient now languishing in a cell for his detention overnight. But now on his own because the last thing Hawk wanted was a witness to back up incredulous claims that toy dolls were held by an open cell hatch, who all talked to him, stating they were his mother. Before their long hair suddenly set on fire as a high-pitched voice cried out, asking him to help them, because they didn't want to be bald again. Later on it was wonderful, before heading out for his team's celebratory piss-up, to hear King cry out like a child. Begging to be left alone when completing his evil deed. Causing a drunk in a cell opposite to call out for a light, after seeing flames. Only to see a smartly dressed man holding a doll with its head on fire laughing loudly, and talking in a funny voice. A story he told everyone for weeks to come, but nobody believed a pissed-up hallucinating, withdrawing idiot.

When Hawk heard his cries and screams, he knew his five pounds had been well spent. Just to make the murdering bastard suffer, all part of his torture to make King crack. To admit to everything at court with a quick easy trial to 'Keep it Simple'. This made him think about an old timer detective who would surely approve of his underhand tactic. After what this caged animal had done over these last forty years. Earlier on King had been told by his bent solicitor to 'remain silent' but now it was rewarding to hear his voice tonight.

As Hawk left a smoky cell area a young officer starting his career, but carrying an injury so confined to indoor duties, looked totally bemused after what he'd just seen and heard. Staring confused at his three much older colleagues, who had nearly finished their careers, for some sort of an explanation. But they imitated the 'three wise monkeys', placing hands over eyes, mouth and ears to send a clear message.

Something he would do over many years himself, until one day he too would be sat, a good few stone heavier, waiting to get out in one piece, with a pension. By then he would also be able to recite endless incredulous tales witnessed first-hand over many pints. Including the one about a six-foot Bunny, who hopped down to their cells all year round. But instead of eggs he handed out beatings to those who had assaulted fellow officers during arrest. Magistrates heard this story many times over the years, as defendants stood marked and bruised before them in Court.

DS Jagger , who organised events for their Sports and Social Club, including its Easter Parade Celebration, had a whisper in his fluffy ear one year. From an irate prosecution's inspector, keeping children waiting for their chocolate treats. Suggesting that perhaps he should stick to only handing out gift-wrapped eggs, and didn't hop down the cells for a while.

Magistrates were now starting to ask him far too many questions, far too often.

37

High Rise Apartment, Manor Estate, Sheffield

A meet in a dimly lit club had led to fumbles in a dark corner, before ending up now, in what appeared to be a bedroom of a high-rise apartment; slowly being illuminated by a rising sun, with dull daylight shining through a net curtain heavily soiled. It hung down from a piece of flimsy plastic rail bowing in the middle, attached either side to rotting window frames. These were almost black in colour, contrasting with the only visible white he could see – that being thin wispy strands of hair, now noticed when shadows retreated, beneath blonde soiled hair extensions – on last night's conquest head.

His 'babe', who had told him in such great lascivious detail what she was going to do to him when they got back to her place – now lay comatose like – facing away from him in a single bed. Hawk could only imagine what she must look like from the front, after seeing a well-faded dolphin tattoo on her sagging, weathered, wrinkly skin. A phantasmagoria image from shafts of light – showing how it hung down from skeletal shoulder blades – suddenly moving, following a cackle of a cough, loud snoring, or some horrendous guttural wheezing.

When daring to lean over to take a look at her face he cringed – sincerely hoping and praying she had collapsed in time, preventing her from following through with promises of sordid deprivation. Hawk glanced down in horror at his genitals that did appear to have peanut butter all over them with faded lipstick smears descending from his chest to waist. Stifling a scream he cringed, placing both hands to his face – only adding to his woes with a rancid smell on his fingers, knowing full well they hadn't eaten a takeaway.

After a celebratory drink following multiple murder charges against Oliver King, he had matched everyone round for round – but this only just took effect on him despite others, being such well-seasoned hardened drinkers – seeing sense to stagger home. Sadly, as always, he needed more, venturing out again all alone before finally finding himself heavily under the influence of pills taken earlier in a run-down salubrious part of their city – but he wasn't alone long before joined, by what now lay next to him.

After making a speedy but silent exit, he walked down 20 flights of stairs with every lift broken, jogging his memory about a crime scene a few weeks ago, found not to be a murder but a death by misadventure. Voices in his head told him once again he had to grow up and get a grip – to take his finger off a self-destruct button before losing everything.

Luckily his car, abandoned at an angle across two parking bays – with its front wheel on a kerb – hadn't been vandalised. Hawk now had an image of her head bobbing up and down in front of his lap when driving, crashing into his mind, running his hand over what he now knew to be a wig with hair extensions. Such a shame he hadn't realised that then or even after – when they had spent ages climbing stairs before things had really gone downhill.

After checking himself out in his cars internal mirror he saw blood shot eyes, also noticing broken capillaries around his nose and cheeks; clearly giving away his drinking habits along with a red glow to his face. Perhaps this would be a blessing in disguise with him beginning to age disgracefully. Hawk wasn't a vain man but knew that even with young attractive women, he had a chance. They were still drawn to him, perhaps his charisma with a soft Irish accent helped – but he knew more than anything else what was going to end everything for him unless he finally got a grip- his dipsomaniac alcohol intake.

His dad and uncles, now long gone bless them, all had this "curse" – when he grew up, before running away with his mother to England. Desperately needing to find a safe haven – with phone calls to loved ones gradually phased out – in fear of being discovered.

This reminded him he had a phone call to make when he was fit enough to hold a conversation, without slurring words or sounding hungover – but his hand out of habit momentarily wavered towards a glove box, where he knew his old well used hip flask would be found full of Irish whiskey. For now though – he resisted temptation for a much needed 'hair of the dog'.

This also reminded him it was a real shame he hadn't managed to walk away last night before he drove an old drunk dog home. Perhaps he was just as bad when all said and done, but surely to God this was going to be his 'Wake up Call' after waking up next to that hound.

Both of them similar when creating false illusions to all those around them – with what they showed to the world on the outside. When inside they slowly self-destructed – as time marched relentlessly against them- with it now gathering momentum and becoming more and more out of step with reality...

38

Beachy View Home, Brighton

He heard the incoming warning signal of 'Nurse Ratched's' leather heels on a wooden corridor floor getting louder – meaning she approached their 'sun room' sounding as though she was on a mission. Andy managed to shuffle back into his chair, just in time to pretend he hadn't been up to any mischief. He made it appear, he was slowly waking from a nap as she entered, heading directly for him and holding a piece of paper in her hand.

"That lovely detective just rang to let you know that all is 'OK'. I made a note of what he wants me to read to you."

"He will never see the light of day again after you gave us a helping hand with our investigation. I will call in person to update you about trial details with a few packets of custard creams as a well-deserved reward because you deserve them. A big thank you from all my team to DS Andrew Laptew. PS: Once a detective, always a detective."

Nurse Ratched couldn't hold back a smile at the thought of him calling in after dropping a little hint when he rang with his message for 'DS Laptew' when letting him know she didn't mind taking things down for him. During a short pause, she had felt herself blush, it had been quite a while, but she would be more than a willing partner if he fancied an older woman to jump on top of him in full nurse uniform.

To see Andy Laptew beam with joy again, made her day – sinking back in his high chair after giving her one of his cheeky smiles with a big thumbs up before nodding at a solitary custard cream left on a plate between the 'girls'. Just like all her other prisoners they slept soundly, mouths open with dentures rattling, almost falling out. She handed his treat to him with a wink and a smile after noticing that yet again he had altered their clock by advancing its hands several hours, so once again he could tease them when waking – that it was such a shame they had overslept after just missed an amazing dinner trolley. Last time he told them it had been one hell of a roast beef dinner with trimmings galore – but he managed to get two down him – rather than seeing it all go to waste.

She knew it kept him going – but sadly, she also knew from his latest scan results read earlier that his tumours had grown significantly, meaning he wouldn't be entertaining them for much longer – possibly with only a few months left to live.

Perhaps he may not get to enjoy packets of biscuits promised – but at least he would die knowing that the 'one that got away' as she had overheard him say to DI 'blue eyes' had been caught by sounds of it. Rarely had she ever shown any feelings or emotions towards any residents, but circumstances prompted her to give his arm a little squeeze, before whispering softly into his ear:

"Enjoy your biscuit, DS Laptew, you are a lovely man – why don't you have a little nap, if your dentures drop out ill pop them back in for you."

Andy Laptew laughed – but he did feel unusually tired today, just like he had done over these last few weeks, meaning that for once he did actually manage to drift off into a deep sleep. But only after eating his reward when once again he pictured a young ginger haired lad giving him a stare, before that final wink, last time he had seen him all those decades ago. When the little bastard continuously played up to his boss, who had fallen in lust with an equally gullible social worker- also believing her 'poor little preyed upon darling', when constantly coming out with such utter bullshit.

If only they had listened to him. Bastards.

39

Faculty of Humanities,
Sheffield City Polytechnic

Steeped in history with furniture to match, he reclined in a beautiful chesterfield chair opposite a mahogany desk. Admiring such a distinctive clock, he noticed it bore a small plaque with only a single letter – this didn't give much away unlike pictures and photos, some family portraits and others abstract. Her personal assistant explained she would be through in a minute, nodding to an annex, adjoining her main study area before then pouring him a cup of tea. He stared down in amazement when offered a large plate of triangular shaped chocolates.

This hit home like a thunderbolt, unable to hide his shock and surprise just as Sophie Ford entered from her adjoining room towards him with her hand proffered for a warm handshake, she looked directly into his eyes saying;

"There you go, 'Tony D', I remember you always pushed ahead of other children – to have first choice from the chocolate tin I always brought to Jean's house, you were on a mission to make sure you got that green foiled chocolate triangle. It was always your favourite, but there was only ever one of them amongst all the other flavours – so you had to fight for it."

As this vivid memory came back to him, he glanced across at a photograph on the desk noticed earlier. Jean Dan stood next to Professor Ford, posing together with a large pearl necklace shared between them, worn around their shoulders; both smiling at a camera giving a celebratory thumbs up.

This was the same necklace worn now, as he felt tears on his cheeks, prompting him to ignore her hand but throw his arms around her instead to give her a loving embrace – almost bordering on a bear hug. This was reciprocated with a squeeze as Sophie Ford whispered in his ear:

"I was there for you then, Tony, when you shared with me what Jean's son was doing to you all, and I'm here for you now. I've read local papers covering in detail all about this 'Sheffield Snuffer' not to mention two Derwent bodies recently found handcuffed in an exposed grave. I'm guessing Oliver Wick as he was then has come back to haunt you as Oliver King?"

Once again, she had managed to shock and surprise him, at one point he had even considered that after over 30 years she would not even know his name when booking an appointment to see her. Let alone remember in such detail with so much clarity, all about her 'chocky chats' doing one to one's with them all, using a treat to break down barriers to gently gain trust. Most of them had told her Jean's son pretended to be a Dinosaur – but they all knew he really was a monster.

Yes – they now needed to chat about another monster that had come back to terrorise them, who needed to be dealt with urgently before it became too late for many. Tony Drummond opened up completely to tell her everything that had happened, for what he thought would be the first time with his 'Acorn Club' extracting revenge against two paedophiles – before a sudden disappearance when 'one that got away' resigned from his job as a policeman, to avoid retribution.

They could now make an obvious link that 'Oliver Wick' snuffed out Jean Dan – using her 'memory box' key to steal handcuffs; but these would connect them to the Derwent bodies – giving his defence ammunition to deflect and undermine the prosecution case – albeit they were young children that acted together to stop abusive behaviour against them.

Professor Ford reacted as would have been expected upon hearing Tony's startling revelations, for what he believed to be the first time. But she had heard this account many times before over so many years from the 'one that got away', who was now stood out of sight only a few yards away in her annex – listening intently to everything that was being said.

She assured Tony it would be her pleasure to help them as she already began formulating in her mind, with her position and contacts, how she was going to avenge this murder of her dear old friend at the hands of a recently incarcerated 'Sheffield Snuffer'. He may be on remand in a prison cell, no doubt under a segregation order – but that wouldn't protect him – because he would most certainly be 'dealt with' especially now Tony had given her a legitimate professional reason to gain access to him.

She was mindful more than most that there were many ways for this to become a reality, as she looked across at a famous print of a painting on her wall done by a Norwegian artist called Edvard Munch. It showed a person stood alone with both hands to his face – on a bridge overlooking a Fjord – with a look of horror on their face.

In her native language it's famous title, meant 'Shriek', its English translation described its distinctive vivid blood red skies above a solitary disturbed figure – with an incredible look of anguish. It was known as *The Scream of Nature.*

Sophie's original surname had derived its meaning from Fjords but she had changed it to fit in better with her acquired identity, when adapting to her new surroundings, to help people in her chosen vocation.

Oliver Wick had done similar – but for evil reasons – to inflict harm, but he would soon find himself in new surroundings with some major changes coming his way by using the man next door. He didn't know it yet but he would soon become a key component of her plan, who for now held back his own cries of torture and pain. After discovering for the first time that his dear mother had been murdered in her own home – by one of those children they were abusing in his village. He now put both his hands to his own face – only just managing to stifle his anguished scream.

40

Holding Cells, Interview Room, Sheffield Magistrate's Court

They were afforded a spacious room with its high ceiling creating an echo, normally set aside for last-minute visits between solicitors and their new clients – before appearing in front of a magistrate when kept overnight on remand. Most of those who had been arrested a day or so earlier now got to speak to someone who was going to help them try to get bail at the very least. Often, they had to help them understand to forget everything they had been promised by the detectives – to explain they must surely have admitted to some of these offences now typed up on a TIC schedule. But when they looked vacantly and asked "what's one of them" – that answered the question – having denied offences charged it supported the fact that all the 'taken into consideration' additional crimes – were obviously never admitted.

When another realisation dawned on them that they hadn't even been interviewed but did remember 'men in suits' bringing them a tea with two sugars – when having a smoke together, and chatting about football for best part of half-an-hour before telling them, "Not to worry, we will sort this all out for you."

Professor Ford sat waiting patiently, after thanking her escort – a gorgeous looking inspector whom she had heard about from Tony Drummond, who had looked her up and down before a subconscious smile of approval, knowing exactly what he was thinking. Tony had used a cover story; they were more than "just good friends" so she played along with it during earlier conversation – telling him she looked forward to giving Tony her report when they dined together in a few nights time.

This 'Hawk' character appeared switched on – he correctly identified her accent as either Norwegian or Swedish after it turned out he had once dated an air hostess, who worked for Scandinavian Airlines, and came from 'one or the other'. Sophie soon levelled the 'I'm a smart-arse score' by telling him Galway always reminded her of rugged terrain – did he miss those amazing sights before moving to the Belfast area?

Hawk clapped his hands – but gave her an uneasy look with a noticeable change in his body language; with even a tell-tale variance in his voice tone. Most revealing of all was a quick eye movement of his pupil to an area associated with memory recall. This indicated a painful unhappy reason for leaving his Emerald Isle – but she wasn't here to psycho analyse him, to open up an unhappy upbringing or to revisit a trouble past – today her full focus and undivided attention would be on a man under guard – now approaching them down a long cell corridor. He wore heavy duty prisoner escort handcuffs, that he kept on glancing down at – until his wild staring eyes locked on Hawk, making the detective quickly move out of his way and leave the room. Coinciding with Oliver King noticeably tensing – then jerking towards him as two prison officers, chosen for their physical stature – took a firm grip of him, telling him to 'calm down'. It didn't take much to see the ill feeling and friction between 'good guy', 'bad guy' with no doubt a confrontational history between Hawk and King. Some shared by Tony D, who had painted quite a picture of his fellow officer. Sophie considered how much the two guys may have in common.

King's escorts sat him down opposite her offering to remain with them. Professor Ford loved this request, allowing her to begin her performance. Explaining that wouldn't be necessary before strategically stroking King's ego by beginning to nod at him and pay him attention in a rhythmic time-spaced, eye contact fashion.

She began by explaining he was innocent until proven guilty, so please remove those ridiculous bulky escort manacles. Her next staged delivery explained her report had to be forwarded directly to his Lordship, and not for a smooth talking Irish detective (with her throwing a glance in the exit direction that Hawk had taken) Everything said here and now with her client (giving ownership and attachment to him) would only be read by the Judge, and not police officers desperate to convict and detect. Who were under immense pressure to get a result. For many reasons her role had to be impartial, as a neutral observer, with no leakage.

Meaning they had to be left alone, and at this point she knew King was hooked by him subconsciously showing he backed and supported an interview. Not only did he now face her but his shoulders were directly aligned to hers, having been drawn in to such an extent he now leant forwards, ignoring his escorts who were authoritarian figures wearing uniforms.

They couldn't be trusted, she could.

Sophie Ford jumped for joy inside, within a few minutes she had already landed this sick murdering bastard.

When alone, she enquired politely to be allowed to call him 'Oliver'. Drawing him even closer like a moth to a flame. She smiled to herself, with this comparison. A man originally called Wick who snuffed women out like candles, including her dear wonderful friend Jean Dan. So for her sake and many others she began to wax lyrical.

She hoped and prayed Jean looked down from above when they spoke together for an hour, only skirting over topics with no real meaning. Totally foreign from her clinical approach during normal detailed assessments, when making copious notes to support her findings. King would find out soon that these would be more than enough to keep him banged up for the rest of his life, but exactly where she wanted him to be, and that wasn't a prison.

Because after writing her damning report when making up 'trigger warning signals' she clearly showed he was clinically and mentally insane. Indeed, one of the worst cases ever encountered in her extremely long and distinguished career. Meaning he wasn't even fit enough to appear at Crown Court. Only one conclusion could now be drawn – to issue a Mental Assessment Custody Order by their trial Judge.

It meant King would be transferred from Prison, with immediate effect, to a secure Mental Asylum for Lunatics. For a month of analysis and further interviews. During this time, a Defence expert witness could attend if King's barrister wished to contest or challenge her initial or future findings.

God willing it wouldn't be much longer now before Oliver King found himself in the company of another Lunatic. Who really wanted to meet him having heard so much about a now infamous "Sheffield Snuffer" But for once in his troubled life he wouldn't want to play Noughts and Crosses with a new opponent.

For her 'fait accompli' Sophie had to meet up next with a man who held a coveted position, no less than their Sheffield Recorder. A highly placed Circuit Judge now overseeing proceedings, after hearing this it really had been 'music to her ears'.

One of several music related clichés to be used when renewing her acquaintance with him after all these years. When he would fully agree with her in-depth report without any hesitation.

Because his learned Judge really wouldn't want her 'favourable report' done many years ago for his Godson, to go public. When escaping a prison sentence after thrusting a drum baton into the eye of another band member. Causing a partial loss of sight after a drunken drug induced fight when rehearsing at university.

His Lordship overstepped the mark to generate enough doubt during his trial to suggest he had suffered a psychosis after several 'adverse childhood experiences' following abuse by a senior pupil at their Public School. Reflected in his bands choice of name 'Handy Prefects' and why performing gigs wearing school blazers.

Sophie had taught his Godsons sister when a student at her University all about the consequences of childhood 'adverse conditions' with a common post-reaction indicated by hostility towards others.

A young ambitious Sophie Ford agreed to support his defence team, to enhance her ever growing portfolio gaining recognition within Academic circles but Sophie discovered following his cross examination and evidence his Godson greatly embellished his answers, following her detailed report. And his Lordship fully complicit contributed to their common cause by influencing the jury suggesting a 'momentary lapse of reason' following flashbacks, diminishing criminal liability.

Yes, if needed to get her way with Oliver King, she would keep on reminding her learned Justice that without 'banging her own drum' too much, she really needed that Order granting. Oh, and by the way how's your godson doing, I haven't seen him since you ended up overseeing his criminal trial. Is he still in a band?

If needed she would even mention about 'keeping an eye out for him' but eventually the Judge would play along, and both of them would end up in perfect harmony.

If he wanted to keep his lofty position and continue to wear his robe and wig, by all accounts worn when meeting up with questionable partners away from court in hotel bedrooms.

41

Arrivals Hall, Manchester Airport

He felt discomfort realising there was still some beach sand in both of his socks – with attempts mid-flight to wriggle his feet out of his shoes thwarted by swelling around both ankles from the effects of altitude.

With that in mind he purposefully avoided looking down at his wife's legs because they appeared swollen at the best of times – but his spirits were lifted in hope and anticipation that any time soon he would hear "such sad news" that whilst away his dear old mother had departed. This would allow his plans to leave take off almost immediately – allowing him to restart his life – with the love of his life, who really understood him – and didn't resemble a beached whale.

After landing – he began to ponder on the value of his inherited home – along with his settlement figure when divorced before noticing just beyond 'nothing to declare' – a group of men all suited up. One of whom looked familiar, perhaps he was that detective who had seemed miles away when doing that elimination interview with Oliver King several weeks ago?

Today though, he seemed a different person, much more alert and livelier, even managing a nod with a wave after making eye contact. He headed towards him, perhaps he was going to break the news to him – but suddenly his world fell apart; making him collapse to his knees after this officer brought his hand up to his face to cover his nose and mouth before saying:

"Snuffing to declare Mr Carter? I have to update you that's not what Oliver King is telling us, I'm guessing it was a case of will power that failed miserably – because your mum, thankfully – can still send her love."

Things had just become a whole lot more uncomfortable for him – feeling that the sands of time were now running out. They sat either side of him, all the way back to the police station, unable to shut him up. If he hadn't been making so many confessions, they may well have been tempted to do an 'Oliver King' and put their hands over his mouth.

42

Exercise Yard, Derby Prison

Banged up in his cell – for 23 hours a day – on a Category A High Risk Wing had helped to focus his mind, in between fitful bouts of unsettled sleep. Not aided by deranged hardened prisoners venting anger towards him, shouting abuse and threats. Normally only visible to them when flanked by two burly members of staff during an escort to a small exercise yard with its wire mesh covering every wall and ceiling.

This certainly added to its 'caged animal' effect, plus he now prowled just like one circling its perimeter edge, helping to focus his mind with every step to make sense of everything going on connected to him, hidden beneath the surface.

Different images from a distant memory suddenly became clearer in his mind as he fine-tuned them all, giving his full attention to focus on what must be a credible link. To connect his fleeting past in Derwent to what had now been put in place by a prosecution team. Obviously hell-bent on having him sent to an asylum following an application accepted by a trial judge, all contained within his rolled-up bundle of papers now held in his hand like a baton.

It all read like a horror story that was a work of pure fiction with its author none other than his 'smiling assassin', who had sat across from him, luring him into her web of deceit. This ran his chain of thoughts back to a 'music teacher' who had chosen his name, as discovered later, that was an anagram of spider.

Who had touched him between his legs as his friend, their babysitter, who became a policeman sat watching, who was Jean Dan's sick bastard of a son. His mind wandered off in her direction, helping him connect up with activities inside her home after 'dinosaur' had moved out to begin police training. He clearly remembered a lady turning up with sweets, who spoke to him softly, telling him there was nothing to worry about, because she had nothing to do with what had gone on, she was there to help him.

His mouth dropped open in shock. He froze still with this recollection, causing him to drop all his papers which blew across an enclosed yard. But like him they remained trapped inside its cage with nowhere to go. Perhaps that may change very soon because he had just made an amazing connection after remembering this same lady speaking kind words about her dear friend Jean Dan at her funeral.

Her distinctive voice resonated over and over again in his head, both back then but most importantly just recently heard again with its same vernacular and tone. Back then as a boy, enjoying his sweets, he had asked if she was from 'darn south'. It had made her laugh out loud, explaining where she came from was much further and in a much colder direction. He remembered she also brought gifts for Jean Dan, which she willingly accepted then displayed with pride – lots of books that were going to help her studies, lined up on a shelf in the kitchen – ironically placed next to the box of draughts – with its hidden meaning and its pieces (when found) possibly allowing you to escape from the evil clutches of others. What a coincidence.

Oliver King ran around a wind-swept yard, scooping up papers, held against wire mesh fences before staring down at the name on this damning psychological profile. It was Professor Sophie Ford who, if his appeal against her report wasn't successful in a week's time, would have him sent to a lunatic asylum with a clear and likely outcome that he would end up staying there for the rest of his life – under her governance.

No doubt it wouldn't take long after that before he did become, as described in her report, a 'deranged psychopath beyond help' – just like all the other mad bastards she also had locked up there.

Once a day, they allowed him a five-minute phone call – unsupervised – and today every second would be needed to update his solicitor, Mr Green. To verbally join up the dots, to complete the puzzle – to show he could connect Tony Drummond and Jean Dan, to Sophie Ford. With a clear picture, now becoming visible – to prove collusion – with their lost friend – a common link. Mr Green had explained to him his theory to support his defence case – if they could stop that first domino from falling in their chain of evidence against him, then others would not topple – meaning the prosecution would fail to convict him at court. Oliver King realised now – they were all making moves against him, playing a game with the rest of his life at stake.

(But Oliver King would never truly fathom the enormity of the final piece of their plan – destined for him. To connect, in a way, that he could never have imagined. Nor – who would be present at the time to make it possible – and be allowed the luxury of watching it happen.)

43

Green Solicitor's, Sheffield

Before leaving his beloved North East after an 'indiscretion' discovered by his wife (thankfully with so many not), Rick Green had been taught by a partner in their firm an important lesson about 'achieving through people', which basically meant you had to decide exactly what needed to be done, but then got another person to do it for you; it was all about delegation, because you couldn't do it all yourself.

In his line of work with such delicate and sensitive enquiries needing to be made, most of which were underhand not to mention potentially dangerous with many serious repercussions and consequences; it was this man sitting and taking notes opposite him today, who excelled in that field. When it came to digging into people's lives, to discover dark secrets or nuances which could be used to great effect to destroy a credible witness- making a mockery of an expert witness, sometimes bringing down a law abiding 'professional', normally in a police uniform or a suit and tie, who would pontificate that their integrity was always 'beyond reproach'.

If you paid enough money to get what you needed, then this brought large rewards at court, exactly why this small, stout, innocuous man who had commanded more money than others- was now going to get paid to help him. Because this particular private investigator used his nickname to promote his services, often telling clients with a sinister smile – 'Achieve your goal, use the Mole'. When it came to digging up past secrets or evidence to assist a defence team or undermine a police prosecution, Mark Jagger was your man, but today, even he looked up from his notebook to stop writing down what needed to be done before asking, "Are you sure about this, Mr Green?"

His terse reply left him in no doubt that 'Tricky Ricky' was going 'all in' to win this game- but he needed to play one hell of a hand because digging up dirt on a few people from a village he remembered called Derwent, during the war before it got flooded, that was fine, even if one was a small-time solicitor and one was a high-flying professor from Sheffield.

But to delve and pry into two detective inspector backgrounds, especially when one was the infamous Hawk, whose reputation preceded him after many prestigious cases at Crown Court, not to mention his own tight network around him- who willingly did whatever was needed to protect him, this was one hell of an ask.

So much so, he put his usual rate up even higher as he cleaned his thick rimmed glasses, making the office appear blurry for a while, but with a far too quick acceptance of his new fee, he clearly saw potential to make a lot of money if he dug down deep enough. He would have to be careful not to dig his own grave, and with this Derwent historical connection that brought a far greater relevance than normal after what was found there. Plus, he really couldn't work out why 'Tricky' was risking pretty much everything for this murdering psycho 'Sheffield Snuffer' bastard.

If there was a hidden reason, then he of all people should unearth it.

44

St Jude's Church, Bamforth

It wasn't often anyone wanted to do a 'graveyard watch' with its historical connection to working through the night to fight off body snatchers, or if anyone buried alive by accident, rang a bell string connected to their coffin to be rescued.

Today, though, Mark Jagger enjoyed his ploughman's lunch in this quaint village pub after getting one hell of a result. He reminded himself when chomping down on a pork pie it was down to his sagacity after hitting upon a clever idea to follow the bodies. After researching events in Derwent before its forced evacuation revealed exhumation then reburial of 68 former locals. They were initially put in an existing graveyard next to its small village church before relocation to a large site opposite where he now ate.

Luckily, they had grouped them together, meaning it had been made easy to identify their relatives and friends who had called over the last two days to pay respects, before laying fresh flowers or doing a clean or tidy around headstones. One in particular looking pristine after being visited and blasted with a strange looking device, by an even stranger looking man.

This had led to some interesting chat with revelations about events and life in and around their village in the early 1940s. All of which was in his ever-bulging folder along with remarkable links between Jean Dan and her now established close friend Professor Ford. They even appeared side by side on a named thesis report, covering a leading breakthrough technique to deal with mental illnesses. It was titled *Pearls of Wisdom*, stemming from a joint police operation from years ago with subsequent work on a main offender who had supplied thousands of perverse photographs of young children. This connection alone would achieve that much mentioned 'domino effect', allowing Rick Green to keep that first piece well and truly standing- but Mole had done what he did best. He had kept on digging a little more because time was money, especially on his new hourly rate affording him to sip on his fine wine that had replaced his usual pint of pale ale.

Perhaps, he may even have a pudding as he read notes made after his chat with a garage owner, Tom Coyne, who obviously looked as though at some point he had suffered a breakdown following his brother's suicide. With an invite back to his garage with several glances at a hand painted sign hung on his workshop wall made many years ago, that really opened up his memories. No doubt as much as those Acorns had all around their beloved tree house, sat high in an Oak when Tony and Sonya had helped make things a whole lot better for them all.

Oliver, the ginger-haired boy from 'down south' got a good few mentions as well, but that hadn't quite made it into his copious notes, because selective hearing was such an important attribute in his line of work, depending of course on who was paying for dinner, fancy wine and plenty more besides.

45

Green's Solicitors, Sheffield

Stroking his ego was the last thing he wanted to do because if nothing else, he would put up his hourly rate even more in future, but even 'Tricky' had to glance across at him with a look of approval. He in turn waited patiently for a response after what he had put together for him, knowing full well himself how impressive it was with lots of hard work paying off, plus an amazing bit of look. Being a clever man, he knew this part of his findings could best be described as 'serendipitous'.

It really had been a 'discovery by chance much to his benefit' after hearing a new barmaid pass comment at his local just before its weekly pub quiz began. He picked up that Hawk was the biggest bastard that had ever walked this Earth after his name was initially voiced by a recently released 'likeable rogue', who after one too many had vented anger towards a bent copper – after stitching him up with a TIC schedule that should have started 'once upon a time'….

It also turned out he featured in their barmaid's emotional background, when Hawk had taken full advantage of her position in the promotion board scenarios; to obtain all he needed to know to get to inspector. After leaving her police job as a civilian she had worked in numerous pubs, then clubs, bringing up on her own what she knew to be his child. He was born with 'vulnerabilities'. This now being a polite modern way of describing a spastic with her attempted suicide by overdose blamed by medical staff for causing her sons 'complications'.

It had cost Mole a small fortune in drinks after finishing her shift to slowly get it all out of her, but as usual he had just won a good cash prize from tonight's quiz single-handedly, so it had all been well worth it, plus it was one of numerous expenses he was claiming.

Guessing his report had now been read in its entirety, Mole broke their silence.

"I would say Vanda, the barmaid, is your best weapon to shoot down this high-flying bird, one hell of a bitter woman who until now has kept quiet, being riddled with self-guilt. There's little doubt that complications were caused after overdosing but if you get her to play ball – he's fucked with his cheating on the promotion boards. Perhaps, they may demote or move him back into a shiny new uniform, but you may consider even letting him know everything you know – but then hold onto it so you can have control over him – if nothing else, initial payback could be given by scuppering this 'Snuffer' case."

Tricky nodded back in agreement, he liked having holds over people, either when free fighting at his Martial Arts Club but better still at work when gloves were taken off to let people really feel some pain.

A 'no holds' barred approach was, without doubt, his best way of tackling Hawk to bring him down, it would certainly take wind from beneath his wings, knowing he had a little 'spaz' of a kid out there, plus with his cheating – he could be suspended or demoted at any time.

Hawk was well worthy of having his own folder tucked away along with many others in his wall safe; until it was needed to teach this Irish cunt a lesson to show him he had messed with the wrong person. Especially if he chose to destroy his credibility as lead investigator at their Oliver King trial with irrefutable evidence to connect them all in a 'tissue of lies' aimed at sending his client to a Loony Bin – in an attempt to cover up their conspiracy of deceit.

King had been right all along with his findings, after being sat on remand before being sectioned. His recollections and theory about his 'profiler' from years ago avenging an old friend was now fully supported.

Thoughts on how to best play his hand for maximum effect was interrupted by Mole.

"I sensed Hawk's X bird has even more against him, something really juicy but she clammed up after alluding to some pills he was popping and a mention of holding onto some evidence that could well and truly finish him. Only a name Bubbles was mentioned, who may be one of his snouts, perhaps a hooker, but when I asked too many questions that was conversation over. It's something juicy, Tricky, my radar tells me that I'm sure if I dug some more perhaps you can really pop his bubble."

Tricky paid off Mole with his much thicker than normal envelope but he didn't mind this outlay because he felt so good. In fact, he would make a call later after checking his diary to book himself a treat when his wife would think he was at a Karate class.

As always what she didn't know wouldn't hurt her- unlike a horny submissive dirty little bitch, he would be hurting in a few nights time once a price for extras had been negotiated.

He really liked this idea though of popping Hawk's bubble after giving Mole the go ahead – to do what he did best in life – and dig up some more dirt for him.

46

C Hall – Private Investigator, Sheffield Office

After pretending to read his Conditions and Codes of Practice forms, she signed them with a steely look of determination in her sad eyes after telling him he had come highly recommended. She was putting her trust in him with so much to lose, being in such a 'delicate' position, because there was no doubt he knew her husband by name. Perhaps with his own 'background' he would be extra keen to get a result 'for old time's sake' to settle many scores.

Retired DS Crowther drew heavily on his cigarette, filling his office with smoke, studying this beautiful lady who was far more than a token worn on an arm, she had done her homework before booking her appointment under a false name. He of all people could relate to this tactic, having lost his identity upon quitting his police career after being called in to see their 'Hatchet Man'. An ACC, who there and then left him with no other option; walk away now with dignity or be thrown out, they had enough on him to make him an offer he couldn't refuse. Thank God that comfy chair had been next to him when he collapsed from the shock of exposure.

He had run with a pack only to be snared, but after licking his wounds for nearly a year he had come back strong but needed to ditch his links to any previous career by losing his name before plying his new trade to a paying public. This had such a hidden irony because it was still those very same connections now rewarding him so well with so much success. He excelled at finding people as requested, more often than not on top of another woman in a high-end hotel, a back street hostel or a back seat of a car when testing out its springs.

His firms 'cover name' for him was a play on the fact that if you paid him his going rate, he would eventually 'see all' to capture it on film to support your dispute, normally a costly divorce. But now with far greater leverage than before, after using his particular set of skills to capture that moment for maximum effect.

This was why solicitor contacts recommended him, because his success was theirs, because they then earned- with a lucrative high-end divorce case to follow, after endless court appearances, letters and phone calls, all adding up before final settlement of bills.

Mick Crowther was more excited than ever since 'retiring' because he was going to take great delight in pulling out every trick in his book to nail a man who for years had been an enormous pain in CID's arse in Sheffield. Since relocating his firm from Newcastle, as rumours abound he had to flee when a crime lord client found out he wasn't only taking good care of him, but also his wife, before and during a remand then prison sentence.

Lisa Green, who sat before him today, had a soft sing song Geordie accent but she was a hardened woman- revealed when her story was relayed. After forgiving his indiscretion from a year earlier for their children's sake to start again after flitting from their palatial home, having to build up another legal business slowly but surely, only to hear rumours that once again her philandering husband was up to his old tricks. This time with call girls who he was paying for what she wouldn't give him, namely extreme sex with excessive demands and aggressive interactions.

But she had done her own detective work, because his evening karate class wasn't held one certain night of the week, but no doubt this was when he was throwing and slamming a dirty hooker around the hotel bedroom. Pinning her down to be sodomised after they had both taken cocaine or whatever pill cocktail he served up to enhance his performance.

Mick Crowther couldn't hide a smile on his face; it really was music to his ears having only recently heard over a few pints with former colleagues that a recent arrival in CID, an inspector who was a match for anyone was on a crusade to 'sort out' the bane of so many detectives' lives, who was their biggest pain in more ways than one.

None other than six-foot-five of defence solicitor Rick Green, a second Dan black belt, hard as nails plus as cunning and clever as any other legal professional they had ever encountered. It was why this Hawk character was on a mission to get rid of him, meaning he may just want to join forces with him soon, when he made him an offer he wouldn't be able to refuse.

Before Lisa Green departed, she dropped her biggest bombshell when glancing down at her signed condition and codes document.

"I will give you a healthy bonus on top of your fees on condition you nail the bastard, it must be possible with who he's fucking now, but I will back it both ways to get a result. Once upon a time he fucked a gangster's Moll, but he assured me her husband's syndicate would not kill him or come after us and our children on account of him holding onto damming evidence, collected over years of representing him. This relates to where a body is buried – he told me it was a nark who 'disappeared' – who didn't quite make a witness stand during his trial, who knew all about laundering their money – using a solicitor with Irish links. I know this will be Brendan, his old boss that's involved. But I think Ricky is hiding from me who they murdered – he doesn't trust me completely. I'm the stereotypical woman scorned. Somehow – a piece of jewellery and a suicide note comes into this hold over a gypsy called 'Mad Dog O'Connor' now in prison. But he is still overseeing all his boys – who are all related, perhaps brothers."

"My husband's practice is alarmed with this 'file of confidentiality' in his office inside a large wall safe, hidden behind our family portrait picture. It has a tumbler locking mechanism, but here's a helping hand for you because if those papers relating to a 'Mad Dog' O'Connor were no longer his protective shield, then at the very least, if he was updated to that effect, you've probably worked out that he would have to disappear- to run for his life."

"This mad dog is a gypsy boy, who once jumped in a pit bare-handed to kill two fighting dogs when young, after a wager he couldn't beat them, so imagine what he will have done to 'Tricky Ricky'. I know he is the only man my husband has ever feared in all his life."

Lisa Green threw an envelope on his desk, thanking him for his codes of practice- as she explained it was only right she gave him codes for her husband's practice. Mick Crowther opened it up to read a note inside with both Alarm and Tumbler Lock codes, along with a front door key. It meant that one way or another Tricky Ricky would be well and truly fucked, either by him, by Hawk or by Mad Dog.

After noticing a glint return to her eyes with even a hint of a smile, Lisa left before he opened his bottom desk drawer to pull out his bottle of whiskey. It was a bit early, but today of all days it was now time to celebrate this prospect of what a not-so-distant future held in store. He worked out a pecking order for contenders on his list, relating to who was having a piece of Green and in which order.

He burst out laughing because he was sure he knew which piece this Mad Dog O'Connor would have; he had no doubt at all that his boys would be giving this dog a bone when they delivered his pecker to him in prison.

It was a well-known fact – that you just don't fuck about with them Gypsies.

47

Pastures Asylum, Derbyshire – Yearly Assessment Hearing

His wooden chair creaked loudly after gently lowering himself into it, clutching his piece of paper to show his panel, sat in front of him why he could now be trusted, to have supervised association with other inmates within their asylum. But they all knew he only asked for a pen to show he could win most of his noughts and crosses. The lovely 'Clock Lady' who recently called to play – had told him how much better he was getting.

He had got off to a far better start than last year when he hadn't controlled his descent – causing his seat to splay out – disintegrating under his 25 stones of body weight. This was after he had ballooned in size over many decades – with his family always giving in to endless requests before visits – to bring a few treats, to help him along.

His mother had overfed him when a child on their farm believing it would make him bigger and stronger quicker, to then be able to help his dad- suffering with a bad back from years of hard labour. After non-stop endless manual lifting in fields, plus in lambing sheds and their piggery where animals had to be constantly carried.

With only sisters before him who fled the farm, to lead a far more comfortable life with men parading them on their arms for show. They were all six footers with their mother's looks- before her face became racked with worry after they battled on for years to survive many harsh winters nearly wiping them out of business.

Buxton Bob, even as a teenager, stood well over six foot but was obese and clumsy after a heavy fall with a head injury that didn't get checked by a doctor for many months, until he kept on falling over. He was found to have had a bleed on his brain with fluid retention on his frontal lobe that had slowed down his thinking, limiting his general understanding of what was going on around him.

Recent reports supporting his application were promising from all his key workers within his unit, full of praise for him with noticeable changes, plus improvement with his attitude and approach to staff and other patients. This had resulted with no incidents or near misses recorded against him for well over a year.

What eventually swung their decision was a detailed summary by one of their most senior physicians, who had told them that as part of what may be her final thesis before retirement, she was experimenting with new calming relaxation techniques. Professor Ford was delighted to report she had made incredible differences to Buxton Bob's demeanour after only a few sessions over recent weeks. It showed his capacity to change and adjust from how he had presented himself over these last 40 years since incarcerated when only a young man.

These findings weren't read to Bob before agreement – to allow him for his first time ever to have weekly interaction but with a caveat; it would be rescinded if there were any contra indications he wasn't coping and dealing or displayed negative traits with his new regime.

Had Professor Ford's report been read out to him then Buxton Bob, even with his limited understanding would have been very confused about how much he had done to impress her. That was because whenever the nice lady in her white coat – had sat with him alone for nearly an hour at a time, all she had ever done was play noughts and crosses as her 'Tick Tock' toy kept moving from side to side.

This was when she kept repeating about someone being 'naughty' so he was 'cross' before, at the end of their games, telling him how much better he was just prior to being taken back to his padded room by guards watching him closely as they always did.

He took that to mean at long last he had improved – winning more games than before and playing 'better' than normal – fantastic to hear after recently losing a few times to himself.

He liked 'Clock Lady' – but she wasn't the best at playing games – but he really loved that noise having learnt how to sound just like it. He could now whisper to himself for hours at a time , 'tick, tock, tick, tock'.

He still wondered who this naughty man was – and why he made him so Cross, Cross, Cross – but she had explained he would soon get to meet him.

48

Pastures Asylum, Derbyshire

Even if Bob could read and write they would still have been reluctant to allow him a pen and paper in his room. As a compromise since being reassessed then moved from a padded cell had worked out well for him. Having normal walls around him allowed his game to be played using a piece of chalk. He could also stoop down to use a small viewing window to take in his only sight afforded to him for nearly 22 hours a day. He would stare out through it to watch inmates with guards moving about on stairwells and balconies being taken to and then returning from their 'recreation'.

This consisted of either a canteen meal or a walk around outside in their exercise yard for an hour; it was his only time he could ever get to smell fresh air when staring out of a large, caged pen, towards rolling hills – miles beyond steel perimeter fences. They were covered with coils of razor wire next to guards in a viewing tower – who were really nice because they waved to him every now and then.

His thoughts raced back to when he was a much younger man living at home with his parents helping out on their family farm. He was happy then with all his sisters spending time with him and asking for help because he was the only boy who was big and strong- so could lift, carry, push and shove far better than them when repairs were made or cattle moved around for milking.

They now came to see him one at a time every week when he was allowed a pen and paper. They were glad because it really helped get through an hour of being sat across from him, watching him draw endlessly another nine square grid. He reminded them at the start of every game that he was Naughty Bob, so went first drawing a nought before they drew a cross, allowing him to win over and over again before telling him they would see him again in a while.

As they drove back to Buxton, they took comfort that with four sisters still well enough to visit it was another month before they had to go through this ordeal again. Bob told his escorts on his return to his cell that his sisters loved him but were not very good at Noughts and Crosses.

Buxton Bob was always excited after visits because his sisters would drop off with security his weekly supply of chalk sticks.

As his door was slammed shut, he eagerly took out a piece having just cleaned hundreds of full nine square grids off his walls earlier, now telling himself out loud he was Naughty Bob so would go first. Guards watched him put a Nought on a grid before passing chalk into his other hand for his opponent to make a Cross.

Later on, after winning his games, he drew circles, dividing them up equally with lots of lines to represent what he remembered to be a darts board but only knew where that number 20 went at the top – high up on his wall.

They had teased him for years about his double top finish. He still had dreams about what happened in that police cell – when coming round with a dart in his hand. Guards teased him that the padded cell block now had dart boards – as he threw pieces of chalk at his – before playing his normal game. When suddenly a lovely guard made his favourite noise – tapping his key on the metal cell door and reminding him to be 'cross' – and the man he would meet soon was 'naughty'.

This new approach had finally sunk in when his nice guard supervised a visit from his sister – who found it hard to believe her ears when she heard him declare that he wasn't Noughts any more he was Cross, allowing her for the first time ever to start play.

Later on at his luxury home, this 'lovely guard' gave Professor Ford a tremendous update – that finally Bob had displayed responsive signs to her hypnotic treatment commands.

Sophie Ford felt overwhelmed with emotion, kissing him passionately, running her finger over his crucifix before saying:

"Well, in that case, let's play a game in bed and I will be naughty for Mr Newman."

49

Ladybower Lake, Derbyshire – Several Weeks Earlier

They ran together side by side in silence, making their way around a well-trodden path, taking them away from Lady Bower Reservoir towards 'Strines', a local beauty spot where they slowly got rid of lactic acid built up after 20 arduous miles of exercise, with a series of shuttle runs, taking in plenty of fluids in order to cool down.

This routine helped her keep in shape, despite taking in twice the normal daily calorie allowance with her high protein diet. It had kept his weight below 12 stone compared to his initial frame of nearly 20 stone when he came to her following their first round of therapy sessions after selling his mum's house, declaring he was moving on' – in his carefully worded letter. A letter of resignation bidding farewell to everyone had been her idea – to allow him a fresh start in more ways than one as he started his life like never imagined or planned with so many changes beyond his imagination. To transform not only in appearance but in his psyche – after he put his trust in her completely.

Within one year of being a recluse, apart from her interaction with psycho analysis, his metamorphosis was accomplished – with even his mentor confounding sheer disbelief; but applied 'Stockholm Syndrome' theory initially to explain how they were drawn together – to then become lovers.

Perhaps her muscular frame with boyish looks helped – but also his changes mentally dovetailed with both their sexual desires for one another; she explained in copious case notes within research studies to record her work, after giving them both nom de plumes before submission.

Indeed, a new identity had been given to him with forged papers with a supporting birth certificate, easily obtained in her position with contacts in both police and social services, where serial offenders and sometimes their victims were given new starts in life; criminals who were no longer deemed a threat to society but needed to be distanced from previous lives or those, who may hunt them down, often press reporters the most determined for a headline story revelation.

Decades earlier a clandestine visit to the Pastures asylum using her pass keys had allowed her to rubber stamp and authorise his application form "Approved" for Mr Andrew Newman to join the staff as an orderly. Her authority carried a lot of weight with nobody questioning his appointment having named her as a reference.

Professor Ford had chosen today's venue for their post run chat very carefully – when she stroked his hair as he lay across her legs with his head cradled on her thigh. They sat in silence as they both looked down at his former sunken village of Derwent which held so many dark sinister memories and events.

Sadly, to be brought back when sharing details provided by Tony Drummond that impacted directly on his hidden past – potentially soon to be exposed about a man who needed to be murdered and with his help. That could happen soon – when he would be able to extract revenge if everything went to plan. She knew his own mother's killer would soon be incarcerated at their asylum – where he had worked as a wing manager for many years – a position she had helped him secure with her elevated standing within this and similar institutions who craved her services and expertise. It meant, if she got King incarcerated, he would possess keys to access not only his cell – but that of a current patient she worked with called Buxton Bob – who really wanted to meet the 'naughty man' King, but for once in his troubled life – not to play noughts and crosses with a new opponent.

With Bob's recent counselling sessions – with a metronome ticking away for hours of hypnotic suggestions, he had no doubt in his mind that this 'Sheffield Snuffer' was a naughty man – which made him so cross – now fully believing he had been sent to their asylum for killing his dear mother, when he visited her at their farm.

Soon Sophie Ford, had to finish this game with pieces taking up their positions – but with a major play still to come. Meaning two players had to be brought together – with neither knowing the other. Buxton Bob had to get access to Oliver King when paired up together on a Sunday – in the asylum's recreation yard – when patients were taken for fresh air and exercise together with a caveat that a guard supervised them.

When she stopped stroking his hair, he glanced up at her smiling before she took a deep breath and gently lay his chain and crucifix over his running top to maximise the impact of her next conversation.

It would be yet another prop to fall back on – to create a positive mind set – only this time not with a patient – but the man she loved.

"Darling, there's something I need to discuss with you."

50

Shower Block – Arrivals, Pastures Lunatic Asylum

As lukewarm water from a shower head hit his face with force, he allowed himself to cry, for his first time since that night he had watched his mother being 'snuffed out' by his dad, all those years ago. Before his warped chaotic journey began on its 'twisted' path, bringing him now to where he found himself with lunatics and imbeciles all around him. This also accurately described staff who he had already met since setting off from prison a few hours earlier after his 28-day order was implemented for detailed psychiatric assessment.

His collection of detailed reports, plus those brought to him by Mr Green over previous weeks had been confiscated, along with every other possession as they explained it was held until assessments were made before deciding if they were allowed in his 'room'. They joked it was being prepared for him, alluding to what a hotel manager may tell a customer as they waited to begin a holiday.

There had been only one member off staff who even bothered to treat him like a 'person' as Oliver King subconsciously made a mental note of his name clearly displayed on his badge, along with his status. So, perhaps as a wing manager he had been promoted for being more professional and civil than many others who were rude and arrogant.

He thought his name was appropriate for others who needed to make some major changes to be more like Mr A NEWMAN – after taking time to explain face to face they would look after him. His cooperation was needed though to work with them – and in return they could watch over him to help keep everyone safe.

Mr Newman felt relieved after Oliver King walked away from him because there hadn't been a flicker of recognition from before – when he used to place a draught in his underwear, or on other occasions when watching him being fondled on a piano stool or indeed when he last saw him before today when mouthing 'You're Next' at his mother's graveside.

How the tide had turned – because he now knew he could be part of a plan to avenge his mother's murder.

He reached inside his shirt to hold her crucifix to run his thumb over its diamond, knowing full well who was going to be next.

51

Exercise Yard – Final Battle,
Pastures Lunatic Asylum

A short walk for a giant of a man, but long enough to put a final piece of their jigsaw in place, to complete its picture for closure as 'Wing Warden A Newman' repeated a rhythmic chant. Only today the beat came from rhythmic footsteps taken on metal balconies and stairwells, timed to coincide as boots landed, but far louder by one of the marching duo. It continued when they approached the exercise yard door, where he then began to generate noise by tapping his key on its frame. To mimic his favourite beat, being reminded one final time, who now stood waiting for him inside.

As Buxton Bob entered, he stared across at 'Naughty Man' who had killed his dear mother, then looked down at an old black and white photograph of her. This had been brought to the Asylum by his sister after Professor Ford had told her it would be a comfort blanket for him following her death from old age. Until recently it had always been held by 'Clock Lady' when they sat playing Noughts and Crosses with her 'Tick, Tock' toy making that noise he really loved to listen to.

Buxton Bob took hold of 'Naughty Man' with both hands, just as Oliver King turned to work out the cause of loud rhythmic tapping noises. With incredible ease he lifted him clean off his feet, before then ramming his head hard against coarse exercise yard brickwork. Instantly his skull shattered, splitting open the back of his head. Before systematically slamming it down onto a whitewashed concrete floor. In perfect timing with the sound of his favourite 'Tick, Tock' machine, chanting along with every dull thud made when Oliver King's head connected, soon turning their whitewashed floor crimson.

"You're Naughty, I'm Cross. You're Naughty, I'm Cross."

After ten chants, with ten dull thuds Oliver King lay motionless with a pool of blood around his head. Before Buxton Bob picked up his photograph to talk to his Mum. He explained that Naughty Man would not be naughty again, but he was still Cross.

As Mr A Newman knelt over the man who had killed his own mother, to run both his hands many times over King's now blood-stained face and his own. To corroborate his future cover story about attempting to save him, with mouth to mouth followed by heart resuscitation, but sadly failed to find a pulse, he had died from his injuries.

Just as Oliver King suddenly opened both eyes wide, with his pupils darting about rapidly, before focusing directly on him.

With blood splattered all around his face it highlighted both pupils, before he gargled and spat blood from his mouth. Then he stared towards a gold crucifix with its small central diamond, now hanging down over him. Only a few inches above his face as distant memories came rushing back.

When a young boy, standing in a busy house full of children, when a kind smiling woman leant forward to read his badge. Telling all the others his name, when this very same crucifix came into view, popping out from beneath her blouse. As King now read this man's badge, who leant over him remembering what his own had said, when pinned on his coat at the train station, after his journey from London.

"OLIVER KING – 10 YEARS"

When he watched everyone, including his soon to become fellow Acorns stick their home-made name badges on, before her son the 'Dinosaur' shook his hand. It now helped him make his final connection on this earth, after joining up so many dots over recent weeks. Including why they had got him sectioned to this Asylum. With a realisation kicking in that Daniel Dan lay in wait for him with his new identity, and such a clever choice of name. After he ran away within days of his mum's funeral to start his life again. He certainly had become a new man.

Who now stared down at him and smiled, just before reaching out before placing both hands over his mouth and nose. As King himself reached up himself to touch his killer's crucifix, that held such meaning for them both, before a final memory from his distant past returned.

His own beloved mother with only clumps of hair on her head, reaching out towards him before his dad 'snuffed her out'.

Oliver King spoke with barely a cackle of a whisper to another son, who just like him, got to avenge his mother's murderer.

"We both turned into monsters didn't we, Daniel, but at least our mothers loved us."

With tears streaming from his eyes after mention of his mother he clamped his hands over King's nose and mouth and pushed down hard with his powerful arms, to watch his eyes flutter, before he died.

Then screaming, after feeling a release, he ran at speed towards the wall to push both hands against it. Leaving blood smears across them, once again to support his cover story. Before walking outside the yard to hit an alarm button next to the entrance door.

With one final stare back inside, before other staff responded at speed, but froze outside, stopping in their tracks. To watch with horror a bored lunatic sitting next to a dead monster, drawing numerous grids on a whitewashed floor using his blood. To tell his lifeless opponent he would go first. Reminding him those were the rules, because like he knew, he was Cross.

'Wing Manager A Newman' didn't have an age on his badge, but it had been well worth a long wait over many years to get his revenge. He cried out to others now stood next to him he had tried his best to help, before holding both arms up with a grimaced look of pain mentioning he may have broken both wrists. He needed to get to hospital for an X-Ray immediately.

In such horrific circumstances it was the very least they could do for him, before they called out their young assistant governor. Who now had a boatload of shit to sort out, because the governor was on holiday, stuck up a mountain and no doubt their young fit canteen manager as well, who accompanied him.

They chuckled away, because it reminded them of that age old work mantra, 'leave it with you kid'.

Buxton Bob upon seeing them all stood outside shouted out, asking if anyone else wanted a game, after beating his dead opponent once again it would seem.

52

Exercise Yard – Crime Scene, Pastures Asylum, Sheffield

An irate Deputy Manager cursed his luck when called out on a Sunday, meaning he now missed his local amateur football match. With no replacement goalkeeper he feared the worst. He couldn't believe his boss had just commenced a two-week holiday in Snowdonia. With his new young girlfriend in tow, their Asylum canteen manager. Who, it would seem, had been serving him up a lot more than could be normally offered from the kitchen menu.

With no contact number, only names of unpronounceable hostels. Where they would stay on an ad-hoc basis when walking steep hills, and admiring sheep, they decided he wasn't as daft as he looked after all. They were unable to contact him so it really had become a classic case of 'leave it with you son'.

His young Deputy held his head in his hands, staring down at a long list of people to contact in accordance with a Manual of Guidance. This detailed what a manager (or Deputies) had responsibility for, clearly set out within a 'Protocol List Best Practice' of actions. Following a Fatal or Suspicious Death Incident within any Asylum. It was a no-brainer it fell into this category, but perhaps in the current circumstances, from what he had been told already, that wasn't the most apt way to describe it.

With their newly arrived inmate, a Serial Killer suspect, known as the 'Sheffield Snuffer' now laid out dead in an exercise yard with a caved in skull. Having had it smashed against a brick wall God knows how many times by another 'patient'. A deranged twenty-five stone psychopath called Buxton Bob who sat crying next to him using his blood to play his favourite game of Noughts and Crosses.

Now meaning acting governor, Marcus Monaghan was compelled to make many phone calls, as per his list before him. He sensed he would be well and truly be criticised if he attempted to cover this one up as 'natural causes' or 'accidental'.

Later on, with initial medical responders confirming no sign of life he waited at the Crime Scene, with a piece of yellow tape stuck across their yard's entrance door. Until a detective having to break off from his Sunday Lunch after calling home for a bite to eat turned up only half-heartedly. Quickly though he raised his game upon realising the identity of the victim but couldn't resist asking a young nervous looking 'stand in' manager, when glancing down at what appeared in blood on the floor.

"Did you get a bit bored waiting for me to turn up mate?"

Beginning to offer an explanation he quickly stopped him by holding his hand up before smiling, thinking to himself:

"Fucking hell, you've got a lot to learn."

After contacting Hawk, who set off to attend immediately, he went through murder scene motions, prior to his boss arriving . Firstly, using a Polaroid camera to photograph everything extensively, before ten staff held down Buxton Bob to have his blood-stained hands and clothing caught on film. Before removing his all-in-one boiler suit style outfit, then bagged up in a brown paper bag and exhibited whilst he kept on repeating to everyone:

"He's naughty and I'm cross, I want to be naughty now. Clock Lady told me I had to punish naughty man."

When DI Shay attended, he kept up with the 'initial shite joke upon arrival' tradition, normally used to relieve upset and tension at some horrendous crime scenes uttering:

"Well, this is insane."

His young detective smiled and had to agree, before telling him about their killers' ramblings when seizing clothing. But they knew they were words out of the mouth of a mad man.

Hawk got an account from a now totally bemused Deputy Manager, who went on to explain that Asylum Incident Procedure had been adhered. An alarm raised within a minute of this incident. A staff member, its Ward Manager, who oversaw their half hour of exercise had gone well above and beyond his duty of care. When entering the secure yard alone without waiting for backup. To find Oliver King beyond help before coming under attack himself from Buxton Bob who pushed him with great force into a wall. Thankfully though he cushioned his impact by reaching out with both hands. Resulting in a suspected broken wrist, but they would get updated after his hospital X Rays and perhaps then he could speak with officers in person.

Hawk's mind raced with so much going on prior to this incident. Surely this couldn't be part of any 'conspiracy theory' to believe Oliver King had been got at by a deranged giant in a lunatic asylum?. Who just happened to be sharing an exercise yard with him? Especially when learning that with low Sunday staffing levels it meant only half hours paired up under supervision, instead of hourly recreation time alone, normally given for high-risk inmates.

When searching Oliver King's cell, he found it bare but luckily his escort officer pointed out that upon arrival "patients" initially had all personal property held in stores. Until deemed fit, following assessments, to be allowed certain items in their rooms.

After collecting his box of belongings from Stores he noticed 'SNUFF KING' had been written across it by one of their bored property clerks. King had brought with him copious files and folders including may letters from his solicitor. Hawk exhibited them all as his, before then calling in at work to have a browse at what King had been putting together when on remand in prison before moved to this asylum.

Following a few hours of reading it taught Hawk a valuable lesson in life. That even when you think you have covered pretty much everything, things are sometimes just not what they seem. He clapped his hands together in recognition of what others had put in place to murder Oliver King. Knowing a brave member of staff who went in 'above and beyond his duty' could also join in with loud applause.

Because there was fuck all wrong with his wrists.

But he had really needed to get out of that asylum quickly, as Hawk considered what his relationship was to their ubiquitous Professor Ford. Without a doubt a genius of a mastermind behind King's murder. Deemed insane by her initially before she obtained an immediate assessment order at the Asylum. Just when this very same professor began working with her new patient Buxton Bob. Suddenly deemed fit for 'recreational pursuits' following his Metronome based therapeutic sessions, copiously recorded in medical notes in his bulging clinical file, now seized pending their investigations.

Hawk raised his glass once again toasting 'Clock Lady' after reading and taking in the ramblings made by a mad man when being stripped off. Who actually spoke with clarity and cognitive recollection. Because these suggestions had been made to him, when no doubt drug induced with a rhythmic 'tick, tock' played to a hypnotic beat as a background noise. This had lasted for an hour at a time with his favourite game being used to induce a mind-set to control his actions.

Very clever, very cunning, very crafty; he really had a lot of respect for her. Such a shame she had never joined the Police, unlike her recent partners in crime who had. Daniel Dan no less, who had gone on to acquire a false identity and certainly had become A Newman in more than name.

Hawk poured another tumbler of whiskey, carefully considering his next move with the other accomplice Tony Drummond. The very same man who had persuaded him and their SIO to assess King's mental capacity. Knowing they would agree but having no idea then she also would be on a mission to seek retribution with King. In her case to avenge the murder of her dear friend Jean Dan.

King had worked this out confirmed within numerous letters between himself and Tricky Ricky; who would have destroyed the prosecution case at Crown Court for maximum impact. With what he knew and had against them he may well continue with his crusade to destroy them, even after his client's death.

Things were now looking a lot worse for DI Drummond, who had cleverly approached their incident room after the bodies were discovered in his old village of Derwent. Applying logic that the best place to hide a tree was in a forest. To protect not only himself but their Acorn Club, who had now given statements to pin blame on King, a mad man who nobody would believe- even if they had got him to court.

But Tony Drummond's future just like their paedophile abusers now looked grave. Unless a lot of things were well and truly buried, never to be discovered, and Tricky Green had a muzzle put on him. He needed to be sorted out sooner rather than later.

53

Operation 'Germ' Reports – Official, Oliver King Papers – Unofficial, DI Shay's Office

Thankfully, he had been able to replace his self-destroyed cut glass engraved tumbler as he now sat alone in his office, sipping malt whiskey. At this time of night it no longer needed hiding in a bottom draw in its box. It now sat on his desk, along with an eclectic mix of forensic reports, several old documents, plus a box full of papers put together by a sectioned lunatic in prison. Sent to an asylum before being murdered under spurious circumstances. Hawk now convinced King was saner than others had made him out to be.

So many secrets hidden out of view with far reaching consequences for so many if released or shared with others – because as always; it wasn't what you knew it was what you chose to do with it, as a voice echoed in his head from a worldly-wise old detective sadly no longer with them.

"Keep it simple, stupid."

A difficult decision needed to be made, which had always been his greatest strength in life having never before shirked responsibility or shied away from making them – even when a young boy in Ireland, before his move to England after sorting out so many wrongs, before being found out, but given a chance to 'move on' – to start again.

Should he now follow suit or deal a heavy blow to fell so many in this pack, who had played their part with both dishonesty and deceit to cover up crimes which carried for them such severe consequences.

The incident room had used its registered name, Operation GERM, to secure a budget code to cover all linked costs for scientific reports – to incorporate any connected expenditures for the joint operation with its neighbouring Force. So

319

this paved the way when attending in person to easily collect everything from a forensics liaison officer. Also helped along following a few flirts and giggles with a false promise to ring her.

He returned with them all after making the one-hundred-mile trip; many different coloured folders labelled; Metallurgy, Arborist, Pathologist now alongside lots of handwritten notes made by both King and Tricky Green categorising, Sophie Ford, Sonya Child, Tony Drummond and last but not least Hawk. With numerous drawings by King, one labelled 'Acorn Club' with a map marking a tree house and a church graveyard with a cross, no doubt indicating recent body discoveries on old village maps.

Correspondence with Solicitor Rick Green that outlined well supported 'concerns' of collusion and underhanded tactics that had been scheduled and prepared for a barrister, and most concerning Hawk knew that since King's murder Green would still pursue the matter, hell-bent on bringing them down to gain his victory at any cost.

Green seemed to be a brave man indeed with his recently discovered 'habits' to take such a high moral stance. Following a recent disclosure by his wife to a divorce solicitor he had used a private investigator to follow and collect evidence, using a horrible little creature called Mole with his detailed findings now in front of him.

DS Crowther had played it clever, knowing Hawk wanted to run Green out of town so he and his team would do all the work. Allowing C Hall investigators to earn good money and no doubt a bonus from Mrs Green when they got a result. She herself could then use it to gain leverage for a decent divorce settlement.

This Mad Dog O'Connor and his band of street fighting brothers sounded a force to be reckoned with, and the thought of them getting hold of Green really could be a favourable option, allowing Hawk to use someone else to do his own dirty work.

Everyone else now appeared to be using everyone else to get what they wanted, so why not follow suit?

54

Graveyard, Bamford, Two Days After King's Murder

Normally he would keep watch for a while from a wooden slatted bench, which bore a small brass plaque in tribute to her life. This routine conducted to make sure nobody saw him, from decades earlier, had also attended to pay their respects to lost loved ones. Even with his new unrecognisable appearance far removed from how he looked back then, when he was last seen in their village, any association with her headstone may have drawn unwanted attention. Even a few innocent questions could prove costly – if they then made a connection.

Today, with what may well be his last visit for years, he departed from his normal routine when immediately upon arrival he tended to a few weeds, then tidied up a gravel edging before removing dead flowers – to replace them with fresh ones. Throughout he spoke softly with his head bowed, initially in prayer, but then giving her an update on his life following so many recent events.

He had so much to tell her, but so little time during which he produced several candles in small holders, which he lit one by one to cast a low flickering light across her well-weathered headstone – allowing its shallow carving to become visible;

Jean Dan

He knew she would have been so proud of him after her intuition had paid off so well – in many ways. He placed his hand bearing a new wedding ring against her stone, to tell her about the next chapter in his life; soon moving to allow his wife to take up a coveted position as head of faculty in Canada. Her final thesis with its remarkable results made up of ground-breaking findings, that drew many job offers.

She had balanced recent events and possible consequences in deciding the time had come to start afresh and move on. Andy Newman could certainly relate to making a decision like that far more than most.

Now holding her crucifix, he stood to let his Mum know her death had been avenged, her murderer dealt with in the most appropriate way, before running his finger over its small diamond. Just when the candles with a gentle breeze building went out one by one. But he managed to smile, feeling at peace with his life and events.

Walking towards an exit gate he noticed a large Oak tree had shed hundreds of acorns. Another symbolic memory from his past flashed across his mind when he looked ahead to see his beautiful wife sat waiting for him in her car.

They sat together in silence throughout their journey to the airport to fly off and put a shared past behind them, to start a new future together.

55

Victoria Hotel, Sheffield City Centre

After putting his car well out of sight from any prying eyes, in the far corner bay of a large private underground car park owned by a luxury hotel, he opened his boot. He collected his case after checking his 'play kit' was in place, containing all sorts of sex toys – with new batteries inserted, along with a few colourful karate belts; perfect for wrapping around wrists and ankles. To spread-eagle her across a four-poster bed – plus creams and lotions to help him do whatever he wanted – not forgetting the pills and powder to make it last for hours.

A taekwondo protective fighting mask for his face was also packed, he was always mindful that he was well-known now in this city. Call girls from this agency may know him by sight, if not by name. Thankfully for his perverse needs they weren't angels – before moving into this line of work more often than not being druggies and young petty criminals. So, if they sent his preferred choice, a woman no older than 20, he had to minimise his risk by keeping his face covered – until he put a blindfold on her or his favourite hood with a mouth hole he would certainly put to good use.

They knew he had paid top money – so a few bruises were allowed, plus he gave them a bonus up front so they never complained or refused 'Mr Lee', one of many names he used to capture his martial arts theme. Once again it meant that as always – he was ahead of the game, thinking it all through meticulously with a cover story and car hidden away under cover.

He smugly thought how you just couldn't be too careful – when he noticed some little miscreant had stuck chewing gum to his tailgate light cluster. Luckily it hadn't set too hard after it flicked off easily with a controlled side sweep with his shoe.

He made his way to a busy reception for his room key whilst popping his first pill before calling the lift – feeling himself get aroused – when admiring such an amazing arse on a fit looking lady stood in the foyer. Maria Whittaker flirted away before getting permission to use a concierge's desk phone – just after giving him a lovely smile to ring her team having heard "Mr Lee" checking in to 'Room 31'.

Her Sgt answered again with a little heavy breathing for a joke, but she knew only too well he fantasised about her before whispering what he needed to know, popping yet another piece of gum into her mouth – with her last piece put to good use, just prior to beginning tonight's surveillance.

She looked forward to seeing photos taken later on, after they burst into Room 31 to capture a moment that would surely be the beginning of the end for Tricky Ricky. Maria then detached from her team and drove to wait for Hawk outside Greens Solicitor's office. With strict instructions to stay put even if an alarm activated, until he jumped into her car, 'getaway driver' now another of her roles she had to perform for him, to secure that long awaited promotion to Sergeant. To be honest she much preferred performing her bedroom roles for him. They were always enjoyable but knew full well nobody yet had managed to cage him. She knew just to enjoy it while she could. Before getting to the next rank, like so many others had done, over so many years.

All a game, just like tonight's activities, but stakes now higher than most, with Hawk on a mission to destroy such a worthy opponent. No holding back, with a loaded deck to stack the odds in his favour. With an "all in" play by Hawk, by orchestrating a 'double whammy' to beat an adversary into submission. Either from a result in his hotel bedroom, or in his own office. Indeed both, if all went as planned.

One way or another Hawk had never been so focused. He would win this game at all costs, to deal with a big man. Who had made an even bigger mistake when trying to outplay him in his own casino.

56

Room 31, Victoria Hotel

It couldn't have gotten any more bizarre – but it just had. Besides Ricky Green wearing his mask – they also now stood all around his bed wearing masks – with theirs being cartoon character party-themed to hide faces from him. Two giants off their surveillance team, both standing well over six foot, and front row rugby players showed they had a real sense of humour. Selecting two of Snow Whites Dwarfs, but tonight, instead of carrying picks, they had chosen to set off to work with baseball bats. They knew his martial arts prowess so had come prepared to 'subdue him' if he chose to fight them. But in his current position he could hardly have managed that. He now lay spread eagled, tied to all four posts of a big wooden framed bed using Karate belts, each one being a different colour. They pulled his own mask up over his head because until then he wasn't even aware six uninvited guests had just joined them, but had to wait for a large young blonde – who they couldn't help but notice wasn't a natural, to stop gyrating on his face and jumped off. After taking in this scene a dwarf really excelled with his humour tonight, saying to her:

"High Ho, what a belting idea."

Once she calmed down and managed to stop screaming, she posed as instructed by squatting over his head, with Green remaining silent his face now in full view. His silence helped by a large plastic bag full of white powder shoved half in half out of his mouth. With him knowing full well he would be in even more trouble if it split and he ingested too much cocaine in one go.

Many photographs were taken as they spoke to taunt and tease him, with several renditions of 'It's off to work we go' while sticking to their agreed cover accent. With all things considered it had to be Geordie tonight, to compliment the sheer enormity of what danger Green now found himself in with his chequered past in Newcastle. With still no idea his night would get a lot worse when discovering other events now taking place elsewhere. 'Aladdin' told him, with his best attempt at Geordie, it wouldn't be long before he would need a magic carpet, to fly far away and never to be seen again. A bemused, shocked weepy call girl had been told to 'get dressed and get gone' after parting her from her lipstick, and they left Green with no uncertainty what this had all been about tonight. Leaving him still tied to the bed having written OK in bright red capitals across his chest. To tell him they had finished their initial enquiries but could return again in the future when once again he least expected it.

After removing masks in a crowded lift DS Copeland returned a spare key for Room 31 to a Concierge, thanking him for his help. It had saved smashing a door down and just as well because it turned out not to be their man. All was OK but he couldn't come down just now because he was tied up, but had asked for Room Service to call with a stiff whiskey on the Rocks. They had left his door unlocked so just leave it for him please on his dresser. He had a decent tip waiting for them.

Outside a very happy, retired DS with a camera hanging down from his neck who had just earned himself a small fortune took them all for a celebratory drink. One big lad told another that surely he couldn't be grumpy about that, before they all made a promise to stop telling shitty jokes.

Well, until they were pissed, by which time Hawk could update them on his progress. Perhaps even buy a few more thank you drinks. They sat in a pub waiting for him and clinked glasses, agreeing he didn't need a mask, already being a character.

57

Rick Green Solicitors, Office Block, Sheffield

Hawk appreciated its carefully chosen position, near to both courts and opposite a cluster of shops selling cheap clothes and hot food. With its main potential draw by far a DHSS signing-on office where thousands of 'pond life' surfaced every fortnight to show they were artistic, when "drawing their giro" before cashing them in at a Post Office- once again close to hand.

This choice of location replicated what he knew about him. Well thought out and clever, using his initiative to allow future clients to see his business, just like with his green key-fob idea. A simple handout but highly effective, used by everyone, and always with you. Especially when booked into police cells, when your world may be about to collapse. Making it a beacon of hope to help get you out of a dark place meaning everyone held it up to a Custody Sgt, asking for Green to attend. Sadly this had been the case with Oliver King as well. They now knew that Green's sons were taken to training at martial art academies and classes that did exist (unlike the class tonight to allow him sordid liaisons) when they were prone to pick up injuries. He couldn't take the whores but did take his boys to King's GP's because this practice covered where he lived. Here Green met without realising it, a man on reception, who would present himself eventually to become their biggest earning client. When discovered to be the Cities now infamous "Sheffield Snuffer" until of course he had been killed.

Tricky Ricky once again over-stepped the mark, like years earlier when breaching safe boundaries in Newcastle with a Gangster, when fucking his Moll. Moving to Sheffield to do similar, but this time trying to fuck over a detective. But one just as ruthless as him, with a far bigger gang at his disposal. Green had dared to go head-to-head, throwing down a gauntlet. One that Hawk didn't hesitate to pick up with a vengeance.

Prior to this challenge he had already put a plan in place, sending in a young female typist, after many had joked about not daring to get to grips with her, because she would throw them about with her Karate skills, even running a self-defence class in their Police Gym. Who became a more than willing volunteer, keen to help him, hoping one day to become an officer herself so Hawk explained it would help her achieve that goal after agreeing to join Green's Club. Being a brown belt provided excellent cover, along with her stunning looks. As he fully anticipated it drew his attention after a flirt then a few carefully fed lines to hook him. Including of course a whispered call from her office phone sharing how Hawk had lost the plot, just smashing his really expensive whiskey tumbler in a fit of rage.

Hawk had staged anger for Green's benefit, when mentioned during their exchanges in the cells, convincing him of her potential value. It would have been a classic "honey pot" tactic to bait him in. But Mrs Greens scorned woman arrival on the scene helped him progress his plan in leaps and bounds. Hawk would now discover with a key in his hand, and codes in his pocket how much of a gift horse she was. Because he now had his own battle to win but other players had now been drawn into this fight who needed his help more than him. When he saw his gum chewing backup park up opposite he got off to a good start, when the key turned its front door lock. Upon entering he soon fed a correct sequence into an alarm panel; confirmed when a soft humming noise fell silent. Hawk saw a Green family portrait and his mind flashed back to happier days when he posed with many loved ones before throwing it all away. Now wasn't the time to get maudlin. The large, mounted picture swung outwards from the office wall to reveal his main prize, a heavy duty safe. With a pocket torch in his mouth, he turned a tumbler dial several times before it clicked, springing open its metal door.

Seriously tempted to remove all his files but he only took two large buff folders marked 'MDO' and 'OK' which he fully expected to find, but was shocked to see how much money he found, no doubt held for criminals until granted bail, or released from sentence to avoid its seizure.

Green would know who had stolen the folders, but he took great delight in leaving him in no doubt when removing his calling card from a rucksack brought with him. To send a clear message he had been well and truly 'fucked over' both in his hotel room earlier and now in his own office, before he carefully placed it on top of the pile of remaining folders.

Because after all, he didn't want to smash yet another expensive cut-glass crystal whiskey tumbler.

Especially not on his pittance of a salary.

58

Rick Green's Office, Sheffield – One Hour Later

Sadly, he soon discovered that what he had believed to be a 'safe haven', his own office wasn't even somewhere he could go to escape, to quickly assess what was happening. His whole world now spiralled out of control with everything he held sacred being systematically torn apart piece by piece as he froze to the spot, staring in horror at what had been placed on top of folders in his safe. With a loud scream of anguish, he grabbed Hawk's calling card – a whiskey tumbler before throwing it across his room, smashing it against a far office wall when suddenly realising only two folders were actually missing.

After thumbing through his remaining ones , despite everything, he couldn't believe one bit of good fortune that had gone his way today. When remembering he was sat at his desk when Mole gave him the HAWK folder. Crammed full with everything he had dug up against him. Unlocking his desk draw he punched the air in delight upon finding he still had what he needed to extract revenge. Hawk had overlooked his possible lifeline.

His mind went into overdrive, glancing down at broken glass from the tumbler. Had Hawk even staged that typist joining his Karate classes? To feed him a line when she rang him before the interviews, to gradually lure him in over time, before then feeling a sting? He slumped down in his office chair with his mind still racing, but it skidded off-track, bouncing his thoughts all over the place. Realising the enormity of just how much danger he found himself in. With his wife now in a strong position to make her demands at will. To stake a dominant claim on everything he owned with her in joint names. Plus plenty more besides- knowing what he had hidden undeclared. He also now found himself at the mercy of a crafty cunt of a detective who now held the upper hand. Not only with any Oliver King related defence tactics, but also over his career.

Soon to be finished if Hawk used those photos to have him struck off. He doubted that to be his primary intention; otherwise surely they could have arrested him earlier with damning evidence to hand? To easily support a possession of Class A drugs charge and conviction. Worst prospect of all facing him – would be the MDO folder being handed to Mad Dog or his brothers, meaning he no longer had any hold over them. He could set his gypsy pack loose to hunt him down. Knowing full well the consequence if found. Did Hawk plan to only chase him out of town? Confirmation came within a minute when his direct-dial office phone broke his reflective silence. When answering to hear a voice with a genuine accent for once tonight, sadly for him though Irish.

"I could have fucked you over better than that young blonde after your exploits in Room 31. Indeed, I could have invited real characters down from Newcastle to hand them a folder."

"Or let them call to watch you perform at that Hotel, making it your last one. As I'm sure you've no doubt worked out there is only one deal I'm going to offer you, so have I got your full attention Tricky?"

Green couldn't stop squeezing the phone until it creaked under pressure from his vice-like grip, before calming himself, so his voice didn't give away both anger and fear.

"I'm all ears Hawk, let's hear it"

Hawk smiled, a good effort but he heard a slight tremor in his voice.

"Firstly, you go nowhere near wifey, soon to be your X. You don't even ring her, from this moment forwards its contact only with your Divorce solicitor and hers. He will be in touch soon, once he stops laughing at those explicit photos we have sent him."

"Secondly, you bury, perhaps the best way of describing it, any incriminating evidence you believe shows 'poetic licence' that we would have used against Oliver King. Anything that may implicate anyone else, with historical murders, and let's be right about it. 'Ricky', he was as guilty as Fuck, so it ends here and now."

"Finally, and purely for my benefit, so take this as a real compliment, you have 24 hours to pack up and move out. Never to return or cause any mischief in the future. Let me assure you big fella, any single hint or suggestion you have and I personally will drive to Newcastle to deliver this folder to 'Mad Dogs' right hand man. Or one of his many enforcers now I know who they all are, being named in that fantastic 'Family Tree' you've made, showing every 'Gypsy

General' below O'Connor. Not to mention the impressive figures for his finances, almost matching the sexy figure of his wife, who I see didn't mind posing naked for you."

"Ricky, there's a wee saying I heard back in the day, when 'boys' in Ireland fought their battles. I think it sums up our little conflict very well, so here you go, answer with one word. Do you choose to 'Comply or Die'?"

Green had no room for manoeuvre or to influence any outcome, despite what he had gathered in his "H" file. With which he had sincerely hoped to strike first using its contents, to do the same to him. He now stared vacantly into space, a defeated man, knowing what the answer had to be.

"Comply."

Hawk's parting words were one final put down, just before he put his phone down.

"So, it looks like I could afford another glass after all, even on my pittance of a salary. It goes without saying everything I have against you is now held by others. Who will deliver it on my behalf if anything untoward happens to me. Get packing and get gone, I will call to your office in person tomorrow to check it's empty."

After ending the call from his bed, it had generated such an adrenaline rush he now found himself fully erect again. Playfully he nudged the soon to be DS Whittaker, jokingly telling her this would be much better than putting chewing gum in her mouth. When glancing towards his groin with a smile, repeating that old police adage "You have to go down, to go up". Later on tonight he knew full well they would join, odds on, a pissed-up Walt Disney cast. And it was a good bet they would tell endless shit jokes for the rest of the evening.

He just knew they wouldn't resist putting their face masks back on, then going back into character.

59

Frame Saver Opticians, Sheffield

Sonya Child's had spotted a horrible little man, known to be an underhand private investigator called Mole, driving past her home. After also seeing him earlier on in the day, when sat in their public gallery at Magistrates Court. She knew who he was, what he did, and indeed whom he worked for. Sadly, it would seem she had become the focus of his attention. This had to relate to Oliver King as Tricky now did what all defence Solicitor's did best, went into attack mode to destroy the credibility of prosecution witnesses. Nobody doubted he would still attempt to discredit and expose their actions from decades earlier and a more recent conspiracy to cover his clients demise.

Was Green considering making an approach at her own home? To assert his all-knowing position of strength by trying to make her turn against her fellow conspirators? Offering her a deal? Either way she updated Tony Drummond who immediately shared this with Hawk, after hearing about his head to head with Green. No doubt just like them Tricky would also be looking at trying to get some dirt on him to gain an upper hand. Tony Drummond knew full well if anyone could make best use of this information his fellow DI was best placed to do so. It was well known that Hawk had declared to teach Green a lesson, they would all benefit by getting rid of him one way or another. Hawk now seemed to keep his cards close to his chest perhaps still reeling from the shock of King's transfer to the Asylum for assessment. Nothing had been said, and no update given, even following King's death, but within a week a serious rumour circulated that Green had vacated his Sheffield office, relocating his business to London. They reasoned that following King's murder at the Asylum he wouldn't be getting a much expected huge pay out. So perhaps sought more lucrative cases in the city with a leading barrister from there who had been scheduled to represent the defence making him a job offer? Or had Hawk won a personal vendetta he spoke about to run him out of town?

Maria Whittaker tried on a pair of thick, black-framed spectacles from a sample display stand in a city centre opticians. They had clear glass in them now to allow customers to see if the style selected suited them. A young, bored shop assistant looked on thinking what a shame this lady hadn't made more of her features Obviously having a great figure, but didn't have a clue how to dress to make best use of it. Plus, such a poor choice of makeup not to mention her flat scruffy shoes and a noticeable slouch.

Watching this lady closely highlighted just what a great bum she had, and this turned out to be a good thing because when staring at that, she hadn't noticed Maria leaving still wearing the ugliest frames she could find. Taken in between this young sales girl looking her up and down. She wouldn't know this extreme dress down would seem appropriate when she joined an ugly little bastard in half an hour. Hoping to make him believe a shy plain girl presenting herself before him would ask to pair up with him at his local pub quiz. They knew he attended there every week on his own, and she would explain her mates had let her down.

They hoped he would find her attractive, because after a few drinks she would then coyly suggest trying out a newly opened Chinese restaurant. But once outside her mates would turn up wearing their dwarf masks before taking him away for a drive to introduce 'Mole to a Hole'. To throw him into on an empty building trench, where in tonight's accent of choice, Welsh, he would be given a clear message. When told laying there begging to be spared, that if he ever repeated what had been passed on to Tricky, they would bury him alive. Too deep down for even a Mole to dig out from.

'Happy' told 'Grumpy' later on, after the deed had been done, when driving away, he had felt quite emotional doing that to him. In fact, it nearly caused him to 'fill up'. They both agreed, yet again, that would be the end of any more shit jokes on that particular subject, before picking up a plain looking bird in glasses to take her for a drink. Like they told her, looking like that if they hadn't bothered then nobody else would have tonight. Maria told them they needed to respect supervision, having just been told about her promotion to Detective Sergeant. Both of tonight's companions commented they simply had no 'fucking' idea how she had managed that, with a few 'there's lovely' thrown in for good measure. It was more than likely she would have a 'yo yo' career, and may well have to go downwards a few times before upwards.

Maria played along, telling them that being good with her mouth had helped and tonight, for old times' sake, that would be demonstrated. With Grumpy joking that would make him extremely Happy, before she chewed her gum and blew out a big bubble. She gave them both her best innocent look, telling them she had no idea what they thought she meant, with a wink. Grumpy narrowly avoided crashing their car, thinking about what may have been coming their way. Stating he really wasn't happy now about her being such a tease.

They were all still laughing when entering the pub for a celebratory drink.

60

Moles Local Pub, Sheffield

It was a brave call, but he had never shied away from anyone as he sat with his back to a wall, twirling his whiskey glass in his hand with empty pint pots left on a table, initially out of arms reach – now moved towards him. If needed these would be used as missiles if worse scenario developed and he came under attack; because he had complied with his request to 'come alone'.

Hawk didn't believe that "Mole" would be that stupid to lure him into a trap, without feeling a backlash. This had already been clearly pointed out to him when he lay in a builder's ditch screaming for his life as two "Dwarfs" stood over him, singing 'Hi-Ho' – pretending they were going to bury the little fucker alive.

Had it not been for what "Grumpy" had heard in and amongst pleas and cries along with ramblings of pity, then he may not have attended here today, but to hear Mole mention he would never disclose about that 'spaz of a kid' had intrigued him – to such an extent he now sat in Mole's local, after receiving a hand-written message signed 'M' within a Chinese menu from a local restaurant. The very same one suggested they visited that night after they left this pub. Only for Mole it became a 'take-away'; with him becoming the main course.

When the small podgy man with heavy framed glasses shuffled towards him Hawk looked beyond him, checking to see if anyone else had also entered. Nobody had, with Mole then placing a tumbler of whiskey in front of him. Picking up on Hawks focus he confirmed straight away that he wouldn't be that stupid, he came alone. Hawk told him he had until both glasses were empty, to say what he had to say before he left, as Mole opened up talking quickly so he could complete his plea.

"I find myself in a precarious position after doing Mr Green's work for him, because he still has a folder containing what could get me killed. I have no control over this after his sudden 'flit', so well done DI Shay, I'm guessing you had a bigger bargaining tool over him, than he had over you."

Hawk's stomach churned, his imagination ran wild, considering just how much dirt Mole had dug up on him. With his many out of office antics making him extremely vulnerable to anyone brave enough to take him on.

"I will share with you what he considers to be his biggest nugget. It's very damaging information I discovered by total chance here in this pub, my local, after chatting to a bar maid who I know for a fact doesn't cover tonight."

"You used her years ago to cheat your internal system to gain promotion before dumping her. Sadly, after that she took an overdose, I take it you must know who I'm talking about." (Nod from Hawk)

"What you don't know is that she carried your child, indeed neither did she until hospital tests confirmed it, but by then it was too late. Damage had been caused to the foetus resulting with your child born 'mentally disabled'." (Mole didn't use his normal descriptive when sat with Hawk.)

Hawk's head dropped before throwing back both whiskeys, but went to the bar to buy himself more drinks. Even one for a nasty little bastard sat with him. But he considered that perhaps he kept the right company – considering his own character traits. Over the next ten minutes they went on to 'finalise a deal' that would benefit his child. Making some calculations before Mole fully agreed to call with an amount allowing at least for her to buy her own place to ease the financial hardship at least. When all said and done the money only represented a small amount of his worth- Hawk had plenty more. Thankfully Mole hadn't dug down deep enough or travelled far enough to uncover many parts of his 'secret life' With this recent gift paid out to Vanda not even half the total taken out of Greens safe. He left him plenty to make sure he had more than enough to travel away to another City – to see if it would be 'third time lucky' for him.

Every cloud though had a silver lining because Hawk told Mole he would be on hand in future to do 'little jobs' for him. Including updates over years to come if anything else became needed for his son's treatments or welfare. Or to pay a little visit to certain people every now and then, but that would be put on a back burner for now. Mole stared down but nodded; he had learnt from the 'mole in a hole' experience that this mad detective wouldn't hesitate to bury him if needed.

Hawk sat in silence, how ironical that after only daughters he had finally managed a son, but one he would never get to know. With yet another whiskey thrown back he had a flashback to his own Dad who had drunk the same way, and pretty much didn't have anything to do with him.

It had gone well for Mole tonight, so he kept it that way, and didn't push his luck by mentioning anything about all her cryptic ramblings about 'Bubbles' or how she knew about his drug addiction. Never wise to upset a complete cunt too much, especially when they were highly volatile and unstable in drink, let alone drugs.

All those details were also included in his folder that Tricky Ricky possessed.

61

Allotments, Bamford

When all the others had finished off their brews after completing endless chores, many of which weren't necessary (but a far better option than sitting at home in front of a television and drinking tea with a nagging wife) he held back from leaving. Tony Drummond now sat alone in front of a communal allotment fire contained in a large metal drum, positioned well away from row after row of vegetables within carefully tended, much loved, still watered plots.

It was unusual for him to be last to leave because he really didn't mind sitting at home with his wife. For Tony it represented a rare treat – but tonight he had far too much business to attend to that couldn't wait. When going to his car boot he subconsciously checked no gum was stuck to his tailgate light cluster. One by one he now retrieved box after box rammed full of files, folders and papers. Removed earlier from office drawers, filing cabinets and his locker from work, with some dating back well over a decade. In his head he heard words uttered many times, over numerous years, normally by defence barristers in closing arguments. When desperately attempting to convince a jury, innocent clients had been subjected to numerous indiscretions by investigating officers. They alleged their trial had been presented with, quite frankly, a non-stop 'tissue of lies' with a 'labyrinth of deceit' to gain an unlawful conviction. So, unless this defendant was found not guilty then it would, once again, sadly represent yet another major travesty of justice.

He had sat so many times with his well-practised look of disbelief, making careful eye contact with 'movers and shakers' on their jury. Normally identifiable as such after watching them throughout long detailed proceedings. They were the ones making copious notes, paying attention to proceedings, with others staring about the courtroom with vacant looks. Tony would nod towards those who would influence others over their deliberations. Plus of course they had good old Betty, a regular jury clerk, a one-time 'popular girl' a paramour for a Detective Sgt from years ago. Soon after joining the jury in their private consultation rooms, she got to know them, to then share many priceless findings 'off the record' Often disclosed over a bottle of wine at her home, happy to have a little male company, even if these days for only just a friendly chat. Betty most importantly remained in their company when discussing daily what they had just heard in court evidence following witness testimonies. When opening up about who they believed or considered to be 'well dodgy'. Tony and other detectives gave looks of incredulity when suggestions were made that investigative officers were dishonest and beyond belief. Officers in the stand would remind the court their 'integrity was beyond reproach' when under oath.

Tony Drummond now fed into an allotment fire hundreds of document bundles, clearly showing 'beyond reasonable doubt' that defence lawyers were exactly right in what they had pontificated about over many years. But knew full well they had already been paid vast sums of money to play a game. Acting like they cared and going through the motions to protest their clients' innocence – when knowing they were guilty as hell. Often joking over after-trial drinks that Hell was where they would all meet up again in future, with barristers asked if their wigs and gowns were fire-proof. Watching pages turn into ash then drift slowly upwards, towards dark skies Tony reflected on whether he could now save himself from his biggest ever threat of appearing before a jury. If arrested on two counts of murder from his troubled past, or conspiracy to murder from his present, despite Oliver King's Asylum death. It had sent his mind racing, hence an 'audit trail of lies' now on paper burning in an attempt to destroy so much. But only if he could also burn tangible connections and links to events well out of his reach, knowing if these became exhibits they would convict him and others.

Ironically those solid 'links' of evidence were found on a set of handcuffs, with his collar number stamped on them. Albeit his dads from years earlier, but he'd inherited number 91 from him. Now a vital part of DI Hawks case file, out of his reach with Hawks exhibits officer having ownership of them. Along with a damning metallurgy report to corroborate a connection to him that couldn't be broken.

Tony stared down at an Acorn in his hand brought to his station by King before his arrest. It brought back an image of Sonya ramming them into her abuser's mouth one by one who lay handcuffed and naked on that church floor.

Another set of handcuffs they used that night would link them all to Jean Dan. That in turn opening up many connections to well respected psychiatrist Sophie Ford who had sectioned King.

A case could easily be presented to show she also wanted King dead, an obvious act of revenge for murdering her dear friend Jean Dan. Her sudden flight quite literally to another Continent corroborating post crime conduct allowing a jury to draw yet another 'guilty as hell' inference.

Many pieces of this jigsaw puzzle had now fallen into place allowing a clear picture to be seen- sadly reading 'Guilty as Charged'. Tony heard movement, then saw a large dark figure approach, to gradually become illuminated by bright flames now feeding off so much paper. Even before his face lit up, a soft voice with its gentle Irish brogue gave away his identity when he spoke.

"You may as well burn these old, decayed acorns with your recent present I see you're holding there from Oliver King. Along with all these detailed scientific reports I picked up earlier."

"Sadly, just lost, like these two old sets of stamped handcuffs. Our old mate Andy Laptew recounted from all those years ago: 'keep it simple', so let's do the same."

"Only this time Tony D between us, we have both dealt in vastly different ways with our murderer. Who was the right man, who can't go on to kill anyone else."

DI Shay made his symbolic gesture first as bundles of statements then several exhibit bags holding all its damning evidence, including handcuffs, were thrown into a large roaring fire, followed by another DI, now with tears streaming down his face, who threw his acorn into ever growing flames. Just about to speak, to try to explain himself, Hawk placed a finger to his mouth because there was no need for Tony to say a word, but he finished off with an explanation for his own actions by saying:

"Let's just say Tony that just like acorns it was an 'open and shut case' which is now finally closed. Who knows, perhaps after your retirement bash in coming months, I will sulk if I don't get an invite by the way, I may well share with you reasons why I'm doing this for you."

"For now, let's just say I once found myself in your position when I was handed a 'get out of jail card' from the unlikeliest of sources, but hey now, that really is a full bottle of whiskey story to be sure!"

Without hesitation, at identical times both men walked towards one another before they embraced, with DI Tony Drummond giving him a big hug, placing his hand over the back of his head, as DI Shay couldn't resist quipping in a strong Irish accent.

"Fir feck's sake Tony, I thought for a moment there yous was trying to snuff me out! Here of all places, I thought you had finally lost the plot."

Despite being such a shit joke, it made them both laugh out loud. Later that night Tony Drummond took great delight in announcing to his wife, when sat in their lounge watching TV, he would retire when his service was up. He didn't want to appeal against a medical report, to remain in the job. Unlike his allotment mates that night they didn't drink tea, instead they quaffed a fair few bottles of wine, clinking glasses over and over again with Tony toasting his new found friend. Without a doubt who had saved him from having to give everyone an incredulous look in months to come, including his trial Judge. But when he was gripping a brass rail himself in a packed courtroom when flanked by two remaining 'Acorn Club' members He sensed they would both keep in touch, because he wouldn't be disappearing completely, having just been given a strong indication a proposal he submitted for an interesting job may well materialise, to take control of a newly formed team. It would shock so many when they found out in years to come what it was, because so many were unaware of his clandestine past with skills acquired over endless years of covert specialist work.

Who knows, one day he may well be able to thank Hawk properly for keeping him out of prison for a life sentence. Perhaps he may buy him a case of Irish whiskey long before then. It sounded like he had a story to tell from his past and after what he had heard, and now knew first-hand about this man, he was sure it would be well worth hearing. In fact he was 'sure to be sure' when raising his glass one final time tonight, before glancing across at an old framed photo of his grandfather and dad. Taken when he was only young, wearing aprons stood outside their village Ironmongers.

Before sadly watching a small ripple appear across his drink, following yet another involuntary movement in his arm.

62

Crown Court, Derbyshire

They adjourned for sentencing, to allow their trial judge to read some last-minute reports from social services and probation as her client stood to give an exaggerated bow to the man in the red robe, after watching all the barristers do the same before the recess. Kelley waved across at his solicitor with a beaming smile, when told earlier on by the prison officers now flanking him, she had dropped off a pork pie for his dinner. It had in fact been two, but it had just become one of those 'caring sharing moments' having taken a share of his food, and they didn't care. Sonya had realised they could well be his last for many years to come, possibly four if their Judge didn't feel lenient today.

What his Lordship would soon read in confidential reports may just help her client. After Kelley 'Kit Kat' Keegan finally opened up about his childhood with his drunken mother. Who sat with her cat purring on her knee watching her young son being abused by one of her many boyfriends. They always called around with chocolate bars for him and a Chinese take away for her, after a skin-full of beer at the local club, having initially first met them on a night out. Where his mother would often strip on stage when much younger, with a silver tray passed around between them all until they collected enough for her to "perform" This meant inviting several on stage to do what they wanted to her, while cheered on by others, hoping they would be invited up next to have a go, in a drink fuelled state.

Sonya had always thought her nickname of 'Silver Annie' related to her distinctive hair colour since being a teenager, when prematurely going that way. Until now- when her sordid past and perverse actions became known. It even explained her sons first ever conviction for killing her cat. With him remembering she loved it more than him, with it sat purring on her knee when violated by other men. Before she then offered him what she had left from her

343

takeaway for supper. One such abuser had found religion after finding an incurable tumour in his pancreas. Who made his peace and gave his confessional from his death bed. To wipe his slate clean before joining God. He named 'Silver Annie' as his conduit back in the day to fulfil his perversions for a bit of chocolate and a carton of take away.

When Annie fully admitted these historical offences following arrest and interviews Sonya had been present representing her. But refrained from giving her any warning signals on her leg to stay quiet. But she did then kick-start detailed reports, now read no doubt in-between slurps of port in Chambers, by his Lordship, served to him by his court valet.

Sonya relaxed outside in a riverside park opposite the court building, eating a tuna sandwich. She fed most of her salt and vinegar crisps to the birds, having still lost her appetite from weeks earlier when shown that Acorn by Tony after breaking the news to her.

Recent events made her consider what, if any compassion, she would be afforded by a trial judge, before sentencing them with a glass or two of fine port inside them. Hopefully they would consider her age and vulnerability and post crime impact allowing a defence of Duress. To ignore their planning and pre-meditation, but they had all just given false statements against Oliver King to offset any involvement. Sadly, with this recent conspiracy as adults, let alone their respective jobs in positions of trust could lead to substantial sentences. Just like with Jean Dan's memory box, once again Oliver King even in death held the key to their futures, if his defence solicitor continued the fight to expose them.

If one domino fell, they all did, meaning a reunion for the Acorn Club and Sophie Ford who sadly may find themselves together again, but in a court dock. Sonya now had a flashback to their treehouse with a sign above its door, she had painted in red with her finger. Now she feared they may all end up caught red-handed. If not by Tricky Ricky perhaps DI Shay with endless tales of his dogged determination hunting down offenders. Sadly, if anyone could, surely he would follow a trail of evidence, well-trodden down, leading directly to herself and others. Upon noticing Tony Drummond approach at speed her heart jumped into her mouth, but then he suddenly hugged her tight and whispered in her ear that everything had just been sorted.

She cried uncontrollably with sheer delight squeezing him tight, but at the same time tried to work out why the hell his hair stank so much of smoke. But she would wait a while longer before asking him, because she was enjoying this lingering embrace far too much.

63

St David's Cathedral, Brighton

Hawk approached his coffin full of regret following the small service. Annoyed he hadn't called to see him earlier just after Oliver King's murder, to update him in person. No doubt Andy would have been 'facking' delighted to know he'd outlived the bastard. But sadly, it transpired, by only a few weeks. He glanced down at a few oranges, and a packet of biscuits, with several missing, placed on a table next to his coffin. A farewell gift from several women at the home including the two weepy old ladies he now watched shuffling slowly out of the church. He remembered them both from when he had called to see Andy. Their poignant farewell biscuit present, next to a card signed from 'Nurse Ratched'.

Now stood there in church brought back so many memories from his Catholic roots in Ireland. Indeed, at one time he may have followed a relative to become a priest, but events and circumstances made him lose faith. Today though, for an old DS whom he could fully relate to more than most, he pulled out his lighter.

In his memory he lit a candle, that only flickered for a moment, before it went out. When a sudden breeze entered the foyer, carrying the distinctive smell of her scent.

Amanda Jayne stood waiting for him to join her as planned, after they had enjoyed several chats since she had initially rung him with the sad update about Andy. Who knowing he neared the end, had written him a letter placed in a sealed envelope. When for once he became serious and clasped her arm, there and then making her promise that she alone would deliver it by hand. Correctly though he had concluded Hawk would be good enough to attend his funeral, because he was 'that sort of guy'. He was indeed, and he nearly cried out with laughter after Nurse Ratched handed him his letter, which he read immediately. Written with an unsteady hand using a fountain pen, also placed in the envelope.

"At least I outlived the 'facker' and well done – I'm sure you got him bumped off inside! I'll bump him off again if I end up heading south myself! By the way I saw her out of uniform at a Christmas Bash at our concentration camp of a home. A few expected her to turn up dressed like Hitler! (Well, perhaps only me!). Believe me, she scrubs up well, I've heard her bang on about you now for ages so, if nothing else this letter will get you two together, but sadly at my expense. I gift you my old work pen, it's comforting to know that at long last it will return into a CID office where it belongs with a 'proper detective'."

PS. Give her one from me because never forget, once you're a facker you're always a facker!

PPS. I hope for once someone listens to me and doesn't ignore what I say!!

Hawk leant forward's to kiss her gently, complimenting her choice of perfume, as he assured Andy in his head that his final wish would be granted. Later on tonight in fact when she would be wearing her uniform with silk stockings and suspenders. He walked her to his car carrying her overnight bag with all its contents that had been discussed many times over the phone. Just like Amanda told him when agreeing to dress up for him in full kit, it was her job to make people feel better, especially when a Night Nurse. She glanced up with tearful eyes to the sky mouthing "farewell" to a bird that had finally flown their nest, to escape them to become a free spirit. Because after hearing him call her Nurse Ratched so often, she had gone to a local cinema to watch her film character.

Now she fully understood that tune he kept on whistling when she walked away from him, normally after a telling off. He had been a likeable bastard, but bad with it every now and then. She wondered if all detectives ended up that way. Surely they weren't all the same, but just like Andy this one now driving her away had the gift of the gab, certainly one hell of a charmer.

64

Graveyard, Bamford

After collecting Tom Coyne from his garage, they could see just how upset he appeared – today of all days; so they drove in silence, only broken when they stood later on around his brothers well-tended grave – with an immaculately clean headstone. He told them what they knew already – that he would have been 40 years of age today, had he not taken his own life. It had been an unselfish act by a young boy; believing he would be helping them – with their plight to kill their abusers.

Tom had really aged, looking much older than he should with a noticeable twitch, indicating what they had thought for a while – that he had suffered a breakdown, but dealt with it in his own way; like most blokes tended to do, in silence and alone.

Tony now understood far better why he had said too much to a stranger, no doubt after noticing the 'AKORN CLUB' painted sign on his workshop wall. Tom had clung on to this as a memory after they had allowed Tim to make one when Sonya's first sign hadn't been fastened tight enough over their small treehouse door – blowing away during a storm. They never corrected the spelling.

Sonya now held Tom's hand as she said her prayers after which, perhaps, as a defence mechanism – when close to tears, he described how he had made a small portable electronic cleaning brush. This explained why his headstone looked so clean, going on to elaborate in detail how a small starter motor taken from a scrapped car worked its head, rotating it at speed.

Before leaving, they placed what they had each brought with them on an impeccably clean grave headstone – before taking him for a meal, a ploughman's lunch at a nearby pub only a short walk away that everyone had raved about, saying how good they were there.

Eventually, a strong wind got up – causing two Acorns placed earlier to blow away; but a shiny 'tanner' coin – cleaned with a rotating headed electric brush, stayed firmly in place, having been stuck on with a quick setting glue from a workshop, still crammed full of anything and everything; until one day he could eventually make use of it – just like his dad had taught them.